struck

INCLUDES *Stupid Cupid*, *Flirting with Disaster*, and *Pucker Up*

RHONDA STAPLETON

SIMON PULSE

New York   London   Toronto   Sydney   New Delhi

SIMON PULSE

An imprint of Simon & Schuster Children's Publishing Division

1230 Avenue of the Americas, New York, NY 10020

This Simon Pulse paperback edition December 2011

Stupid Cupid copyright © 2009 by Rhonda Stapleton

Flirting with Disaster copyright © 2010 by Rhonda Stapleton

Pucker Up copyright © 2010 by Rhonda Stapleton

For information about special discounts for bulk purchases, please contact Simon & Schuster Special Sales at 1-866-506-1949 or business@simonandschuster.com.

The Simon & Schuster Speakers Bureau can bring authors to your live event. For more information or to book an event contact the Simon & Schuster Speakers Bureau at 1-866-248-3049 or visit our website at www.simonspeakers.com.

Designed by Karina Granda

The text of this book was set in Adobe Caslon.

Manufactured in the United States of America

2 4 6 8 10 9 7 5 3 1

Library of Congress Control Number 2011932810

ISBN 978-1-4424-2862-1

ISBN 978-1-4424-4545-1 (eBook)

These titles were previously published individually by Simon Pulse.

This is dedicated to my children, Bryan and Shelby, who remind me every day how much fun it is to make people laugh. And Chad, I'd be remiss if I didn't tell the world how awesome you are, and that I look forward to more Breakfasts in America with you. (Ha, you just got Supertramped!) Seriously, though, I love you all, and am blessed to have such a wonderful family.

This is also dedicated to my parents, Pat and Ron, and to my sister, Lisa. You have encouraged me every step of the way, and I'm grateful for it. I couldn't have asked for a better support system . . . or a goofier one. ☺

Lastly, I want to dedicate this to YOU. Yes, you. Thank you for reading this, and I hope you enjoy this very goofy, but heartfelt, story of love.

contents

STUPID CUPID

chapter one

"So"—Janet glanced down at my résumé—"Felicity. You'd like to be a matchmaker. Can you go into more detail why?"

Because my mom threatened bodily harm unless I get off my lazy butt and get a job. No, that wouldn't do. Better to try for the more professional approach.

"Well, I believe in true love," I replied. "I think everyone has a match out there—some people just need a little help finding that special person. I think it would be fun to do that."

Janet smiled, her bright, white teeth sparkling in the soft light pouring from the window. "Good answer. That's what we believe too. Here at Cupid's Hollow we want to find true love for everyone."

I nodded, trying not to fidget with the clicky end of my pen.

This was my first real interview, and I was determined not to let my twitchy thumb get the best of me. After applying for a thousand jobs (and getting a thousand rejections), I'd found a tiny ad on the back page of Cleveland's *Scene* magazine: TEEN CUPIDS WANTED FOR MATCHMAKING COMPANY. CALL FOR INTERVIEW.

It was a cute angle to advertise for employees in that way, so I called. Two days later, here I was. In all my nervous, sweaty glory, working it as best as I could so I wouldn't look or sound like a total idiot.

"So, you're a junior," Janet said. "And what school do you go to again?"

"Greenville High. Go, Cougars!" I cheered, then winced internally at my dorkiness. Oh, man, that was way lame. Like she cared about our school mascot. *I* didn't even care most of the time.

"Um-hm," she said, her face unreadable. She flipped through the notepad on her lap and scribbled furiously on a page.

Crap, did I blow it already? Three minutes into the interview and I'd sunk my own battleship.

"And you're available to start work . . . ?"

"As soon as possible," I spilled out, heart racing. Maybe this could still work out.

"Have you ever used a BlackBerry or similar handheld technology before?"

"Well, my mom has one, and I've used it a little bit." Okay, that was an exaggeration, as I've really only *seen* her use it, but I'm sure I could figure it out if I needed to.

Janet wrote more notes. "I assume you've never participated in or worked for a matchmaking service before?"

"Um, no." I thought fast. "But I did help my brother set up his Match dot com profile."

My brother is four years older than me and is a cop. Trust me, not a good combination. He's insane. I can't count the number of times he's flashed his stupid badge at me in front of my friends, threatening to haul me in if I mocked his authority again. Total dork.

"Okay, last question. This job requires a certain level of . . . confidentiality." Janet looked straight into my eyes, her face serious. "Confidentiality for our clients, as well as for our own technologies and processes. You'd have to sign a document promising never to share our information with anyone outside the company. Would that be a problem?"

I swallowed. What was I getting myself into here? Was this normal?

Geez, chill, Felicity. She wasn't asking me to sew my lips together and join a convent. They probably just didn't want other matchmaking companies to steal their ideas or customers.

I nodded and put on my most serious, trustworthy face. "Sure, no problem." A thought popped into my mind. "Wait, I'm only seventeen. Is the contract legally binding?"

She shot me a smile. "Good question. It's binding as far as our concerns go."

"Okay, then." Not that I'd be spilling any industry secrets, anyway, so I wouldn't have to worry about that.

Janet finished writing, then uncrossed her legs and smoothed her prim, plum-colored skirt. She stood and stuck out her hand. "Well, we'd love to have you join our team. Welcome to Cupid's Hollow, Felicity."

I bit back my squeal and shook her hand. "This is so awesome. Thank you!"

She grinned. "Why don't you come in tomorrow for the training session."

I thanked her profusely, slipped on my thick winter coat, and left the office, turning back to give the building one last glance. The outside itself was nondescript, just an old brick exterior with lots of windows and a thin layer of late March snow perched on top. But the inside held the key to my working future.

My first real job. I was so excited, I did a little booty shake in the parking lot. I couldn't wait to tell everyone I knew! If I'd had a cell phone, I could have called my best friends Maya and Andy instead of waiting until I got home. With a job, though, I would now be able to use my own money to buy one.

I hopped into my mom's dark green Camry, cranked up the heat and the radio, and headed home, taking the long way through the suburbs instead of driving on Route 480. Mom had let me borrow the car for the interview, but made me swear a solemn oath that I would not go anywhere but to the interview and back, would not pick up any hitchhikers, and would stay off the freeway at all costs.

"Mom," I said as soon as I threw open the front door, "I'm home. I got the job!" On the front porch I stomped the loose snow off my heels, then stepped into the foyer and gingerly slipped out of my boots. After tucking them into the corner of the tiled entryway and hanging my coat in the closet, I added, "And no, I didn't track snow in the house." I knew what she was going to ask, because it was the same thing every time.

Mom darted out of the kitchen, wearing a white apron over

her dress pants. Other than a small smudge of flour on her cheek, she looked pristine and composed, as usual. "Congratulations!" she cried out. "I'm so proud of you." She leaned over and kissed me on the cheek.

My mom is surprisingly domestic—she's as assertive in the kitchen as in her workplace, where she's in the accounting department. God help any of the company's clients who are late on their payments, because my mom hounds them until they pay, just to shut her up. She runs our household the same way.

When we were younger, my brother and I used to call her the House Nazi. Neither one of us was stupid enough to say it directly to her face, though—I liked my mouth right where it was, thank you very much.

"Thanks, Mom. What's for dinner?" I asked. "I'm starving to death."

"Fried chicken, but it's not ready yet. You should go call Maya and Andy with your good news. They'll be thrilled."

"Yup, I'm heading up to my room now." I tossed the keys on the small table in the foyer. "Thanks for letting me borrow the car."

She winked. "Well, now you can save up and get your own, can't you."

Gee, I'd suspected she'd say that. Now that I had a real job, I could predict the answer for everything:

Need new clothes, Felicity? Want to go see a movie with your friends? Well, it's a good thing you've got a job now.

I darted up to my room, flung myself across my bed, and grabbed the phone off my nightstand, dialing Andy's cell.

"Andy's mortuary. You stab 'em, we slab 'em."

Andy Carsen is my best friend. She and I have been close since kindergarten. Sometimes, though, I feel a bit jealous of her. Her folks aren't as harsh as mine can be. And Andy, of course, has a cell phone, just like everybody else I know. I swear, I must be the only teenager in the free world who doesn't have one. But now that I had a job, that was going to change.

"Hey, it's me."

"So . . . ?"

"I got the job!"

She squealed. "That's awesome! Now you'll finally have spending money, and we can go shopping more and buy those cute jeans you wanted and—"

"Whoa." I laughed. "I haven't even gotten a paycheck yet."

"So, how does this gig work? Will you make those geeky

videotapes of people, or is it an online dating thing?"

Hm. I hadn't even bothered to ask. "Actually, I don't know. I was so excited I got the job, I just took off before she could change her mind."

"You're ridiculous."

"You say that like you're surprised. Anyway, tomorrow I've got training, so I'll let you know."

We hung up, and I dialed Maya Takahashi, my other BFF. Maya moved to Cleveland when we were in middle school, and though she's completely unlike me or Andy in just about every possible way, we clicked. Maybe it was the way she quietly snarked on the preps her first day of school that made me instantly love her. From then on, the three of us have been nearly inseparable.

"'Lo," Maya said into the mouthpiece, her mouth clearly full of food.

"Hey," I answered. "I got the job!"

"That's great. I knew you would."

I heard her chew a few times, so I held the phone away from my ear to let her finish the bite without subjecting me to it. Delicate, she was not, but that was Maya for you.

"Sounds like you're busy," I said. "I'll let you go."

"Sorry, I'm totally stressing over here and trying to multitask by eating and doing homework at the same time. I almost bit off my pen cap! And then, after dinner, I need to practice my solo."

Maya's a fantastic trumpet player, in addition to all her brain talents. Though I'm not a huge fan of the school band—nerd alert, anyone?—Andy and I do support her and go see all her performances at the school's basketball games. I know she'd do the same for us.

"Okay, hope you get it all done. Talk to ya later."

After we hung up, I turned on my PC and logged on to my blog. I made sure to lock it so it was a VIP entry only—Andy, Maya, and I usually shared entries with only each other.

I'm so excited. Now that I'm a matchmaker, maybe I can even learn some tips to make Derek fall madly in love with me.

I sighed. Derek Peterson's the hottest guy on the face of the earth. Every time I look at him, my heart squeezes up, and I forget how to speak. Not that he ever talks to me, anyway. He's a smart jock who runs with the AP crowd (shame of all shame, I'm only in honors, not advanced), but we have art class together.

Of course, that's my favorite class, even though I end up spending the whole time trying not to get busted for staring at him. Or drooling.

I bet half my blog was filled with his name. I'd been crushing on him since the first day of freshman year, when I saw him walking through the hallway at school. Not that he'd noticed me, but it didn't matter. One look at his beautiful smile, and I was a goner.

Derek Peterson-n-Felicity Walker 4-ever

Mr. and Mrs. Derek Peterson

Felicity Walker-Peterson

Felicity Walker-Peterson, M.D.

Felicity Walker-Peterson, President of the United States

Felicity Walker-Peterson, America's Next Top Model

Well, that was fun. I saved and closed the blog, then quickly checked my e-mail (nope, nothing new, except from my spam buddies telling me I won the Irish lotto—lucky me!). Time to start my homework to avoid being grounded for getting anything below a C.

The next day at the office, Janet handed me a hot-pink PDA. "Here ya go," she said. "Your LoveLine 3000. Please take care of it. It's the key to your job."

Whoa. It was possibly the most tricked-out PDA I'd ever seen in my life. There had to be some serious dough coughed up for these puppies.

I sat in the plush green chair across from Janet's cherry wood desk, flipping on the device and looking at all the buttons. "So, what's this for? Are we supposed to schedule the customers' first dates or something?"

She tilted her head and gave me a funny look. "It has the e-mail addresses of everyone in your territory, which in your case is Greenville High."

"Wait. I'm matchmaking my school?" I didn't know yet if that was a good or a bad thing, so I tried to keep my voice calm and neutral.

"Absolutely. That's part of the reason we're hiring. We decided to try a new venture and let people matchmake their own peer groups. After all, who better to be a cupid for a teen than another teen?"

"Good point." Most of my classmates would die laughing if an adult tried to help them find a date. And with good reason.

I mean, no disrespect to anyone, but "great personality" can only get you so far in high school.

For instance, look at me. I've got personality practically oozing out of my skin, but I've only had one boyfriend ever. And he dated me so he could get closer to Andy. I should have picked up the clue phone when he always wanted to do group things—with her tagging along, of course. And here I'd thought he was just getting to know my friends.

Andy, of course, has no problems getting a guy's attention. She's hot, smart, and funny, but she's also extremely picky, so she doesn't date a lot. And she's 100 percent loyal to her friends, so my ex's strategy to get closer to her backfired, to say the least.

Poor Maya, on the other hand—the girl's sharp as a tack, captain of the debate club, lead trumpet in the marching band, but can't get a date to save her life. In fact, she can't even get a guy to notice her. Not that she'd even admit to wanting a boyfriend.

And not that she isn't cute enough, either. It's just . . . she's busy. And kinda shy. But still, I couldn't exactly picture her signing up with a dating service for help. That just isn't how it's done.

Janet delicately cleared her throat. "Felicity, this is no small thing. It's taken the company thousands of years to evolve and perfect our technology, but I like the way the PDAs work so far."

"I'm sorry, what did you say?" I must have misheard her. Maybe I needed to pay better attention to this training session instead of thinking about me and my friends' dating disasters.

"Trust me," she continued, chuckling, "you'll like using this much better than the bows and arrows of yesteryear. The misfiring possibility alone made the job more difficult than it needed to be. And the PDAs are far less cumbersome to carry."

I swallowed hard. Okay, I hadn't misunderstood. The lady was obviously a loony-bird.

And I was now employed by her.

I glanced at the door, trying to think of a polite way to get the hell out of there.

Janet paused, looking at me. "Are we on the same page here?"

I slid my eyes back to her face. "I—I'm guessing not." Because I was on planet Earth, and Janet was obviously circling somewhere around Jupiter, floating on a pink cloud with rainbows, bunnies, and fluffy kitty cats. And a whole lotta bathtub-created meth.

No wonder they always warned us to stay away from drugs.

Janet spoke slowly. "You do understand you're a cupid now, right?"

chapter two

"I'm . . . Cupid?" I squirmed in my seat.

She laughed hard for several seconds. "What? No."

I sagged in relief—I *had* misunderstood her.

"You're not Cupid. You're *a* cupid. There's more than one of us, you know."

"Well, okay, then." I stood before she could do something else crazy, like carve my name on her hand with a ballpoint pen. "It's been really nice meeting you, but I should go now."

Janet squinted at me, then stood, as well. "You're a skeptic. That's okay—almost all new hires are. Follow me."

She paced across her office and opened the door, hurrying into the hallway. Did she really expect me to follow her? This was my perfect chance to escape. I flung my coat on, struggling to slip my arms through the armholes as fast as I could. After snatching my purse from underneath the seat, I stepped outside of her office, then paused.

What if she was telling the truth? What if she really could prove to me I was a cupid? Or, more likely, what if she was loony but harmless, and I was missing out on the second half of a really great story to tell Andy and Maya? Before I realized what I was doing, I found myself heading down the hallway too, following the *click-clack* of her heels and trying to keep up.

I hoped I wasn't walking blindly into my own death. Mom would be so pissed if I did something dumb like that.

We hoofed it to the end of the hall and swung a left, going into a windowless room. Janet closed the door behind me.

"Take a look around," she said.

The glint of gold caught my eye immediately. There had to be millions of dollars' worth of antique weaponry here—namely, bows and arrows.

Janet picked out one bow and arrow and, quicker than the blink of an eye, pointed the arrow at me, firing it right into my chest.

"Aaaaaaah!" Squeezing my eyes shut, I touched my tingling chest and looked down. No arrow sticking out of my heart. Not even a hole. The arrow had disappeared. "What the—?" I choked back the fearful sob building in my throat. "That's not funny. How'd you . . . ?"

She offered me a chagrined smile. "Sorry, but that's quite possibly the most effective way to show you. Magical arrows. They disappear when they hit their target. I told you, it's real." She hung the bow back on the wall. "Oh, and don't worry. You won't be falling in love. A matching arrow also has to be fired at someone else for the love spell to work. It's kind of like completing the electrical love circuit. That weird tingle you're feeling should wear off in an hour or so."

All I could do was gape as Janet led me out of the room and shut off the light, then locked the door behind us. We headed back to her office, me much more somber than before.

How was this even possible? How could she fire an arrow at me and have it disappear? I'd seen her shoot me with my own two eyes. But nothing had hit. I touched my chest again, the tingle reminding me I hadn't imagined things.

It seemed like there was no way to rationalize the incident other than to realize maybe it was true. I was Cupid. No, wait, *a* cupid.

About a billion questions flew into my head. How long had Janet been a cupid? How was she chosen? Was the knowledge just handed down from one cupid to the next? How did this all get started in the first place?

Then, it hit me: This had to be the coolest thing ever to happen to me. Even better than when I won tickets from a radio station to see Panic! At The Disco in concert—from the front row, thank you very much.

Yeah, this crushed that little triumph right into the dust.

"Do I get wings?" I asked. If so, I hoped I got to pick out a pair of pretty ones. Maybe a nice sage green or pale purple. Or maybe she'd touch my back and they'd sprout out of my spine.

I shivered at the odd thought.

Janet snorted. "I wish. Unfortunately, that's a myth. Cupids can't fly. They're just imbued with magical properties for matchmaking."

Magic. It couldn't exist . . . could it? My tingly chest taunted me with the answer.

A sudden thrill of excitement shot through me. Oh my God, I couldn't wait to tell every—

"Nope," Janet said, sitting back in her executive chair. She chuckled. "I can read your face like a book. Looks like it's time to go over the rules."

"Okay." So being a cupid came with rules, just like everything else. I guess it made sense—you wouldn't want employees going crazy all over the place and hooking up people and chickens, or anything else weird like that.

"Rule number one. No one can know you're a cupid. Not your mom, not your best friend, not anyone. Sorry, but it compromises our anonymity. It's in the contract you signed, so don't even think about admitting it to anyone outside the company, ever, or else . . . well, let's just say don't."

I nodded in agreement. "Okay. I'll definitely keep my mouth shut." It would be hard, because I knew me. I'd want to spill the beans to Andy and Maya. But I wasn't about to double-cross a woman with magic arrows.

Weird. My friends and I never had any big secrets from each other. I hoped this wouldn't cause any issues. I'd have to come up with something to tell them about my job that wouldn't cause more questions.

Janet glanced at the PDA in my hand. "Oh, and don't lose your LoveLine 3000 or show anyone what's on it. If someone else tries to open it, it'll have only your school schedule, nothing else. We installed a custom security system, just to cloak the data." She smirked proudly.

Geez. This stuff was no joke. "I'll keep it close to me."

Janet nodded in approval. "Good. Now, rule number two. Only match your target to one other person at a time, making sure all matches meet the minimum-compatibility requirements of at least three common interests—but the more commonalities, the better. One pairing at a time, and if the love match doesn't last after the magic wears off in two weeks, you can try pairing the target with someone else."

"Okay." I took a mental note to write all of these rules down later.

"And last, rule number three. While you remain in our employment, you're not allowed to matchmake yourself. Sorry, it's a conflict of interest."

Well, crap. My dreams of Derek and me growing old together and holding hands on a rickety porch swing flushed down the drain right before my eyes. Because without a little magic, that was never going to happen. I sighed deeply. "All right."

"Great." Janet beamed, her mauve lipstick perfectly framing bright white teeth. "You are required to make at least one match per week, but the more matches you make, the better chance you'll have of creating lasting matches. Your minimum quota is one lasting match a month."

Only one a month? This was going to be a piece of cake. "Okay, so how will I know if it's a lasting match?"

"Lasting love matches keep going after the magic wears off in two weeks. We offer bonuses for those, so that's where the real money is. It's in your best interest, then, to pair up suitable people from the start."

"Okay, I see."

Janet opened a drawer in her desk and rummaged through it. "Be sure to read your instruction guide before attempting to create a compatibility chart or client profile. Your LoveLine 3000 has the capacity to store thousands of profiles, so start doing some investigatory work, and match well. But, most importantly, trust your gut. Aha, here we go." She pulled out a thick pamphlet and gave it to me.

"This is the guide on how to use the PDA to matchmake," she continued. "Basically, you'll send an e-mail to the target, and carbon-copy the compatible love interest. When they open the e-mail, it'll appear blank, but *Bam!*" She wiggled her fingers in the air. "Love at first byte. Get it?"

I forced a laugh. "Yeah, I get it." Sounded easy enough. I could totally do this.

Janet handed me her business card. "Call me if you get into trouble. And take it slow until you feel comfortable. *Read the instruction guide*—it'll help." She smiled. "Any other questions?"

I scrunched up my face, thinking. "Actually, yeah. If customers aren't paying for us to matchmake them, how does Cupid's Hollow make any money?"

She laughed. "We get sponsorship from companies that most benefit from love matches—the floral industry, the greeting card companies, and so on. They fund us, and we fund them. It works out nicely."

Sneaky. I never would have thought. "Makes sense, I guess."

Janet stood. "Okay. Well, if there aren't any other questions, go out there and make some matches!"

After third period the next day, I tossed my biology book and matchmaking instruction guide into my locker, grabbed my bagged lunch, and slammed the locker door, trying my best not to feel guilty for once again ditching the required cupid reading. I still hadn't gotten past the first few pages of the manual, which was littered with snoozeville statistics and compatibility rules . . . and about a billion teeny, tiny charts.

I consider myself a pretty smart person, but the material went right over my head. Did Janet really expect me to get all this stuff?

The highest quotient of compatibility cofactors increases optimal relationship longevity, give or take a 3 percent margin of error based on certain established external parameters, blah blah blah.

And that was just on page one.

After spending two hours last night reading the same few paragraphs over and over, I'd finally just decided to forge my own matchmaking path as best I could. I'd work on making minimum-compatibility matches for people I didn't know well and do in-depth matches for closer acquaintances.

This would increase my overall chances of a lasting match and save on research time, to boot. I mentally patted myself on the back for coming up with this brilliant strategy.

I whipped out my PDA and leaned back into the corner of an edge locker and a wall, scrolling through the profiles I'd been working on that morning. I'd never have expected how much pressure I would feel to make my matches good ones. This was serious stuff.

I'd spent all morning in between classes scouring the halls before picking my first target: Britney Nelson, a new sophomore at our school, who didn't have a lot of friends yet. However, she was cute and seemed pretty nice. I figured it shouldn't be too hard to find her a date, especially with the help of some cupid magic.

I knew who Britney was because of gym class, but we weren't close friends, so it made her the perfect choice for my first "cast the net wide" match. I could test out my cupid powers on her without being biased. I needed total objectivity to try this stuff out.

From scrutinizing her in the hall and oh so subtly peeking in her locker while she was moving stuff in and out, I'd already figured out a few key things to start her profile:

Name: Britney Nelson

Age: 16ish?

Pets: Dog, as evidenced by short, wiry hairs on her black pants. Either that, or has really hairy legs. I choose to go with the first option.

Interests: Robert Pattinson—his picture's plastered all over locker. Also loves the color pink.

Style: Girly, but casual

By examining the evidence, I'd come to the conclusion that Britney's a girl who needs a sensitive guy, one who will appreciate her femininity.

Now, to find a match for her. Eyes still on my PDA, I stepped into the line of hallway traffic.

A hard shoulder slammed into my back, and my lunch flew out of my hands. A strong, tanned hand darted out, grabbing the bag just before it hit the floor. Luckily, I kept my grip on the cupid device. Janet would so not be thrilled if I broke it on my very first day.

"Sorry," a deep voice behind me said. "Are you okay? I didn't see you."

With fumbling fingers, I pocketed the PDA, then turned around to gaze up into piercing green eyes. Derek's eyes.

"I—I, yes, I'm fine. Thanks." A slow burn crawled up my throat and across my cheeks.

He frowned, a crease between his dark blond eyebrows. "You're . . . Andy, right?"

I bit back a sigh, trying not to rub my sore shoulder. "No, I'm Felicity. Andy's friend."

He nodded, giving me a wry grin. "Oh, sorry. I always see you two together. I'm easily confused, ya know. Football and all that—probably knocked some brain cells out." He paused. "Aren't you in art class with me too? I never hear you talk in there."

He'd noticed me? I perked up. "Yup, that's me. Quiet as a mouse." And übercliché, too. *Ugh, why do I say these stupid things?*

"I'm Derek." He handed me my bag with a smile. "Okay, see you later."

"Bye." I waved at his retreating back. Oh my God, I couldn't wait to tell Andy and Maya.

In the cafeteria, I settled at my regular table beside Andy and Maya, unwrapped my turkey sandwich, and tried to refocus. Okay, back to business. I needed to match Britney up with someone. But who?

The question stuck with me throughout lunch, though I tried to act like everything was normal. Andy, in between bites of pizza, talked to me and Maya about some jerk in her homeroom who broke up with his girlfriend by having his friend dump her. So not cool. But even though I nodded and rolled my eyes and said "what a loser" at all the right parts of the story, I was only half listening. My brain was focused on cupid business.

I was tempted to ask Andy and Maya who Britney should

date, or to pry them for info that I could add to her profile, but Janet's rules kind of scared me. I was better off trying to figure this out myself.

I finished my sandwich and balled up the trash, proud of myself for not breaking down and getting a slice of pepperoni-laden pizza. As tasty as Andy's lunch had looked, I didn't need a greasy skin breakout, since junior prom was coming up soon. Of course, I didn't have a date, but neither did Andy or Maya, so I figured we could always go as a group.

While the girls kept chatting, I wandered over to the trash cans to pitch my garbage. My heart fluttered when I thought about how romantic it would be to dance with Derek at prom, even just once. I'd be sitting at the table with Maya and Andy, telling them a funny and clever story, and he'd walk up to me, a shy smile on his face, and say—

"Hey, don't throw that can away. You can recycle it."

I jumped, startled out of my daydream. "Huh?"

Matthew Cornwall, a guy from my biology class, pointed to the empty soda can in my hand. "There's a recycling bin by the front doors."

"Oh, right."

He smiled. "Thanks. Sorry to scare you. Just trying to do my part, you know." He walked away, waving hi to another guy and starting up some conversation.

Hm. Matthew seemed pretty decent—he knew how to apologize, after all. Plus, he wasn't a total jerk in class and usually had smart commentary on the lessons . . . and caring for the environment was a good quality too. Maybe he'd make a good match for Britney.

When I got back to the lunch table, I told the girls I'd meet them after school as usual, then headed over to where Matthew was talking and squatted at a nearby table, trying to look casual while eavesdropping like mad.

I turned on the PDA and created a new profile.

Name: Matthew Cornwall

Age: 17

Pets: Has a bird. Remember him talking about it in biology.

Interests: Recycling, obviously

Style: Tree-hugger

But what else?

I leaned my ear in his direction as he talked to the other guy.

For a few minutes they did nothing but go on and on about school sports. I added that to his interests list and tried not to die of boredom as they argued the finer points of one of our basketball players' stats. Then, a perfect tidbit came up.

"Hey, did you catch the opening band at Peabody's last Friday? They were awesome." Matthew grabbed a folded piece of paper out of his messenger bag and handed it to his friend. "Here's their flyer. My cousin knows the lead singer. They're playing again next month. You should go."

"Thanks, I'll try," the guy replied, stuffing the flyer in his back pocket.

Aha, so Matthew likes indie music. Peabody's is well-known in downtown Cleveland for featuring small local bands, and it was obvious from the enthusiasm in Matthew's voice that he enjoys going there.

Indie rockers are sensitive, always crying about something or another, aren't they? I went to Britney's profile, looking over what I'd found about her. Both she and Matthew have animals, and it's a well-known fact that pet people tend to like other pet people. And I was guessing that they're both the sensitive type. But what would be my third minimum trait?

Hm. They both attended Greenville High, so that could count as one common interest, couldn't it? Well, I'd make it count. Besides, after they got together, I was sure they'd find lots more in common.

Yup, it was time to do a little matchmaking.

Using the PDA, I created a blank e-mail to Britney and carbon-copied Matt.

My stomach flipped in nervousness. Before I could talk myself out of it, I hit send.

My first love match—signed, sealed, and e-mailed.

chapter three

TGIF! Friday is our weekly sleepover night, and I was currently perched over the edge of Andy's queen-size bed as I painted my toenails Slutty Red. That wasn't the "official" name, but whatever.

"Okay, so dish, ladies," Andy said, rubbing the green tea mask—oops, sorry, *masque*—on her face. "Whaddaya think of that Britney girl who Matthew's suddenly dating? I mean, I never even saw them talk before, and now they're practically dry humping in the hallway? What's up with that?"

I stifled a giggle at Andy's vivid but accurate description of my successful love match. Now that I was a bona fide cupid, I wasn't even grossed out by couples' smooshed-against-the-lockers Public Displays of Affection. Matthew and Britney had been locked at the lips ever since I sent the e-mail, and I couldn't have been happier about the match.

"I think it's gross," Maya said, her nose wrinkled. She pulled her long, dark hair into her trademark ponytail, grimacing at her reflection in the hand-held mirror.

"You would," Andy teased.

Maya stuck her tongue out at Andy. After dabbing clumps of masque all over her thin, pale face, she continued. "Well, who wants to see people groping like that? Get a room. I'd rather be with a guy who knows how to act like a gentleman." She paused. "Though at least Britney and Matthew seem to really like each other. They've both been beaming all week. What do you think, Felicity?"

I swallowed, suddenly nervous. As much as I wanted to 'fess up, I had to play surprised. Which meant lying to my best friends—not a fun task. I was a terrible liar, and I knew they would see right through me.

"Oh, yeah. I thought it was weird too," I said, trying to play it cool, even though my hand was shaking. "But definitely great for them."

Damn, I messed up my pinkie toenail. A big glob of Slutty Red clumped on the toe knuckle. "Hey, I need the nail polish remover."

Luckily, my friends were both too caught up in beautifying

themselves to notice my fibbing. Andy tossed me the bottle with the tips of her fingers, trying not to get green tea masque all over the cap. "Here ya go."

"Thanks. Well," I said casually, "you never know when love will strike."

Maya shot me a weird look. "Speaking of, what's going on with your job? Have you started yet?"

"Yeah." Quickly, I brought into my mind the story I'd rehearsed. "It's a lot of paperwork so far, but I've been learning the fine art of matching profiles by observing some of the pros."

In a way, that was true. I'd rented some older movies, like *Clueless*, *Emma*, and *The Wedding Planner*, to put me in the right frame of mind and maybe give me some ideas.

Maya nodded thoughtfully. "Well, maybe once you're there for a while, you'll move up and get to do some of the good stuff." She grabbed a washcloth and headed into Andy's bathroom. Yet another reason to be jealous of Andy—she had a full bathroom attached to her room, including a luxurious, claw-footed tub.

My mom wouldn't even let me keep my curling iron in our family bathroom, since she said it junked it up. However, lucky Andy's girly stuff was strewn all across hers.

"That sounds cool," Andy said. "So much better than my stupid job." She hustled into the bathroom to rinse the masque off her face as well.

That was one thing about Andy I actually didn't envy: her job. She works as a waitress at The Burger Butler, one of those cutesy, gimmicky restaurants with a franchise in every big city. Unfortunately, she has to wear a butler uniform when she serves her customers, right down to the white gloves and bow tie. God only knows how many times she's gotten called "Jeeves" on a daily basis or had her tuxedoed butt grabbed by some pervy old man. She doesn't have to work—her parents are happy to buy her whatever she wants—but it's important to Andy to be independent and more self-reliant.

"Yeah, but at least you get free food," I pointed out.

"Like I want more burgers," Andy said, coming out of the bathroom and patting her face dry with a plush purple towel. "Besides, do you know how bad all that grease is for your complexion? I don't need any more breakouts."

"Please. You hardly need to worry about it." I finished up my toenails. There—picture-perfect. Too bad Derek would never see them. "You have gorgeous skin. Besides, your booty alone is the ultimate guy magnet."

"If all it takes to get a boyfriend is a big booty, then guys should be knocking down my front door," Maya said, coming out of the bathroom and flopping on the floor. "But they'd have to notice me first. I'm just way too nervous to talk to them the way Andy does."

Oh. My. *God*. I just got the best idea in the world. I could find a love match for Maya! Why didn't I think of that before?

Maya needed an ego boost, stat, and I had just the magic to make her dreams come true. Besides, it would be way more fun and fulfilling for me than pairing off people I don't know very well.

This was a seriously good use of my new cupid powers. Why shouldn't my friend have a great boyfriend? If I couldn't date Derek, at least Maya could be happy. I'd just have to live vicariously through her love life.

"So, Maya," I said as nonchalantly as possible, screwing the nail polish lid tightly closed, "what kind of guy are you looking for? I mean, obviously you want someone who appreciates junk in the trunk."

Maya laughed, stretching her legs out and flexing her toes. "Well, I want a smart guy who's involved in school activities, like I am. I want someone who respects me and doesn't just think about how to get in my pants. Someone who likes to have fun. And someone who isn't too macho to hang with me, or to call me to talk."

Andy snickered. "So basically, you want Prince Charming."

"Well, I guess having a white horse would be a bonus too." Maya laughed again and flung the towel at her. "Smart-ass."

"Pass the potatoes, please," Rob said, "or I'll have to arrest you for resisting an officer."

My dad chuckled, handing him the bowl of garlic mashed potatoes. "Funny."

So not funny. Rob always cracks way too many stupid cop jokes every time he comes over. My mom insists on my brother joining us every Sunday for family dinner. She says our family needs to keep in constant contact in order to stay close. I guess it's a carryover from her large Italian family.

Frankly, I think I'd feel closer to Rob if he'd stay farther away.

Rob had brought a new "flavor of the week" with him, some fake-blond chick with poofy hair and a poofier chest. I don't know where he finds these girls, but this one looked like maybe he'd picked her up for prostitution on the way here and decided to bring her to dinner instead of to jail.

Blondie giggled. "Oh, Robbie, you're too cute." She swatted his arm with her long, acrylic nails painted neon pink with tiny crystal jewels on the tips.

I think I just threw up a little in my mouth. "Hey, *Robbie*, can you pass the dinner rolls over here?"

Rob shot me a glare. "Here." He tossed me the bread basket and kicked me under the table.

"Mom," I whined, ducking a hand under the table to rub my sore shin, "call the child-abuse hotline. I'm being beaten up by my own brother. And a cop, too. For shame—always sad when the good ones turn bad like that."

This time, *she* gave me the evil eye. I shut my mouth. Some people just don't appreciate genuine humor.

"So," Mom said, turning her attention to Fluffykins, or whatever her name was (I didn't bother to learn them anymore, since women came and went out of my brother's life with alarming speed), "where did you say you and Rob met?"

"We met on LoveMatesForever.com," she said around a spoonful of mashed potatoes. "I thought he was so dreamy. Plus, he wasn't, like, forty or anything. I'm sooooooo tired of those old guys hitting on me."

My dad nearly choked on his bread roll. I bit back a laugh. *Nice job, dumb-ass.* In one fell swoop she'd insulted both my parents, who were in their early forties.

Hey, if things didn't work out for Rob and Fluffykins—and that was a sure bet, because things *never* worked out for him—maybe I could use my matchmaking skills to find him a real girlfriend. But then I'd have to get close enough to him to observe him, and that would seriously bite. There are only so many times a day a girl can be called "butthead" by her brother before wanting to kick him in the joeys.

"Did you know Felicity works for a matchmaking company?" my mom said, trying hard to keep her polite smile in place.

Oh, crap. I should have seen that one coming.

"No way!" Bleach Blonde squealed, her bright red lips flying open. "Which one? I've joined, like, every one out there."

Rob shifted in his seat. I guess I'd feel uncomfortable too, if my date continued with the rampant stupidity.

"Well, it's a little one," I replied. "I doubt you've heard of it. I just started, so I'm not doing any of the good stuff yet. Mostly paperwork."

She squinted her heavily lined eyes at me. "Try me."

"Cupid's Hollow."

"Oh." She scooped another pile of potatoes on her fork. "Never heard of it." After chewing a bite, she glanced at Rob, then patted his hand. "Guess I don't need to worry about that now, do I, Snookie?" *Giggle, giggle.*

I shoveled the rest of my dinner down fast. I had to get out of there, now. "Excuse me," I said, carrying my plate into the kitchen before anyone could beckon me back. "Gotta go do some homework."

That was one good thing about still being in school—I always had homework to serve as a ready-made excuse for getting out of crappy family events.

Up in my room, I picked up the PDA and flipped through the many, many entries I'd made yesterday, trying to find the perfect match for Maya. There were a few candidates who seemed good and who met the minimum-compatibility requirements, but I still wasn't sure who to choose. I resolved to follow the top candidates around for a day so I could observe them as much as possible and find the perfect one.

After all, we weren't talking about any old target here. This was one of my best friends!

• • •

Monday morning, I was rarin' to go. The first thing I did after stepping inside the front doors of Greenville High was flip on my PDA and run through the entire male population of the junior and senior classes about a billion times. After much scrutiny, I finally narrowed the candidates for Maya down to three possibilities: Josh Wiley, the drum major of the band; Ben Johnson, the announcer for the school's basketball games; and Quentin Lovejoy, the editor-in-chief of the yearbook.

All three of those guys were highly involved in school activities, one of Maya's big criteria, and just as importantly, I'd never heard complaints from other girls about them being total buttheads. Plus, they were all cute and smart, so putting them at the top of the lineup made total sense.

Therefore, my mission was to pay special attention to these three lead candidates for Operation Hook Maya Up and determine who was most worthy of my friend's affection.

As I gathered further profile data throughout the day, watching the guys closely, my initial thoughts were confirmed. All three would be great for Maya. The more I observed of the three of them, the harder it was to choose among them.

In art class, my last class of the day, I sat in the back corner, doodling absentmindedly on the corner of my latest project, a pencil sketch of a pile of books. I was too wrapped up in matchmaking Maya to even stare at Derek's gorgeous face from under the shield of my eyelashes, like I normally did (although he did acknowledge me in class today with a nod and smile). I needed to figure out which guy would be the best choice for Maya, but the decision was overwhelming me.

How could I pick just one of them?

Then, still staring at the books in my drawing, I had a sudden realization. Maybe it wasn't fair of me to make the choice for her— didn't Maya have a right to choose for herself which guy she liked best? I stopped doodling and pulled out my PDA, nestling it in my lap, then turned it on and opened up the e-mail program.

I typed in Maya's e-mail address and then carbon copied Josh, Ben, *and* Quentin. Matching all of them up like this was so against the rules—but then again, didn't Janet tell me to trust my gut? Surely the "gut" clause trumped the so-called "rules"—right?

And my gut was saying loud and clear, "Hedge your bets, Felicity! Send it to them all." I mean, what are friends for?

Time for Maya, with a little help from me, to get the kind of attention she deserved. Drawing in a deep breath, I hit send.

chapter four

When the bell rang dismissing school for the day, I dashed to the front doors to meet Maya for our after-school study session. We were prepping for a test in first-period English on *The Grapes of Wrath*. I'd actually read this one and was ready to go, though the ending grossed me out.

Breast-feeding an old guy? Nasty. Who decided to make *that* a classic?

Andy, who was outside yapping with Maya, wasn't going to get her nerd groove on with the two of us, since she wasn't in me and Maya's English class. However, it was tradition for the three of us to walk home together.

We headed down the icy sidewalk. Luckily, Maya's house was only a few blocks away. In thin pants, I was freezing my buns off. I rubbed my hands together, then crammed them in my coat pockets, wishing I'd remembered my gloves.

"Did you hear?" Andy asked, shouldering her backpack a little better over her coat. Her breath huffed out in little clouds.

"Hear what?" I asked, eager for her to dish details. Andy always had the good scoop.

"Mallory Robinson was flirting way hard with Derek today at second lunch. Jenny Mack was sitting across the table from them, and she told Amanda West, who told me. Mallory's probably doing it just because she knows you like him."

My stomach clenched. "God, seriously?"

Mallory Robinson was my mortal enemy, and if there was a way for her to make my life miserable, she was after it. It looked like flirting with Derek was a new addition to her "let's torture Felicity" list.

"What are you going to do about it?" Maya asked me.

I shrugged.

"I know," Andy volunteered. "You should tell Derek you like him before that piece of trash steals him away."

Man, I wished I could. If only the cupid law was different. But I couldn't just throw some e-mail love his way and make him come running to me. And without the cupid magic, he barely knew I was alive.

"I don't know," I said. "I guess I'll figure something out."

This sucked. The one guy I'd been in love with forever was off-limits.

Or was he?

Janet had told me I couldn't matchmake myself. But that didn't mean I couldn't be available if *he* wanted to date *me*, right? If I could get him to fall for me without using the magic, it wouldn't be breaking any cupid rules.

But how on earth was I going to do that? I needed to think about this more. There had to be something I could do to make Derek notice me. If he ended up with Mallory, I swear I'd spontaneously combust.

Once Maya and I arrived at her house, we darted inside, waving bye to Andy, and ran upstairs to her bedroom. Maya hopped onto her computer to check e-mail, as usual.

However, this time was different. I'd get to watch my love match in action.

As she booted up her PC, my heart pounded, and I realized my hands were shaking slightly. What if I messed it up? What if she realized what I was doing? What if the triple-match strategy backfired, and the guys all fell for each other instead of for Maya? I stuffed my hands in my pockets to keep from showing my nervousness. "Um . . ."

"Hold on a sec, Felicity. I got e-mail."

I sat on her bed and nodded, holding my breath for what seemed like an eternity.

Maya double-clicked with the mouse, then froze. She stared at the monitor. After a moment, she shook her head, blinking. "What were we talking about?" she asked, rubbing the middle of her chest.

It worked! She must have been feeling the same tingle I'd experienced when Janet hit me with the arrow. "Oh, you know," I said oh so casually, "just talking about guys."

She spun in her seat and looked at me, a dreamy smile on her face. It almost freaked me out—I'd never seen her look . . . blissful before. With her face so soft, she almost looked like a different person.

"You know who I like?" She sighed, putting her hand to her heart. "Josh Wiley, Ben Johnson, and Quentin Lovejoy."

Bingo.

That afternoon, after studying with Maya and running home quickly to change clothes, I bummed Mom's car and made my way to Cupid's

Hollow headquarters, where I was scheduled for my first one-on-one meeting with my boss to discuss the state of my cupid affairs for the week.

Janet had been pretty friendly during my interview and training session, but now that I was a true employee, I quickly found out that she could be plenty intimidating when she wanted to. She sat at her desk like a dictator at a podium, peering down her nose at me. Or maybe she just seemed extra scary since I was terrified I'd get fired for having already broken a rule in my first week on the job.

Trying to remain as calm and professional as possible, I filled her in on my pair-ups for Britney and Maya, using generic statements for Maya's match and carefully omitting the part about having carbon-copied all three guys.

With a brisk nod, Janet said, "Sounds like you've done a good job so far, Felicity." She wrote a note in her ever-present notebook. "So, you made one match last week and one this week. Way to go."

I shifted in my seat. Nervous as hell, I'd dressed to impress in my best outfit—a semisheer white blouse, lacy white tank top, and deep blue A-line skirt. Unfortunately, the skirt was also made of the itchiest fabric known to mankind.

I'd bought it because it was super cute, but every time I wore it,

I ended up scratching myself like I had fleas. Not very attractive.

"Thanks," I said to Janet. "It's been fun so far."

"Well, why don't you hand over your LoveLine 3000 so I can upload your information into the main computer. I can also port updated e-mail addresses to you this way."

At her words, my heart stopped beating and nearly jumped out of my chest. I hadn't realized she'd actually want to *see* the matches. If I handed her the PDA, she'd know instantly that I'd matched Maya up with three guys, thus breaking a cupid rule. Would she buy my "gut" reasoning?

Instinct told me not to find out.

"I'm sorry, I left it at home," I said, pasting on a huge, fake smile. With my heel, I subtly nudged my purse—the one that currently held said PDA—under my chair. "That was so stupid of me. I can bring it in next time, though. Will that work?"

"Sure," she replied, "but please bring it in then." She glanced at her watch. "Okay, you're free to go. I'll see you next Monday."

Sweet, blissful relief surged through my limbs. Thank God I'd have time to delete Maya's match and claim it was an "accident."

I stood and shook her hand. "You got it!"

"If you feel comfortable with it," she said as I slid my arms into my coat, "try upping your quota to two matches this week."

I nodded. "Absolutely. I can do that."

"Oh, wait." She flipped through a manila folder on her desk, then handed me a check. "Here you go. I'll be paying you weekly at our meetings."

I grinned widely. "Thanks!" *Sweet!* It wasn't a land mine, but I'd earned this paycheck. And I was doubly happy to find out I'd be getting paid weekly.

After the meeting, I hopped in Mom's Camry and pulled out of the parking lot, giddy with relief. I'd managed to avert certain disaster and keep my awesome job. Janet had praised my matches and even upped my quota. And tomorrow, I'd get to witness the biggest payoff of all.

Boy, would Maya be surprised when the three guys started wooing her! I couldn't wait to see her happy face.

I was seriously the best friend ever. Of course, Maya would never know I was the reason for her dating surge, but that didn't matter. It would be my little anonymous contribution to the whole "pay it forward" concept.

About a mile from my house, I shifted the car into the right lane. Suddenly, a wailing siren appeared from out of nowhere behind me, and blue and red lights flashed in my rearview mirror.

But I wasn't speeding or anything! And I'd even used my turn signal (which, I freely admit, I sometimes forget about). Crap, I was in serious trouble now. Mom would kill me for getting a ticket while driving her car.

"Pull over!" a loud voice barked over the police car's megaphone.

With shaky hands, I sucked in shallow breaths and did as instructed, parking on the side of the road. I dug into my purse to find my license, barely able to concentrate. I was in such deep sh—

The megaphone interrupted my thoughts. "Ma'am, we know you're using the marijuana!"

I clenched my jaw. I'd know that irritating voice from anywhere.

Pissed off, I hopped out of the car, stomped to my brother's cop car, and stood by his door, hands on hips. I cussed loudly, scaring an old lady crossing the street. She blinked at me and walked faster, trying to get away from me.

"Geez, Rob, you scared the piss out of me!" I yelled. "I thought I was in real trouble. You're such a jerk."

Rob and his partner were in the front seat, bent over laughing. Rob straightened, then said through the megaphone, "Stop cussing at me or I'm going to have to take you in."

I shot him the most evil glare I could muster. "Stop pulling me over!" I shouted at him through the window. "This is the second time now you've done this to me. It's still not funny."

He rolled down his window and stuck his head out. "Then, ma'am, stop driving in this city."

"But I live here!" I turned on my heel and headed back to the car.

"And, ma'am," Rob hollered to my back, his voice ringing loud and clear throughout all of Cleveland, no doubt, "lay off the spray tan! Your skin's starting to look orange."

I whirled back around and stomped toward him, unable to control my rage. "If you pull me over again," I said, pointing my finger in his face, "I'll tell Mom about the time I caught you making out with Cindy Masterson in Mom and Dad's bed when you two were supposed to be studying."

His jaw dropped. He tried to cover up his fear, but I could see it in his eyes. "You wouldn't."

I leaned close to his face, then widened my eyes and blinked rapidly, gasping. "Mom, it was awful! He was touching her under her shirt! I didn't know *what* to do!"

Rob stared at me for a long moment, then tipped his hat. "Have a nice day." He drove off in a hurry.

chapter five

Tuesday morning, I walked with Maya to school, shuffling carefully along the slick, snow-encrusted sidewalks. Sooty gray clouds hung low in the air. *Great*—more snow was surely coming. Cleveland in March sucked hard. But my thoughts were quickly taken off the weather and returned to the huge success that was Operation Hook Maya Up.

Case in point: Josh, the drum major, was already waiting outside the front doors, his gaze scouring the grounds. When he saw me and Maya walk up the front steps, he waved, his breath coming out in rapid puffs at the sight of her.

"Hiya, Maya," Josh said, a smile plastered across his face. It was dorky, for sure, but still pretty darn cute. Bright pink spots tinged his cheeks and the tips of his ears, and I wondered if it was from the cold or from the excitement of seeing Maya. "Need help with your backpack or trumpet case or anything?"

Without waiting for an answer, he snagged both items in question. His body now laden with an instrument case and two backpacks, he looked like a lovesick bellhop.

"Oh, hey, Josh," Maya said, her lips wavering in a small, surprised smile. "Thanks for the help." She snuggled deeper into her thick black coat.

This was definitely friendlier and less tongue-tied than Maya normally was around guys, but she didn't seem as head over heels for Josh as he was for her. Interesting. Given the way the magic had worked with Britney and Matthew, I'd half expected Maya and Josh to be playing tonsil hockey by now.

Maya headed up the steps, and Josh teetered by her side, ignoring me completely.

"Oh, hey," I mumbled to Josh's back, a little miffed that he couldn't even bother to say hi or acknowledge my existence. "No, I'm fine, thanks for asking."

"Do you always talk to yourself?" a guy's voice said.

I turned gingerly to my right, trying not to slip on any icy patches lingering on the school steps. It was Derek, leaning against the concrete stair ramp, bearing a deep smirk as he looked at me.

My heart did that funky pitter-patter it always does when I see him. "Oh, h-hi." Gee, stuttering is sexy. My oh-so-witty reply was sure to dazzle him.

Derek slid up beside me, and we headed into the building like everything was normal. As if we did this all the time. I felt like everyone's eyes were on me, though in reality, no one probably gave a crap about me and who I walked with.

I looked for Maya among the clusters tromping through the hallway, but she was already out of my sight. I hoped everything was going okay with her and Josh. Luckily, I'd have a chance to talk to her in our first-period English class, as well as at lunch. That is, if I managed not to pass out from forgetting how to breathe, due to the distraction of Derek's incredible hotness by my side.

"Well, see ya," Derek said, taking off down the hallway to the left.

"Okay," I croaked, waving bye to him with waggly fingers. I headed to my locker. Damn, I should have had something more clever to say than "huh-hi," or "okay." *Stupid Felicity.* This was not the way to get his attention. I grabbed my books from my locker and took off for English.

Maya was already in the classroom, sitting straight up in her seat.

She waved me over beside her, eyes wide, mouth shaped like an O.

"You won't believe what just happened," she breathed. "Josh asked me out. On a date. For tonight! Can you believe it? He's so sweet."

At least someone's love life was going the right way. "That's awesome," I said, pushing my own Derek woes out of my mind. I had a job to do, and Maya was a part of that. Plus, I was utterly thrilled for my friend and wanted to make sure she knew how excited I was. *Focus.* "What kind of date?"

"He wants to take me to dinner and a movie. I think we're going to go see—"

"Shh," Mrs. Kendel interrupted, the permanent scowl deepening on her face. I turned away from Maya and faced forward in my seat. Our teacher was not a good person to piss off.

Mrs. Kendel handed out the *Grapes of Wrath* test to every student, the gold bangles on her right wrist clanging with the repetitive motion. "It's time to pay attention. This is not an open-book or open-note test. You have thirty minutes to complete the exam. Please use a number-two pencil and write legibly in the short-answer portion. You may beginnnnnn . . ." she drawled off, staring at her thin gold watch in silence for several seconds. "Now."

As I read the first question and filled in my answer, I glanced at

Maya from the corner of my eye (no, I wasn't cheating). I took in her faded jeans and black sweater, her pale, unmade face, and her dark hair tied back with a black ponytail holder. I swear, Maya's wardrobe was filled with so much black, Death himself had to be jealous. I tried to observe her with an unbiased point of view, to see her not as a best friend, but as a professional cupid.

Hm, if one of these love matches was going to last past the two-week love-glow period, which would be a total win-win for everyone involved, we were gonna have to do some makeover changes, stat. Maybe during lunch we could do some wardrobe replanning, and this weekend, I could take her to get her hair cut and highlighted—

A knock on the classroom door startled us all. I looked up and saw a guy peering through the glass panel, scanning the room. It was Quentin, the yearbook editor and love match #2 for Maya. His eyes lit up when he saw her beside me.

"Mr. Lovejoy," Mrs. Kendel said, ripping the door open with a meaty hand, "can we help you, sir? We're in the middle of a test."

"Sorry, Mrs. Kendel," Quentin said, unable to tear his eyes from Maya, "but this couldn't wait." He stepped past the teacher and crossed the room, stopping in front of Maya. He took her hand in his, then dropped down on one knee, tugging a folded piece of paper out of his back pocket with his free hand. "I wrote a poem for you, Maya. It took me all night to compose it."

Maya's jaw, along with every other jaw in the classroom, hung open. "You did? For me?" she pulled it together to ask.

"Mr. Lovejoy, we don't have time for this nonsense," Mrs. Kendel said. She opened the door wider. "You need to leave."

"But if I don't get to read my poem, my heart will die," Quentin said, swallowing hard. I'd never seen a guy that serious about love in my life. "It'll only take a minute. Please."

"Come on," one of the girls in class said. "Let him read the poem!"

"Yeah," others started chiming in. "Let him read!"

"Zip it!" Mrs. Kendel barked to the class. She looked at Quentin. "You have thirty seconds, starting now."

"Thank you!" He looked at his paper and began to read, pouring emotion into his voice. "Ode to Maya." He paused dramatically. "The sun rises and sets in your fair face. Being near you makes my heart race. Your laughter, wit, and style are so bright, I'd love to take you out tonight."

Oh, God. That was the cheesiest thing I'd ever heard in my life. It took him all night to write that? I'd hate to see the first few drafts of that puppy.

Apparently, the guys in the class agreed with me, judging from their loud guffaws. "Way to go, lover boy," one ribbed. "That'll get you laid for sure."

"Hush, Mr. Packard," Mrs. Kendel snapped.

Tom Packard's girlfriend elbowed him in the side, and he grunted loudly.

"Shut up, you jerk," she cried, her voice thin and watery. "That was the most romantic thing I've ever seen. How come you never write *me* poems?"

Quentin ignored them both, focusing solely on Maya's ever-reddening face.

"Say yes!" someone shouted.

"Yes, yes, yes!" girls chanted.

Blinking rapidly, Maya nodded, smiling. "Sure, that sounds good."

The class broke out in applause. You'd think he'd just proposed to her, the way he jumped up and hugged her, almost knocking her out of her chair.

"Well, now that that's finished, you can leave, Mr. Lovejoy," Mrs. Kendel said, attempting to regain her control of the classroom. But even she looked moved by the gesture. Who would have thought beneath that withered skin of hers beat the heart of a romantic?

With one last wink, Quentin slipped out the door, a modern-day Romeo who had likely just won the heart of every girl in class, and turned Maya into an instant celeb.

I stared at the closed door, stunned. Wow. This cupid thing was way more powerful than I'd realized. I tried to go back to focusing on my English test, but really, who could concentrate after a display like that?

One thing was for sure: Quentin and Josh had it bad for Maya, even worse than she seemed to have it for them. And given the pattern, I'd be willing to bet that Ben, the third match, would be the same way.

Now I could see why Janet had discouraged group matches like this. It seemed the guys' love was much stronger than Maya's, since it was aimed only at her, but her love was weaker since it was divided among the three of them.

Maybe that wasn't such a bad thing, though. At least Maya would be in her right mind when all three of them tried to date her.

I scrawled out the short answers on my test with a half-assed effort, not caring at the moment about the woes of the Great Depression. Then, I stopped writing mid-sentence. Maya had told Josh and

Quentin she'd go on a date with each of them—tonight. Crap. So much for staying clear-headed.

When Mrs. Kendel called time, we all put our pencils down and handed our tests up the rows. I took the opportunity to lean over and talk to Maya. "Hey—isn't your date with *Josh* tonight too? You just double-booked!"

She gasped. "Oh, no. You're right! What was I thinking?" Her face fell. "I just got so excited at being asked out. And I really like them both."

I couldn't blame her. After a dating dry period of, oh, her whole life, it's no wonder she got that way. It would be like starving for sixteen years, then being taken to a buffet and getting wooed by the steaks. Or something like that. "We'll figure it out," I said.

Mrs. Kendel shot me and Maya a small glare, then went over to the chalkboard and started writing. "Okay, let's go over the test answers together."

The rest of the period flew by fast, as did the whole morning. I mostly zoned out in my classes and fretted over the Maya dilemma, not sure what to tell her. How would we figure out which guy to ditch tonight? And what would we do if Ben demanded a date with her too?

At lunch, Andy met up with us, sliding into a seat beside Maya and unwrapping her food with gusto. "Hey, girls," she said between bites of a burrito. "How are things going?"

Maya inched in close to her. "You won't believe my day!" She filled her in on the Josh-and-Quentin love-fest.

"Geez, that beats my day by far." Andy shook her head, a new admiration for Maya lighting her eyes. "What, do you have a guy magnet or something on today?"

Maya shrugged. "I don't know. Just my lucky day, I guess. Right now, though, I have to figure out which date to postpone." As she spoke, her voice wavered, and her face grew paler, if that was even possible. She slumped in her seat. "But what if I cancel with one, and he changes his mind and decides he doesn't want to see me at all?" She groaned and leaned forward, thunking her head in her hands. "I like them both! I don't want to have to choose."

"I wouldn't worry about them losing interest," I said, patting Maya on the back. "They both seemed pretty smitten." Of course, I knew she'd have two weeks of their undivided attention, but there wasn't any way I could say that without giving away trade secrets.

Andy tilted her head and twirled a strand of hair around her pinkie, considering the situation. "There's no way to know that for sure, though. Guys are so hormonal. Maybe it's better not to tempt fate."

We sat in silence for a moment. Then, Andy snapped her fingers. "I think there's only one solution, Maya—you'll go out with both of them, tonight." She looked at me, and I recognized that expression in her eyes. It was stubborn determination. "And Felicity and I will help you juggle your two dates."

chapter six

And that's why, on a Tuesday night, when I should have been home doing quadratic equations, or washing my hair, or anything else in the world, I was listening to my iPod and staring at the back of Josh's slightly shaggy head of hair in the darkened movie theater. He'd just crammed another fistful of popcorn into his mouth, nodding in enthusiasm as blood spurted from a severed arm on the screen.

Ew. I popped a Whopper in my mouth and sucked on the chocolaty coating, reveling in the taste. I couldn't believe I'd agreed to this scheme, but Andy had worked her magic over lunch and talked me into it. I'd even pointed out to her and Maya that things like this never worked right except in the movies, but Andy was convinced we could pull it off.

Besides, Maya had looked so hopeful about the idea, I just couldn't say no. This was, after all, sorta kinda partially my fault, if only in a strictly technical and by-the-book kind of way. I'd broken a cupid rule, so I had to help clean up the mess.

Well, at least I wasn't the only one on recon duty. Andy was doing the exact same thing with Quentin in the next theater over. We'd agreed beforehand to stick to the guys like white on rice while Maya bounced back and forth between them.

The girl in the seat beside me elbowed me in the arm for the four hundredth time, and I shot her an evil glare, trying to reclaim my armrest. Not that she was paying any attention to me, since she was too busy cramming her tongue in her guy's ear.

Which I normally wouldn't care about, if she weren't making revolting slurping sounds every time. *Slurp slurp. Giggle giggle. Slurp slurp.* It was disgusting.

I cranked up the sound on my iPod and sank into my seat, two rows back from my target. Josh had taken Maya to the six thirty showing of *He Knows Who You Are*. It was a horror piece of B-grade crap starring some fluffball Hollywood hoochie of the month. This actress couldn't do a scene without either losing an article of clothing or tripping over a blade of grass as she screamed in overexaggerated fright.

The movie was cheesy, and a bit on the gory side, with limbs being hacked off left and right. Totally not my thing. So I entertained myself with my iPod on shuffle and kept my eyes carefully trained on Josh.

Not that he'd moved from his seat. He was an easygoing date, for sure. In the forty minutes we'd been in the theater, Maya had already excused herself twice, as we'd planned. Before the dates, Andy had mapped out a route plan and time-share schedule, and the three of us had come up with a whole list of reasons for her to sneak out of the theaters.

We'd also decided Maya would have coffee with Quentin before their movie and go into the theater with him. And then, right before the other movie would start, she'd duck out to meet Josh and head into *their* theater together, alternating back and forth at regular intervals during the flicks. At the end of the movies, she'd tell Quentin good night and have dessert with Josh afterward. Equal time for equal dates.

I had to hand it to Andy, she was unbelievably good at scheming. The master planner, indeed. If I ever got in a situation where I had to date two guys at the same time, I knew who to go to.

Yeah, right. Like that would happen.

I took a sip of my Coke, downed another couple of delicious Whoppers, then skipped to a more upbeat song to tune out the stupid actress's piercing scream in the movie.

Forty-three minutes in, and it was Maya's turn to be with Josh again. She was leaning into his side, whispering something in his ear. His shoulders shook as he laughed at whatever she said, and then he reached an arm over and wrapped it around her, tugging her closer.

A lump clogged my throat as I watched them. I was both happy for Maya and a little sad for myself. It was a bittersweet feeling knowing I was helping her find love but not being able to do a darn thing about my own pathetic love life.

Plus, I felt really bizarre watching them, like I was some kind of pervert. I mean, what kind of person goes to the movies alone and watches couples like this? Lonely old men? Yeah, it was the good-friend thing to do, but this was still a bit awkward.

I'd damn well better get some Twizzlers out of it, at least. I wished for the ten billionth time that year that I owned a cell phone. Then at least I could text Andy to see how things were going on her side.

After another few minutes of watching the movie, Maya said

something to Josh, then crouched and hustled her way out of her row, slipping down the steps and out of the theater. Josh leaned back in his seat and took a draw from the ginormous Styrofoam cup, focusing on the film.

I wonder, what excuse did she use this time? Phone call from her mom? Soda spilled on her shirt? More popcorn? A pee break? And how many excuses had she burned through by now? We still had an hour left in the movie, and I didn't want her to run out.

I looked down at my iPod and scrolled through the albums. Who did I want to listen to now? Maybe I'd play some old music. I had the *Grease* sound track in there, which I'd snagged from my mom's collection and uploaded on a whim. I clicked it, listening in amusement to John Travolta and Olivia Newton-John croon about summer lovin'. Maybe in a few months I'd have my own summer love—preferably one named Derek.

Another scream ripped through the theater, and I jerked slightly in my seat in shock, looking up at the screen. The hoochie was lying on a bed, strategically covering her surgically enhanced, heaving bare chest with her perfectly manicured hands as some guy in a black trench coat stalked closer and closer, leering in anticipation. I love Maya, but she truly has terrible taste in movies.

I glanced down at Josh to see his reaction . . . but he wasn't there.

My heart stopped beating for a second, then slammed hard in my chest. Oh God, where was he?

Leaning forward in my seat, I scoured the dark theater as best as possible. Josh was nowhere to be found. He must have slipped out when I was daydreaming about Derek.

Crap!

Way to go, Felicity. I had one job tonight, to keep an eye on Josh, and I'd already blown it.

I yanked out my earbuds and crammed the iPod in my pocket. Time to get out of there and find Josh . . . before he could find Maya with Quentin.

Okay, calm down. I forced myself to take several deep breaths. He was probably just getting a reload of popcorn, or something like that. Maya and Quentin were safely in another theater, and Josh would have no possible reason to go in there. Maya wasn't scheduled to emerge from the other movie for at least five more minutes. Nothing was going to go wrong.

I rose from my seat and tripped over the legs of the make-out slurper beside me.

"Excuse me," I mumbled, not bothering to wait for a response. I headed to the end of the aisle, then ran down the stairs and out of the room.

The lobby was bustling with people shuffling through lines to get popcorn, tugging children's hands to keep them from disappearing. I saw three shaggy-haired guys horsing around near a coming attractions cardboard cutout, and a guy I recognized from the basketball team on a date with a redheaded cheerleader. But no Josh.

Where could he be?

A hand clamped down on my shoulder. Heart in throat, I spun around. It was Andy, and she looked unusually freaked out, her breath coming out in short bursts. She tucked a strand of hair behind her ear. "There you are!" she said. "Josh just went in the bathroom!"

I heaved a huge sigh of relief. "Oh, thank God. I thought I'd—"

"Quentin's in there already, *and he just finished a jumbo Coke!*" she blurted.

Oh, no. No doubt they'd see each other in there. After all, guys don't pee in individual stalls like girls do, do they? No, they have those urinal thingies they line up against.

And if they saw each other—I mean, if they saw each other's face, not their guy parts—they'd probably start talking . . . and then, they'd surely find out both of them were on a date with the same girl.

"Where's Maya?" I asked, trying to keep control over my shaking voice.

"She's still in the movie. We gotta do something, now." Andy's hand clutched my shoulder harder, her fingers digging under the bone.

I flinched under her killer grip. "Hey, that hurts. Okay, okay, I'll fix this."

I eyed the men's restroom, and a sick thud of realization hit the bottom of my stomach. There was only one way to keep this thing from escalating.

Drawing in a deep breath and screwing up my courage, I marched straight ahead and pushed the men's bathroom door open with a mighty heave.

"Oh, man!" I squealed as I rushed in. "I gotta pee like crazy!"

I froze dead in my tracks. The row of men all lined up in front of the urinals turned, wide-eyed, and stared at me in shock.

Including Quentin and Josh. They were standing right beside

each other. Neither one was throwing punches, so I must have burst in on time.

"Aaaaaah!" Quentin gasped when he saw me, turning away from me to zip his pants. His hands moved so fast, I hoped he wouldn't accidentally catch "it" in the zipper.

"Felicity?" Josh said in a horrified tone, then followed Quentin's lead quickly when he realized I could almost see his junk. "What are you—"

"Omigodthisisn'tthewomen'sbathroom!" I blurted in a rush, my words tripping over each other. I didn't have to fake the nervous edge in my voice. "I'm so sorry!"

Urinus interruptus accomplished, I backed out of the bathroom and let the door swing shut behind me, then plopped with shaky legs down on the bench against the wall, right beside Andy. That was quite possibly the weirdest, nastiest experience of my life, and I wanted to take a super-hot shower to scrub off the dirty feeling.

"Did you get there in time?" Andy asked. "What were they doing?"

As if in answer to her question, Quentin and Josh both rushed out of the bathroom, almost running in the opposite directions to their respective theaters.

With a visible sigh of relief, Andy nodded at me in approval, a smirk curling the corner of her mouth. She didn't even look surprised about my rash idea, and I wondered how many men's bathrooms she'd gone into . . . or, even worse, thought I'd been in.

"You're good," she said to me, rising from the bench. "Okay, we gotta go finish this date. We'll talk later." She took off running behind Quentin.

I took my time following Josh back to the theater—I didn't want him to think I was a stalker—and filed back toward my row, sinking deftly into my seat. Even Slurpy McGiggle's skanky make-out sound effects didn't seem as gross as what had just happened.

Pushing my earbuds back in, I turned on my iPod and waited the rest of the date out. Operation Hook Maya Up was turning out to be crazier than I'd ever imagined.

chapter seven

The next day, I arrived at school with the furry hood of my winter coat tightly wrapped around my face so only my nose and mouth showed; I was nervous about being seen by Josh or Quentin. I just knew they thought I was some kind of bathroom peeper, and I didn't feel like facing them this morning. My only hope was that they were still so blinded by love (or so embarrassed at having been caught with their zippers down) that they wouldn't bother to mention the encounter to anyone else. The last thing I needed was for everyone at school to be laughing at my expense.

Luckily, the dates had ended well enough last night. Maya had said good night to Quentin (with a hug in the lobby) before her movie with Josh ended. She'd then headed out for post-movie dessert with Josh. Both guys had also asked Maya out again. Thankfully, instead of accepting on the spot, she'd promised to call them and set the dates up in the near future. And she was still equally smitten with them both, so it was totally worth my embarrassment to see Maya coming out of her shell like this.

I looked down the hall as I shuffled into the building and spied Maya standing frozen in front of her open locker, her jaw dropped to the floor. I hurried over, wondering what disaster had happened. Had Quentin and Josh found out about their double dates somehow and left Maya breakup notes in her locker? Or had she somehow figured out that her sudden luck with guys was due to cupid magic?

When she saw me, she grabbed my upper arm, her eyes wide and slightly buggy. "Felicity," she breathed, "you won't believe it. You know Ben? Ben Johnson?"

Oh, Ben! In all the madness with Quentin and Josh, I'd forgotten about pairing him up with Maya too. Duh!

Come to think about it, I hadn't seen him in school at all yesterday. "What about him?" I asked her.

Maya thrust a folded note into my hand. "Read this."

I unfolded the paper and read the scrawling handwriting.

Maya,

*I was sick yesterday, so I didn't get to ~~see~~ talk
to you, but you were all I could think about. I
would like to have lunch with you today. My treat.*

~~Sincer~~ Love,

Ben

"Wow, he wrote 'love,'" I said. I knew he was under the cupid spell, but I was still surprised.

"I know," she said, still breathy. "I just can't believe it. I always thought he was cute, but I didn't know he'd noticed me."

"So I take it you're saying yes?"

She took the note back and pressed it against her heart, her shiny mouth sliding into a slow smile. Wait—was Maya wearing *lip gloss*?

It was sheer, but yes, I detected a hint of glossy pink tint on her lips. And now that I was looking closer, her eyelids had a touch of light brown eye shadow on them.

"Are you wearing makeup?" I asked, dumbfounded.

She shrugged, a blush creeping across her cheeks. "Just a little. Why, does it look bad?"

She put the note in her pocket, then lifted her hand and went to wipe the gloss off her mouth.

I grabbed her arm to stop her. "No, don't do that. It looks . . . great. I was just surprised, that's all."

Even her traditional ponytail seemed a little nicer today than usual. She'd curled a few loose strands of hair around her face.

"This is crazy," Maya said, shaking her head. "I can't believe that three guys—" She jerked in surprise, then dug into her pocket. "Hold on, I think someone's texting me. Must be Andy."

She flipped her cell phone open, clicking the buttons a couple of times, and scanned the message. Then, her smile grew bigger.

"That was Quentin, thanking me for the date last night. He said he can't wait to see me today!" She closed the cell and looked at me. "This is so overwhelming. Why is this happening to me?"

Impulsively, I hugged her. "It's happening because you're an awesome person, and boys are finally starting to notice that," I said, pouring my heart into my voice.

"Well, thank you for helping me last night. You and Andy are a godsend," Maya whispered into my shoulder.

Another pair of arms wrapped around the both of us. "Hey, I wanna join the love-fest too," Andy cooed, squeezing us tightly.

We laughed.

"How come you're so late getting to school today?" I asked her. "Usually you're here before we are."

Andy grimaced and released us, rubbing the small of her back. "I'm exhausted, that's why. After I got back from Maya's dates last night, Mom made me practice yoga positions with her for an hour. I collapsed in bed without even setting my alarm. I think the dog actually woke me up."

Maya snickered, shaking her head. "Yoga, huh? Your mom is so trendy."

"Yeah, it's her new hobby of the month. She walks around in yoga pants and a tank top all day, breaking into new poses every couple of minutes. My dad is threatening to stick her out on the lawn if she doesn't stop."

We all erupted into laughter just as the first bell rang. Time to hustle. English class would wait for no man—or teen girl, in my case.

Mrs. Kendel practically pushed me and Maya in the room, then closed the door behind us.

"Ms. Takahashi," she said to Maya, looking down at her over her nose, "I trust we won't have any further disruptions in class today? No one bursting into the room bearing a Candygram, breaking into song, or other declarations of love?"

Maya shook her head and reddened slightly as the students around us tittered. She took her seat, and I sat in mine beside her, shooting her an empathetic look.

The teacher strolled up and down the aisles, handing out our next novel. *Jane Eyre*, by Charlotte Brontë.

Almost in unison, the guys in the room let out a miserable groan when they saw what we were reading.

"Come *on*," DeShawn Wallace mumbled, thumping the book down on his desk. "Can't we read something that's not a *romance*? Those are so boring. 'Oh, I love you so much, my darling!'" he said in a falsetto, batting his eyelashes.

DeShawn is the very embodiment of the quintessential arrogant, irritating male. Every time he speaks, I can't fight the massive eye-rolling.

My intense dislike of him started back in fifth grade, when

he'd pantsed me in front of the class. Because of that underwear-flashing debacle, it took years for people to stop calling me "Fruit of the Loom."

So, my hackles went up instantly at DeShawn's words.

"And what's wrong with romance?" I said, unable to bite back the snippy edge in my voice. "Maybe if you read these kinds of books, you could hold on to a girlfriend for longer than a week."

Okay, that wasn't nice. I instantly felt a twinge in my stomach for being so hostile in reply. Yeah, DeShawn was a jerk, but his insult hadn't been aimed at me directly . . . just at my line of employment. Besides, he didn't know I was a cupid. I needed to stop taking him so personally. "Look, I'm sorry, but—" I started.

"Oooooooh," one of the jocks behind him interrupted me, laughing hard. He slammed a palm in DeShawn's back, shoving him forward. "Burned!"

"Zip it, everyone," Mrs. Kendel said, shooting me a quick frown, then turning her attention to DeShawn. "Mr. Wallace, if you don't care for my choice in reading material, perhaps you'd like for everyone to read *War and Peace* and write a report on it, instead."

She dug into a drawer in her desk, grabbed what was quite

possibly the biggest novel I'd ever seen, and slammed it down in front of DeShawn.

I stared in disbelief. No one else but Mrs. Kendel would threaten a sixteen-year-old that way . . . and mean it.

DeShawn's lips pinched together. He shook his head slowly. He had to be feeling the heated burn of the entire class glaring at him. *Jane Eyre* was definitely the better, quicker read, and no one wanted his big mouth to blow it for us.

"No?" Mrs. Kendel asked him, then snagged up the tome. "Then I trust we'll let me decide what's right for the class." She turned around, stuffed *War and Peace* back in her drawer, and headed for the chalkboard.

While Mrs. Kendel's chalk squeaked out biographical details about Charlotte Brontë on the board, DeShawn shot me an angry glare. Like I'd made him rant about romance. Oh well, I was disgusted with him, too. What is it with guys like that? What he needed was a good girlfriend to straighten his sorry self out.

At that moment, a beam of pure enlightenment hit me. I was totally the best person to distract DeShawn from his own obnoxiousness and help him experience true love. It was the perfect comeuppance. Mr. "Romance Sucks" was going to be the next on my list for matchmaking. He'd probably be way less annoying—and way more vulnerable—when he was head over heels for someone. And it would be highly amusing to watch him get all mushy-gushy in looooooove.

In fact, I bet he'd be desperate to pick up any tips possible on how to hang on to a girl. I could help him with that, too.

I chuckled to myself and grabbed my notebook. This cupid job was full of perks I hadn't considered before. Hell, maybe I'd find matches for all the disbelievers in school, just to teach them how wrong it was to snub romance.

A pale-faced Ben was waiting for Maya outside the room, almost bouncing in eagerness to see her. His nose was red on the end from being sick, and his eyes were puffy, but he didn't seem to care. And judging from the way her face lit up when she saw him, she didn't mind either.

"Maya!" he said, smiling. "Get my note?"

She nodded shyly.

"Great. I gotta head to class, but I wanted to see you first." He started to lean in close to her, then jerked back, as if unable to decide what was appropriate. Finally, he just grabbed her hand and pumped it up and down enthusiastically, then took off down the hallway.

Maya busted up giggling. "Did he just shake my hand?"

"Hey, he was just nervous," I said, laughing. "I can understand that. You know, you *are* a super hottie today."

"You sure are," Josh said to Maya from behind her. He slipped right in between her and me, turning his back to me.

"Oh, hi Josh!" she said, then started down the hall with him, not even noticing me anymore. "I didn't see you there. How was chem lab?"

I slowed my speed, letting them walk off together. I'd already had enough fun being the third wheel and didn't relish jumping back into it anytime soon. I shifted my notebook and *Jane Eyre* to my other arm and headed toward my locker, keeping my eyes peeled in case I was lucky enough to catch a glimpse of Derek.

Beside the stairs, I noticed Matthew and Britney, my first cupid match, standing close together. Matthew stroked the side of her face with his palm, then planted a small kiss on her forehead.

Britney sighed, a satisfied smile on her face, and took off upstairs. A week and a half in, and the magic clearly was still going strong.

Two of Matthew's buddies snickered as they approached him. "Dude, I can't believe how whipped you are," one said, shaking his head.

"Yeah, yeah," Matthew replied, rolling his eyes. "Laugh now, but we'll see how you feel when you find someone."

The three of them headed down the hall.

A warm feeling of joy swept over me. Look at what a great job I had done with the two of them! Matthew was enamored, totally swept off his feet for Britney. And she was obviously just as wrapped up in him.

Man, it hurt to be this talented at matchmaking. I wanted to proclaim right there in the hallway, *See those two people? I helped them find love!* Of course, I couldn't, so I settled for a tiny squeal under my breath.

"You okay, Felicity?" a guy's voice asked from right behind me.

I spun around, nearly smacking headfirst into Bobby Loward. I bit back a sigh.

Bobby Blowhard, as everyone in school called him, was a weird guy, to say the least. And he was about five foot two on a good day, which put him at eye level with me.

He also had a severe case of short-man's syndrome. You know, where little guys act big and tough in order to make up for their lack of height. So he wore his brown hair in a "tough," spiky style and pumped iron a lot.

Well, I assumed he did, anyway. He was always talking about how much he lifted. I couldn't count the number of times he rubbed his arm muscles in front of me, yapping on about all the reps he'd finished that day.

Like I, or any other girl in school, cared. Poor, delusional Bobby.

"Hi, Bobby," I muttered, trying not to look irritated. Or make eye contact with his black mesh shirt.

Ew. I mean, come on—I could see his little man nipples poking through the holes. How was that even allowed? I thought clothing you could see through was against school rules. He should get sent home.

"I totally blew out my quads yesterday," he bragged, moving even closer to me. "Did three hundred pounds on the leg press." He looked down at his thighs and flexed the muscles. "Gotta keep in top shape, though, if I'm gonna top my own wrestling record next year."

"Gee," I said, wracking my brain for something nice to say. "Well, good luck." Rocking up on my toes, I looked over his shoulder, trying to plan my escape. Being trapped in a conversation with Bobby Blowhard was as bad as doing your own dental surgery, sans anesthesia.

And I should know—I mean, about dealing with Bobby, not about the dental surgery. He and I shared two classes together, health and math, so I always had to hear him spout off about something.

For some reason, Bobby had a crush on me. Maybe because I tried to be nice to him, even though he was odd. I kind of felt bad for him, since most people couldn't stand him. But it just figured. The one guy in the entire school who actually liked me had to be Bobby Blowhard.

He leaned in closer, now flexing his pecs at me too. If I didn't know better, I'd think he was having a seizure, with all the body twitches going on right now. "So, Felicity, what are you doing this weekend?"

Oh, God. Was he going to ask me out on a date?

I backed away, trying not to flinch at his creepy smile and dancing man-boobs, then glanced at my watch. "Oh, geez. Would you look at that? I gotta run. My American history class will probably start any minute, and I'm sure everyone will be inside soon. See ya later!"

I smiled and waved, turning to walk at breakneck speed. Time to get the hell out of Dodge before being guilted into something I didn't want to do.

chapter eight

I ducked into American history, relieved by my narrow escape. No way did I want to get stuck going on a date with Bobby. And to ask me in front of everyone in the hallway, where people could overhear him? What if Derek saw Bobby leaning that close to me and assumed we were a couple? He'd probably never consider touching me after that. Okay, not that he was considering it, anyway, but still.

I flipped open my notebook and history book. We were wrapping up a lengthy discussion on the Great Depression—my English and history teachers liked to coordinate their lessons sometimes. Stupid me, I'd forgotten to read the required chapters last night because of going on Maya's date, but luckily, Mr. Shrupe went over everything in the book, so I didn't stress too hard.

Mr. Shrupe stood in front of the class, wearing his requisite white dress shirt, brown plaid sweater vest, and brown pants. His brown hair was parted perfectly on the side and slicked down across the top of his head. I swear, it would kill the guy to throw a little zazz in his wardrobe. He must get color-coordination tips from Maya or something.

"Today, we're going to wrap up our discussion about the—" Mr. Shrupe paused, waiting for the answer. No one replied. "Great Depression," he filled in, his voice droning. "That's right."

A couple of students groaned in misery, but he didn't seem to hear. Mr. Shrupe was certainly focused on history, if not fashion.

He wrote a few key words about the Great Depression on the board:

stock market crash/Black Tuesday
dust bowl
the New Deal

"And the Great Depression mainly occurred during the—" He paused. No answer again. *Duh.* "The nineteen thirties. That's right."

To keep from stabbing myself in the eye with my pencil from the sheer torture of enduring this lecture, I grabbed my PDA and nestled it in my lap. It was time to distract myself with something useful—making more successful love matches. If I could find more well-suited couples like Britney and Matthew, I'd be floating in bonus money in no time at all.

As visions of all the new shoes and super-hottie clothes I'd buy danced through my mind, I flipped through my database to find DeShawn's profile, which apparently I'd filled out on a mega-cranky day:

Name: DeShawn Wallace
Age: 17
Interests: Himself
Style: Jock (and smart-ass)

Okay, I needed a bit more to go on than that. I forced myself to think of anything positive about DeShawn. It took me several minutes, but something did finally pop up: He likes to crack jokes. I added "sports" and "strong sense of humor" to his profile.

Who could I pair DeShawn up with? I flipped through the profiles of all the girls in my database. One, oddly enough, jumped out at me:

Name: Marisa Dwight

Age: 16

Interests: Poetry, romantic encounters, journaling. Loves Shakespeare, as well.

Style: Smart, but popular

Marisa's a smart chick who is leagues above everyone else. She has perfect skin, can rock a poetry slam like nobody's business, and has legs longer than my entire body. She can also spout Shakespeare sonnets at whim and is probably going to one of those Ivy League schools when she graduates next year.

Could the two of them make it work as a couple? Well, Shakespeare was a great comedy writer, right? Plus, he wrote all those sword-fighting scenes . . . couldn't that count as a sports interest?

And, most importantly, dating Marisa would give DeShawn something positive to aspire for. He'd be inspired to learn the finer arts of wooing, an activity that could only do him some good. A smart, pulled-together girl like Marisa was exactly what he needed.

A small part of me whispered that I was stretching this one big-time. But then again, hadn't I stretched it with Britney and Matthew? Look at how well that worked . . . lightning could strike twice, couldn't it? Or three times, if you counted Maya's matches. I told my doubting inner voice to shut it.

I composed my love match e-mail to the two of them and hit send, then put away my PDA and tried my best to focus on the rest of Mr. Shrupe's lecture.

I couldn't wait to see what happened when Marisa and DeShawn fell in love.

"Is spring really just around the corner?" I mused aloud to my mom that evening, running my finger along Target's shelf of fake green plants. "Because it sure doesn't feel like it."

Mom nodded, studying a ceramic green vase closely. "It'll be warm before you know it," she replied, flipping up the bottom of the vase to check out the price.

We'd decided to go browsing at Target, just to get out of the house for a while. Or at least, that's what I'd told her when I'd suggested the idea. In reality, I was scouting around for the perfect twenty-fifth-anniversary present for my folks, as the big day was less than a couple of weeks away.

Typically, my folks keep their celebrations low-key, so Rob and I don't normally get gifts except for the big milestones. But whenever those anniversaries have come around, I've procrastinated on getting them a present, waffling on what would be the perfect way to congratulate their lasting love. And every idea I've come up with has always been way too cliché or expensive.

So, my wishy-washiness inevitably meant me running out to the store the night before and getting them a card and some kitschy gift. For their twentieth anniversary, it was a Scooby-Doo head you could grow moss on, and a pair of soup mugs (I know—über lame, but in my defense, my parents love soup).

And this time was gearing up to be no different. Everything I'd looked at was either the wrong color, cost an arm and a leg, or was something they already had. Shopping for a couple is hard, especially my parents.

We made our way over to the clothing department. It seemed I wasn't going to have any luck tonight spotting them a good gift.

Well, I'd just borrow my mom's car in the next few days and hit another store without her.

Having come up with this tentative plan of action, I headed toward the aisles of bathing suits, ready to check out stuff for me. Sometimes, if I hit Mom on a good day, she'd splurge and buy me clothes.

"I can't believe they already have bathing suits out on the rack," I said.

Mom *mm-hm*'ed me noncommittally. Tough to tell whether she was feeling generous tonight or not.

I flipped through the bright, multicolored swimsuits and bikinis. Maybe there was something hiding on the rack that would make me look both super stacked and super skinny. Not likely, given the lovely pear shape of my body, but hey—a girl could hope.

Also, I was desperate for warmer temperatures to come, so maybe buying a bathing suit would remind the weather gods to send a little bit of sunshine our way.

My mom wrinkled her nose in disdain as she took in the teeny-tiny swimsuits in the juniors' section. With the tips of her fingers, she picked one up, her eyebrows shooting clean up into her hairline.

"This one's nothing more than hot-pink dental floss," she gasped, shaking her head. "Felicity, I don't want you wearing these. Can't you get a nice one-piece that will fully cover your buttocks?"

"Mom," I groaned, wishing she'd keep her voice a little quieter. She was such a prude. Besides, nobody says "buttocks" other than our health class teacher.

"I'm not going to wear one that shows everything, okay?" I said, trying hard to keep the whine out of my voice. "I just want to look nice."

Mom walked over to a rack in the women's section, which was right beside the juniors', thoughtfully studying the wares. "Look, this one has a lovely cover-up wrap," she cooed, holding up a bathing suit that had to have come straight from the 1920s, complete with thickly knit fabric in horizontal blue and white stripes. "And this one has shorts!"

Great. Just what I needed—to look like a grandmother. I mean, no offense to my grandma, who's the coolest woman I know, but I'm not in my seventies, for crap's sake.

I grabbed an adorable red two-piece suit, then took off down the aisle. "Going to the dressing room, okay?" I threw out over my shoulder.

After pulling shut the changing room door, I stripped to my bra and panties as fast as I could, then slipped on the two-piece. Surprisingly, the boy-cut bottoms fit nicely. I checked it out in the mirror, trying to ignore the panty lumps under the fabric.

The halter top, however, was too big. I'd inadvertently grabbed a size C-cup. Damn my non–C-cup chest! Maybe Mom could bring me the next smaller size.

I threw my coat on over the bikini, quickly slipped into my tennis shoes, then tiptoed to the front entrance of the changing room.

"Mom," I whispered. No answer. I tried again, a bit louder. "Mom, you there?"

"What do you need, Felicity?" she asked from about thirty feet away. She was still looking at old-lady bathing suits, probably trying to find me one that came with a turtleneck.

"Can you get me a different top?" I asked. "It's the dark red bikini halter top on the front rack."

"Sure thing," she bellowed back. "What size?"

I groaned and glanced at the lady working the changing room, who stared back at me with a slightly hostile look on her face. She looked like she trusted me about as far as she could throw me. And she certainly wasn't offering to help.

"Thirty-four B," I said as quietly as possible.

I heard Mom snort. "Did you say thirty-four D? With those little apples? Let's not delude ourselves, honey. You're more like an A-cup."

The dressing room attendant smothered a chortle behind her hand.

My entire face flamed with heat. "Mom!" Could this get any worse? "I said B-cup!"

"Felicity? Is that you?" a devastatingly familiar voice said from the guys' department, which was located just to the right of the women's changing rooms.

As if in a horror flick, I turned slowly, the blood draining from my face. Yup, my worst nightmare, come to life. Derek, the boy of my dreams, the hottie who had captured my heart, the guy I had been trying desperately to make notice me all year long, had just heard me announce my chest size. And probably my mom's "little apples" comment too.

I waited for my life to end. No such luck.

Derek placed the black pinstriped dress shirt he'd been looking at back on the rack, then came over to me in a slow, sexy saunter. At that moment I became acutely aware of the unfortunate fact that I was dressed in nothing more than a loose-fitting halter top, a lumpy bikini bottom, my coat, and a pair of sneakers. *Très* sexy.

I smoothed a hand over my hair and tried to look relaxed, like I always hung out in bikinis and winter coats and knew I looked fabulous. "Oh, Derek. I didn't know you shopped."

He chuckled, raising an eyebrow at my words.

"I mean, I didn't know you shopped here. At Target, I mean," I stumbled, wanting to kick myself for sounding so stupid. Time to cram my tennis shoe in my mouth. "Do you come here often?"

Someone, stop me from talking!

"Honey, I found the perfect—" My mom stopped dead in her tracks, staring at Derek in blatantly open interest.

Oh no, here it comes. The Target Inquisition.

"Hello," my mom said to Derek in a deceptively gentle voice. With one hand aimed at me, she thrust into my arms the smaller red halter bikini top, plus a wretched one-piece covered in hot-pink paisley, then stuck out the other hand toward him.

"Are you one of Felicity's . . . friends?" she asked, her beady eyes taking in my embarrassed look. "I'm her mom. Nice to meet you."

Derek, bless his heart, just smiled wider and shook her hand heartily. "I'm Derek. I go to Greenville High too."

Okay, time to end this introduction before I was forced to pray for a fiery meteor to hit the store.

"Well," I interjected, "I'm trying on bathing suits, so I'd better get back to it. It was nice seeing you, Derek." I pasted on my fake huge, bright smile.

He smirked, then nodded. "See ya, Felicity." With that, he strolled off toward the electronics department.

I tried not to watch him walk away, knowing my mom would totally harass me for staring at his cute butt. Instead, I turned back into the dressing room, stripped off the bikini, and threw on my regular clothes, too depressed to even try on the smaller top.

How was I ever going to face him again after the way that went down? And why do these things always happen to me? I'd spent so long practically worshipping at Derek's feet, wishing I could snag his attention.

Well, this was *not* the way I'd wanted to accomplish that goal.

chapter nine

"It was so mortifying. I'll be scarred for life. My future therapist should thank my mom for all the shrink bills I'm going to run up," I whined, studying my freshly made-up reflection in the small handheld mirror.

Maya, Andy, and I were sprawled out in our jammies at Maya's house for our TGIF sleepover. Her parents had gone to bed a couple of hours ago, and I'd just finished sharing the Target bikini debacle with the two of them.

"And the worst part is," I continued, digging into the Clinique gift bag of makeup samples I'd received for buying another much-needed bottle of facial lotion, "Derek heard my mom say I was probably only an A-cup. There's, like, no way to do damage control on that."

"That's worse than him seeing you dressed in a lumpy bikini

bottom and falling-off top?" Andy asked, so not helpfully.

I tried to smile. "Don't forget the winter coat too. That really pulled the whole look together."

At least that was the only disastrous thing that had happened since then. The last couple of days I'd kept myself busy with homework and tried to avoid Derek at all costs. Which was virtually impossible, given that we shared a class together. The best I could do in art class, then, was keep my eyes firmly fixed on the project at hand, a linoleum cutting on the subject of our choice that we would use to make prints.

I'd found a picture of a woman's face in a magazine to do for mine. She was reclining, her face turned in a three-quarter profile toward the viewer. It was challenging, required my full attention, and thus was a godsend.

However, I'd sensed Derek's eyes on me every once in a while. Or maybe that wasn't really happening and I'd been just hallucinating it, because I'd refused to look up and risk eye contact. But my Spidey senses had been tingling.

"Poor thing. Did you at least have shaved legs?" Maya asked, scrutinizing my face. She grabbed the eye shadow container and took the applicator in her hand, sliding a bit more of the dark brown shadow in the crease of my eyelids.

I kept my eyes closed and stayed motionless, not wanting to lose an eyeball. "Yes, thank heaven for that," I mumbled.

"Well, that sucks. Your mom kills me sometimes. And I thought mine was bad." Andy took a swig of strawberry wine cooler, then passed the bottle into my hand. She had smuggled it from her parents' house, and she and Maya were taking turns sipping from the bottle.

Honestly, I was surprised Maya was drinking any, since she wasn't a party girl, but I guess she felt comfortable enough around us to give it a whirl.

"I don't want any, thanks," I said, setting the bottle on Maya's nightstand. "The last thing I need is to get ripped." I hadn't been to a lot of parties, but I'd been to enough of them to know how stupid people looked when trashed.

"Ripped from a wine cooler?" Andy snorted. "Right. Honey, we're sharing the bottle. It won't be enough to give any of us more than a buzz, at most."

She had a good point. I took a tiny drink, the sweet liquid bubbling instantly in my mouth. "Hey, that's pretty good," I said, handing it back to her. "So, Maya, how was your first week as a love goddess?"

"Hardy har," she said, rolling her eyes. "I'm hardly a goddess."

"Don't underestimate yourself." Andy took a sip of the wine and passed the bottle to Maya. "You've managed to attract *and* sustain the attention of three hotties. That's no small feat."

She shrugged, taking a sip. "Yeah, I guess it's not too bad. It's just a lot to juggle. Ben's taking me out tomorrow afternoon for lunch and a movie, Quentin's meeting me for ice cream that evening, and Josh wanted to have Sunday brunch." She put the bottle down and sighed. "How am I going to choose between them? I feel bad for putting it off, but I like all of them."

"I'm sure you'll figure out something," I said. "But in the meantime, we can go over your schedule one more time to make sure we covered all the bases, if you're still feeling nervous about it."

On Thursday, I'd helped Maya come up with a plan to keep her love life balanced. It was an intricate chart, woven with incredible skill and finesse, breaking down which day and after which period she'd walk with each guy, with whom she'd share lunch, and on which nights they would date. I had to say, I'd outdone myself. Even Andy gave me kudos on the plan.

And the best part was, since Maya was dividing her attention equally, we could keep the rumor mill at bay, because there was no one guy she could be attached to. All in all, a success, if I did say so myself.

And not just with Maya's love match. Britney and Matthew were still going strong too. I'd overheard them in the halls talking about some indie band they'd seen on Wednesday night, holding hands and smiling into each other's faces. They still looked crazy about each other.

Even DeShawn's and Marisa's match was working out great so far. I'd noticed the two of them spending a lot of time in each other's company. She walked him to class every day, and they sat together at lunch, heads tucked closely together as they talked. Even though her friends weren't thrilled about the pairing, given the glares they gave DeShawn behind his back, Marisa didn't let it deter her from being with DeShawn.

And, much to my amusement, DeShawn now spent our English classes poring over *Jane Eyre* and listening to what the other students—females, especially—had to say about the romantic aspects of the book. Was he taking mental notes? Even our English teacher noticed the difference in his attitude, commenting on how quiet and attentive he was lately. I think she suspected him of brewing something sinister in his mind, but I knew the truth.

As for me, I secretly reveled in having brought DeShawn and Marisa together, a love match against all odds. I was getting really good at this. No wonder Janet had hired me—maybe I had a natural flair for romance and love.

Even though I still hadn't read the cupid guidebook or followed the rules to the letter, everything seemed to be working out great. Following my natural instinct was clearly way better than going by the book. After all, this was love, not rocket science.

A weird sound outside Maya's window caught my attention. I paused and cocked my head. "Did you guys hear something?"

A few tinkling thuds hit the window right when I finished my words.

We all jumped, and I let out an involuntary squeak.

Maya leaped from the floor and dashed to her window, peeking between the slots of her blinds. "What was that? What if it's a burglar?"

"It's not a burglar," Andy said, rolling her eyes. "What are they gonna steal, your trumpet?"

Maya leaned closer to the window. "Oh my God," she whispered, her voice suddenly breathy and soft. "It's Josh. He's here! Do I look okay?" She grabbed the mirror from my hand to study her reflection, checking the makeup job I'd done for her.

"Josh?" Andy stood, her eyes wide in surprise. "What's he doing here?" She pulled up the blinds and threw open the window, letting in a swift, chilly draft of air.

I grabbed a blanket to ward off the cold and cover my French poodle pajama bottoms. I'd already been spotted in one mortifying outfit that week, and once was enough. "Hey, close that window. It's fricking freezing!"

Andy stuck her head out. "Josh, stop throwing rocks!" she hissed. "You're gonna wake up Maya's parents!"

Oh God, she was right. That would be extra bad, especially since we had a wine cooler up here. What if Maya's parents found it? What if they had us arrested for teen drunkenness and we were thrown in jail?

My mom would never let me out of the house again. I'd have to quit my job, and maybe even be homeschooled, locked away in my bedroom with no outside contact. I'd never get to see Andy or Maya or Derek again.

I grabbed the bottle and thrust it toward Andy. "Pour it out," I said, my voice shaking. "And hide the bottle. I don't want Maya's parents to bust us with it."

"Andy, is that you? Where's Maya?" Josh's voice carried up into Maya's second-floor room.

Maya peeked her head over Andy's shoulder, shivering slightly as another gust of cold air swept into the room. "Hi, Josh. I'm right here," she said, waggling her fingers at him in greeting. "What's going on?"

Andy slipped away from the window, then handed me back the bottle. "I'm not pouring it out. That's wasting good wine. Just chug it."

"It's a cheap wine cooler—I'd hardly call it 'good.' And I'm *not* chugging it. *You* chug it." My luck, I'd be the one person in the world to get alcohol poisoning and die from chugging part of a wine cooler. How lame would that be?

"Maya," I heard Josh say, "I couldn't sleep. All I could think about was you. So I snuck out to see you."

Andy took a big swig of the wine, then leaned back out the window. "Josh, that was so sweet!"

Maya shot her a look, and Andy backed off.

"Geez, I wasn't being a smart-ass. It really *is*," she mumbled, plopping down on Maya's bed.

I stood up and peeked over Maya's shoulder to see Josh staring up at the window, his neck craned up. He clutched a bouquet of a dozen roses in his hands.

"He brought you flowers too?" I said, surprised. "Wow, that *is* sweet."

No one had ever snuck out and given me flowers at midnight. Or at any time, really.

"Who else is up there with you?" Josh asked Maya. "Are you having a party?"

I stuck my hand out the window and waved at him, then quickly pulled it back in, rubbing warmth back into my frozen fingers. Damn, it was cold out there. How could he stand it? I guess the power of love was warming him from within. Gag.

I could understand the compulsion, though. I'd probably stand out all night in an arctic blizzard if it meant getting a chance to talk to Derek one-on-one. Okay, that was an exaggeration, but just a little one.

"That was Felicity," Maya said to Josh. "I'm having a sleepover."

"Felicity? Oh," he said, his voice uncomfortable. I knew he was remembering the bathroom incident at the movies.

Yeah, I didn't want to think about that, either. I stepped back to let them talk, sitting beside Andy on the bed.

"I brought you flowers," I heard him say. "Can you come to the door?"

"I can't. My parents' room is on the first floor." Maya's voice was filled with regret.

"Maybe he can fling them up here," I suggested.

"Good idea," she said to me, her face brightening. "Can you throw the flowers up to me?" she asked Josh.

"I'd really rather see you," he hedged. "But if you want them, here they are. Catch!"

We heard him huff as he tossed them up, and then a smashing thud as the bouquet hit the window, next to Maya's head, then fell back to the ground.

"Ow!" Maya gasped, clutching her brow. "I got scratched by a thorn! And I dropped the flowers!" She backed away from the window.

"Here, let me see it." I checked out Maya's war wound. It was a small scratch right in the middle of her forehead. A bead of blood bloomed at the spot of the injury.

I grabbed a tissue and wiped it away, pressing the tissue to the scratch. "It's . . . not that bad," I fudged.

"Are you sure?" Maya's face was pale and drawn. "Wait, what if this is an omen? A sign that I shouldn't be with Josh? What do I do now?"

"Maya, are you okay? Maya!" Josh's voice got louder, more anxious.

Andy leaned out the window. "Shh! She's fine. Hold on a sec." She turned to Maya. "Just go down and see him for a minute. Let him give you the flowers the right way instead of making him throw them at your face."

"But my parents—" Maya protested.

"Just be quiet about it, and don't stay down there forever. You'll be fine," Andy said. She pushed Maya toward the door, then leaned out the window. "She's coming down."

Andy and I sat on the bed while Maya snuck downstairs. Andy shook her head. "That girl's a mess. I hope when she picks one of them, she'll settle down into being a bit more normal."

"So, who do you think she should pick?" I asked.

In all honesty, I'd had no indication from Maya on which guy she liked best so far. All three of them were different, and all appealed to various aspects of her. With Josh, Maya was able to discuss and enjoy weird and off-the-wall movies or music, because he was into that too. Quentin brought out her romantic nature through discussions of literature, art, and poetry. And she loved that Ben reached outside his comfort zone to show her his feelings.

But she showed the same level of affection to each of them and talked about them with equal excitement and uncertainty, so there were no external indicators to show me which one she preferred.

I could see, though, that the attention from the guys was causing a slow but definite change over Maya. I'd never seen her fuss over makeup before. She smiled more in public now, walked down the halls with more confidence and bounce. She'd never seemed so comfortable in her skin before. But then again, she'd never had a guy try to bring her flowers at midnight before either.

"I don't know." Andy shrugged. "It's hard to tell. She's her own person, and even if I like one guy better than the others, Maya won't be influenced by anyone else when making a decision as big as that."

I nodded. "Yeah, I guess you're right." That was, after all, why I'd wanted to let her choose for herself in the first place.

After another minute, we heard the bedroom door creak open. I lunged to cover the wine cooler with a blanket, but it was only Maya, her entire face aglow. She held the bouquet in her arms, pressing the blossoms to her face.

"Aren't they beautiful?" she said, her eyes shiny. "I've never had anyone bring me flowers before."

At that moment, I realized what a vast difference being in love (well, at least, one-third in love) did for Maya. She looked flushed, a bit erratic, but very, very pretty. Even with the little bloody dot on the middle of her forehead, she looked great.

But it was not just loving someone. It was *being* loved by that person—or those people—in return. Having someone reciprocate those feelings made everything feel right.

"They really are gorgeous," I said, rising to go hug her and smell them for myself. After all, those roses were probably the closest I was going to get to that all-encompassing kind of love.

chapter ten

"Bye, Rob," my mom said, holding the front door open with her hip as my brother headed out the house after dinner that Sunday. She squeezed him close. "Don't be a stranger," she added, her tone slightly chastising. "We never hear from you during the week. You *can* call us, you know."

"Yeah, yeah," he mumbled. He gave my mom a peck on the cheek and clenched the large bag of leftovers in his hand. Mom always sent him home with food, which was a good thing, because Rob couldn't cook to save his life. When he wasn't eating Mom's food, he probably had takeout every night at his apartment. Which was also a good thing, because it kept him from burning down his place.

Rob had come alone to Sunday dinner this week, no date in tow.

I figured the blond fluffbag had already dumped him. None of us had even bothered to ask where she was, that's how cynical we were about his love life.

"Thanks again for dinner," he said. "See ya guys next week." He took off down the front steps.

Mom closed the door behind him, then darted into the kitchen, probably to microwave a bag of butter-laden popcorn, as she did every Sunday night.

"It's almost eight, Becky," my dad called to her from the living room. He sank onto his plush dark brown recliner, clicking the TV on with the huge cable remote, then pushed up the footrest using the handle on the side of the chair.

"What's on tonight?" Mom asked, returning from the kitchen bearing a bowl of popcorn and settling onto the couch.

"Not sure. Let me look." He turned on the cable guide, scrolling through the list of shows.

It was my parents' tradition after Sunday dinner to watch a movie together. They'd been doing this religiously every weekend for as long as I could remember. When I didn't have homework to do, I'd join them if I was interested in whatever movie they were watching.

Mom often picked the old romantics on the American Movie

Classics channel, laughing at the sharp banter between the leading couples. I loved watching the antics of those early Hollywood actors too.

My dad, however, tended to be drawn to epic movies like the Godfather trilogy. Mom hadn't loved these, but I'd gotten totally caught up in the drama of that infamous Mafia family, the Corleones. Watching those people spend money hand over fist made me wish I had a more exciting home life, but I guess being surrounded by danger and destruction isn't really such a good thing.

As thrilling as it would be to be the daughter of a mob boss, we were all better off with my dad working in the mortgage department of the bank. A bit on the boring side, yes, but less prone to death.

"Hey, Dad," I said, snagging a handful of popcorn from Mom's bowl, "what are you two doing for your anniversary?" Maybe if I pried into their plans, I could get an idea for the ultimate present.

He shrugged, continuing to flip through the channel guide. "Probably the same thing we do every year. You know I love El Rincon's enchilada platter."

Mom eyed the TV. "Maybe we can check out that Japanese

restaurant in North Olmsted, instead. Oh, flip back to the Turner Classics," she said, waving her finger at the screen.

Dad blanched. "I hate sushi."

"How do you know if you hate it?" Mom must have realized how edgy her voice sounded, because she gave a small smile. "You've never tried it. You might like it." She put the popcorn bowl down on the coffee table.

Dad gave a grunt in reply and kept his eye on the screen.

Yikes. This was no help at all. If they kept bickering like that, their milestone anniversary wasn't going to be much to celebrate.

I chewed on my handful of popcorn. Come to think of it, when was the last time I saw the two of them dress up and have a special night out on the town? They basically only ever went out together one night a year on their anniversary, and even then, they could barely be bothered to make the night romantic.

I racked my brain to remember their past dates. One particular anniversary came to mind—when Rob and I were little, our sitter cancelled at the last minute. So Mom and Dad took us to Chuck E. Cheese for their anniversary because Rob pitched a fit and refused to eat anywhere else.

That night got even worse when Rob pulled off the Whack-a-Mole hammer and thwacked me over the head with it, causing a flurry of screams and tears. The jerk. He was built for a life of whomping on others. He'd make a fantastic prison warden, for sure.

Now that I was older, I could appreciate how bad that must have been for my parents. Spending your anniversary with two whiny kids? Sucksville.

Year after year of their anniversaries flipped through my mind, a never-ending series of nonspectacular non-events. Dinner at a Chinese buffet. Dinner at El Rincon. Dinner at home because I had the flu. Dinner at a Chinese buffet. Dinner and a movie that my dad hated and griped about for weeks after. And my all-time favorite . . . dinner at Burger Butler, when Rob did a fake burp and ended up puking all over Mom.

A sudden alarm darted through my veins, and I stared at the two of them, taking in their attitudes about their own anniversary—especially my dad's utter unwillingness to try something new. Was the magic gone for them?

Wait, had the magic ever been there in the first place?

I thought about the love matches I'd made at school, the rush of feelings sparking almost visual fires between my couples. Even

Maya, who was only one-third in love, had more chemistry with the three guys than my folks had together.

Had my parents ever been like that? Looking at them now, one wouldn't think so.

Wait. A flutter of excitement tickled inside my chest. I hopped out of my seat and flew upstairs, turning my PC on as I ran an utterly inspired idea through my mind.

I logged into my blog, making it a diary entry so that I was the only one who could see it, then started to type.

I think I figured out what to do for my parents. Finally! Maybe the best gift I can give them for this milestone anniversary isn't one bought in a store—though I'll still get them a card, of course.

Maybe in this case, the gift of love is much more needed. And I'm the perfect person to help with that.

I could send my mom and dad the love e-mails, and not even count it as a love match—it could be a side project. As a cupid, I've learned to appreciate romance in general, especially lasting matches. Why should my folks be any different?

I continued with my diary entry.

The big question is, will it work between two people already in a relationship?

Well, there was only one way for me to find out.

"So, why is Jane Eyre drawn to a man like Mr. Rochester?" Mrs. Kendel asked our English class bright and early on Monday morning. She paced up and down the aisles, her long skirt swishing around her thick legs. "Rochester is gruff, rude, sometimes downright hostile . . . and yet, she falls in love with him." She stopped and scratched her chin, her head tilted. "What does this say about Jane and, even more importantly, what does it say about society and women's expectations during Jane's time period?"

Silence. Either no one knew the answer, no one cared, or no one was awake enough yet to articulate any halfway decent thoughts.

I raised my hand.

"Miss Walker," Mrs. Kendel said to me with a small smile, almost looking grateful that I was going to take a stab at it. "Please, go ahead."

"Well," I started in a hesitant voice, "even though Mr. Rochester is far from perfect, Jane feels he's perfect for her." Out of the corner of my eye, I noticed DeShawn staring at me with an odd look on his face.

At that moment, a profound thought hit me—DeShawn was kind of like Mr. Rochester. Gruff, rude, and sometimes downright hostile, but there had to be goodness deep inside. Maybe Marisa would be his Jane. How romantic!

"Mr. Rochester's made mistakes. He did things that embarrassed people unnecessarily," I continued, thinking about DeShawn and the unfortunate pantsing incident, "but Jane can see he's a good man on the inside. He just needs to work harder on showing her he deserves her love, long-term."

Yeah, I was laying it on a bit thick, but I hoped my words were getting through to DeShawn. After all, I didn't think Mrs. Kendel would appreciate me outright saying that Mr. Rochester-slash-DeShawn needed to stop being an ass permanently if he was gonna keep the love going. Though Deshawn and Marisa's relationship was solid right now, there was no guarantee it would continue that way—especially if he converted back to his old antics after the spell wore off.

Just this morning, when Marisa and DeShawn had split ways to head to their separate classes, I'd overheard Marisa's friends giving her flack again for being with DeShawn, saying she could do better than him. To be honest, I think most of us—and maybe even Marisa herself—knew this was a precarious pairing. Because of that, I felt obligated to do my part and steer DeShawn in the right direction. Hopefully, he'd pick up the hints I was throwing his way.

DeShawn looked away from me, staring at his notebook. He rubbed a hand over his jaw, deep in thought.

"Thanks, Miss Walker," Mrs. Kendel said. "Those are valid points. I think you'll see this novel also reflects how the Victorian society viewed relationships. Rochester has the upper hand, both as a male and as Jane's employer. As we read on, we'll see what happens to change the dynamic of this relationship and how the power shifts from Rochester to Jane."

The rest of the class period went by fast. When the bell rang, Maya gave me a quick hug, then darted out the door to meet Ben, who was scheduled to walk her to second period.

"Hey," DeShawn grunted at me after the guys around him left the classroom. "You're a girl, right?"

Gee, was it that obvious? Swallowing my instinctively snarky reply, I simply nodded.

"If a guy wanted to impress a girl—a smart girl—and really

show how he . . . cared, what could he do?" DeShawn's hands fiddled with the hem of his shirt.

Oh. My. God. DeShawn was asking me for love advice! It had worked—I'd gotten through to him!

I grabbed my books in the calmest manner possible, cradling them in the crook of my arm. I needed to weigh my words carefully—one wrong phrase could screw everything up.

"Well," I said, "for a girl like that, a guy should appeal to her heart *and* her brain. She'd appreciate someone reaching her intellectually."

"But how? Should I buy her something, like a book?"

We headed out the door, him walking beside me. I never thought this day would come, the day DeShawn and I would walk side by side down the hallway like friends. It was like a UN peace treaty had been signed between two warring countries, and it was all because of the cupid spell.

Amazing, the power of love.

"Well, you can buy her presents," I answered, "but smart girls really appreciate gifts that come from the heart." I paused, trying to think of the best answer. What would be the perfect gift for her? "Mari—um, smart girls often love handwritten poetry. I mean, you saw how well it worked for Quentin on Maya."

He cringed. "I can't write that junk."

I nodded, feeling unexpected sympathy with him. "Honestly, I can't either," I confided. "But if you care about someone, isn't it worth trying something difficult to prove your feelings?"

"I guess so." By the tone of his voice, he didn't sound too convinced.

"Hey, what about haiku?" *Oh, Felicity, a brilliant idea!* I congratulated myself. My words spilled out in an excited rush. "Those are short and easy to write, but very poetic. They're only three lines long, but they pack a lot of punch." Boy, my tenth-grade English teacher would be proud to hear me now.

DeShawn gave me a seemingly indifferent shrug, but I could tell by the look on his face that he was considering my suggestion. "Yeah, I remember. So, I should just write about flowers and sunsets and other girly stuff, right?"

I smothered a giggle with an exaggerated cough, pressing my clenched fist to my mouth. This was not the time to laugh. "Yup, that's right." I stopped in front of my American history class. "Well, this is my room. Good luck on the poem!"

"Later." DeShawn walked off.

I stared at his back for a moment before heading into class. That. Was totally. Surreal.

chapter eleven

"Felicity!" Maya called to me from outside her locker, waving frantically. When I got there, she leaned in and whispered, though not very quietly, "Wait till you hear this—Quentin wants to take my picture!"

"He does? What for, HottieTeenHoochies.com?" I teased her.

"Shut *up*." She slugged me in the upper arm, ignoring my cries of protest. "No, Quentin wants to feature me in the 'movers and shakers' part of the yearbook. He thinks the school should learn more about me and my accomplishments."

"Oh, that's so cool!" I said. "He takes really good pictures."

Maya paused, biting her lower lip, and her face fell a little. "Hm. Now that I'm thinking about it, maybe that's not the best idea. After all, I'm not like the divas around here who can wear sweat pants and no makeup and still look hot."

"Hey, no talking like that," I said, frowning. "Andy and I think you rock. Quentin thinks you're awesome. So do Ben and Josh. Just remember that." I could tell by how strongly they felt about her that their love would probably last past the spell, whichever one she finally chose, so I was confident in pointing this out.

Maya scrolled the lock on her locker door, shrugging a little. "I know you're right. I'm just panicking about this. I need a clear sign of which guy is the right one for me."

"Maybe you can get your palm read," I joked. "And you can also learn what college you'll go to and how many kids you're gonna have."

"That's actually not a bad idea." Maya flicked off the lock and tugged the door open, then sucked in a quick, startled breath. A flock of small, brightly colored helium balloons flew out of the tight locker space and up to the ceiling. It looked like a circus clown car being evacuated, there were so many balloons fleeing the locker.

"Oh my God!" she gasped, her eyes wide.

"Look! Balloons!" several people in the hallway said as they snatched at the thin white ribbons. Most of them handed the balloons back to Maya, though few jerky guys held on to theirs—probably to pop them behind whatever unsuspecting girls they could find. Idiots.

One cute guy handed Maya a couple of balloons back. "Here ya go," he said, a deep dimple in his right cheek as he shot her a smile.

"Oh, thanks!" she said to him, a bright blush staining her cheeks. "What a crazy surprise!"

Interesting development. Now *other* guys are flirting with Maya too? Must be something to this budding self-confidence of hers.

"Soooo," I drawled after the cute guy walked off, shifting my attention back to the bundle of balloons Maya held in her shaky grasp. "Who did that? Is there a card or something?"

And how did he get into her locker? I thought to myself. That part was a bit creepy, though I knew the gesture was meant to be sweet.

Maya poked her head in the locker, looking around. "I don't see any—oh, wait." She withdrew, holding an envelope. She peeled it open, staring at the contents for a moment. Without a word, she handed me the card.

I peeked at the front, a picture of two purple cartoon rabbits cuddling on a puffy pink couch. The card's inside was just as cheese-laden:

I got an idea—
Let's be snuggle bunnies!

Oh, gag. Who got paid to write this kind of crap? I tried my best not to roll my eyes as I read the handwritten inscription:

I hope these balloons brighten up your ~~mom~~ day!
Love,
Ben

I looked up at Maya. "Wow," I finally said.

She nodded slowly, then dramatically sighed, pressing her free hand to her chest. "No kidding. Wasn't that the sweetest thing ever? Maybe this was my sign—maybe *Ben* is the one. There's something about his quiet, deep nature that really draws me in. And these surprises he leaves me shows me I'm on his mind."

"It was very thoughtful of him," I said, nodding. "But we gotta head to class, so you'd better put the balloons back in your locker."

"Oh, good point," she said, scrunching up her nose. "I can't take these to anatomy."

It took both of us pushing to get those damn balloons in there, though a couple wouldn't fit. We picked the three smallest to pop, tossing the deflated balloons into the garbage bin a few feet away. How the hell had Ben fit all these into her locker in the first place, especially with Maya's trumpet case hogging up a large portion of room? He must have spent some serious time and effort.

The bell rang. Uh-oh, time for art class.

"See ya," I said to Maya, waving good-bye as I took off down the hall.

I headed my way to art, both dreading and looking forward to it. It was almost a delicious sort of torture, seeing Derek's striking face, hearing his low chuckle when someone said something that amused him. And when he laughed, his bright eyes crinkled in the corners. He was magnetic, and I just couldn't seem to get enough of him . . . even in spite of the bathing suit incident.

Inside the classroom, I grabbed my linoleum cutting and tools from the art shelf and slipped into my seat. Derek came in shortly after, heading right to the art shelf as well.

Staring intently at my carving, I picked up the V-shaped knife, drew in a deep breath, then started digging into the shell of the ear I was etching.

"Can I sit here?" Derek asked from out of the blue, startling the crap out of me.

My hand jerked slightly, cutting off a bit too much linoleum. Whoops, there went the tip of her ear. Van Gogh would be proud.

I glanced up, up, up into his glorious sparking eyes looking down at me, and gave him a crooked smile.

Hello—speak, idiot!

"Um, why do you want to sit by me?" I blurted. Oh, geez, that sounded dumb. And rude. Why did I grill him about it instead of simply saying yes? I was a glutton for punishment.

He nodded his head toward his usual spot. "My spot's taken." Sure enough, some other guy was perched in Derek's usual chair.

"Sure, go ahead." I tugged the chair out for him, the feet squeaking across the floor.

He sat in the seat beside me, putting his project and sketching pencils on the table. He was still finalizing his picture before beginning to trace and carve his linoleum square. His project was an apple orchard scene on a farm, trees sprawling across the countryside down to the horizon. A rickety barn rested in the back right corner. The picture was good—very good.

God, was there anything Derek couldn't do? Hell, he could

probably jump right into a pilot's seat and land a freaking airplane if he wanted to.

"That's amazing," I said, a little breathless. I slid my hand over my own linoleum cutting, trying to obscure it from his vision. It wasn't horrible, but it certainly didn't compare to his work.

He chuckled, picking up a pencil and adding more definition to the tree nearest the bottom of the picture. "It's not that great, but thanks. I need to do a little more work on the shading."

I nodded, then looked back at my work. We did our art in companionable silence for a long stretch of time, and I found myself glancing back at him again and again. "So, why did you pick an orchard scene?" I finally asked him.

"Well, this was what my grandpa's farm looked like. I used to go there as a kid all the time and run between the rows of trees."

"Really?"

He laughed. "No, not really. I just thought it sounded more interesting than the truth. Actually, I saw the picture in a magazine and just picked it to draw." Then, he looked at me, a small grin still lingering on his face. "I guess I just like apples."

Apples? What did he—

Clarity came to me in a whirl of mortifying light. Derek was teasing me about my mom's comment in Target on my "little apples."

Or, wait. Was he ... flirting?

The last bell of the day rang, and I dawdled out of the art room, wanting to prolong my time with Derek as much as possible. It was crazy, this compulsion to be around him. To keep him talking to me. Not that I seemed to say anything remotely intelligent when I did get him into a conversation.

I pushed my art project back in its spot on the shelf, shooting Derek's retreating figure one last glance, then gathered up my belongings and made my way back to my locker. There had to be a way to make Derek notice me that would not make me look like a dumb-ass this time.

I bet I could ask Andy and Maya to help me come up with something that didn't relate at all to my cupid matchmaking techniques. Then, Janet couldn't complain, because I wouldn't have done anything against my contract.

I shrugged into my coat and grabbed my backpack, then made my way through the school doors. Andy had to run an errand for her mom, and Maya had a date right after school, so I was hoofing it alone. The grounds were nearly emptied, except for a few people lingering on the steps.

A heavy thud, followed by rustling around the corner of the school building, got my attention.

"Careful!" I heard a guy say. "Don't squash that piece of cardboard. It's in perfect shape. We can recycle that."

"Sorry, honey. I'm—trying my—best," a girl replied, sounding breathless.

Curious, I rounded the corner to find Matthew and Britney, my first matchmade couple, waist-deep in two of the school's garbage dumpsters.

I stopped mid-stride at the sight. Britney had dark smudges across her face, from God only knew what. Her nose was red-tipped from the cold air, and she had clumps of unidentifiable stuff in her hair.

From his garbage bin, Matthew flung a few more pieces of garbage out onto the parking lot. "I can't believe people threw this away," he muttered to Britney, shaking his head. "Look at this!" He waved a small glass bottle in one gloved hand. "Do you know how easy it is to recycle glass?"

"What are you guys doing?" I asked, trying to keep my repulsion at their garbage-digging activity out of my voice.

Britney stopped mid-dig and stood up. "Oh, hey," she said to me, smiling. "Matthew likes to go garbage diving once a week and pull out the recyclables. So he asked me to join him today after school."

Was this a date? As for me, I'd rather have dinner and a movie, but they looked happy and were being productive, so I guess that's what counted.

"Well, that's great," I finally said.

"Actually, it's scary how much recyclable stuff I find in here," Matthew said to me, his eyes boring into mine. "If we don't take care of our environment, no one will." He stopped and raised one eyebrow. "You *do* recycle, don't you, Felicity?"

"Oh, absolutely," I answered quickly, instantly feeling a twinge of guilt. Okay, that wasn't the absolute truth, because I knew for a fact I wasn't *this* active about it. But I did throw old paper in the paper recycling bin—didn't that count for something?

Besides, I didn't have to dig through garbage to help the environment. There were lots of ways to pitch in and reduce, reuse, recycle. I totally avoided aerosol cans, so I was saving the ozone in my own way.

"That's great. Wanna help us out?" Matthew asked. "We still have a couple of garbage bins to go through." He pointed over to the two furthest garbage dumpsters, their lids flung open to reveal a mysterious pile of grossness.

"Ah!" Britney suddenly cried out, clinging to the side of her dumpster. "I think I slipped on something in here. Anyway," she said to me, righting herself, "it's not so bad once you get past the smell."

Ewwww. Yeah, that was appealing. I'd heard the nose was quick to adapt to stinky scents, but I didn't see how one could adapt to the school trash smell.

I lifted up the sleeve of my jacket, glancing at my watch, while secretly trying to cover my gagging mouth. "Oh, I'd love to," I choked out, "but I gotta head home. You know how parents are when you're late."

Not that my folks were home this early, but there was no way I was going to dig through the school garbage dumpsters. I saw the kinds of things people threw away, and no way did I want to reek like that.

"Okay, later," Britney said.

"You two have fun," I replied, heading back around the corner. I heard more stuff being flung onto the ground and shook my head.

To each his own, right?

chapter twelve

When I got home, I keyed the front door of my house and pushed it open, shuffling through. I needed some peanut butter fudge ice cream therapy, stat. The confusion over Derek's ambiguous words in art class had run round and round in my head throughout the rest of the period, and then on the walk home from school. Even in spite of Britney and Matthew's gross garbage-digging date.

What was going on with Derek? Was he actually trying to flirt with me, or was I just reading what I wanted to hear into the conversation? Why were guys so hard to interpret, anyway?

Regardless of his intent, I was seething anew over my mom's snarky public commentary on my chest size. Boy, was she gonna hear about it when she got home.

I pulled off my boots and hung my coat up, slogging into the house with my backpack over my shoulder. Right after ice-cream therapy, I needed to call Andy and dissect every word of the discussion. Maybe she'd help me find clarity.

Andy was pretty good at what I liked to call "guyomancy"— where you picked apart everything a guy said to interpret his true meaning. I couldn't count the number of evenings we sat on the phone and practiced this mystical art as old as time. Of course, it was usually more about Andy's dates than mine, but whatever.

This time, we'd have some good Derek stuff to talk about before I went to my weekly meeting with Janet in a couple of hours.

I dumped my backpack on the couch and headed toward the kitchen. I happened to glance over at the stairs. A pair of Dad's black socks was draped carelessly on the plateau of the lowest step. They must have fallen out of Mom's laundry basket. I snagged them, then walked up to toss them into their bedroom. Geez, and there were Mom's panty hose, the toes drooped over the top step.

Maybe it was time for her to get a new laundry basket, given how much stuff was falling out. The House Nazi would go ballistic if *I'd* left my socks on the stairs. Nice double standard, Mom.

I grabbed the pantyhose too, then turned the corner at the top of the stairs and froze. Two pairs of naked feet were stretched out on the ground, sticking out my parents' bedroom doorway.

What the . . . ?

I heard a low chuckle. The toes on the small pair of feet wiggled, then rubbed along the inner arches of the big pair of feet.

Understanding cracked me over the head like Rob's Whack-a-Mole mallet. Those were my parents' feet!

"Aaaah!" I screeched.

The feet froze in place, then scrambled inside the room.

"Felicity, is that you?" my mom asked, her voice slightly muffled.

Horrified, I dropped the panty hose and socks in the hallway and booked it down the steps, almost tripping over my own feet. I grabbed my purse, threw on my shoes and coat, and ran out the front door, escaping into the brisk air.

As I headed down the sidewalk to Andy's house, I scrubbed my hand over my face. Maybe a few years of therapy would scrub that horrific image out of my head. Likely not.

I could just imagine that conversation now:

"Sex is natural," the doctor would tell me, her soothing voice like a balm to my grossed-out feelings. *"It's wonderful for two people to share."*

"But . . . but . . . they were on the floor. What were they sharing, carpet burn? And, hello, they knew I was coming home after school." I'd grab a tissue and cry for a few minutes, dabbing the corners of my eyes.

"That's it, cry it out." She'd pat me on the back. "You're making fantastic progress. Another decade or two of therapy, and you'll finally be almost normal. Oh, and here's your bill for the month," she'd say, handing me the invoice. "Wanna just sign your car over to me this time?"

Yeah, maybe even therapy wouldn't reduce the trauma. I strolled up Andy's walkway, cramming my hands into my coat pockets. I'd talk to her about it.

I stood on her stoop and lifted a fist to pound on her door, then paused. Maybe dumping this on her wasn't the best idea, after all. Why would she want to hear about my parents' extracurricular activities? I wouldn't want to hear this kind of pervy info about her folks, especially given her mom's inclination toward the super-freaky side of life. No need for everyone to be scarred.

Besides, this had all come about because of me and my brilliant anniversary present idea. The only reason my parents were all makey-outey all of a sudden was because of the love e-mail I'd sent them.

I had no one to blame but myself for this catastrophe.

Before I could walk away from Andy's house, though, the front door opened, with Andy herself in the doorway.

"Hey," she said to me, smiling. "Whatcha doing here? That's freaky, because I was just getting ready to call you. Mom didn't need me to get her a new yoga mat, after all. Thank. God." She dramatically rolled her eyes, then studied my face, no doubt seeing the utter misery etched into it. "Hey, you okay?"

"Remember this moment, Andy." I glanced at my watch. "Monday, three twenty-five p.m. This is the day I found out firsthand how much my parents like to—" I couldn't even finish the sentence. A wave of sickness rolled through my stomach at the memory of their rubbing feet, their giggles.

God, someone kill me now!

"Oh, noooo," Andy said, her eyebrows shooting straight up into her hairline. "You didn't catch them . . . ?"

"Andy," her mom said from inside the house, her light voice lilting over to us. "Close that door, would you? It's getting drafty in here. And come help me with this new pose. I can't get my leg up far enough."

Andy held a finger up to her mouth, fake gagging. "Fine, Mom,

I'll be there in a sec!" she shouted over her shoulder.

"Gee, that sounds like fun," I teased.

In a low whisper, Andy said to me, "Right. At this point, I'd rather bust my parents doing it than help my mom stretch her leg over her head. Maybe it's time to act on our old plan to join the carnival?"

I smothered a laugh. When Andy and I were in fourth grade, we'd mapped out what we thought was the perfect plan to run away from home. Of course, since we were only nine, it involved asking our parents to make us enough sandwiches to last us until we found jobs at a traveling carnival.

In retrospect, it wasn't the best idea ever, but the concept still had merit, given the current icky situation.

"Sounds like you got parental issues of your own to deal with right now," I said, shaking my head in sympathy. "Wanna meet at Starbucks this evening after I get out of my work meeting? Around six?"

"Okay, I'll see you there." Andy gave me a quick hug, then headed back inside.

I turned around and headed home, knowing it was time to face the music. When I rounded the corner to my street, my mom and dad were leaning out the front door, clad in long, thick black bathrobes. They peered down both sides of the sidewalk.

When Mom saw me, she waved her arm. "Felicity!" she yelled, her brows pinched together in concern. "Are you—were you—"

I nodded, unable to fight back the shudder as I got a flashback of the naked rubbing feet. "I am, and I was, thank you very much."

I broached our front steps and stopped.

She grabbed my arm and tugged me in. "It's freezing. Come inside."

I grudgingly followed her into the living room and plopped on the couch. Dad closed the door, and then they both stood in front of me, staring down.

"It's okay, sweetie," Mom said to Dad, resting a hand on his arm, "I can take it from here."

He whispered something in her ear, rubbing his hand up and down her arm. She giggled, her cheeks burning bright red.

"You're such a cad!" she said with a laugh, pushing him out of the room.

My gag reflex threatened to give. "Mo-o-o-ommm," I groaned. "You're grossing me out." What the hell had I done? That e-mail was a huge mistake. I'd had no idea they'd go from being normally indifferent, asexual parents to acting like a pair of horny teenagers.

Mom sat on the couch beside me, a smile lighting her face. It was almost creepy, because I'd never seen her so . . . glowing. "Felicity, when a man and a woman love each other—"

I held up a hand. "Ew. Don't go there. We had this talk a long time ago, remember?" I'd actually known about the birds and the bees for ten years now.

That's right. I got the sex talk at age *seven*. I was just an innocent young lass then, not knowing that The Talk lay in wait for me.

I remember one day in second grade, I'd asked Dad the meaning of "jumping her bones," a term I'd overheard Rob say to one of his friends. Dad's face had instantly paled, and after sucking in a few deep breaths, he'd mumbled something under his breath before pushing me out of the room.

But the very next night, Mom had knocked on my bedroom door, instruction books in hand. For the next hour and a half, she'd proceeded to burn the worst possible images ever into my tender young retinas.

But I'd taken her lesson to heart. I was now too freaked about pregnancy and worried about getting an STD to even think about putting out.

In front of me, Mom sighed, her shoulders sagging in relief. "Oh, good," she said. "Anyway, your father and I are sorry you had to see that. We love you." She kissed me on the cheek, then traipsed upstairs, giggling again.

I sank back into the couch with a groan. Was this what I had to look forward to every day?

The next two weeks couldn't go by fast enough.

"Thanks for meeting me," I told Andy as we stood inside the doorway of Starbucks. "I needed to get out of the house for a while. My parents are driving me crazy, so I told them I was going to go study with you for a little while."

Actually, my parents were fine with me being out of the house, as it gave them more alone time.

Ick. *Not* going to think about that right now.

Andy hugged me, and her laptop bag bumped against my side. "No problem," she said. "I wanted a break from my house, too. Mom's driving me insane with this yoga crap." She paused. "You know, it's too bad Maya's out on a date. I'm sure she's having more fun than we are, though."

We hopped into the coffee line, right behind a couple of

businesswomen in matching dark blue pantsuits. They took about a billion years each to order a half-caff double whippy mocha java thingamajig.

Good grief. I kept it simple for the poor barista and got an iced mocha. Andy ordered her standard black coffee, no sugar or creamer.

Yuck. I don't know how she drank those. I'd be shaking like crazy from that much caffeine overload, not to mention be sick to my stomach. Plus, I like a bunch of sugar. But black coffee totally fit Andy's personality: straightforward with no messing around—what you see is what you get.

When our drinks had been prepared, we snagged a table near the back. Andy pulled her laptop out, plugging it into the outlet beside her.

"It sounded to me like you needed some cheering up," she said, a mischievous smile on her face as she flipped open the laptop, a present from her mom and dad for her birthday this year. "When you're down, I know there's one thing that always cheers you up."

"And what's that?"

"Our favorite activity—besides ripping on people at school, of course. Ripping on your brother." She booted the computer up, then opened Internet Explorer and went to LoveMatesForever.com.

I giggled, sipping through the straw and drawing in a sweet, delicious mouthful of mocha coffee. "You kill me!"

"I know, but it's a surefire way to make you laugh." Andy typed in the required search terms and drew up my brother's profile. Then, she pulled the lid off her coffee to blow lightly across the top.

"Ewwwwww," I said, pointing at the opening line of Rob's profile and fighting my gag reflex.

Single Man ISO A Real Chick

Yeah, brilliant Rob had set this one up on his own, without having me help. And it was painfully evident. My God. No wonder he was bringing hookers over to the house. As scary as Fluffykins had been, she was likely the cream of the crop who had contacted him, based on what he'd written here.

I'd hate to see some of the other women who'd been drawn to his profile.

Andy snorted as she scanned the opening line too. "Wow, that's so appealing. And flattering too. Rob wants a *real* chick this time, as opposed to the blow-up ones who won't stay hidden in the back of his closet."

At least Rob did one thing kind of right. The picture in his profile was him graduating from the police academy. It was a good, flattering shot, especially since women love men in uniforms. Not that Rob was a real man or anything, but I could see why people might think that was attractive.

"Hey, look," I said, "he cropped me and Mom out of the picture." Rob's arms, which had been wrapped around our shoulders, were chopped off the sides of the image. Nice.

"Soooo, you said on the phone that you had a saucy encounter with Derek today," Andy said, shooting me a sideways glance with one raised eyebrow. "Care to talk about it with Auntie Andy? Maybe it'll help take your mind off your parents getting their freak on."

"You suck," I said, my gag reflex threatening to give. "I'm going to hurl on you if you keep that up."

"Sorry," she said, not looking apologetic in the least.

"Anyway, the whole thing in art class was insane." In between sips of coffee, I explained the discussion between Derek and me.

"Very intriguing," Andy finally said, rubbing her chin in an exaggerated sage-like manner. "Yes, given the evidence you've presented, I definitely think he was flirting with you. The apples comment was to let you know he'd noticed you in more than a 'friendly' way. I don't think he was making fun of you at all. Don't sweat that."

"You think?" Hope fluttered anew in my stomach. Could it be true? Could I have a real chance with Derek?

"There's no doubt in my mind. He's intrigued by you, possibly because of how striking you appear in a bikini." Before I could speak, she held up her hand and cut me off. "I'm kidding, okay? But keep throwing yourself in his line of sight, and Derek will start flirting even more. That's how guys work."

"How do you know?"

"Guys are actually fairly predictable, so I know certain techniques work with them. It's just like with advertising. Keep putting a product in the forefront of your buyer's mind, and he'll remember it. Look how well it works for mops and cleaning stuff—those theme songs get stuck in your head whenever you see their commercials."

"Gee, thanks soooo much for comparing me to a mop," I said in a droll tone. "Nothing says 'I'm sexy' like washing pasta sauce stains off the kitchen floor."

"Oh, stop it. I'm telling the truth. Plus, you're not like some of those skanks at school who practically rip their clothes off in front of Derek to get his attention. You stay classy, and don't resort to stupid tricks like that. He'll see how cool you are whenever he's around you."

That was actually a good idea. If I kept myself near him more, hopefully wearing all my clothes and not babbling like an idiot during those encounters, he'd be sure to see the real me. And even better, no cupid magic would be involved.

"Thanks," I said, greatly heartened. "I think I can do that. You're full of wisdom."

"No problem. I try." Andy took a sip of her coffee, then looked back at the computer. "Oh. My. God. Check out what your brother wrote here, in the section on what he's looking for in a 'chick.'" She dropped her voice low to mimic my brother: "'Do you like long, moonlit walks on the beach?'"

"Dude, this is Cleveland in March," I interjected, biting back a laugh. "And what beach is he talking about? It's not like we're in Miami."

"'I'm looking for someone who isn't afraid to be a real woman,'" Andy continued. She looked over at me, rolling her eyes. "God, you know he totally means someone who enjoys wearing miniskirts and tank tops in the winter."

I snorted. "You called it. Hey, speaking of dating, how are things with you? I haven't heard you talk about any guys in a while."

She took a draw from her coffee, then gave a sarcastic laugh. "That's because I'm on a sabbatical from guys. They're all morons."

"Not all of them," I pointed out. "Some of them are totally awesome."

"Oh, that's right," she said, fluttering her eyelashes at me and clasping her hands in front of her chest. "Derek is oh so dreamy and super-duper *fabulous!*"

I laughed. "Andy, I will hit you if you keep that up."

"Seriously, I think Derek's great for you. And one of Maya's guys will likely turn out to be perfect for her, if she ever figures out which one she likes best. Or who's the best kisser—whatever works for her. But as for me, I'm on a break. At least for right now. I'm tired of being hit on by jerks who don't care about anything but themselves." She shrugged casually and took a drink. "Not that it stops me from looking at eye candy, though. Hellooooo, hottie." She nodded her head toward the attractive college guy, wearing a

Baldwin Wallace College sweater, walking through the door.

"I guess I can understand why you feel that way." It made me sad, though, thinking of Andy swearing off love, but after all these years, I knew how she worked. Her super pickiness in guys had her saying no to dates all the time, so it wasn't like swearing off guys right now would change her life *that* greatly.

Still, I hoped she'd come around and start wanting to give love a chance again. I didn't want to force her into a love match if she didn't want to be in one, because I respected her feelings. But that didn't mean I don't want her to have a great boyfriend eventually.

And hopefully sooner, rather than later.

chapter thirteen

The first thing I noticed outside of school Tuesday morning, as I headed up the sidewalk to the front steps, was Britney, perched alone on a bench. Her head was buried in her hands, and she was crying her eyes out.

"Hey," I said to her in a gentle tone as I approached, "are you okay?" I sat on the bench beside her, my butt instantly freezing on the cold wooden seat. Ick.

At the sound of my voice, Britney sniffled loudly, lifted her head, and wiped her eyes with the back of her glove.

"I'm fine," she answered, giving me a watery-thin smile. The rims of her eyes were blood-red, and dried tear tracks streaked her pale cheeks.

She was obviously upset, but not wanting to talk, and I didn't feel comfortable pushing her into it.

"Want me to get Matthew for you?" I asked.

At my words, Britney's tears started anew. They slipped down her face, landing in large plops on her slick blue jacket. She dropped her face back into her hands.

"I d-don't know what's going on with Matthew," she blurted out, her voice muffled by her gloves. "He was supposed to pick me up for school today, but he never showed up. I tried calling him, but he hasn't answered my voice mail or text messages. I don't understand—this isn't like him."

"Maybe he's just sick?" I suggested. Digging around in garbage wasn't the most sanitary hobby around, so he could have caught some kind of bug.

She sighed, shrugging her shoulders lightly. "Maybe that's it." She didn't sound convinced, though.

Even so, if he were sick, why wouldn't he text her back? That's not the action of someone in love.

Oh, no. Maybe Matthew *wasn't* in love anymore. I quickly did the math and realized that, yup, the spell was due to wear off today. How could I have forgotten? With all the madness around Maya's love life, as well as matching up DeShawn and Marisa, hyper-analyzing Derek's every word, plus dealing with my hormone-driven parents, it completely slipped my mind.

"I'm so sorry," I said, a thread of guilt twisting around my stomach. How did this relationship fail? They'd seemed so wrapped up in each other for the last two weeks. Was Matthew really trying to ditch her? What could I do?

"I'll be fine, thanks," Britney said, sniffling again. She rose. "I'd better get to class." She shuffled away, her body hunched over.

I chewed my thumbnail, deep in thought. Maybe everything would still turn out okay. After all, it could just be a simple mis-understanding, a small fight, one that could be fixed through some effort. Even if Matthew was no longer under the love spell, he still must care for Britney a little, right? All I knew was I certainly didn't want to be responsible for Britney's heartache.

In all the time I'd been a cupid—well, these past two weeks, anyway—I hadn't considered the downside to the job: the fact that the couples I paired up might *not* stay together forever.

Once that realization hit me, it opened the floodgates, and the bad thoughts kept coming. What if *none* of the couples I'd matched up stayed in love? If Marisa dumped DeShawn, he'd probably become even more insufferable than he'd been in the first place, and even more down on romance.

What if, next week, Maya ended up alone and bitter? What if none of the guys stayed in love with her, or she ended up not wanting to be with any of them? She'd withdraw even further back into herself, and I'd never get her to go on a date again.

No, I wouldn't accept defeat. I'd make sure Maya and Britney and DeShawn ended up happy, damn it. I was a cupid, and it was my job to help people find lasting love! I was gonna see what the deal was with Matthew, and then I'd take it from there.

Feeling reinvigorated, I rushed up the walkway to school. Maya was already waiting inside the doors for me, a big smile on her face as she clutched her trumpet case. Her hair hung in light waves down her back instead of being pulled up in a ponytail, and she was wearing a light green sweater and cute low-rise jeans.

But even more important, above all the makeover changes she'd been making, she looked happy, totally oblivious to whatever fate awaited her next Monday.

No, I couldn't fail her.

"Hey, where's your morning escort?" I asked. At this point, I couldn't keep the schedule straight anymore. But since I planned it out myself, I didn't want to admit that, so I kept my words vague.

She shrugged. "Quentin had an emergency yearbook meeting, so he had to come in early. I told him I would just walk myself and see him before class."

"So, are you still thinking balloon-man Ben is 'The One'?" I asked.

"Well, I was, but then Josh and I had such a fun time hanging out last night that it made me think he's the one to choose. We're planning to go see this new horror movie next weekend." She sighed. "But then, when Quentin called to say he couldn't walk me this morning, we had the best phone conversation, and I—"

The first bell rang, interrupting her romance saga. We headed inside with the rest of the students, trying not to be jostled to death in the chaos of the hallway. Homemade posters covered the walls and lockers, courtesy of the pep squad, encouraging students to attend the basketball game at the end of the week against our rival team, Lincoln High.

"Are you ready for your big solo at the game on Friday?" I asked Maya.

She groaned, moving the trumpet case into her other hand. "Well, I've been practicing, but not as much as I should. I just haven't had time, with all the dates lately. Anyway," she said, changing the subject, "how was your evening?"

"Not bad. I read a few chapters of *Jane Ey*—ooph—" My words were interrupted as I slammed in the back of a tall guy in front of me, who'd suddenly stopped dead in the middle of the hallway.

Wobbly, the guy spun around on the balls of his feet, trying to right himself as he examined me. "You okay?" he asked in a rush. He swiped a hand across his forehead to move a strand of shaggy black hair out of his eyes.

Giving him a small nod, I tried to regain the breath that had whooshed out of me at the impact.

"Sorry about that," he mumbled. "Some girl stopped in front of me, and I didn't want to run into her. I didn't know anyone was right behind me."

"Hey," Maya said, "aren't you in my French class? You're the new guy, right?"

His cheeks turned a deep red, and he nodded.

Aw, poor guy. No wonder he was so jumpy and embarrassed. It sucked being the new kid at school. Ooh, but as a cupid, I'm the perfect person to help him out. I should try to find out more about this guy so I can start a profile in my PDA. Janet had encouraged me in our weekly meeting yesterday to keep working on new matches.

Yeah, this guy needed me, and I'd make it my job to find him the perfect love match.

"I'm okay, really," I told him, feeling generous. "No worries."

Quentin came out of nowhere just then and pushed in between me and Maya to stand in front of her. A digital camera dangled around his neck.

"Hey," he said to her, giving the new guy a glance, then dismissing him by completely turning his back to the guy. "There you are! I want to take some shots of you with the morning light. Let's plan some time tomorrow morning, okay?" He grabbed Maya's elbow and led her off toward our English class.

I turned back to the new guy, but he was gone.

With a tired groan, I sank into my seat between Maya and Andy at the cafeteria table, grabbing a bright green apple from my brown paper lunch bag. What a long day, and it was only lunchtime. I was also keeping an eye out for Matthew so I could see what was going on with his love match. The issue plagued the back of my mind, chewed at my conscience.

Yeah, I was so ready for spring break next month. Not that I was going to do anything fun. Mom wouldn't dream of letting me escape Cleveland to go somewhere south, where the sun might possibly shine more than five minutes a day.

I looked at Maya's lunch tray, glad I'd brought a PB&J sandwich and chips. There was no way I'd touch the meat loaf surprise. Ick. God only knew what lurked in those little brown loaves of doom, but I guarantee it wasn't real meat.

"You guys are coming to the game on Friday night, right?" Maya asked. "And then, sleepover at Andy's?" She picked up her fork and poked at the "meat" loaf, her nose wrinkling in disdain.

I took a bite of my apple, then said around a mouthful, "I'll totally be there." Not that I knew a damn thing about basketball, of course, but I could support my friends with the best of 'em.

"The chance to watch you seduce the rest of the school with your mad music skills?" Andy teased. "I wouldn't miss it for the world."

"Hardy har." Maya threw a balled-up napkin at Andy, who cackled evilly in response.

"Maya," Ben said, suddenly appearing beside her and me. He stared down at her, his face rapt. "Hi."

"Ben!" Maya smiled at him, then peeked at her watch, a deep

crease between her brows. "I'm . . . surprised to see you. Don't you have a different lunch period?"

She glanced at Andy and me with alarmed eyes, blinking rapidly. Apparently, it wasn't Ben's turn to eat lunch with her. Crap.

A small flash of irritation shot through me. What was it with these guys, just eating up Maya's time whenever it was convenient for them? Between Quentin's obsessive photo shoot, Josh's midnight visit, and Ben's awkward-but-cute-but-creepy locker invasion, the girl barely had room to breathe. The boys were totally not sticking to the schedule.

Maybe there was a lesson to be learned in this—I guess guys in love can't be controlled, after all. Definitely good to know for future reference.

All four of us stared at one another in awkward silence. Ben's cheeks reddened as he shuffled from foot to foot. He obviously wanted to sit down beside Maya, but I refused to move over.

Actually, I was trying my best to figure out how to nicely get him to leave, before Maya's *real* lunch date showed up. Time was of the essence here.

Andy cleared her throat. "So," she asked Ben, "you stoked about Friday's game?"

"Game?" Ben echoed, not peeling his eyes from Maya. "What game?"

Andy's eyebrows shot up clear into her hairline. "Um, the big basketball game. The one you're supposed to be announcing . . . ?"

"Oh," he said with a nervous chuckle, his flush deepening down his throat. He finally looked over at Andy, shrugging slightly. "Yeah, right, *that* game. Sure, it'll be fun." He whipped his head to look at Maya. "You're gonna be there, right?"

Geez. The old Ben always seemed so pulled together and on top of things, on or off the microphone. This new, in-love Ben couldn't even remember when the game was. Could my love spell have changed him this greatly?

As I looked at Ben, trying to figure out how to get him away from the table, I noticed Josh weaving his way through the crowd, heading straight for our table.

Oh, hell. Things were about to go from bad to worse.

"Excuse me for a sec." After putting my half-eaten apple on the tabletop, I jumped up from my seat, darting right over to Josh.

"Hey!" I said to him in my oh-crap-I'll-just-distract-him-with-my-utter-perkiness voice. "I need to tell you something urgent."

Josh peered over my shoulder, probably trying to keep his eyes on Maya. "Yeah, what is it?"

I racked my brain while continuing to block his path with my body. *Think quickly!* "It's about Maya."

That got his attention. He halted in his tracks, eyes on me. "What about her?"

"Well, Maya's nervous about her solo on Friday. Since you're a fellow musician, I figured you're just the guy to help. Have you thought about . . . making her a mix CD or something? Maybe it would inspire her and soothe her worries."

Ugh. Stupid, stupid words poured out of my mouth in a rush, but I couldn't make myself stop. I had to give the girls time to ditch Ben.

Josh tilted his head, considering my suggestion. "She does love music," he murmured, scratching his chin. "But I don't think a CD is going to be enough to show how I feel." After a long moment of silence, he snapped his fingers, then gave me a wide, excited grin. "I got it. I know just how to make her feel better. I'll go get started right now!"

Turning, he took off through the cafeteria, bursting out the double doors into the hallway.

Well, that wasn't exactly what I'd intended to do, but whatever. It worked. I headed back to the table and plopped back down in my seat. Ben had been evacuated, leaving just the three of us again.

"God, that was too close," I said, propping my elbows up on the table and leaning my head into my hands. I couldn't wait for this dating madness to be over.

Maya groaned, her brow furrowed. "Yeah, this is way crazier than I ever dreamed it could be. I can't keep it straight anymore, and I'm still no closer to figuring out which guy I like most." She bit her lower lip. "My poor day planner is jam-packed, every day, but I'm still searching for a sure sign of which guy is the right one. I seem to like them all equally—like, whichever one is right in front of me is my favorite at the time."

A horrible, sinking feeling hit me as I stared at her overwhelmed face. What had I gotten Maya into? Since none of the guys knew about each other, Maya was doing a constant juggling act. At least the spell would be over in less than a week, and Maya could make a completely clear-headed decision then.

"Man," Andy said, shaking her head, "I'm getting tired just looking at you. Maybe you should take a break from dating a bit."

"I can't. I don't know how to explain it, but whenever I think about cutting back, I just feel completely drawn back to them. It's like I'm under some kind of spell."

"Yeah, a spell of loooooooove," Andy drawled, pointing her wiggling fingers at Maya.

My heart accelerated to about five thousand beats per minute, but Maya just rolled her eyes at Andy and kept going. "I'll just make this work somehow. It's only been just over a week. I'm sure I'll be able to decide soon, and then things will be more normal. The more I see of each of them now, the faster I'll be able to choose the right one . . . right?"

The bell rang, dismissing us from lunch.

"Time to skedaddle," Maya said, sliding out of her seat and balancing her tray in one hand. "See ya after school, guys."

I dunked my apple core in the trash and shoved my chips and sandwich back in the paper bag. So much for using lunch period to occasionally eat lunch. The sacrifices I made for my career. Well, maybe I could grab a candy bar from the vending machine later.

Andy and I headed down the hall to health class, where we were talking about the importance of adequate nutrition for teen development.

I thought about my uneaten sandwich and sighed. *Yeah, tell me about it.*

chapter fourteen

"There's Quentin's little photo slut," a not-so-subtle stage whisper said as Maya and I walked toward the school's front doors at the end of the school day.

We both turned in unison. There was my archenemy Mallory, surrounded by three of her tanorexic, fake-blond diva girlfriends.

All four of them were wearing matching pastel snow parkas and low-slung jeans with thick, white fuggly boots that they clearly considered cool. Their heavily made-up eyes raked over Maya, a snobbish sneer on their collective faces.

A surge of anger throbbed in my gut, and I clenched my fists at my side. "Ex-*cuse* me?" I said, hostility freely ripping through my voice as I aimed my glare straight at Mallory. "What did you just say?"

She blinked her bright blue-contact eyes at me. "I don't know what you're talking about." She turned to her friends. "Come on, let's go."

"You're not leaving without apologizing to Maya," I said, stepping in her path.

At my movement, Mallory's eyes about bugged out of her head. Then, her hot-pink lips pursed in disgust. "I'm not apologizing for anything," she spat out. "If anyone owes anyone an apology, it's you, for stabbing me in the back."

"This again, seriously?" I asked with a heavy sigh, rolling my eyes to the ceiling, "I told you, nothing happened between me and James—*two years* ago, I might add."

"That's not what I heard," Mallory said. "And my *real* friends have no reason to lie to me."

Her vapid blond shadows nodded their heads in agreement.

What the hell did they know? They only knew what Mallory told them.

Not that anyone could tell now, but during freshman year, Mallory and I were way close. We shared a bunch of the same classes, half our wardrobes, and all of our secrets as well. Between the time I spent at Mallory's, Maya's, and Andy's houses, Mom complained I was never home.

All was going great until Mallory got a bug up her butt and decided out of the blue that I wanted to steal James, her boyfriend at the time. As if I would *ever* make a move on another girl's boyfriend, let alone a close friend's boyfriend, let alone *James*.

But Mallory ditched me in an instant, without even asking to hear the truth. And then, she turned her back on Andy and Maya too, when they refused to believe her paranoid rants. Unbelievable.

She and James broke up a few months later, but I have a sneaking suspicion Mallory never got over him.

I crossed my arms over my chest. "Well, whatever you heard was wrong. I tried explaining that to you, many times."

Actually, I'd never understood her attraction to James in the first place. I always thought he was a pretty dumb guy. He was the person in class who made armpit farting sounds and laughed too loud at how clever he was. I liked to think I could hook up with someone smarter than that.

Besides, Mallory knew how I felt about Derek, and she *should* have known I would never backstab a friend.

She held up her palm at me. "I don't care, and I don't want to talk about it." She turned and scrutinized Maya, shaking her head as if she didn't like what she was seeing. "I just don't get it. Why you?"

With a parting look of disdain, she pushed between Maya and me and strolled through the front doors outside. Her airheaded posse quickly followed.

Maya remained frozen in her spot, her jaw clenched tightly. "What did I ever do to them?" she asked me through gritted teeth.

It took me several long moments to calm my blood pressure down before I could answer her. I had to seriously fight the urge to run after them and clock Mallory square in her perky, stuck-up little nose.

"You didn't do anything," I finally said. "Mallory hates me because of the James thing, and she hates you for being my friend." I paused as I replayed Mallory's words in my head. "Well, and apparently they've heard about Quentin's plans to feature you in the yearbook, and their heads are exploding with jealousy."

Maya pulled the loose strap of her backpack over her arm and up her shoulder. "Come on," she said, her voice flat. She tugged on my arm and led me out the door. "Let's just go home."

I wanted to give her the "don't let them get to you" pep talk, but it was apparent by the look on Maya's face that she didn't want to say anything else about it.

We walked back to my house in total silence. Andy was going to meet us there, since she had to run home first.

I trudged beside Maya, fuming over Mallory. Ever since our big confrontation freshman year, I'd tried to just ignore her, but that didn't stop her from picking on me every chance she got. Once, she even wrote "Felicity is a slut" on my notebook when I got up out of my desk to go to the bathroom.

I squinted and sucked in a deep breath, pissed off about the past all over again.

Friends came first, period. No exceptions. That's why Maya, Andy, and I had set that cardinal rule right after the Mallory fiasco: We'd never let a stupid guy come between us, ever. And because we felt secure in that rule, we knew we could help each other with whatever dating woes hit, like Maya's current love problems.

Maya and I turned up the driveway of my house, and I put my key in the door, tentatively pushing it open.

"Mom?" I hollered, hoping she and Dad weren't swinging from the chandelier or christening the kitchen counter. My poor nerves couldn't handle another incident, and I definitely didn't want to subject my friends to it.

Silence greeted us. Nobody was home.

Thank God. At least I could get a mini-break from their public displays of affection. If I had to see my dad squeeze my mom's butt one more time, I was going to lose it.

"Come on in," I said to Maya, heading over to check the answering machine. There was one message from Mom, saying she and Dad wouldn't be home until later, but would bring dinner.

"Want something to drink?" I asked.

"I guess." Maya shrugged halfheartedly, her eyes cast down as she tossed her backpack on the floor beside our living room couch.

"Hey, I know—want me to set up a hit on Mallory?" I asked, trying to make her smile again. "I'll hire someone to break her kneecaps. Actually, I bet we'd get a line of people at school offering to do it for free."

She chuckled, plopping down on the couch. "Sure, that'd be great."

I dug into the fridge and grabbed us two Diet Cokes, then headed into the living room. "Let's get down to business," I said, handing her a drink. "We got some big-time studying to do."

We spent the next half hour discussing the ins and outs of *Jane Eyre*. Mrs. Kendel had warned us she'd be giving a short-answer quiz on the book, so we wanted to be prepared.

Maya had originally been scheduled for an after-school date

with Quentin, but when I'd pushed for her to study with me, knowing that that date would mean less study time for her, she of course had followed the rule: Friends come first. Quentin could wait until later to do some nature shots of her.

A heavy pounding on the door startled me. I jumped up and answered. It was Andy, bearing snacks.

"Oh, thank God you're here," I said with a big, dramatic sigh, taking the bag. "I'm starving. I thought my stomach would start chewing on my own spinal cord."

"Funny, funny. And I'm so glad to see you too," Andy said. She slipped over to the couch and sat beside Maya, the amusement on her face disappearing as she wrapped an arm around Maya's shoulders. "Hey, I heard you guys had a big scene with Mallory and her skank-gang today after school. Everything okay?"

Maya shrugged her shoulders. "I'm fine," she mumbled.

"Geez, the rumor mill works fast." I groaned, ripping open the bag of Doritos. I popped a super-cheesy chip in my mouth, chewing fast. "She was just being a jerk, as usual. I'm sure it was her time of the month or something."

Andy drew in a short breath. "I'm not so sure about that," she replied. "The rumor mill's also churning out some trash-talking stories about Maya and her dating life. I tried to dispel them as best as possible, but gossip is flying all over the place."

Maya's mouth flew wide open. "People are talking about me? I don't get it. Why do they care?"

I plopped back down on the couch beside Andy, cramming another chip in my mouth. "Because some people have nothing better to do than make up crap about people."

Mallory was so going down for this, if it was the last thing I did.

Andy nodded in agreement. "Mallory and her clan are just pissed that Quentin's featuring Maya in the yearbook instead of showing a thousand photos of their hoochie selves."

An angry flush burned Maya's cheeks. "They can have the whole yearbook, for all I care. I just wanted to spend time with Quentin. I *so* don't need this right now."

An utterly brilliant idea came to mind, a way to make love conquer all *and* get them off Maya's back. God, I was so, so good. Call me Saint Felicitas.

"Don't worry anymore about it," I told Maya, smiling. "I'm gonna take care of this. You just focus on your solo. And figuring out your social life, of course."

She and Andy shot me curious and slightly worried looks, which I waved off.

"I won't be breaking her kneecaps, I promise," I said, laughing. "I'll just nip the rumors in the bud. She won't be talking about you any longer."

Because instead of having time to spread malicious gossip, Mallory was going to be too busy focusing on the new love of her life . . . Bobby Blowhard.

The plan was so brilliant, it was scary.

"And speaking of rumors," Andy said, leaning in, "what's going on with Matthew and that Britney girl he was dating? I heard she was crying outside of school this morning. Did he dump her?"

Maya's eyes widened. "That's awful."

My stomach flipped over as guilt clutched me in its grip again. "Yeah, it—it is." Gah! With all the lunch drama, I forgot I still hadn't seen Matthew at all today. "Have you seen him?" I asked as casually as possible. If there was any news to be had, perhaps Andy had heard something.

She shook her head. "Nope. I don't have any classes with him."

Darn.

Well, there went that idea. I made a mental note to keep digging for information on Matthew. It was almost certain their love match was a failure, though, and I dreaded talking to Janet about it next Monday. She probably wouldn't take the news too well. But I wanted to confirm it before I told her.

"Love comes and goes so quickly sometimes, doesn't it," Maya observed, shaking her head sadly.

Unfortunately, it sure did.

The next morning, Wednesday, was surprisingly warm, with temperatures breaking the fifties. Finally. I was anxious for spring to actually show itself. As I stared wistfully out the window of my English class, I almost yearned to prance around freely outside, except I knew the mud factor would be crazy gross right now, what with all the melting snow.

The quiz at the beginning of class had gone well. Mrs. Kendel showed unusual mercy and only gave us a couple of short-answer questions. And thank God, they were all from the material Maya and I had read yesterday.

So I'd finished up early and was busy mentally traipsing around outside, waiting for everyone else to be done.

"Miss Walker." Mrs. Kendel's sharp voice interrupted my

wandering thoughts. "Would you like to join us for class today in both body *and* mind?"

The smart-ass answer would be, *Yeah, right,* but considering I needed to pass her class to eventually graduate, I meekly nodded.

Other students tittered at her verbal smackdown, and I forced myself to focus the rest of class. I noticed DeShawn taking notes as Mrs. Kendel talked. Was he working on the haiku for Marisa? When the spell wore off, would he change back into his buttheaded self, or would love continue to conquer all and keep him different than he used to be?

When the bell rang, Maya and I flew out the classroom door—Maya to meet her escort to the next class (Ben this time), and me to see if the newest love match I'd made last night had worked.

As I considered the Bobby-Mallory setup, I knew a part of me should feel guilty about pairing them, but I had to be honest. I didn't feel bad at all. In fact, wasn't it selfless of me to give my worst enemy a chance at love?

And who was I to say it wouldn't work, anyway?

The profiles I'd written on Bobby and Mallory were finely crafted works of art, to be sure. I should consider becoming a novelist, given the way the words had come out of me in an almost inspired fashion. Instead of commenting on their massive egos, I'd written that both had a healthy sense of self. I also said they were both engaging conversationalists, as well as passionate about physical well-being.

Yeah, I had a gift.

Besides, all of that word-smithing was for Janet's benefit as well, since surely she'd be scrutinizing my pairings. I'd lucked out and avoided being caught matching Maya with three guys, and Janet hadn't said anything about the e-mails I'd sent to my parents, but I wasn't about to take any more chances—this job was just too much fun, and it had way too many unexpected side benefits. Plus, having a new love match would show her I was still working hard.

I spied Bobby standing about twenty feet away, his back pressed against a locker as he scoured the halls. Suddenly, his eyes lit up, and a huge grin broke out on his face. I'd seen that smile before—it was the look he usually reserved for *me*. Wow, was it refreshing to not be the recipient this time.

"Mallory! Mallory!" he yelled as loud as possible, frantically waving his hand. "Ma-a-a-a-alloryyyyyy!"

Biting my lower lip to keep from bursting out in laughter, I ducked into a classroom doorway and watched the scene unfold.

Mallory noticed Bobby hollering—it was kind of hard to miss it, and pretty much the whole hallway stopped in stunned silence at his ruckus.

She gave her giggle-squad an apologizing shrug, then waved them away from her. "Go ahead. I'll meet you at lunch," she said.

They stared at her retreating figure with heads tilted to the side, not believing she was giving them the brush-off for Bobby Blowhard.

For once, I totally could relate to them.

"Hey," Bobby said when Mallory got there. "You know, you've been on my mind a lot lately. Um, this morning, I mean."

Hah. I bet so. The effectiveness of these love matches never failed to amaze me.

Mallory nodded enthusiastically. She briefly stared at her feet, a blush spreading across her cheeks. "Yeah, I was thinking about you, too," she replied, licking her lower lip and daring a glance at him through her eyelashes.

Bobby's pecs began their instinctive mating dance, bouncing in some kind of rhythm only he could hear. "Wanna meet me in the gym later? Maybe we could work out together," he said, eagerness pouring into his voice.

Students around them were frozen in place and openly staring, not even bothering to hide their shock. Not that I could blame them. The school's biggest snob, hooking up with Bobby? It was a tale for *Ripley's Believe It Or Not*. A few people actually giggled out loud.

Mallory ignored them all, focusing solely on Bobby. She nodded in assent and brushed his upper arm with her fingertips, smiling at him with an earnestness I hadn't ever seen in her before.

Wow, she was definitely smitten—I don't think she'd even looked at James like that, back when they were together. It was kind of weird to watch, honestly.

The bell rang. Students groaned, but dashed off to class, their whispers about Mallory whirling all around. This would definitely end any talk about Maya, since this was way juicier stuff to focus on, witnessed firsthand.

Problem? Solved. Go Felicity!

"I gotta go to class now," Mallory said in a breathy voice, waving bye to Bobby. She backed away slowly, eyes still locked on his until she bumped into an open locker door. "I'll see ya."

He watched her leave. "Bye, Mallory!" he screamed to her departing figure at the top of his lungs.

Holy crap, their relationship was going to be even better than I'd imagined.

chapter fifteen

Constellations glow,
but their shine cannot compare
to your inner star.

"Wow, DeShawn," I said, utter surprise stunning me for a moment. "This is a really good haiku. Did you write this by yourself?"

DeShawn had found me lingering in the hallway after Bobby and Mallory walked off and immediately thrust his poem into my hand, grunting that he wanted me to read it.

I leaned back against my locker, rereading the scribbled poem on the crumpled-up piece of notebook paper. A part of me was sure he must have stolen it from somewhere. It sure didn't sound like the DeShawn I knew.

He nodded in response and gave me a halfhearted shrug, looking a little unsure as to whether or not to believe my compliment. "Thanks. I worked hard on it. Think Marisa will like it?"

I blinked. "She'd be an idiot not to," I blurted out, almost scoffing at the idea of her not being taken in by these romantic words. "It's fabulous."

What girl *wouldn't* be flattered by such a lovely poem? I'd practically stab someone in the face for a poem like this to be written about me.

I handed DeShawn back the piece of paper, suddenly feeling peppy and excited about his love match. At least one coupling was working out well. And thank God for that. I hadn't spotted Matthew at all since seeing Britney cry Tuesday morning, so I was unsure of what to do in that area.

DeShawn folded the paper and crammed it in his back pocket. "Gotta go. Later," he said, taking off down the hall without a care in the world.

I turned back to my locker, grabbed my American history book, and headed to my boring class, dragging my feet the whole way. On a more positive note, I now had something awesome to tell my cupid boss Janet in our Monday meeting.

She'd probably think DeShawn's love poetry was cool too.

Then, I noticed Matthew himself, a few feet ahead of me down the hallway. He was resting a palm against the wall, leaning in close and talking to Britney. Sweet, blissful relief swept through me at the sight of the two of them together.

No, wait, that wasn't Britney. This chick had darker hair than Britney and was wearing one of those granola dresses, with brown, hemp-looking fabric. Even her dirt-brown sandals looked like you could smoke them.

Matthew laughed at something the granola girl said. He stroked the side of her face with his palm, then planted a small kiss on her forehead.

The same gesture he'd done with Britney when I'd seen them in the hallway together last week.

My stomach fell. Guess it was official. My first failed love match—signed, sealed, and flushed down the toilet.

I heard a sharp gasp from behind, and turned to see Britney stop in her tracks right beside me. She stared in horror at Matthew for a long moment, then ran into the bathroom, the heavy door closing behind her.

The bell rang, signaling it was time for us stragglers to dash into class. I shifted on my feet, unsure what to do. The love match was technically over, and it was out of my hands, but I felt horrendously guilty leaving Britney in such disarray.

After all, it was my fault for pairing the two of them in the first place.

With a light push, I gingerly headed through the bathroom doorway. "Britney?"

I heard a sniffle in the last stall. Then, Britney shoved the stall door open. "Oh, it's you," she said, blinking rapidly to clear the tears out of her eyes. "Sorry, you seem to catch me in the worst moods lately."

"I don't mean to be so nosy, but I saw you run in here. You wanna talk?" I leaned back against the sink counter.

She moved toward the sink too, then turned on the faucet and splashed water on her eyes. "Nothing to talk about, except my boyfriend and I broke up yesterday, and he's already moving on to someone—" Her words broke off with a sob.

I had a sudden impulse to hug her, but held back. We really didn't know each other all that well. Instead, I settled for nodding empathetically. "That sucks. I'm sorry to hear that."

"I guess he got tired of how different we were. I tried to be someone he wanted, but I just wasn't enough. I even dug through garbage for him even though I hated it, just because he'd wanted to." Her voice sounded bitter, even as it seemed weak and unsure. She was probably experiencing the full spectrum of emotions right now.

As for me, I had one overwhelmingly strong feeling: guilt. Britney's words about how different she and Matthew are stabbed me right in the stomach. And what's worse is that she was right. It was my job to ensure compatibility, and I messed that up royally.

I had no idea what to say to her in response.

Britney studied her reflection in the mirror, then dug into her purse to pull out concealer, dabbing it around her eyes and gently rubbing the makeup in. Her eyeballs were still red, but the eyelids didn't look so rough.

"Maybe I just need to try harder," she said. "Maybe I can win him back."

I bit my lower lip, studying her face. What would Oprah say to her right now? I tried to channel the queen of talk therapy.

"You know," I said slowly, "that might work for a while. But what happens if you 'slip up' again, even accidentally? Is it worth constantly walking on eggshells, afraid you're gonna ruin the relationship?"

"Yeah," she hedged, "but I hate to give up on something I've worked on. I feel like a quitter." She cast her eyes down, her shoulders slumped.

"But you're not a quitter. You're just being smart and getting out of something that isn't working. Even if you're giving one hundred percent of yourself into a relationship, it's still only fifty percent."

Holy crap, I was even more profound than I realized. I was really getting into this counseling stuff. It wasn't going to earn me any lasting-match bonuses, but at least I was undoing some of the damage I'd caused.

She stared at me for a moment, a light of hope flashing in her eyes. "Yeah, maybe you're right."

It was sorely tempting to pair Britney up with a new match and give her a quick romantic boost with another guy, but she needed time to focus on herself and her own needs before diving back into a relationship. I made a mental note to give it a month or so, then try to find Britney a better match.

I stood up, pushing my shoulders back. "Damn straight, I'm right! I think you should spend more time working on *you* instead of trying to get him back. Screw Matthew. Viva la independence!"

Britney nodded, a smile growing on her face. "Viva la independence," she echoed.

"You know, I haven't seen Josh in school since the lunch fiasco yesterday," I said to Maya, then took a big swig from my water bottle. After reading an article on the effects of artificial sweeteners on the complexion, I'd decided to cut my soda intake. Which was totally going to kill me, because I hearted caffeine so much, I wanted to marry it, but one had to make sacrifices for beauty.

Maya nodded. "It's all good. He texted me earlier to say he's caught up in some super-urgent project, but wanted me to know he's still thinking of me. Wasn't that sweet?" She grinned at Andy and me, then glanced at her watch. "Oh, crap, I forgot." She quickly packed up her stuff and stood. "I made a lunch appointment with Absinthia today to have my cards read."

I spat my mouthful of water all over the table. "Say what?"

Absinthia's real name is Karen Mack. She's one of those kids who cuts class like she's allergic to school, preferring to discuss poetry and the futility of life with all the other moody kids. She usually hangs out under the bleachers and smokes like a freight train.

I had no idea she did fortune-telling too, but I guess it was a better career choice than folding T-shirts at the Gap.

"She's going to read my tarot cards. Maybe her insight will help me figure out which guy is right for me." Maya looked sheepish. "It couldn't hurt, right?"

Andy rose, balling her napkin up in her fist and tossing it on her tray. She grinned madly. "Oh, no way am I missing this."

Well, I wasn't going to be the odd man out. "Count me in too." I'd never seen cards read before except on those late-night TV infomercials (*You'll soon be fifty bucks poorer, so call this number—woooooooooh*).

This would be very interesting, to say the least.

We shuffled out of the lunchroom and slipped outside, heading to the track field bleachers. Sure enough, the usual crowd was there, evidenced by the puffs of smoke rising through the seats. I heard a heated discussion going on, something about symbolism in Kafka's work.

Maya led us under the bleachers and over to the group, Andy and I on her heels. The goth kids stopped their conversation, several of them staring at us. I shuffled in place, suddenly feeling awkward.

"Absinthia," Maya said in a soft tone, "I'm sorry I'm late."

Absinthia turned, her heavily lined eyes raking over the three of us. The chains on her black wide-legged pants rattled with her movement.

"Time's relative, anyway," Absinthia said in a low voice, shrugging. She tapped the ash off her cigarette onto the ground. "Did you bring the money?"

Andy scoffed. "You're paying for this? How do you know she's even the real thing, Maya?"

Absinthia raised one eyebrow, eyeing Andy, and took a deep drag of her cigarette. "And what makes you so sure *you're* the real thing?" she said, the smoke curling out her mouth. She sneered. "At least I'm not just a product of the media conspiracy to turn teenage girls into robotic breeding machines."

One of the guys in the group nodded enthusiastically at Absinthia's words. "Exactly. Why look like every other cookie-cutter teen?"

Andy opened her mouth to reply, but I interrupted.

"Hey, this is Maya's decision," I said calmly, wanting to defuse the situation before it got out of hand. "But can we move somewhere else to do this?" I didn't want everyone and their mom staring while Maya threw her hard-earned bucks in the garbage.

Absinthia shrugged and smashed out her cigarette on the heel of her black boots, then rose, leading us back across the field and under the eaves of the school building. She plopped down at a nearby picnic table, and the three of us sat across from her. What an interesting group we must have looked like.

Maya handed her a folded bill. "Can we get started? Lunch is going to end soon."

Absinthia pulled a wrapped pack out of her large pants pocket, then unfolded her deck from the soft, blood-red fabric. She flipped through the cards and pulled out certain ones, then put the rest of them away.

"We're going to use just the major arcana deck for you," Absinthia said. "I need you to think about what your concerns are. Close your eyes and have a specific question in your mind." She shuffled the remaining chunk of cards, then put the deck down on the table. "Okay, split the deck for me."

Maya did so, and Absinthia put the two halves of the deck back together, then fanned the cards out.

"Please draw three cards," she intoned.

Maya drew in a deep breath and reached a hand out. I detected a slight shake in her fingers as she picked out three.

Absinthia flipped over the first one. "This is your past," she said, pointing to the card. "It's the hermit. You spent a lot of time inside yourself, skeptical of things around you." She shot a big grin to Maya. "A girl after my own heart. You're quite the antisocial thing, aren't you."

Maya chuckled. "Yeah, I guess that's a good way to put it."

Andy snorted. "Huh. Ya think?"

I elbowed Andy in the side, and she shot me a glare, but quieted down.

"There's nothing wrong with getting some quiet time to sort things out," Absinthia continued. She flipped over the next card, a man and woman embracing each other. "This is your present, representing the lovers. You're currently in the throes of making a big decision."

Goose bumps rose across the surface of my arms.

"Whoa," Andy breathed. "That's freaky."

Maya gasped. "Oh, that's it! But what do I do?"

Absinthia nodded knowingly. "What this card is really saying to me is that you need to follow your gut, even if it's scary. You may be led to believe there's a certain ..." She paused, weighing her words. "A certain path that's right for you, but it may not be the one you're supposed to be on. You need to forge your own path, look at your instincts, or else you won't be complete."

"I know," Maya said with a heavy sigh. "I just don't know what that path is."

My heart went out to her. This was obviously tearing her apart. Would it have been better for me not to give her the option to choose?

"Don't the cards give her any guidance on what to do?" I asked.

"She already knows the answer, deep down inside," Absinthia replied. "She just needs to articulate it, make it happen." She flipped over the third card. "Hm," she said, pursing her black-colored lips. "This is your future. The moon card. It seems you're in for a bit of a wild ride, so get ready. There are probably going to be some ups and downs for you, but just hang in there and ride it through."

Maya groaned. "Great."

The bell rang. Time to get back inside.

I patted Maya on the back. "Hey, it could have been worse. At least you didn't get the death card, right?" I teased, slipping off the bench.

"Actually, the death card isn't the bad one. The one that causes all the troubles is the tower. That one's all about drastic upheaval." Absinthia bundled her cards back up and tucked them back into her cloth, then rose from the bench. "I gotta run."

"Thanks again," Maya said, her voice dejected. "I'll think about what you said."

Absinthia gave her another smile. "Thanks for the business," she said, then pulled out her cigarette pack, smacking the bottom to force one out the top hole. She plucked it out and headed back to the bleachers. "See ya."

Andy, Maya and I headed inside, quiet as we all considered Absinthia's words. She'd said Maya already knew what she wanted to do.

For Maya's sake, I hoped that was true.

chapter sixteen

"Settle down!" Principal Massey bellowed as over a hundred juniors spilled into the auditorium bleachers that afternoon for the last period of school.

About once a month, our school held assemblies for the different classes, and today was the juniors' lucky day. The other half of our class had had their assembly the period before—unfortunately for me, it seemed Derek was with that other group. No chance for drooling over him. Boo.

Principal Massey pointed at a jock, clad in his football jersey, who was lingering in the hallway with his girlfriend and scoring some kissy-kissy time before the assembly. "Harper, get in the bleachers, sir!"

"Fiiiiine," he groaned. Reluctantly, he gave his girlfriend a last kiss and shuffled his way in.

With the stealth of ninjas, Maya and I slipped into a crowded section, making sure there was no room around us. After the lunchtime tarot card reading, we'd decided to avoid any hints of favoritism with whichever of her guys would be at the assembly by giving them no chance to sit with us. From what I could tell by scouring the bleachers, only Ben was in here with us, and he was already parked in a seat and talking to some other guys. It was apparent he hadn't seen us.

Whew. Fortune was on our side.

And even better, Marisa and DeShawn were right behind us, so I could oh-so-casually listen in on their conversations and get an idea of how their relationship was going. Sadly, I noticed Marisa's friends were not even sitting with them, letting her and the whole class know exactly how they felt about DeShawn.

Given my rocky past with him, I could understand their hesitation to believe in the new DeShawn, but I knew better than anyone how love could change a person.

"Today, our assembly will be on sexual harassment." Wearing low, thick black pumps, Principal Massey paced in front of the bleachers, keeping her eyes firmly on all of us. I think she was afraid that given the nature of the topic, there might be some rambunctious behavior. She was probably right.

"Mr. Johns, who works with the guidance counselor's office for our school district, will be speaking to you," she continued. "Please give him your full attention." She waved him to the front and took a seat nearby, where she could watch all of us.

"This is so going to suck," I whispered to Maya. "The guys who are the most likely to harass girls aren't going to pay any attention, anyway."

She nodded. "No kidding."

Mr. Johns stepped forward, standing in front of a large TV. He was the skinniest man I'd ever seen in my life. A stiff breeze could probably sweep him right out a window. He was clad in all black, including a black beret perched jauntily on the side of his head.

I'd never seen anyone wear a beret before. It was so bold and uncaring about modern-day conventions, it was almost hip.

Almost.

"Hello, everyone," he said, his mouth splitting into a huge grin. The gap between his front two teeth looked big enough to drive a car through. "Thanks for coming to the assembly today. We're going to be discussing sexual harassment, which means unwanted sexual advances toward the victim. Does anyone know some of the different types of harassment?"

The room was silent. I heard a few under-the-breath mumbles between DeShawn and Marisa, but I couldn't understand what they were saying. I shifted in my seat, trying to lean a bit closer. Casting a quick glance over my shoulder, I saw their hands clasped together and their heads leaned in close.

Aw, how cute! They really did make a great couple.

Mr. Johns took our silence in stride. "Well, there's one kind where someone in power harasses a victim. It may be a teacher, a coach, or even one of the administrators."

I heard someone whisper, "Like who, Massey? Right." A couple of people chuckled.

Principal Massey cleared her throat and sat straight up, her slitted eyes scanning the crowd to see who was talking.

"Anyway, that person in charge would use his or her power to sexually harass someone," Mr. Johns continued, his voice boisterous and absurdly perky, considering the subject matter. "Another kind is a hostile environment, meaning the victim would be in an environment that was threatening. Harassment isn't just touching. It can include inappropriate words, looks, or behaviors that are unwanted. I've brought in a video that I think will help show you what harassment is and how you should handle it."

Principal Massey rose and shut off the lights. Mr. Johns clicked the large TV on, then pushed in the video tape. The fact that it wasn't a DVD filled me with a sense of dread. This was not going to be fun.

After fast-forwarding for a minute, he let the video play, stepping to the side and turning up the volume.

A narrator's deep voice boomed through the auditorium, and a bunch of us jumped at the startlingly loud sound.

"Meet Jane!" the narrator proclaimed. On the screen flashed the image of a teen from what had to be the nineteen seventies. She was wearing plaid bellbottom pants, and the neckline of her pastel blue shirt had exaggerated collar points that I thought until now was just a costume effect for hippie outfits.

Jane strolled down the hallway, her long brown hair swishing behind her as she waved at people. She reminded me of Marcia Brady from *The Brady Bunch*. Jane stopped in front of her locker. A jock, bearing helmet hair and a smarmy smile, swaggered up behind her.

"Jane's your average teenage girl. She's hip, and she likes to have a good time."

I heard several snickers from around me. "Yeah, I heard that about her," one guy said.

Maya giggled at the comment. "I don't think this video is working," she whispered to me, shaking her head.

The narrator continued, "Bradley also likes to have fun, but Bradley is about to make a big mistake."

Bradley sidled up to Jane's side. "Hey, there, groovy chick," he purred, rubbing his hand up and down her arm.

Jane froze, her face an exaggerated mask of horror. "Bradley, I'm not comfortable with that," she said. She turned to face the camera as the scene around her froze. "But what do I do about it?"

I couldn't bite back a snort of laughter. Was this for real?

"Pay attention," the principal barked to our group. In return, there were several loud chuckles.

I heard Marisa whispering, "They won't even turn around and say hi." Her voice sounded low, broken.

Instantly, I sobered up and tried to block out the sounds of the stupid video. The friend situation was getting worse for her, and it seemed like it could cause real trouble.

"What's their problem?" DeShawn said. "I'm tired of being judged by those bit—"

I heard Marisa draw in a quick breath.

"Sorry," he mumbled, sounding sincere. "I know they're your friends. I just hate how they act."

My stomach tensed. If DeShawn didn't keep himself in check, Marisa might finally listen to her friends and dump him when the spell wore off next week. She might be in love with him now, but I knew all too well how that could disappear in the blink of an eye.

I turned my attention back to the video, all the while trying to figure out if there was anything I could, or should, do.

"Omigod, thank you guys sooooo much for this," Maya said, kissing me and Andy quickly on the cheek and giving us chips and drinks. "Here are some snacks, on me."

After the junior assembly, which Principal Massey had ended early due to the exponentially increasing heckling, Ben had finally spotted Maya and asked her if they were still on for tonight's date at the bowling alley. Maya had agreed, but later asked if Andy and I could come and spy on one last date. She wanted us to help her see if Ben was the guy she was supposed to choose, especially since we'd already observed her dates with Quentin and Josh.

There was a pool table at the bowling alley. And where there was pool, there were cute college guys for Andy to scope out. So of course, we were glad to help.

"Go have fun," Andy said, shooing Maya away from our spot. She crammed a chip in her mouth. "We'll watch and give our professional diagnosis. Ben's not supposed to know we're here, anyway. Don't give us away!"

Maya flitted over to Ben, who was tying on a pair of rental shoes. She gave him a kiss on the cheek.

"They really do look cute together," I said, snaking a chip from the tray. "Then again, she looks cute with Quentin and Josh too. I don't know how she's going to choose one."

"I know." Andy and I watched as Maya showed Ben the right way to hold the ball. Following her lead, he released it down the lane and knocked over eight pins. She hugged him tightly, giving him a big smile.

"They all seem like good guys," Andy said. "If I were her, I'd just keep dating them all. Why not? You get three times the love and attention."

"You would not," I scoffed, rolling my eyes. "You won't even date *one* guy, much less three."

"Good point." She took a drink of her soda. "Anyway, my mom would choke me if I brought that many guys around. 'None of those boys are good enough for you!'" Andy said in a high, perky voice, mimicking her mom.

"Well, you *are* quite a catch," I said, waggling my eyebrows at her.

Even though I was teasing, it was true. Andy was gorgeous and fun, and I hoped she'd give love another chance soon. She deserved to be happy.

"Enough about me. Let's focus on Maya," she said, shaking her head at me with a chuckle.

Observing Maya with Ben showed us a lot. She really was different with him than she was with the other guys—quiet, but with a steady sort of confidence.

"Hey there," a large man holding a cue stick said, interrupting us as he came over to Andy. He had to be almost as old as our parents. And even better, he sported a mullet that flowed down his back in delicate ringlets. I'd never seen such carefully coiffed hair in my life. "You wanna play a game with me?"

I felt a shudder ripple through me. Any kind of game this guy wanted to play would probably result in him doing some jail time.

"No, thanks," Andy said, giving him a polite smile and turning her attention back to Maya.

Pervy Mullet Man turned his attention to me. "Well, what about you?"

Gee. As sorely tempted and flattered as I was to be chosen second, I was going to have to pass. "No, thanks."

"Come on," he said, thrusting the pool cue toward us. "It'll be fun. I'll even pay for the first game."

"We're busy," Andy said, no longer smiling. "Bye." She stared hard at him until he broke eye contact, shrugging his massive shoulders.

"Whatever," he said, sidling away and mumbling under his breath.

"God, what a creep. Thanks for sending him off," I said to her. Andy was good for that, though—she wasn't afraid to tell it like it was.

"I think Jane, the Sexual Harassment Hippie, would have had a few choice words to say to him," she said. "She would have sent his groovy self packing."

I chuckled. "Yeah, we should have taken our lead from her."

Mini crisis averted, we turned our attention back to Maya and Ben. After a few minutes of studying their body language and discussing it with Andy, we saw Ben digging in his coat pocket, proudly handing a gift over to Maya.

Her eyes widened in surprise, and she quickly tore the wrapping off. It was a Magic Eight Ball.

"Whoa," Andy said. "Now that's uncanny. Especially since she just saw that psychic chick at lunch."

"No kidding," I breathed. I had to admit, I was a little freaked out.

Maya seemed to be experiencing the same sense of shock. She stared at the gift, her mouth in a perfect O shape.

Ben nodded, saying something to her.

Maya squeezed her eyes shut and tilt the ball over, shaking it from side to side, then righted the ball and looked.

I had a feeling I knew what she'd asked. And judging by the fallen look on her face, she didn't get the answer she'd wanted.

After a couple more rounds of bowling, Maya kissed Ben good night and came back into the billiard area to do a post-date report.

"Wellllllll," Andy drawled, "it was a good date. He seems really into you, and whenever you were talking, his attention was solely on you. Totally sweet."

"And you know," I interjected, "it was also totally crazy that he gave you a Magic Eight Ball. So what did you wish for?"

"Of course, I wanted to know if he was The One. Know what the message said?" Maya paused dramatically. "'Ask again later.'"

I giggled, shaking my head. "Figures."

"Even if the ball didn't help give me any good answers, I had a great time with him," she said, biting her lower lip as a happy flush spread across her cheeks. "He's not a bowler, but he's always willing to push outside his comfort zone for me. I just adore that about him."

I peeked at my watch, stifling a yawn. I was so lame, but I hadn't been sleeping well lately due to my parents, the make-out bandits. "Maybe you can sleep on it and get some clarity tomorrow. And the Magic Eight Ball may have some better answers then too," I teased.

"Good idea." She hugged us both. "Thanks again, guys. I owe you."

"You sure do. We got hit on by a guy with an Ape Drape, and it was *not* pretty," Andy said.

"*You* got hit on. *I* got your leftovers," I said, giggling. "Not that I wanted his attention or anything, though."

We gathered up our stuff and headed to Andy's car. During the drive, she and Maya dissected every minute of the date to see if they could find any signs that would illuminate a clear path for Maya. The fact that Ben had given her an eight ball was the closest thing they'd seen to a "sign." But since the eight ball didn't give an answer to Maya's question, nothing was totally clear yet.

I sat in the back, quietly remembering Absinthia's words about Maya being in for a rocky ride. Hopefully, with me and Andy helping, those rocky times would be fast and relatively painless. After all, there was no way we'd let our friend get hurt or let down.

I perked up a bit at the thought and joined in their conversation, ready to push these worries out of my mind once and for all.

chapter seventeen

A whisper of a giggle slipped under my bedroom door, and I groaned in misery, glancing groggily at my alarm clock. Twelve thirty in the morning.

God, were my parents at it *again*? What were they, rabbits?

This was getting old, fast. Every time they had a moment together, they were all over each other. It was good for their relationship, sure, but bad for my beauty sleep.

I grasped for my iPod on my bedside table and popped in the earbuds to block out the sounds of *amour*, pressing the iPod on and cranking up the first song that I found. Every night since I'd love-matched my parents had been like this. They had to be taking some kind of uppers to make it through each day, given how little sleep they were getting. Totally gross.

I'd planned to get good rest, since we'd probably not get a wink of sleep during our sleepover at Andy's after the game tomorrow night. So much for that idea.

With a huff, I sat up in bed, put the iPod on my bedside table, and headed to my computer desk. If I wasn't going to sleep, at least I could update my poor, neglected blog. I turned the PC on, then hopped on the Internet and set the blog post to private diary entry.

I feel like I'm surrounded by weirdos, and it's all my fault. My parents keep copping a feel on each other, Maya's turning to psychics for dating advice, and Bobby Blowhard won't stop doing these crazy romantic gestures for Mallory.

Today at school, I walked by the gym and saw her proudly wearing a headband he'd embroidered his name onto. Yes, I said embroidered.

It was the craziest thing I've ever seen.

I snickered at the memory of Mallory's blond hair pinned to her head by the homemade pale blue sweatband. And just to make things complete, he'd even given her matching wristbands. How thoughtful.

She was probably going to regret wearing those when the spell was over, because I doubted her friends would let her live it down, ever. I hoped Quentin had snapped a photo to preserve it for posterity in the yearbook.

I chewed on my thumbnail, then continued typing.

I'm worried I made a big mistake pairing Maya up with three guys at the same time.

Maybe this was why Janet warned me not to matchmake like this. Because it's hard enough to make love work with one other person, much less three.

At least the spell will be ending on Monday, and things will finally calm down.

I hope.

I loaded the entry up and closed out of the Internet browser. With a quick push of a button, I turned the computer off, then crawled back into bed and tucked the pillow firmly over my head.

Things were finally quieter in the house, and I needed to be prepared for whatever awaited me tomorrow.

"Where's Maya?" Josh panted on Friday morning, gripping my upper arm to stop me from heading into American history. He looked like a mad scientist or a crazy Mozart-wannabe, his hair wild and spiky, his eyes about bugging out of his head. "I finally finished it, and it's amazing!"

I twisted my arm out of his grip as gingerly as possible. "Finished what?"

"Never mind." His eyes scoured the hallway. "I need to find Maya. She'll understand."

"I think she's already in class. Maybe you can catch her when it's over," I answered, studying his eyes to make sure he wasn't on drugs. I thought I read somewhere that people addicted to crack had different-sized pupils.

Josh's pupils, fortunately, seemed okay.

"Yeah, maybe." He tapped a finger on his chin. There was ink all over his hand, and it left a smudge on his face. "No, wait. I have a better idea. Okay, don't tell her you saw me. I'll surprise her tonight, instead."

I had no idea what he meant, but given how odd he was acting, it was probably better to go along with it. "You got it," I said in a soothing tone. "Mum's the word." I pretend to zip my lips.

"Good. This'll be our little secret," he whispered with a quick, conspiratorial wink, then took off running down the hallway.

What the crap was that all about?

I shook it off and went into social studies, where Mr. Shrupe was walking up and down the aisles, putting sheets of paper face-down on our desktops.

My stomach lurched, and I mentally smacked my forehead. Oh, no, a stupid pop quiz! And I hadn't done the required reading last night.

I slipped into my desk and flipped the quiz over, analyzing the questions closely. Part multiple guess, part short-answer. Maybe I could fake my way through enough to pass.

Right off the bat, question number one stumped me. So I picked C for the answer. I progressed through the rest of the first half of the quiz in a similar fashion, trying to mix it up a bit whenever I didn't know the answer.

When I got to the short answer portion, I tried to bluff my way through, making sure in the last question to also compliment

Mr. Shrupe on his choice of a lovely blue tie today. I figured a little butt-kissing couldn't hurt.

After a half hour, we handed up the tests and moved on to discussing something-or-another. Yeah, bad me, I wasn't paying much attention. Instead, I tried to push the imminent F I was sure to get out of my mind and focus on work instead.

If I could do it all over again and match Maya with just one guy from the start, which of the three would I choose? Honestly, I still wasn't sure which guy was right for Maya. Maybe Quentin? He was definitely enraptured by her, what with the constant photographs and the poem he wrote. But then again, Ben was super sweet with her, and always seemed willing to try the things Maya loved, like bowling or sushi. And Josh . . . he'd shown up at her window at midnight, and obviously was planning some big surprise for tonight.

I just hoped Maya would make the decision that was best for her. Absinthia's prophetic words wouldn't leave my mind, and I bet they were weighing on Maya too. Tonight at the game was the first time all three of Maya's suitors would be in the same room at once, and I had a feeling that would be interesting, to say the least.

I slogged my way through to the last period of the day and then headed to art class, heart in throat as usual in the excitement of seeing Derek. I think I'd die if he knew how strongly he affected me. Could he see it in my eyes?

Art class went by fast. I completed carving my square of linoleum, the woman's profiled face as good as I could make it, then got the roller, ink, and paper out to start making some prints. And all the while, I peered at Derek, studying the features that were by now as familiar to me as my own.

The small freckle below his index finger knuckle. The light blond strands of color streaked through his hair—earned the old-fashioned way, through outdoor activity. The set of his strong shoulders. The light creases around his mouth when he smiled. Everything about him was just amazing, and he seemed oblivious to it. Which made him even more amazing, in my opinion.

Derek's eyes suddenly connected with mine. My heart squeezed hard in my chest at the unexpected eye contact. I tore my gaze away, embarrassed at having been busted.

Stupid! I chastised myself. *Way to be subtle there, Felicity. Why not just fling yourself across his body and beg for him to love you, while you're at it?*

The bell rang, and I gathered up my project, crammed it in the art shelf, then ran toward the door. It was time to escape with whatever dignity I had left. But of course, Derek was standing to the left just inside the doorway, talking with a couple of jocks.

"Yeah, I'll be at the game tonight," he said to them. "Should be a good one. I wanna see that guy Greene get crushed by our defense."

The other guys nodded. "We've really brought our game this year."

Oh, geez. Even as my stomach fluttered in excitement, I dragged in a pained breath. It was going to be hard to focus my attention on Maya, knowing Derek would be there.

I pushed through the door and plodded down the hallway to the front doors of the school, chewing my lower lip as I pondered another tortured night of Derek-gazing. This was getting pathetic.

Wait a minute. I squared my shoulders. I was a professional cupid, damn it! Maya and my other matches were my priority, not my hots for Derek. I needed to stop this, now.

An arm looped through mine. It was Andy, wearing her customary grin to greet me.

"Hey, hottie," she said. "Maya's practicing her solo, so she won't be walking with us."

"Oh, that's right."

We proceeded down the school steps toward my house.

"How's your job going, by the way?" Andy asked, sliding a sideways glance at me. "You never talk about it. Do they have you matchmaking anyone yet? Helping beer-bellied forty-year-old truckers find true love?"

How was the job going? I had a wild urge to tell Andy everything, from Britney to Maya to DeShawn to Mallory. Even the part about my icky parents. It would be such a relief to dish the whole saga to my best friend, to solicit her support and advice. But of course, I couldn't. I had an oath and all that.

Instead, I offered her a casual shrug. "Actually, I've been moved into the invoicing department. I have a knack for numbers, I guess."

Andy snorted. "You, loving math? Wow, that's . . . surprising. And what are things like at the office? Any crazy coworkers or hot guys? Anything good you can dish on, or is it all boring stuff?"

I said the first words that came to mind. "Well, the only thing big going on around there is the impact of the constant postal rate increases. Let me tell you, it's getting ridiculous to mail stuff out anymore."

I saw the exact moment in my reply that Andy zoned out, her eyes glazing over.

"Oh, that's nice," she mumbled.

Heartened by her bored response to my fake rant, I continued, pouring enthusiasm into my voice. "Do you have any idea how many one-cent stamps I've had to purchase? Or how many customers have sent mail to us that we had to pay on because they didn't attach the appropriate postage?"

It was an inspired performance, really. One worthy of an Oscar. But a small part of me flinched on the inside, knowing I was lying to everyone around me. And what was worse, I was getting better at it.

I wasn't sure if that was bad or good. Maybe a little of both, truth be told.

"Yeah, that's great." By the droll tone of her voice, I could tell Andy wouldn't be bugging me about my job anymore.

Another tiny crisis averted.

That night, Andy and I nestled into our seats on the school's worn wooden bleachers, scoping the crowd to see who was coming to the game. It was a nice turnout of students, parents, and members of the community, and the bleachers were filling up fast. Nearly every student in attendance, including me and

Andy, wore our school spirit shirts—the one with our mascot, the Greenville Cougar, plastered across the front.

I instantly did a Derek check, trying to see if he was here yet without being disgustingly obvious. After a couple of minutes, I saw him stroll through the double side doors, a plastic bowl of nachos in one hand and a large drink in the other. He headed to the opposite end of our bleachers and blended into the crowd, out of my line of vision.

My heart did its usual pitter-patter, and I tore my eyes away from his direction.

Okay, fine, you saw him, I admonished myself, heat tingling my cheeks. *Now, get over it.*

A guy whose face looked a little familiar moved past me to sit in the upper bleachers behind us, holding a slice of cheese pizza and a large bottled water. Oh, wait. He was the guy I ran into in the hallway . . . literally! I made a mental note about his food choices so I could add it to his profile, once I finally learned his name.

"Hey, check it," Andy leaned in close and said, "there's Maya."

Carrying her trumpet, Maya filed in with the rest of the pep band and slipped into her assigned seat with the band, in the bottom left corner of the bleachers. She looked around and, when she spotted the two of us, she waved.

We waved in response, blowing her goofy air-kisses, and Maya winked, then turned her attention back to the band director, who was getting the band warmed up.

The cheerleaders lined up in two rows on the floor right in front of Andy and me, waving their pom-poms like mad.

"Let's go, Cougars!" they cried out in unison, several of them jumping up into air splits to touch their toes. "We've got the spirit! We're number one!"

Andy turned to me and made an overly perky face. "Like, omigod, let's totally go, guys!" she cried out, pointing her index and middle fingers in the air. "We're number two, y'all! Rah rah rah!"

The head cheerleader shot Andy a glare, tossing her head in a disdainful whoosh that sent her ponytail swirling. Whoops, she must have overheard Andy being a smart-ass.

In a loud voice, the cheerleader said, "Okay, guys, everyone repeat after me!"

I tuned her out, instead watching as the two basketball teams filed onto the court to throw some practice hoops on each side of the court. I tried not to roll my eyes too hard at the self-pimping going on, what with the muscle flexing and extremely far hoops.

Ugh, snoozeville. I hate basketball so much.

At least things in boyland were going smoothly so far. Since each of Maya's guys would be handling different facets of the basketball game (Ben announcing, Quentin snapping photos, and Josh playing in the band), and Maya would be occupied playing in the band, we figured things should stay level.

Matthew and Granola Girl passed by us to sit on a bleacher between us and the band. They were holding hands, looking like two hippie peas in a pod. I felt a little dumb that I'd actually thought he'd be good with Britney, since clearly Granola Girl is exactly the kind of girl he should be dating.

Britney, I noticed, wasn't in sight—I guess she decided to give the game a pass. Well, she really was better off without Matthew. When she was ready to date again, I was totally going to find the perfect guy for her.

A weird, screeching feedback sound nearly split my head in two as the microphone in the announcer's booth turned on, and then Ben's booming voice rang through. "Good evening, everyone, and welcome to the playoff game between Greenville High and Lincoln High."

I noticed Maya beaming at the sound of Ben's voice. She gave the announcer's booth a small wave.

Applause filled the room, and the basketball players for both teams shuffled off the court onto the sidelines.

A rustling sound crinkled over the microphone, like maybe Ben shuffled some papers. "I'd . . . like to take a minute to thank Parma Pizza for the concession food available for purchase at tonight's event."

More polite applause. Then, Ben cleared his throat and said, "And one last thing. Let's all give a big hand to our Greenville High pep band. Most notably, Maya Takahashi, who is playing a trumpet solo tonight."

Andy and I jerked our heads over to Maya, whose face grew as red as a beet. Maya sank down in her seat, staring at her trumpet. As much as she liked Ben, I knew she was mortified because of the sudden attention being aimed at her.

From out of nowhere, flash after flash of camera shots from Quentin's camera bombarded Maya. "Hey," I heard him say, zooming in on her with his monster-huge lens, "lift your face, Maya. I can't get a good shot!"

Poor Maya bit her lower lip and looked up as Quentin continued his shots. She looked utterly embarrassed, and I couldn't blame her.

Then, the double doors to the gymnasium flew open, and Josh barreled through and made a beeline for the band, looking like he hadn't slept in a year and a half. His shirt was rumpled beyond belief, and I swear he had a twelve o'clock shadow. In his hand, he clutched a pile of papers.

My stomach sank in dismay. Crap, I'd forgotten about his surprise for Maya.

I had a sneaking suspicion that maybe tonight wasn't going to go as smoothly as we originally thought.

chapter eighteen

The first quarter started with a loud buzzer. Andy and I quickly started our crowd-scoping, since we lost interest in watching the game about three minutes into it. There's only so many times I can watch people run back and forth across a court before I get severely bored.

"Oh my God, look," Andy said, tugging on my sleeve. "It's Bobby Blowhard, and he's with Mallory!"

I almost choked on my drink when I saw Mallory and Bobby walk in together, bearing nachos and drinks. They were wearing matching purple muscle shirts, though at least Mallory wore a tank top under hers. She led Bobby toward her group of friends, just a couple of rows down from us.

"Hey, girls," she said to them, beaming. "Sorry we're late. We came straight from the gym." She and Bobby sat down beside them, and with her now ever-present sweat band, she wiped a bead of sweat from Bobby's brow.

"Thanks, babe. You hungry?" Bobby asked Mallory. "You should try taking in some calcium after that killer workout." He held up a cheese-laden nacho and fed it into her mouth.

She opened wide for the chip, then sucked on one of Bobby's fingers as it passed her lips. "Mmmm, delicious," she mumbled around his finger.

Her friends stared at the two of them like Mallory had sprouted an eyeball in the middle of her forehead. And the hostile, horrified looks they were throwing Bobby were even worse.

Not that Mallory noticed. She preferred to gaze soulfully into Bobby's eyes as he twitched his chest muscles at her beneath his shirt. Honestly, the sleeves had been cut back so deeply, I could see his armpit hair sprouting out from under his arms, like he had two midgets in a headlock. Nice.

Andy shook her head. "I thought I'd seen everything, but Mallory and Bobby? That's the weirdest. Can you imagine the children those two would make together? They'd never do anything but exercise and stare at themselves in the mirror."

I snorted at her description and smirked at my successful revenge. "Love knows no boundaries, I guess."

The buzzer sounded, ending the first quarter, and our side of the auditorium broke out in cheers. I guess we were winning or something.

"Go, Greenville High!" Ben said over the loudspeaker. "Ladies and gentlemen, let's hear it for trumpet player Maya Takahashi and the rest of the pep band! They're doing a marvelous job, aren't they?"

With his words, the pep band started to play the school fight song.

We all cheered along, saying our rah-rahs at the appropriate times. The song ended, and I saw Josh stand up, handing out papers to the band members. He took his place by the band director, whispering in her ear for a moment. She raised one eyebrow, skepticism written all over her face, but nodded her head.

"Hey," I said, nudging Andy. "I think Josh is up to something."

"This song is dedicated to someone special," I heard Josh say to the band. "Someone who needed a little extra . . . inspiration tonight. This one's for you, babe," he said directly to Maya, winking at her.

Josh raised his hands in front of the band and began to conduct.

A soft flute melody floated over to us, and then the clarinets started. Soon, the whole band was chiming in, their volume rising and falling with his gestures.

Maya stared in shock and awe at Josh, utterly surprised by the song he'd written for her.

And oh God, was it sappy. I think I got diabetes just from listening to the sugar-laden melody. It sounded like cheesy elevator music. The old people in the crowd were eating it up, though, their wrinkly hands clapping out of rhythm with the song.

Andy shook her head, grimacing in mock horror. "Oh no he didn't."

"Yessss," I exhaled, scrunching my face up in misery. "Yes, he did."

This must have been the big secret he'd wanted to spring on Maya. Well, I guess it could have been worse. At least it was just a song, right? And most of the auditorium didn't know that Maya was the inspiration for the crappy sap. I mean, he could have streaked across the court with "I love Maya" written on his butt cheeks.

After what seemed like two hundred years, the music finally finished, the dying strain of a tuba an odd, jarring ending. The parents and grown-ups in the crowd applauded heartily. Most students, however, didn't bother with manners, instead snickering and whispering among themselves, or even laughing outright.

The basketball game continued, and Josh headed over to quickly talk to Maya. While she was still covered in a full-face blush, I could tell she was thanking him by the nodding and smiling.

The other team's coach asked for a quick time-out, and the band director leaped up to guide the pep band in more upbeat songs. Josh dashed from Maya over to her, talking in her ear again as she conducted. She shook her head *no*, and he waved the sheet of music in her face, pointing at it.

Oh God, was he asking her to play the love song again? Surely one time was more than enough.

The band director ignored him and led the band in "Hang on Sloopy," the tune played in every high school and college sports game in the entire state of Ohio. Everyone stood and sang O-H-I-O in the appropriate spots, except for Josh, who plopped down in his seat and stared straight ahead, jaw clenched tightly.

"Wow, look at Josh. He looks pissed," I said to Andy.

She nodded. "That didn't go well."

The band took a break, and the band director headed over to talk to a group of teachers lingering by their side of the bleachers.

One of our basketball players faked left, but got tripped up trying to dodge someone, and wiped out. He held his ankle and grimaced as the refs blew their whistles and the coach ran on to the court.

The players all huddled around the injured guy. Andy and I strained to see what was going on. And then, I blinked in surprise as the audible strain of flute music started up from the band. Josh's love song, again?

Half the crowd turned its attention back to the band, including Mallory and Bobby, who actually seemed to *like* the music. Their arms were locked around each other's sides as they swayed to the sound. I heard a few kids around me make gagging noises.

"They're playing this again?" some guy behind me grumbled loudly. "Come on, play the fight song. This ain't prom, it's a basketball game!"

"This is bad," Andy groaned, smacking her forehead. "I wonder if Maya's digging it. I can't see her face right now."

I stared in horror and embarrassment as I watched Josh, guilt twisting in me. I couldn't believe he was conducting Maya's song again, and it was totally my fault because of the love spell. He was trying his darndest to woo her, but wasn't he going to get in trouble for—

At that moment, the band director realized what was happening and thundered up to the pep band's bleachers, stopping the music dead in the middle of the wobbling flute solo.

"You're done," she shouted to Josh in disgust. "Get out of here."

Josh shot one last, lingering look at Maya before stomping away from the pep band, still clinging to his magnum opus. His eyes flared with heat, and he looked like he would spit fire any second.

I popped out of my seat. "Come on," I said to Andy, pulling her up with me, "we need to get Josh to chill out before he does something even more rash."

"I'm with ya," she said, her voice filled with worry.

We wove our way down through the bleachers and caught up with our target.

"Hey," I said, grabbing his elbow, "why don't you sit with us? There's room." With my free hand, I pointed up at the bleachers.

Josh exhaled heavily through his nostrils, which flared wide open. "I guess."

"Plus, it's a pretty good view of Maya," I said.

With that, he seemed to perk up. "That won't be so bad, then."

We ushered him up there and parked him in the middle between us. He stared dead ahead, and I could hear his molars grinding in his clenched mouth.

"Hey," I said perkily, trying to distract him, "your song was great."

"You think so?" he mumbled.

"Absolutely!" I shot a look at Andy behind Josh's back, mentally encouraging her to talk it up too.

"Ohhhh, riiiiiight," Andy drawled, nodding in an exaggerated manner. "Yeah, it was amazing. I know Maya was so moved."

He rubbed his jaw, and his shoulders visibly relaxed as he pondered our flattering words. "Yeah, I guess she was, wasn't she." He shot a glare at the band director. "Too bad I was cut off so rudely."

"Oh, I know," I said in a soothing voice. He was still irritated, but the edge of his anger was vanishing. Thank God. The last thing we needed was him causing a scene. Again.

The buzzer rang, and the cheerleaders flooded the floor as the basketball players left. They performed a dance routine, flashing their bloomers every two seconds as they kicked their legs impossibly high into the air. Once the routine was done, they waved their pom-poms and danced off the floor.

The loudspeaker crackled, and Ben's voice came through. "Greenville High, in the lead at the halftime break." He cleared his throat, and I heard his voice shake. "And now, we have a special treat for you. The lovely and talented Maya Takahashi is going to perform her trumpet solo. Everyone, please give your undivided attention to this gifted star musician."

I rolled my eyes. God, could he lay it on thick.

En masse, the whole crowd turned to the band. Josh tensed beside me as he stared, unblinking, at the object of his love. Quentin, standing in front of the band, snapped about four billion shots of Maya.

The band director waved for Maya to rise. Maya stood from her seat, her hands slightly shaking. With the trumpet's mouthpiece pressed to her lips, she took a deep breath.

"Wait!" Ben's voice cried out over the microphone, bouncing off the auditorium walls. "Before you play, Maya, I just had to say in front of everyone that . . . I love you. IIIIIII looooove youuuuu!"

The crowd gasped and stared at Maya, who dropped her trumpet in surprise. A loud *clang* echoed throughout the room as her instrument hit the bleacher and fell to the floor.

Beside me, Josh froze, his body becoming like a brick.

"What did he just say?" Josh spat out.

Andy and I exchanged glances. "Uh-oh," she whispered.

He jumped up from his seat and shouted, "Did he just say he loves Maya?" With a quick spin, he ran up the bleachers to the announcer's booth.

OhGodohGodohGod. My stomach flipped over itself, and I just knew I was going to hurl all over the people in front of me.

"Andy," I said frantically, tugging on her sleeve, "we have to stop him!"

"What are we going to do, jump on him?" Andy rubbed her scrunched-up brow with her fingertips. "What a nightmare."

Maya stood in place, still looking stunned. Her eyes pleaded with me and Andy to help.

"Fight! Fight! Fight!" students around us chanted, thrusting their fists in the air.

Great. Josh was going to beat the living crap out of Ben, and it was all because of my wishy-washy matchmaking.

Before I could blink, I saw Quentin book it at breakneck speed up the bleacher, hot on Josh's heels. Oh, of course—because two guys fighting wasn't going to be enough drama for the evening.

I whipped around to follow the two of them up to the booth, ignoring Andy's light grip on my shoulder to keep me in place. This was my responsibility, and I needed to think fast on how to fix it.

"Guys!" I panted as I wove in between people, reaching for the back of Quentin's shirt. "Guys, stop. Hold. On!"

I got to the booth just in time to hear Josh say, loud enough for everyone to hear over the loudspeaker, "What the hell are you doing, telling my girl you love her?"

"Your girl?" Ben squinted his eyes in confusion. "Who's your girl?" He turned off the loudspeaker.

"What? Maya, of course," Josh answered, his voice scathing. "Who else would I be talking about?"

"Why are *you* two talking about Maya?" Quentin butted in, a sneer on his face.

"Guys," I said, stopping to drag several short, ragged breaths into my starved lungs before continuing. "Let's talk. For a second. Everyone. Just stay. Calm."

All three ignored me, as did the crowd, still chanting for a fight.

"Back off, man," Josh said, slitting his eyes at Ben and Quentin. "She's mine."

"Like hell," Quentin said, taking the camera off from around his neck and placing it on the announcer's table. "She's mine!" In the blink of an eye, he smashed his fist hard into Josh's face.

Josh's head jerked backward from the blow.

The crowd nearest us, seeing the blow, gasped in unison. Then, people burst into a furious uproar, voices buzzing all around us.

Oh, no! Oh no, oh no, oh no, this can't be happening. I tried to step in the middle of the three of them, but someone tugged on the back of my shirt.

"Felicity, don't!" Andy said from behind me. "Stay back, or you'll get hit!"

Josh touched his nose gingerly as a thin stream of blood trickled out. He pulled back his fist to hit Quentin, but Ben grabbed Josh's arm.

"She's mine!" Ben yelled. "No fighting over her!" With closed eyes, he started swinging blindly at both Quentin and Josh, his hands glancing off the sides of their heads.

From out of nowhere, a swarm of teachers and parents rushed the announcer's booth, and the guys were pulled apart. In the rush to evacuate the area, I was jostled to the side, falling hard on my hip. A smash of pain surged from the bruised area, and I yelped.

"This is unacceptable! You're all suspended!" the principal bellowed to the guys.

Josh, Ben, and Quentin were separately led back down the bleachers, surrounded by a posse of grown-ups. I could see the guys straining their heads to spot Maya, but from what I could tell, she wasn't in her seat anymore. Was she still here?

A high musical note pierced the air, sustaining for several

seconds. The crowd turned to the sound, then froze in place.

Was that . . . Maya? I spotted her. She'd moved to the middle of the game floor and was facing the crowd, playing her solo.

I was floored. The old Maya from two weeks ago would have melted in a puddle of embarrassment. But this new, more confident Maya had managed to push the fighting and drama aside and was currently playing a kick-ass solo.

As she performed her piece, her fingers flying with deft skill, the crowd remained eerily silent. I'd heard her play before, but never had it been with such strength. Such confidence.

After another minute or so, the last note burst forth, then stopped. Maya pulled the trumpet from her mouth, dragging in a deep breath.

The crowd went wild, screaming with approval and applause.

Maya nodded her head slightly in thanks, then turned and exited the auditorium without a backward glance.

My hip aching in pain, I dropped my head in my hands, fighting back the shaky nerves that threatened to take over. What a nightmare I'd caused.

How was I ever gonna fix this?

chapter nineteen

With a heavy sigh, I put my key in my front door and dragged myself into the house. After the basketball game disaster, Maya had called Andy to tell us she just wanted to go home and sleep, so we'd decided to cancel our TGIF sleepover.

Honestly, I couldn't blame her, as I was feeling a little shell-shocked myself. So, I'd just headed home . . . alone, with my horny parents. Great, more fun times for me. The only way this evening could get any better would be if a meteor suddenly hit our house.

I took off my shoes in the foyer and made my way into the living room. Mom and Dad were cuddling on the couch. The room was dark except for the flickering screen of whatever black-and-white movie they were watching.

"Oh, you're home?" Flashes of light from the TV flitted across Mom's surprised face. Her hair was slightly mussed, and I realized I must have interrupted them mid-makeout.

Gross. Every teen's worst nightmare, now my daily existence. Just another one of my brilliant matchmaking ideas. At least the spell wouldn't last forever. Right now, that was my only saving grace.

I fought the urge to shudder. "Yeah, I'm just going to bed." I slung my purse over my shoulder.

"But I thought you were staying at Andy's tonight," Dad said.

"We decided to hold off until next week." I shrugged like there was no problem. I didn't want to share the basketball game drama with them. "Not a big deal."

"Well, that's too bad," she said, glancing at Dad with a tender smile on her face. "Your father and I just got back from that Japanese restaurant. He treated me to a date, and it's not even our anniversary yet—wasn't that nice of him? The food was fantastic."

Dad shrugged, sliding a strand of Mom's hair out of her eyes. "It was okay, I guess. I liked it more than I thought I would."

"So why did you go, then?" I asked him.

"I knew it would make your mom happy," he said. "And why wait until our anniversary to show her how much I care?"

She made love-sick eyes at him. "Oh, Stephen."

"You're worth it."

They kissed. UGH. I took my cue and booked it upstairs. After tossing my purse on my computer chair and draping across my bed, I buried my face in my bedspread and replayed the whole evening in my mind.

Why had things turned out like this with Operation Hook Maya Up? Was there something I could have done to prevent this disaster? I mean, besides not having orchestrated it in the first place. It was obvious by now that I should have just picked one guy from the start and run with it. But they'd all seemed so right for her.

I thought about the events of the last two weeks. All three boys had made Maya feel special and important, but she'd run around like a chicken with its head cut off, looking more and more frazzled every day.

I rolled over onto my back, pondering Dad's words. He didn't want to go to the Japanese restaurant, but he'd gone because my mom had wanted it. My parents' relationship since the cupid spell had blossomed in a direction I wasn't thrilled about, but it was showing me something I hadn't thought about before.

Real love was giving, compromising with someone, like what

my dad did for my mom. Maya and the guys had all bent over backward to do stuff for each other, but it wasn't the *right* stuff, the one thing to truly make her happy. None of the boys seemed to complete Maya with his presence the way Mom and Dad did for each other.

I grabbed my nightclothes together and headed to the bathroom to take a quick shower, a bit more enlightened than before. This selflessness thing was definitely something to watch for with my future matches. Maybe keeping these new ideas about love in mind could help me even learn to predict how well my matches would turn out.

This cupid job wasn't as easy as I'd first thought, but I was totally figuring it out. My future matches were going to be so much better now—I just knew it.

School on Monday came and went, with Maya nowhere in sight. She hadn't returned any of my calls over the weekend, so Andy and I had spent the lunch period fretting over Maya's state of mental health.

Was she buried in her bed under her blanket, crying her eyes out? Was she blaming me and Andy for our dating advice? Worry picked away at my nerves, making me edgy and tense.

To make matters worse, Andy told me she had found out Maya's guys had been suspended for a week. What a mess. At least the spell would end today, so things could level out for everyone involved.

Art class had offered me no happy reprieve, either. Derek wasn't in class today because of some other school project, so I slogged through the period bored and without my daily visual stimulation.

When the bell rang, I exited the building by myself. I noticed Britney leaning against the wall, her back facing me.

"Hey," I said to her as I approached.

She turned and smiled. "Oh, hey, Felicity."

A loud clanging sound rang out from the side of the building. I peeked my head around the corner. Sure enough, there was Matthew and his new girl doing his favorite pastime, garbage diving. They were enthusiastically tossing recyclables out of the bins, their cheeks bright red from the cold sting of the air.

"So . . . how are you?" I asked Britney, studying her face. She didn't seem overly distraught, nor did she look like she'd been crying. In fact, she looked serene.

"You know, I thought I'd be more upset seeing them together. But honestly, I'm just happy I'm not in the trash." Her smile grew bigger. "Let them have their bonding time together. That just doesn't work for me."

"I don't blame you," I said, chuckling. "There are better ways to spend time than smelling like a landfill."

"Well, I'm heading home. See ya." Tossing one last look over her shoulder at Matthew, she shook her head, then walked off.

I walked home too, feeling better for the first time in days. Yeah, Britney's matchmaking didn't end romantically, but it did end happily. She was moving on, finding her inner strength. That was definitely something I would share in my weekly work meeting tonight.

"Seems like things are moving along for you," Janet said to me later that afternoon, propping her elbows on her desk and steepling her fingers. "You made another match last week, right?"

I nodded, trying to keep my nervousness under control. Though Janet didn't know exactly what had happened with Maya's matchmaking, I'd 'fessed up that Britney's coupling didn't work out, and that Maya's pairing also failed.

But to help take the focus off all the bad, I'd made sure to talk about how DeShawn had shown positive progress over the last twelve days while paired with Marisa, how closely knit Mallory and Bobby had become, and how Britney had changed too.

Janet smiled. "Well, I'm proud of the work you've done so far."

My heart thudded in surprise from her praise, and my shoulders sagged in relief. "Really? Thanks. It's been a lot harder than I expected."

"It sure is. You should have seen me the first few months I began to matchmake. I was a total wreck, afraid every couple I'd paired up would fail."

"You?" It was hard to imagine the pristine, perfectly composed Janet as anxious. She was the pinnacle of self-confidence.

"Absolutely." Janet winked. "We all start out unsure of ourselves. But I have something to help take your mind off your matchmaking woes." She flipped open a folder on her desk and handed me a paycheck.

Yay! Getting money perked me up a bit. "Thank you." I stuffed the check in my purse. "So, you're not upset that some of my couples didn't stay together?"

Janet leaned toward me. "You know, I've made many people fall in and out of love during my time, and every pairing I make continues to surprise me. Our ability as cupids to cause that . . .

spark, that instant connection between two people, doesn't guarantee a couple will stay together." She paused. "One thing you should always remember, Felicity, is that love isn't a science. It's not predictable, though we'd like it to be. And love can work out between even the unlikeliest of people, as well as fail spectacularly between couples who seem ideal for each other."

No kidding. And Wednesday would show me if one of those unpredictable couples, DeShawn and Marisa, would make it or not.

Still half asleep on Wednesday morning, I headed into the school building, taking off my jacket and cramming it into my locker. I took out my *Jane Eyre* novel and headed to first-period English, praying Maya would be there. Yesterday had also come and gone still without a word from her, and I was starting to get sick from worry.

Maya still wasn't here. I slipped into my seat and anxiously watched the door, drumming my fingers on the top of the desk. I didn't know what I was going to say to her, but I needed to do something.

The bell rang, and Maya came through the door just in time,

much to my relief. She parked it in the seat beside me. I tried to catch her attention, but she was busy getting her notebook and class supplies out. When I leaned over to whisper to her, Mrs. Kendel saw me and gave me the evil eye, so I straightened back up and faced forward.

Why wasn't Maya looking at me? Maybe she'd realized I was involved in her love-life disasters and was furious with me.

Oh God, what if she'd found out I was a cupid? This week was getting worse and worse.

Mrs. Kendel started class talking about *Jane Eyre*, but I didn't care. Once my paranoid thoughts had taken over, they wouldn't let me go.

Maya scribbled quickly on a piece of paper, then ripped it out, folded it up, and deftly slipped it to me.

Heart in throat, I read its contents:

So sry didn't call. Bad few days, but better now.
Tlk after class?

I nearly cried in sweet relief. Maya didn't hate me, and it didn't appear that she'd figured out about the cupid stuff. I wrote *Yup!* on the bottom of the page and handed it back to her, then opened my novel, ready to focus on the lecture.

In between taking notes, I kept a close eye on DeShawn too. The spell had worn off today, but his quiet demeanor gave me no indication of what was happening between him and Marisa. Talk about a killer poker face.

Were they still together? Had her friends convinced her to dump him? Maybe after class, I could keep my eyes peeled for Marisa in the hallway.

When the bell rang forty minutes later, I gathered my stuff and moved out the classroom door, tugging Maya along with me.

"You okay?" I asked her, scanning the hallway quickly for Marisa to see if she'd meet DeShawn. I didn't see her, so I focused my attention back on Maya.

She nodded slowly. "I am now. I just needed some down time."

"I'm sorry." And I was. It had to have been a rough weekend for her. Poor Maya.

"Hey," Andy said, popping up between us. She hugged Maya, then pulled back, a frown on her face. "I've been worried about you."

"Sorry for the disappearing act." Maya smiled. "I fretted over the guys all weekend about what to do. If I should call them to apologize and explain so I could patch everything up. But when I woke up on Monday, it was like I didn't feel that . . . pressure anymore. That overwhelming desire to be with them."

"That's crazy." Andy shook her head. "But probably better for your sanity."

"I know it," Maya said. "All this time, I've been worrying over which was the perfect guy for me, and then I realized: None of them is. It was fun to date them, but maybe the reason I couldn't choose which one to keep is that none of them was all the things I want in a boyfriend. But I wasn't ready to face everyone at school yet because of Friday night's incident, so I told my mom I was sick. Luckily, she let me stay home."

"I think I understand what you mean," I said, wondering if the guys had also fallen out of love when the spell wore off, or if they'd continue to fight over her and try to win her back.

"So what now?" Andy asked. "Are you planning to date any of them again?"

"No, I think I'm done with them," Maya answered. "I liked their attention, but none of them were quite right for me, though it seemed like it at first." She paused, then said, "Hey, can you guys hang on a sec?"

Maya darted across the hallway to talk to a familiar-looking guy who was standing by the lockers. It was the mysterious new guy from her French class, the one whose name I needed for my profile.

"Um, do you have yesterday's assignment?" Maya asked him.

"Whoa," Andy whispered to me. "Is that *our* friend Maya, going up to talk to a guy?"

"It would appear so." The Maya from two weeks ago never would have done that. I loved seeing this new boldness, this confidence in her.

"Damn, I gotta run to class. Fill me in later on everything that happens," Andy ordered, hugging me quickly. She disappeared into the hallway.

"Oh, hey," the guy said to Maya, surprise flushing his cheeks a deep red. "Yeah, I do." He dropped his backpack onto the ground and hunched over to dig into it. Books and papers filled with writing were crammed in there. How in the world did he find anything?

"Here you go," he finally said as he stood, thrusting a piece of paper at her. Did I detect a slight shake in his hand?

"Thanks," Maya replied, giving him a small smile. She drew in a deep breath and swallowed. Her eyes darted to the ground, then back to him again.

Wait, was Maya flirting? I leaned back against the locker, watching the melodrama of teenage life unfold right before my eyes.

"So, maybe we can get together sometime and study for the French test," Maya continued. "If-if you want, I mean." Her cheeks turned a light shade of pink.

The guy nodded, giving her a toothy grin. "Yeah, I'd like that. Maybe we can meet today?"

"Let's meet tonight at Pizza Hut at . . . seven? We can eat and study."

"Okay." He grinned even wider, if that was possible.

Maya headed back toward me, then threw out over her shoulder to the guy, "See ya then."

I nestled my books in front of my chest and regarded her with one eyebrow raised. Well, well, well. This was an interesting turn of events.

"What was *that* all about?" I probed, understanding full well what was going on. Mama didn't raise no fool.

She shrugged a bit too casually. "Oh, nothing much. He's Scott Baker, from my French class. We're going to study together tonight."

"I see." And suddenly, I realized that Maya probably had been interested in this Scott guy before I hit her with the Operation Hook Maya Up love spell. After all, this sudden awareness of him hadn't come out of nowhere.

Whoops.

Well, she hadn't told me, so there was no way I could have known before pairing her up with the other guys.

But all's well that ends well, right? At least things were going in the right direction for her now. And the spell did play a part in that.

I knew, though, that things didn't end that well for Quentin, Josh, and Ben, even if it wasn't my fault how crazy they got under the spell . . . well, not 100 percent my fault, anyway. Besides, I totally learned my lesson. Once the guys were off suspension, maybe I could start to make amends by finding them appropriate girlfriends—one for each of them, of course.

Maya and I moved back down the hallway, splitting up to head to our respective classes. Across the hallway from my American history classroom, I spotted Marisa standing with her friends.

Instantly, I stopped mid-stride, then darted in front of some nearby lockers to scope the situation.

"—too bad," Marisa was saying to them. "DeShawn's changed. I've seen the difference in him, even if you refuse to believe it."

So Marisa was still in love, even after the spell wore off? Sweet bliss! That was one half of the battle.

One of her friends shook her head, her arms crossed in front of her. "He's just putting on an act."

"No, he isn't," Marisa replied, her lips pursed and her brow furrowed. "Look, I know you guys care about me, but I need friends who support me, even if they don't agree with what I choose to do." She hitched her books on her hip. "I hope you'll think about that."

Marisa stepped into the hallway toward DeShawn, who reached out and took her hand.

I watched the two of them walk off into the sunset. Okay, they were just heading to their classes—but still, it felt romantic and utterly fulfilling to see their fingers tightly woven together as they strolled down the hall.

I was amazed. Marisa had stood up to her friends and chose what she felt was best for herself. She hadn't caved to their pressure.

And just as cool for me, I'd made a match last past the two-week spell! There was hope after all, both for love and for my matchmaking career. And, oh yeah, for my wallet.

I slipped into American history. Once I got into my seat, I dug my trusty PDA out and created a quick profile for the new guy Scott Baker, then sent a love e-mail to both him and Maya. Just to nudge things along a bit.

I pushed the LoveLine 3000 back into my bag and leaned back with a satisfied smile while Mr. Shrupe started class. Things were going to be better now, I just knew it. Quentin, Josh, and Ben would be out of suspension tomorrow—and now that the love spell had worn off, their lives could go back to normal too. That had to be a big relief to them.

I just hoped they'd be able to let it go and not stay mad at each other. And if not, I'd find a way to make that happen.

Of course, I couldn't just sit back and rest on my laurels. More love matches had to be made. After all, the DeShawn-Marisa match had worked, so I knew I had the ability to make good couples. And if that weren't enough proof, my parents' renewed interest in each other, to put it politely, was icing on the cake.

And if their relationship ever flagged again, I could do another love match for my folks to spice things up a bit . . . and then send myself on a two-week trip so I wouldn't have to watch.

I flipped my social studies book open and wrote in my notebook as Mr. Shrupe scrawled across the chalk board, wiping a chalk-dusted hand on the left butt cheek of his brown pants. I bit back a giggle. Good old Mr. Shrupe—at least he never changed.

While Mr. Shrupe droned on, I peered out the window and saw Derek walk by outside with a group of jocks, his letterman jacket hugging his upper body nicely. He laughed at something one of the guys said, a dimple creasing his cheek. My heart slammed in my chest at the unexpected pleasure of seeing him.

Derek sauntered off with his friends, and I drew a heart-shaped doodle in the margin of my notes. Watching Maya grab the bull by the horns and ask Scott out had inspired me. If I was going to snag Derek for myself, I needed to bring my A-game. I knew he would be the perfect guy for me.

It was going to be a challenge, since I couldn't use my cupid skills, but aren't the best things in life the ones you worked for?

Absolutely. And I was totally ready.

FLIRTING WITH DISASTER

chapter one

"There are lots of fun ways to have a good time at a party without drinking!" Mrs. Cahill, our health class teacher, hopped up on the end of her large desk. She crossed her legs beneath a flowing brown paisley skirt.

A few people chuckled at her words, and I bit back a laugh myself. At least she was enthusiastic about her topic. It was hard for me to scrape up enthusiasm for anything on a Monday, but Mrs. Cahill never lacked any.

"So, what did you guys list?" Mrs. Cahill asked. "Let's share a few of our choices with the class. Now as I said before, I won't be collecting them. This is for you to take home and hopefully implement in your life to encourage a lifestyle that avoids alcohol."

Yeah, right. I was sure most of my classmates would instantly give up partying because of a list made in health class. That was *totally* plausible.

I glanced down at my paper. Our in-class assignment was to write ten "fun" things to do that didn't involve alcohol. Out of my ten items, six of them involved staring longingly at Derek, the guy I've been madly in love with since freshman year. No way was I going to say that out loud, though.

James Powers thrust his hand into the air, a smarmy grin on his face.

"Go ahead, James," Mrs. Cahill said. "What did you write?"

He made a big show of holding up his paper in front of his face. "Ahem. I put, 'have sex.'"

His buddies around him guffawed, and several girls tittered behind their hands. I rolled my eyes. Mrs. Cahill should have known better than to call on James.

"Oh my God, James!" one girl whispered, giggling. "You're so crazy."

Mrs. Cahill blushed and pressed a hand to her beet-red cheeks. "Well, that's ... not quite what I meant."

Mallory Robinson, my mortal enemy and the bane of my

existence, turned and whispered something to her friends, Jordan and Carrie. Jordan nodded briefly in response, but Carrie barely looked at her. They both turned their attention back to James. Mallory's face fell. She quickly recovered and started writing in her notebook.

I smirked. The dynamics between Mallory and her friends had changed ever since I'd set her up last month with Bobby Loward, a.k.a. Bobby Blowhard, the biggest weenie I'd ever known. It was still the most talked-about love match around school, even though the magic had worn off and Mallory and Bobby had split up a few weeks ago.

Of course, nobody else knew that there'd been magic involved in their hookup, let alone that I was the cupid responsible for the match. Total secrecy was the first rule of my job at Cupid's Hollow. I wasn't allowed to tell a soul that my hot-pink PDA was used to matchmake my classmates using the latest in handheld technology—love arrows shot through e-mail.

Not that anyone would believe me if I *were* allowed to spill the beans. Though maybe the ridiculous pairing of Mallory and Bobby Blowhard would be convincing proof.

Mallory's friends hadn't treated her the same since. It didn't matter that they'd broken up the day the spell wore off. The damage was already done.

My only regret was that I couldn't step forward and claim credit for what was surely an act of humanity: keeping Mallory's stuck-up nose out of my best friend Maya Takahashi's dating life by giving Mallory a relationship of her own to focus on. But the cupid contract I'd signed meant I couldn't spill the beans—and frankly, I feared my boss Janet too much to screw around with that.

"What about spin the bottle, then?" Mitzi, one of the flaky chicks in our class, asked. "That's just making out, not actually *doing* it."

Andy Carsen, my other best friend, bit back a laugh. She leaned over and whispered to me, "I think the whole point of the exercise was to *avoid* bottles."

"No kidding," I said quietly, shaking my head.

Mrs. Cahill looked over at me. "Felicity, since you feel like talking, do you have anything to add to our conversation? What did you write down on your list?"

Whoops. I glanced at my paper, reading aloud an entry that wouldn't totally humiliate me for life. "Um, play poker."

Not that I knew how to play, but I don't think that mattered to her. At least I didn't say something that involved being naked.

"Good answer!" Mrs. Cahill beamed at me. "Card games are a fun and healthy alternative to drinking at a party."

"What an ass kisser," I heard Mallory whisper to her friends. They giggled.

Andy spun around in her seat and stared hard at Mallory until she looked away.

The bell rang, dismissing us from class.

"Make sure you hold on to those lists," Mrs. Cahill said loudly over the bell as we all rushed to evacuate. "Especially since we're nearing prom season."

"Thank *God* that's over," I said to Andy as we walked down the hall. "I swear, that class gets weirder every day."

"No kidding," Andy said. "I don't think Mrs. Cahill was expecting those responses. She should know James by now, though. He's always going to give the most obnoxious answers he can think of."

"You know, I'd feel bad for her if she hadn't given us this dumb assignment in the first place."

I hated health class with the fiery passion of a thousand burning suns. It was possibly the most boring, ineffective course I'd taken to date. The only good thing about it was I didn't have to take gym anymore, one of the other most terrible classes ever.

I was so not athletic, and it was highly unfair that I was forced to participate in events that made me look like a dumbass. Ever see me dribble a basketball? Once you did, you'd understand my plight.

But health class was not much better. For one period every day I was trapped in a room with both James and Bobby. And even worse, with Mallory, who took every opportunity to shoot me nasty glares across the room, or make snotty comments to her friends.

In between shooting me the evil eye, Mallory would sneak peeks at James, who was her boyfriend freshman year. She was probably wondering why they weren't still together. Um, maybe because she was a total cow. Not that James even noticed her anymore. He was too busy trying to show the whole class how very funny he was.

Fortunately, Andy was in there with me. She helped make the time go faster with her dry humor.

"Hey, Felicity, that was a good answer," Bobby Blowhard said, appearing out of nowhere and sliding in between me and Andy. "I didn't know you played poker. What's your favorite kind? I like Texas Hold'em."

Fortunately for us, and all of mankind, Bobby wasn't wearing his usual mesh workout shirt. Instead he had on a tight black spandex top. I suppose it was his way of enticing people to look at his muscles, but I can't say it worked on me.

"Actually, I don't really play," I mumbled, trying not to be rude, but also not wanting to encourage him into further conversation.

Bobby was . . . overbearing, to say the least. I'd noticed that once the cupid spell wore off him, he lost his attraction toward Mallory and instantly regained it toward me.

Lucky, lucky me.

"Oh." Bobby paused and flexed a little. "Well, maybe I could teach you sometime. I know lots of card games, actually, and—"

"Hey," Andy interrupted, "it's time for us to head to lunch." She grabbed my elbow and led me away.

"Okay, see ya!" Bobby bellowed to my back.

I gave him a halfhearted wave as Andy and I darted down the hall.

"I owe you," I told her gratefully. "Cokes are on me."

We headed to the cafeteria and made our way through the lunch line to our usual table, where Maya was already waiting for us. She was holding hands and talking closely with her boyfriend of almost a month, Scott Baker.

I swear, the guy looked like he had a permanent flush whenever he was around Maya. It was cute, even if it was a little goofy. But it made me happy to see her with a guy who was perfect for her.

After the fiasco of matching her up with three guys at once, I'd learned the hard way that it was much better to do a one-on-one pairing. Much, *much* better. Maya had started dating Scott after that, and they'd been going strong since. Of course, I had sent them a cupid e-mail to encourage their attraction (not that they'd needed it).

And just as cool, I'd recently received my second bonus check for a lasting love match. Score!

"Hey," Andy said, plopping down beside Maya. "How's my favorite couple today?"

"Oh, hey guys!" Maya shot us a big smile. "How are you? Anything good going on?"

"Not too much," I said. "Except in health class James said he wanted to have sex instead of drink at a party, and Mrs. Cahill about had a heart attack." I sat on Andy's other side and started noshing on my burrito.

Maya shook her head. "Yeah, that sounds like him. And more exciting than my morning."

"Actually Maya got an A on her French test," Scott interjected. "She beat all of us with the top score. She could probably teach our class and put Monsieur LeBec out of a job."

Maya shrugged, blushing. "I guess you're just a good study partner," she replied. She glanced at her watch, then stood. "Oh, I gotta go. I told Mr. Seagle I'd help him set up the chem lab today before class."

"I'll go with you," Scott said, automatically rising beside her.

"You two lovebirds have fun. Try not to coo all over each other," Andy ribbed.

Maya shot her a fake glare. "Funny, funny."

She and Scott headed out of the cafeteria, glued to each other's sides. I couldn't help but grin at the sight of them.

"If I didn't love Maya so much, I'd be super jealous," Andy said, watching them go. "She looks so happy."

I jerked my head to look at her. "Jealous? Really? I thought you'd sworn off love."

Andy bit her lower lip. She drew lines in her creamed corn with her fork. Why the school was serving creamed corn with burritos, I'd never know.

"I thought so too," she said with a sigh, "but seeing how good they are together makes me think maybe I'm missing out on something."

My heart rate kick-started to about a million beats a minute.

Andy had been on a self-imposed sabbatical from guys for a while now and hadn't shown any interest in dating. So this was the opportunity I'd been waiting for—to hear her say she was ready for me to find her a love match.

Okay, not that she knew I'd be matchmaking her, but whatever. I knew I could do the job justice. After all, Maya and Scott were still going strong, as were DeShawn and Marisa, an unlikely couple I'd paired on a whim who seemed to beat all odds and make it work. That relationship had also changed DeShawn's bad attitude, and he wasn't the überbutthead he used to be.

I just knew I could help Andy find love too.

"Yeah, Scott seems like living proof that there are nice guys out there," I said casually.

"No kidding. If only we could all be so lucky. She snagged herself a good one." Andy took a bite of her food, then shot me a pointed look. "Not that *you* won't be that lucky soon, with you-know-who."

My stomach flipped over in excitement at the thought of Derek smiling at me the way Scott smiled at Maya. God, would there ever be a time when Derek didn't make every part of me feel utterly, painfully alive? A time when I wasn't a total wreck, wishing I could get him to see me as the perfect match for him?

For the thousandth time since taking the cupid job, I rued the fact that I couldn't matchmake myself.

"Well, who knows what'll happen with that," I said, biting off a big hunk of my burrito. I chewed and swallowed before speaking again. "Our plan of me repeatedly throwing myself in front of him hasn't seemed to work yet."

Not only had Derek *not* fallen head over heels in love and dropped down on one knee to ask me out on a date, things hadn't progressed much further than the casual conversation stage we had been at for a couple of months now. It was slow torture, and yet I was putting myself willingly through it every step of the way.

"Well, maybe we'll both be surprised." Andy shot me a crooked smile. "Maybe love will strike us both out of the blue."

I grinned back. "If it can happen for Maya, it surely will happen for you."

Because I'd sure see to it that it would.

That afternoon I made it my primary mission during my classes to select the lead candidates for Andy's love match. Holding my tricked-out PDA just out of the teacher's line of vision, I flipped through the profiles I'd stored in it and found two guys I thought might suit Andy and that Maya and I might not mind having around.

First was Tyler Macintosh, a cute guy who plays drums in a local band. He's popular and always has a big crowd around him wherever he goes. His light brown, wavy hair looks casually tousled without any effort, and he's always smiling and laughing with his friends. Andy could definitely appreciate his positive attitude and enthusiasm.

The other guy was Jacob Simpson, a superhot, smart guy on the soccer team. I didn't know much else about him, other than he's really, really attractive, with big dimples in his cheeks, and black hair. Oh, and a soccer player. Duh, me. Anyway, he truly is the perfect blend of brains and brawn, and Andy tended to like a good combo of both those elements.

Yes, these were promising initial character notes, but I still needed to flesh out their profiles before I chose between them. I wanted to do right by Andy . . . and to cover my butt with Janet, my boss at Cupid's Hollow, by making sure the match would meet the minimum compatibility requirements. Luckily, I had classes with both guys, which made it easy to add notes into my LoveLine 3000.

During anthropology, while Mr. Wiley scrawled furiously across the chalkboard, I tucked my PDA into my lap and continued enhancing the profiles I'd created for Tyler and Jacob.

Name: Tyler Macintosh

Age: 17

Interests: Loves music—carries drumsticks everywhere in back pocket. Also into performing, and likes to bang drumsticks on his desk when teacher's gone. Good sense of humor. He cracked a funny joke today about night-shift waitresses at Waffle House.

And he totally checked out Andy at lunch when she walked by. But then chewed his sandwich with mouth open. Ew! And did "seafood" to another guy. Obviously likes attention.

Style: Casual rocker

Name: Jacob Simpson

Age: 17

Interests: Sports and fashion—likes to wear soccer socks and shin guards, even when not in a game. Into fitness and has nice butt—go, Greenville High soccer hotties! Also checked out Andy at lunch. Gee, surprise.

Made crack about "large" girl in anthropology class. :-(

Style: Preppy sports guy

At the end of the day it looked like seafood and drumsticks won out over tight soccer tushie. While Jacob might have been cuter than Tyler, the fat joke he made wasn't cool. I felt bad for the butt of his joke, Justine, who'd just stared straight ahead in class and pretended not to hear him.

I shot Jacob a glare when I caught his eye, just to show I disapproved, and I made a mental note never to matchmake him to any of my friends. The jerk.

Yeah, Tyler was the no-brainer choice here. I'd seen Andy check him out once or twice before. Plus, it didn't hurt that Andy was wild about musicians. She had pictures of drummers from several bands plastered all over her notebooks.

Surely it had to be fate.

I composed my e-mail to Tyler, CC'd Andy, and sent it. When they opened the e-mails, they'd fall in love instantly, matched together for two weeks of bliss.

Awesome. I couldn't wait to see Andy happy in love.

chapter two

"I ran out of light blue. Can I share with you?" Derek picked up his painting and moved beside me, settling into the seat on my right.

My heart nearly stopped in my chest, and I put my paintbrush down to keep my shaking hand from dripping paint all over the art class table. "Oh, uh, of course."

I pushed the tempera paint toward Derek. We were doing monochromatic self-portraits for our newest art project, and he and I had both coincidentally chosen the color blue to paint ourselves in.

Okay, it was no coincidence. I was an unabashed paint stalker. Once I saw Derek go for the blue tempera paint tubs, I did the same. Besides, painting myself in those hues would only echo the blue longing in my heart for him.

Oh, gag, that was over-the-top gross. When did I get so sappy? Why can't my brilliant wit and sparkling conversational skills ever come out too?

Why does Derek bring out this side in me?

He and I worked in silence for a good twenty minutes, painting in perfect harmony. I was aware of his hard thigh, an inch away from mine under the table. It was so tempting to shift just slightly in my seat, just enough to brush against his leg.

Geez, snap out of it! I was acting like a love-crazed freshman, not a mature, self-controlled professional cupid.

I forced my attention back to my self-portrait, scrutinizing what to do next. I'd already drawn the outline and was filling in the blue hues to add shading and depth.

"Your sense of proportion is really good," Derek said out of nowhere.

I looked up at him, blinking rapidly. "Who, me?"

He grinned crookedly, one eyebrow shooting up at me. "Yes, you."

"Oh. Okay."

I mentally smacked my forehead. That was smart. He'd given me a compliment . . . a weird one, but a compliment nonetheless. Maybe I could act like I had half a brain.

"I mean, thanks," I continued. "Yours is . . ." I looked closely at his painting, trying to find the right compliment to give him back. Everything looked fantastic—he'd even captured his own strong jawline and the wave of his hair perfectly.

"Your painting is just incredible, Derek. You're really talented." I finally said, daring a glance at his face.

"Thank you." His eyes locked with mine for a moment, and I felt a crazy, impulsive urge to spill my feelings. Would he freak out if I told him how badly I had it for him?

Was there any chance he could feel that way too?

Only one way to find out. I parted my lips to speak, willing myself to let whatever needed to be said just flow out of my mouth.

"Okay, the bell's going to ring any second," our art teacher said, his low voice cutting me off. "Pack up your paints and put your projects away, people."

Derek closed the light blue paint tub. "Thanks again for sharing your paint." He lifted his wet canvas and moved toward the art shelf, totally unaware of how close I'd come to confessing my undying love.

What was I thinking? Just because Derek had looked into my eyes so boldly, I'd suddenly wanted to tell him all those embarrassing feelings I had for him.

I had to be losing it. That was not one of my better ideas, and if it weren't for the art teacher, I'd have made a total fool out of myself.

I packed up my stuff and darted out the classroom door, weaving rapidly through the students in the hall to escape. I didn't know how much longer I could handle this, but something was going to have to give.

When I reached the comfort of my home, I darted upstairs and hopped on my computer, booting it up. I created a blog entry, locked just for Andy and Maya to read:

> *I almost did the dumbest thing today, guys. I was*
> *thiiiiiis close to spilling my guts to Derek. Honestly, I*
> *don't know why! There was just something about the*
> *way he was looking at me. Gee, I must love torture.*
> **sigh**

"Felicity, you here?" I heard my mom call from downstairs.

"Yup, I'm in my room."

"Can you come down and help with dinner? I'm making enchiladas tonight. You know how your dad loves Mexican."

I tried not to roll my eyes. Ever since I secretly matchmade my folks last month as an anniversary gift to help them renew their affection for each other, they've been super lovey-dovey. Okay, not nearly as bad as they were while under the two-week spell, but still. I could do without all the gooey attention they give each other.

"I'm coming," I said, posting my blog entry and closing my PC down. I could only imagine what comments the girls would leave when they read my post.

I shuffled downstairs, rolling up my sleeves. I probably should have put a bib on, given how messy I tended to get when cooking. Not my mom, though—she was always pristine and pulled together. Sometimes I wish I could be like her . . . until I start remembering what a control freak she is. Yeah, not my style.

Mom pointed toward the stove, where the frying pan was already perched, a pile of tortillas on the countertop beside it. "I need you to fry those up and dip them in the enchilada sauce," she said.

"Okey dokey."

We worked in silence for a few minutes—me frying like a diner cook and Mom preparing the filling.

"So, what's going on with school? Any guys tripping over themselves to date you?"

I scoffed. "Right. Because I'm such a beauty queen."

"Hey, don't sell yourself short," she chastised, pointing a finger at me. "I happen to think you're very pretty."

Well, that was nice of her. Mom wasn't one to dole out compliments a lot, so I knew she meant it.

"Thanks," I said, hoping my earnestness rang through in my voice. "I wish—" I stopped myself, not wanting to go into how badly I wanted Derek to feel the same way I did.

Mom, though, must have known what I was going to say. She nodded her head, shooting me an empathetic look as she filled the tortillas and wrapped them into cylinders, lining them up in neat rows in the baking pan.

"Guys don't always pick up on things when they should, especially when it comes to matters of the heart," she said. "You know, back in high school, it took a while for your dad to see me as more than a friend."

"Really?" Mom never talked to me about how she and Dad ended up together. And I never asked, not wanting to pry, but also trying to avoid the ick factor of thinking about my parents in that way. "I always figured you two were instantly in love." I popped the last tortilla into the frying pan.

This time she was the one who scoffed. "Hardly. For a long time your dad was oblivious to anything but football. I had a crush on him for a full year before we started dating."

"So, what changed, then?" Mom can be a little stuffy sometimes, but maybe back then she had a trick or two up her sleeve on how to get a guy's attention.

She stopped folding enchiladas, dropping her voice and leaning in to me. "Honestly, I don't know. One day he came up to me out of the blue and asked me on a date. We've been together since."

I chuckled. Someone must have hit him with Cupid's trusty arrow. "Funny how that works."

The front door opened. Mom wiped her hands clean on a dish towel, then winked at me. "Speak of the devil. That must be your dad." She headed out of the kitchen, and I heard her say, "Hey, honey. We're making enchiladas."

"Fantastic. Thanks!" he exclaimed.

Kissy sounds came from the living room. Oddly enough, I didn't feel as horrified as I normally would. I guess hearing that Mom went through the same kind of rough time I was in made me feel a little less squicked out. It also helped that they were fully clothed and not getting it on. Thank God.

I finished making the enchiladas, poured sauce over them, and sprinkled on the cheese, as Mom had been doing, then popped them into the oven. I could be the good daughter and give them a minute to themselves. It wasn't like I was getting any romantic moments of my own anyway.

"This was such a great idea, Tyler, to have a group date!" Andy proclaimed later that evening. After a good half hour of loving gazes, she finally took a moment to peel her eyes away from Tyler to look at me, Maya, and Scott, all seated around a table in Starbucks and holding steaming coffee cups. "Thanks again for coming out with us, guys."

"You're welcome," Maya said with a smile, giving Andy a knowing look. "Like we'd say no to you." She took a sip of her drink, then snuggled into Scott's side. He lifted an arm and wrapped it around her.

I wiggled over a little bit to give them more room.

Andy and Tyler started whispering to each other again, their faces mere inches apart. I looked at the two of them with half amusement, half pride, knowing the love spell I'd cast on them earlier today had obviously done its job. They'd been inseparable all evening.

As soon as I'd finished eating dinner, a breathless Andy had called me, saying Tyler had asked her out on a date for tonight. But she'd already planned to chill with me and Maya at Starbucks and had regretfully let him know. Therefore, Tyler had suggested all of us get together as a group.

Of course Maya and I agreed—that's what friends do for each other. Besides, it was painfully obvious Andy was desperate to go out with Tyler, and it was a great opportunity for me to view the newly made couple.

So there we were, in Starbucks, where happy couples in love cuddled, sipping coffee and whispering sweet nothings in each other's ears.

Oh, wait, except for me—a.k.a. "the fifth wheel."

I had never felt so painfully out of place. My discomfort was highlighted by the lovey-dovey smiles passing every millisecond between the two couples.

Not that I wasn't thrilled for them, because I totally was—I'd matchmade them, after all, and I took a great sense of pride in the job I did. It's just that watching Scott and Tyler so enraptured with my friends made me realize I was never going to have that with Derek, no matter how much I tried to fool myself.

It was pathetic, really, to keep chasing after a guy who wasn't going to look at me that way. *I* was pathetic.

Let it go for right now, Felicity, I ordered myself. Right now was about Andy, not me. I needed to buck up and hide the little green monster lurking deep in the back of my brain. This was not the time to be jealous of my best friends. They couldn't control Derek or his feelings.

And actually, neither could I.

Maybe it was time to move on from my crush on Derek, once and for all. Because as long as I let myself think about him romantically, I knew I'd always be hoping there was a chance to make it work. Why keep torturing myself like that?

"What's wrong, Felicity?" Maya asked. "You have a big frown on your face."

I forced a smile. "Oh, nothing," I replied. "I . . . burned the roof of my mouth on my coffee. You know how badly that hurts."

Maya nodded in empathy. "I sure do. Scott and I went to a movie last week, and I actually burned my tongue on the nacho cheese in the theater. Nacho cheese—who knew it could even *get* that hot?"

Andy leaned over toward Tyler and whispered something in his ear. He sucked in a quick breath, nodded, then kissed her.

Yeah, it was time for me to go. These lovebirds needed their privacy, and I felt like a perv watching them.

I glanced at my watch. "I gotta run. I need to cram for my

English quiz tomorrow. You know Mrs. Kendel will crack the whip on me if I don't do well. And that's not half as bad as my folks would be." I slid out of the booth before anyone could protest. "Have fun, you guys!" I said in an overly bright voice.

"Bye!" Andy said. "I'll talk to you tomorrow, 'kay?"

I gave her and Maya a quick hug, waved to the boys, then took off from Starbucks, heading to my mom's car in the unseasonably warm late April air. I slid into the driver's seat and headed home, a plan formulating in my mind.

I needed to find Derek a girlfriend. If he was unavailable to date, I would be forced to move on. Maybe I could even find love somewhere else someday.

I almost laughed out loud. I knew that wasn't likely to happen, but I needed to do something drastic to get over him.

I pulled into the driveway, then exited the car and headed inside the house. I trudged to the kitchen.

"Thanks for letting me borrow the car," I said to my mom, dropping the car keys into her open hand. "I think I'm going to go study for a little bit."

She pinched my cheek with her other hand, smiling. "My little studious girl."

I rolled my eyes, laughing. "Oh yes, you know me. The total nerd."

"Well, don't forget to fold and put your laundry away," Mom said. "I left the basket on your bed."

I saluted her. "Sir, yes sir!"

She swatted me. "Get out of here, smart mouth."

Upstairs in my room, I popped in a CD, then grabbed my PDA and turned it on. Perched on the side of my bed, I stared hard at Derek's profile, the pixels taunting me.

Name: Derek Peterson

Age: 17

Interests: Excellent athlete in football. Highly gifted artist. Witty sense of humor, and very intelligent. In all honors classes. Drives a Chevy Cavalier. Is superfriendly to everyone.

Style: Casual jock

Okay, think this through. Who would be the perfect match for Derek?

I lay back on my bed, closed my eyes, and blindly grabbed for my pillow, plopping it over my face. I needed to shut out all distractions, including Justin Timberlake, who was currently crooning in the background.

I sat straight up in bed as a flash of inspiration hit me, the pillow falling onto my lap. What if I paired him with Britney? She was a nice, attractive girl I'd set up in my very first cupid match. That pairing didn't work out, because the guy had turned out to be totally wrong for her, but Britney had survived the heartbreak and grown more confident and outgoing since then.

It would be a good way for me to make reparations for pairing her with an utter bonehead the last time. And I knew Derek would treat her right, because that's the kind of guy he was. He'd be the best boyfriend a girl could have.

Surely she'd make Derek happy as well. He deserved to be with someone who would strive hard to keep their relationship working. Someone who would appreciate how amazing he is.

I swallowed down the lump in my throat. This would truly be the most generous gesture I'd ever made in my life.

I turned on the PDA and drafted the blank e-mail to Derek, then quickly flipped through the address book and carbon-copied Britney. Closing my eyes, I pressed send, ignoring the twisted feeling in my gut.

I was setting Derek up to be in love with someone else.

I opened my eyes and glanced back at the LoveLine 3000.

Maybe I could matchmake another couple to help take my mind off Derek. I did, after all, have a weekly quota to fill. *Who's been single for a while?* I sorted my profiles and came up with a name at the top of the list: James Powers.

Oh, geez. The comedian himself, with no girlfriend? What. A. Surprise.

With a big sigh, I flipped through the list of students until I found someone who might like James. Mitzi from health class would be perfect—she was a total ditz and always giggled at everything. Maybe she'd think his armpit farts were funny. And I just so happened to know that she and her boyfriend broke up a few weeks ago.

I sent them the love e-mail, then turned off my PDA. I'd had enough matchmaking for the day.

chapter three

The next morning when I got to school, it was deserted. Well, there were cars in the parking lot, but no people roaming around outside like usual. Maybe school was canceled, or maybe there wasn't supposed to be any school today. That would be a nice surprise.

I checked my PDA's calendar to make sure it wasn't a teacher's in-service day. Nope, all was normal.

Cautious, I stepped toward the double doors, waiting to see if something weird would happen. A sudden cheering sound to my right caught my attention, so I headed in that direction instead. The sound had come from the track field.

Wow. Hundreds of students—and teachers—packed the

overcrowded bleachers, waving and hollering. Was there a morning track meet I didn't know about?

I pushed through the crowd and made it to the edge of the wire fence surrounding the track. There was only one person out there, running laps.

Derek.

"Oh my God," a student whispered behind me, "isn't he the hottest? Why didn't I ever notice it before?"

A guy beside her nodded enthusiastically. "Look how well he runs," he said, awe practically oozing out of his voice. "One foot in front of the other. No tripping. You'd think he invented the sport of running with those skills. No wonder he's so good at football. Think I can get his attention?"

"As if," a girl with a nose stud and purple hair said, her tone huffy. "Derek walked past me earlier this morning and said hello. It's obvious he's interested in *me*." She sighed deeply, unable to peel her eyes off him.

I spun around, my eyes raking the crowd. All these people were here to watch Derek run? What was going on here? Since when was our school so wrapped up in running?

"Dude," some guy said, "Derek is the best. Don't know why, but I just . . . feel the urge to be around him."

His buddy, a big burly guy, nodded in response. "Me too. Weird, huh?" He glanced around, his eyes taking in the group of students pressed against the fence, all watching Derek run laps. "Seems like everyone else here does too."

A sinking feeling plopped into the pit of my stomach. Something told me this was probably my fault.

I withdrew from the crowd and dashed into the school building. After looking around to make sure I was alone, I opened my LoveLine 3000. I looked at the sent messages. Okay, the love e-mail to James and Mitzi went fine. I scrolled down to Derek's e-mail.

And found that I'd accidentally CC'd the entire school.

Oh, crap.

"Hey, Felicity," Bobby Blowhard said from right behind me.

I crammed the LoveLine 3000 into my pocket and spun around, nearly smacking into him.

I bit back a sigh. "Hey," I mumbled in response. Bobby was the last person I'd wanted to see, and the tight, sleeveless top he was wearing was a vivid reminder of that.

I was trying to formulate an escape plan when a thought hit me. "Wait a minute—how come you're not outside with everyone else?"

He shrugged. "I don't know what the big fuss is. So Derek can run. Big deal."

It didn't make sense. If the whole school was now in love with Derek, why wasn't Bobby out there too?

"Don't you still have e-mail?"

"Sure, but my computer crashed a couple of days ago, and I can't get on there. Anyway, I'd rather talk face-to-face." He gave me a big, wolfish grin and leaned toward me. Like that was going to lure me to the dark side. "Why, did *you* want to talk?"

I bit my lower lip to keep from laughing. Oh, great. No wonder he wasn't all over Derek's ass. And of course it was my typical luck that *he* was the one person in school who hadn't checked his e-mail.

"I'd better go," I said, moving away from him toward my first-period English class. "Mrs. Kendel gets mad if we're late." I darted off, throwing a quick "bye" over my shoulder.

The rest of the day was just as odd. Classes went on as usual, but in between classes, Derek's name must have popped up in every conversation I heard, between both guys and girls, students and teachers:

"Derek's so handsome. I love the way he styles his hair."

"Derek said he and I are going to play some football tomorrow night."

"Guess what? Derek touched my arm today when he was reaching around me to grab a Coke. His hands are *so* warm."

And so on.

Not that I was eavesdropping. They just made it very easy for me to listen.

One good thing I noticed was that the other love matches I'd already made weren't affected by the Derek e-mail. Probably the rules about this were explained in my cupid user's manual, but that thing was waaaay too long and complicated for me to be expected to read. Maybe once a one-on-one love match was made, it would stick until the sparkles wore off, no matter what other arrows were shot—or e-mails sent, in my case.

That was a good thing in some ways, but had one drawback I hadn't predicted: If I wasn't listening to people moan forlornly about Derek, I had to listen to Andy rattle on and on about Tyler.

And talk, she did:

"Oh my God, Felicity, did you see the way Tyler answered Mr. Wiley's questions so fast? He's so smart—who knew he was soooo good at anthropology."

"Tyler looks so good in Abercombie and Fitch."

"I love the way Tyler holds his drumsticks."

"Tyler blah blah blah . . ."

Help. I'd created a monster!

My only consolation was that he seemed as equally in lurve as she did. In classes and at lunch he spent most of his time staring moony-eyed back at her.

Even art class didn't give me the thrill it normally did. We finished our monochromatic portrait early in the class period. Our art teacher, Mr. Bunch, then set up a still life for us to draw with charcoal . . . and proceeded to spend the entire hour giving Derek one-on-one instruction, praising his "profound" and "innovative" techniques with the charcoal stick.

Mr. Bunch started getting possessive of Derek's attention, which was kind of creepy. One guy in class complained because he didn't get a chance to hover over Derek and was immediately sent to detention.

Derek smiled and treated everyone fairly, but I could tell he wasn't nearly as in love with everyone as they were with him. Which made sense—his love was divided among the entire student body. Sans me and the couples I'd matchmade. And Bobby Blowhard, of course.

The last bell rang. With a heavy heart and a guilty conscience—after all, I'd caused all this mess—I gathered up my materials, slung my backpack over my shoulder, and plodded my way to the library. Andy was *supposed* to study for our health quiz with me today, but during lunch she said she was going to listen to lover boy's band practice for some upcoming party, so I was on my own.

I found a thick wooden table in the very back and opened my book, turning to the chapter where I'd left off yesterday. I read the first few lines of the page about four times, but couldn't concentrate. I closed the book and dropped my head into my hands.

I'd made such a huge mess of things. Again. What if Janet fired me?

Or, even worse—what if she sued me?

I swallowed hard and slouched in my seat, glancing furtively around me at the empty room. Did anyone suspect I was to blame for the Derek lovefest? What if they sent me to jail for messing around with people's lives like that? If it isn't illegal to screw around with people's hearts in that way, it should be.

I'm way too soft to go to the joint. There's no way I'd make it.

Oh, crap. Another thought hit me. Janet was going to see that I butchered this job when she looked at my PDA at our weekly meeting. And something told me this wasn't a mistake I should try to hide. Maybe it would look better if I came to her and fessed up instead of waiting to get busted.

I plunked my elbows onto the table, then cupped my head in my hands. This had all started because I was trying to do a selfless act. Note to self: Next time, just be selfish.

A shuffling sound got my attention. I lifted my head and saw the very object of my desire—and everyone else's—dart into the room. Derek.

My heart almost jumped into my throat.

When he saw me, he froze. I could see the panic written on his face.

"Oh, sorry," he said. "I, um, just needed a place to study. Alone."

I sighed, disappointment spinning in my stomach. He thought I was just another groupie. I gathered up my materials and stood. "Be my guest. You can have the room. I won't tell anyone you're here."

Derek tilted his head and looked at me oddly. "Really? Oh. Well, you can stay if you want to."

"Um, okay," I said with a cool nod, trying to squelch my nerves. I just needed to play it casual. After all, I was alone, with Derek, in the library. No one else was around.

And I couldn't even drool all over him.

With a sigh of relief, he plopped into the seat opposite me at the table. "Sorry," he said, digging through his faded blue backpack. "It's been a weird day for me, in case you didn't notice."

I laughed and sat back down, pulling out my book again. "So I saw. You got girls hanging all over you."

He shook his head. "Not just girls. Guys, too. And teachers." Derek leaned forward, his eyes sparkling as he gave me his trademark crooked smile.

"Must be your cologne, huh?"

"Maybe. Eau de Derek must be a popular scent today." He laughed again, then looked at the book I had. "Oh, I had health class last year. Mrs. Cahill's quite a character, isn't she?"

I rolled my eyes. "Yeah. Now, we're talking about cholesterol and what clogged arteries look like. This book has some of the grossest stuff I've ever seen. I swear, I'll never eat meat again."

"I said the same thing. Two weeks later I was back at McDonald's. Obviously didn't last too long."

Holy crap, what planet was I on? I mean, look at me. I was sitting in the library, having a normal conversation with the guy of my dreams. And he seemed to like talking to me, too!

Maybe I really did have a chance with him. Maybe he and I could—

"I'm so glad you're here," Derek said, interrupting my thoughts. "It's nice to have someone around who just wants to be a friend."

And instantly my heart deflated. I swallowed hard and tried to recover from the crushing blow of the "just friends" curse.

"Oh, absolutely," I said, nodding like an idiot. A bobbing-headed idiot.

I was no closer to dating him than Bobby Blowhard was to dating me.

chapter four

Janet shook her head and looked at my PDA. "You sure did a number on this one. I can't even see how you copied everyone in the school."

I blinked rapidly, embarrassed. I felt so guilty about my error that I'd driven over to Cupid's Hollow to see her as soon as I left the library, asking her for an emergency meeting. Thankfully, she'd been able to fit me in.

"I'm sorry," I whispered, trying to swallow down the lump in my throat. "I'm so stupid. Is it fixable?"

She glanced up at me. "You're not stupid, you made a mistake. Don't worry about it. The magic will wear off in a couple of weeks, just like it does with every other love match."

I exhaled, the tension easing from my shoulders and neck. "Oh, thank God. I was afraid I'd created something very perverted . . . and permanent."

Janet scoffed. "Permanent? Hardly. Ever heard of the sixties' lovefests? The famous Summer of Love? Well, that was partly my fault."

"Really?"

"Absolutely. You're not the only person to ever make a mistake, you know. I was toying around with ways to create love matches other than bows and arrows and decided it might be fun to try adding the magic to Kool-Aid . . . not realizing *everyone* would be sharing it. I got some unexpected results from that experiment."

I watched her smile, her eyes staring off into space. Obviously, she had some good memories. I couldn't imagine Janet as a carefree hippie, though. It was so far removed from her current personality, which leaned more toward uptight.

"Yeahhhhhh, those were the days." Janet shook her head. "Anyway, that was a long time ago, and we've gotten better at matchmaking since then."

"Well, I'm glad to hear I won't cause any permanent harm."

"You didn't, but try to be more careful next time." Uptight

boss-lady mode was back. She scrawled something on her ever-present notebook, then glanced back up at me. "So, what are you going to do to fix the problem?"

Good question. "Wellllll . . . ," I drawled, trying to think fast, "what if . . . what if I started matching all those people up with each other? Since Derek's love for them isn't equal to theirs, maybe I can distract them with a new romance?"

Janet rubbed her jaw. "Interesting idea. Actually, that just might work. Since it's not a direct one-for-one match, the magic is probably more vulnerable. It might be worth a shot to try that tactic. Let me know how that works out for you."

"Okay, I will!" I sat up in my seat, suddenly excited. Things weren't hopeless, after all. Thank God, I could still fix this!

I made a new mental goal—to make as many love matches as I could in the next two weeks. Yeah, I had, like, more than three hundred couples to make, but I could do it, right? Nothing was impossible, especially if Janet gave me the go-ahead.

"Just make sure all the new matches meet the minimum compatibility requirements so the magic will take. Willy-nilly pairings won't cut it here. Is there anything else?" Janet asked, glancing at the clock mounted on the wall.

"Um, no, that was it."

"Great." Janet stood and smoothed her skirt.

Guess that was my cue to leave. I thanked her for being so understanding and headed home, careful to drive five miles under the speed limit so my stupid cop brother couldn't decide to play head games with me. He had a tendency to pull me over whenever he wanted, just for laughs. It drove me absolutely nuts.

Once I got home I popped into my room, draped across my bed, and opened my PDA, ready to make some love matches. Considering the magnitude of the job I was facing, I'd need a system to ensure the best quality matches possible in the shortest period of time.

So, I'd match people in their own classes—freshmen with freshmen, sophomores with sophomores, and so on. That would make life so much simpler.

But first, I'd match up couples who I knew were interested in each other. Pairs I'd noticed flirting with each other sometimes, or checking each other out in the halls.

Unfortunately, that list was small. I matched up the dozen or so obvious couples within just a few minutes, then stared at my huge profile list. So many people to pair off!

I spent the next hour making couples as quickly as I could. I got through about forty before my hands started to cramp from working on the PDA. So I put it down and stretched my aching fingers, then picked up the phone.

I dialed Andy, ready to chat with my BFF and see how her love life was progressing. Also, I wanted to get her take on the library encounter with Derek.

"Hello?" she said.

"Andy, it's me."

"Hey, Felicity. Hold on a sec, 'kay?"

"Oh, okay."

The line clicked, and then Andy's voice came through. "Hey, honey, that's one of my friends. I'm going to get her off the line so we can keep talking, okay?"

My throat closed up, and I forced my voice to stay low and even. "Andy, it's still me. You didn't click to the other line right."

She gave an uncomfortable chuckle. "Oh. Sorry, I'm just right in the middle of a really good convo with Tyler. I'll give you a call later tonight, okay?"

"Yeah, sure," I mumbled, my face burning.

We hung up.

I couldn't ignore the twisting sensation in my gut. Ditched. For a dude.

Andy had just broken our unwritten rule . . . again. First she'd bailed on our health class study date, and now this.

I shrugged and swallowed down the uneasy feeling that I was losing one of my best friends. She never would have done this before.

Well, things were different now. And since I was the one who had matched her up, I had to deal with it.

Maybe Maya would have better perspective on the issue. I picked up the phone to call her, but promptly hung it back up again. I needed some face time, and I knew Maya wouldn't ditch me. She'd be shocked to hear how the phone conversation had gone, but she would know how to smooth things over and make me feel better.

I dashed down the stairs, threw my coat and shoes on, and booked it to Maya's house. The snow, piled along the sidewalks, was finally almost melted because of the bright sunshine, but everything was slushy and gross. Luckily, the jaunt to Maya's house was fast.

I knocked on her door, and it opened just a second later. Maya's mom, Mrs. Takahashi, nodded to me.

"Oh, hello, Felicity," she said, smiling politely. "Please come in. Maya is upstairs."

"Thank you," I said, careful to scrape the crud off the bottom of my shoes before taking them off in the foyer and placing them in a shoe cubby.

I heard a heavy series of thuds as Maya flew down the stairs.

"Oh, hey!" she cried out, her face splitting into a huge smile. She ran over and hugged me tightly.

Tears pricked the back of my eyes as I hugged her back. "Thanks for being so warm and welcoming. It's nice to know when I'm actually *wanted*," I said, unable to hide the edge of sorrow—and, to be honest, irritation—in my voice.

Maya pulled back, studying my eyes. The smile slid from her face, and she frowned. "Hey, what's wrong? Did something happen?"

I swiped a hand across my eyes. "Wanna go up to your room and talk?"

She nodded, leading me upstairs and into her bedroom. I saw her trumpet on her bed.

"Sorry if I interrupted your practice," I said as I sat in her computer chair. Maya's fastidious about her daily trumpet time. But then again, that's why she's so good.

"No problem," she said generously. "I can always pick it up again later. Now, what's going on?"

I sniffled, then explained the phone diss that had followed the study session ditch. Maya remained quiet as I talked on and on, expressing my frustration over Andy's attitude change now that she had a boyfriend.

Maya nibbled on her lower lip. "I can understand why you felt hurt by that," she finally said. "You know, though, Andy had been single for a long time. So maybe adjusting to a new boyfriend was a bigger transition for her than any of us had realized."

"I guess that's true," I acknowledged, spinning the computer chair back and forth as I chewed on her words.

Andy has always been überpicky about guys, so she doesn't date a lot—at least, not seriously. I couldn't remember the last time she'd had a real boyfriend. I guess I'd gotten used to her being around whenever I wanted to do something. Maybe that was a bit selfish of me.

"Give it a little time," Maya coaxed. "Things will level out with her, just like it did with me and Scott. I know she'll find balance. She remembers who her friends are, and she won't forget us—she'll probably call you later to apologize for brushing you off."

"You're a good person. Okay, I'll give it a little more time and be more patient." I stood and hugged her. "Now, go practice your nerdy music."

She rolled her eyes, tucking a strand of long, black hair behind her ear. "You're just jealous."

"You're probably right," I admitted. "You're so talented at everything."

We headed back downstairs, and I left her house, feeling a little better. Maya and Andy are opposites—Andy's fiery, spunky, and bold. Maya is calm, soothing, and steady. Her advice was like a balm to my raw nerves, and I tried to keep in mind what she'd said: Andy would level out eventually. I hoped she was right.

I shuffled through my front door, mentally gearing up to make more matches.

"Oh, good, you're back just in time," Mom said, spraying the coffee table and rapidly wiping it down. "I need you to run to the store and pick up a few things for dinner."

Great. Fixing all my messes would have to wait.

chapter five

Wednesday morning at school I slipped into my first-period English class, taking my typical seat beside Maya. Contrary to what Maya had said, Andy never did call me back. But in the spirit of being the bigger person, as well as a responsible matchmaker-slash-friend, I decided to let it go.

I glanced around the classroom. Most of the students were buzzing about Derek and how attractive he looked today in his dark orange shirt. But in the back of the room I noticed a couple I'd paired yesterday sitting beside each other, holding hands, and whispering into each other's ears.

My matchmaking had worked! There was hope after all.

"Let's get class started," Mrs. Kendel finally said. She handed out the new novel we'd be discussing in class—*The Scarlet Letter*.

Several students groaned when they saw the title.

"That's enough of that," Mrs. Kendel barked, pointing a thick finger at all of us. "This novel is not only relevant to the time period in which it was written, it's relevant now. It shows a culture that shuns a scandalous woman for not confessing the identity of her child's father. And moreover, it shows a woman trying to not let society define who she is."

For the next half hour we talked about the setting of *The Scarlet Letter*. I had to keep my hands busy taking notes so I wouldn't be tempted to grab my PDA and make more matches. Mrs. Kendel wasn't someone who would let something like that go—she'd surely snatch the PDA out of my grasp and keep it in her desk drawer for the rest of the week.

The bell rang, and Maya and I gathered our stuff and left class. I noticed DeShawn, one of the first guys I'd matchmaded, slip out the door to greet his girlfriend, Marisa. He kissed her on the cheek, and with fingers wound tightly, the two of them made their way down the hallway, waving hi to Marisa's friends as they joined the couple in their walk.

I guess they'd decided to give DeShawn a fair chance, after

all. Well, that was good. When I'd first paired the couple, Marisa's friends tried their best to encourage her to break up with him. But holding true to her love, she stuck with him.

"I'm so glad they're still together," I said to Maya, nodding my head toward them.

"No kidding. DeShawn's so different since dating her," she said. "I think she's been a good influence on him."

"Absolutely. I think—" I stopped as the hallway started to buzz with abnormally loud activity.

Then I realized why. Derek was coming down the hall, surrounded by a massive group of students and teachers.

"And speaking of different, what's up with that?" Maya said. "I don't understand why everyone is all over Derek. Didn't you tell them he's your guy?" she asked, her tone teasing.

I snorted. "If only it worked that way." I shrugged casually, trying to say as little as possible to not give away the real reason Derek was the center of everyone's attention. "I guess he's just the flavor of the week. I'm sure things will chill soon enough."

And now that I knew how I could help remedy that, I was going to be a busy, busy girl, making those new matches—not just for the students, but for the teachers!

• • •

"So, what are you reading today?"

I glanced up from my novel, my heart racing. Since my matchmaking mistake—okay, *massive blunder*—Derek and I had been meeting at the library after school, just to hang out. Today was Thursday, our third meeting in a row.

Nothing was set in stone, as we hadn't officially declared we'd meet, but I'd shown up every afternoon this week just hoping our "date" would keep happening.

It did.

And it was the biggest thrill and most crushing disappointment of my life.

After all, Derek only saw me as a friend, like he had said. And technically, I should only want to be friends too. Though to be honest, I hadn't managed to move past my romantic feelings for him at all. Spending these afternoon sessions with him was only making me more smitten.

What could I do?

I ached to be close to him, so friendship was the best chance I had right now.

I shot him a smile. "It's *The Scarlet Letter*." I set the book down.

"I didn't think you'd be here. Don't you have about a billion people trying to date you right now?"

He laughed, sliding into the seat across from me and plopping his backpack onto the table. "I had almost fifty love notes crammed into my locker, asking me out for Friday night." He dug into the bag and pulled out a huge pile of folded pieces of paper.

Holy crap, he wasn't kidding.

"Well, I'm sure this will go away soon enough," I said. And if I did my job quickly enough, it would.

He opened the note on top, covered with red lipstick kisses. "'Derek,'" he read aloud, "'when Mr. Stephanides asked who had read last night's homework, and you raised your hand, I just knew I wanted to be around you. You're such a smart guy. Wanna go out tonight?'"

"Wow."

He sighed and looked up from the paper. "Yeah, no kidding. I can't date them all. I do like them, but there just aren't enough hours in the day."

I tried to smile, but my stomach flipped as I thought about my private blog. All those entries with Derek's name written over and over. Was I really any less pathetic than the people who wrote him these notes?

Well, at least I wasn't sending them directly to him. And that's because I was a class-A chicken.

"It's hard to keep coming up with good reasons to say no, though," he continued.

I shrugged. "Just figure out something else to do and tell them that, unfortunately, you're busy, but thanks. That way, you can be nice about it and tell the truth without making them feel bad."

His face brightened up. "You're right. That's a good idea. What are you doing tomorrow night?"

Every skin cell froze in anticipation. "W-who, me?"

"Wanna hang out? We could catch a movie or have dinner or something. It would be nice to chill with someone not psycho. You know, as friends."

As *friends*. I was beginning to hate the *F* word. Blech. But since I was desperate to be closer to him, I immediately answered, "Yeah, that would be fun."

Now that we'd talked it was time to get down to studying. After cramming the love notes back in his backpack, Derek grabbed his laptop and anatomy text. I glanced back at my novel, pretending I was reading and being studious. In reality I was watching Derek's hands as he typed his notes.

He had long, strong fingers. Clean, short nails. Lean, muscled forearms. I had a sudden flash of imagining those hands on the small of my back as I was pressed up against him, dancing slowly at prom. He'd slide his hand up my back, caressing my shoulder blade, to rest those strong fingers on my neck, leaning me closer . . .

I had to stop this. I fervently dug through my brain for a question to ask him. Anything to get my mind off Derek's hands.

"So," I said, clearing my throat, "do you have any brothers or hands?"

A startled look swept across his eyes. "Huh?"

A slow burn crawled up my face when I realized what I'd said. "Er, sisters, I mean. Sisters."

Derek smiled. "Two brothers and two sisters, actually. They're all younger than me, though, so I have to keep them out of trouble."

I stared at him in shock. "There are *five* of you? At least I only have one brother—he's crazy enough. Wow, how does your mom find time to do anything? And how do you get a moment of quiet in all that chaos?"

Derek laughed. "Yeah, there's no privacy in our house. Our family is Catholic, and my mom is apparently pretty fertile," he said with a mock grimace. "She and my dad just smile and say, 'the more the merrier.'"

I chuckled. "At least they have a good attitude about it."

Derek got a thoughtful look on his face. "I try to do what I can to help. That's why I have to work so hard at football. I need to get a scholarship so I can go to college next year. With that many kids, they can't afford to pay for me."

I nodded, feeling a sudden swell of pride that Derek was opening up to me about his home life. I was learning new stuff about him every day, and he was just as cool as I'd suspected. "My parents are super tight with money. My mom won't give me money for anything, which is why I had to get a job."

"Oh, really? What do you do?"

"Um, I work for a matchmaking company. Filing and paperwork and such."

He stared at me for a long minute. In fact, it was so long, I started to feel a bit weird. Maybe he thought it was odd for me to work there.

Or, even worse, maybe he suspected that the Derek lovefest somehow led back to me. Crap.

"That's interesting," he finally said. "Maybe you can find matches for everyone in school, then, so they stop hounding me."

I gave him an uneasy chuckle. He had no idea how close to the truth he was. "Yeah, I'll get right to work on that. So, do you work anywhere?" I asked, eager to divert attention away from my job.

"Well, I work part-time at my dad's sports store." He smiled. "We're pretty athletically oriented in my family."

"I'm terrible at sports, but I was the goalie on my elementary school soccer team."

"Oh, that's cool. Did you like it?"

"I got bored really easily," I said with a laugh. "Unfortunately, I was more interested in catching worms and butterflies than actually defending the goal." I shook my head, smiling. "Needless to say, I was asked to refrain from playing the next year."

"Aw, that's too bad," he said, trying to keep a straight face. "I'm sure you were cute to watch."

My lips got tingly excited from the compliment. "Well, my mom didn't think so. Like I said, she's pretty tight with spending dough, so you can imagine what a waste of money she thought it was."

Derek shrugged. "Sounds like most moms, actually. Mine's no different."

I rolled my eyes sympathetically.

We studied in silence for another half hour. Derek studied his work, and I studied him. The last few days, I'd gotten to know him a little better not only by asking questions, but by watching him.

When he was deep in thought, he rubbed a hand across his jaw. While taking notes, his forehead crinkled, and he got a little line between his eyebrows as he typed. He was so unbelievably cute.

I thought about what he'd just said. Four siblings total—that had to be hard on him. Forced to be responsible, to be accountable for what the others did. My esteem of him went up another notch, if that was even possible.

Compared with Derek's, my life was a picnic. All I had to worry about was myself. My pain-in-the-butt brother was out of the house and on his own, even though he did come over a lot. And my parents would at least help pay for part of my college.

I bit back a sigh. God, how I looked forward to whatever Derek and I were going to do on Friday. Even though it wasn't a real date, I had a feeling it was going to be an interesting evening.

chapter six

"I just don't get this book," Maya said to me later that night. With a groan, she closed *The Scarlet Letter,* rose from my bed, and started pacing the floor. "Why wouldn't Hester just tell on the guy who got her pregnant so she wouldn't be thrown in jail and viewed as a slut by her whole town? It was as much his fault as it was hers."

I squinted my eyes, flipping through my copy of the book. "It's kind of romantic, actually, that she's willing to face public scorn to keep their love a secret."

"I guess. I just wish he'd been there more for her, like she was for him. She did everything he wanted of her." She glanced away.

Maya wasn't normally this downhearted. Something had to be bothering her.

I put my book down. "What's wrong? Is there trouble with Scott?"

"Nothing's wrong." She sighed. "Actually, Scott gets better every day. He's the most thoughtful guy I've ever known." She shook her head, as if to dismiss her thoughts, and shot me a smile. "Anyway, let's start figuring out the symbolism in here so Mrs. Kendel will think we're utter geniuses."

I was tempted to push the issue and ask more questions, but decided to let it go. Maya would talk when she was ready, and if there was a problem with her relationship, I'd figure out a way to fix it.

Hopefully, she was telling the truth.

"Okay," I finally said. "Maybe we can get our discussion on this book over before Andy arrives." A glance at my watch confirmed what I'd feared. "Though she's already a half hour late."

"Maybe she had some stuff to do for her mom," Maya offered, sitting back on the bed. "You know she sends Andy on some wild errands, like to find crazy herbs or vegetables for whatever trend she's into now."

"Yeah, maybe." I pushed down the irritation that had been growing in me since Andy first ditched us for Tyler and I tried to focus on *The Scarlet Letter*. But only half my brain was there, while the other half was wondering, *Where in the world is she? Why hasn't she texted Maya or called?*

"Okay, here are the symbols I wrote down in my notes," Maya said, reading back over her paper. "We have the big scarlet *A* on her chest. Um, the *A* stands for adulterer, though Hester eventually grows to wear the symbol with a sense of pride and refuses to leave town. But what does Hester's daughter, Pearl, symbolize?"

I shrugged halfheartedly, not really caring about the drama of Puritan America.

"You know, you should just call her," Maya suggested.

"I don't see why I should keep having to reach out to her. She should have been here. On her own. *Without* me having to nag each and every time. And if she's standing us up, she should bother to call and let us know." I crossed my arms over my chest. "Besides, I wanted to talk to her about my date—er, nondate date—with Derek. I thought all of us could go out together."

"And we still can," Maya said. "If you just call her. She could have a very good reason for not being here."

"Maybe you're right." I wanted to believe Maya, wanted to feel like my friend wasn't ditching me yet again—and for a guy, at that.

I grabbed my phone from my bedside stand and called her. No answer.

"Hey, Andy," I said to her voice mail, trying to keep my voice light and nonreproachful, "it's Felicity. We were supposed to meet at my house for studying tonight. I wasn't sure if you forgot. Maya's here too. Anyway, give me a call." I glanced over at Maya, who nodded in encouragement for me to continue. "Um, I also have some news I wanted to talk to you about."

I hung up.

"Good." Maya smiled. "She'll call you back. In the meanwhile, let's get back to business."

"So what were we talking about?" I asked, trying to refocus. Maya was showing great patience with my griping, so I didn't want to keep blabbing on about Andy and end up irritating Maya in the process.

Maya and I studied for another hour, then called it a night. She went home to have dinner and finish the rest of her homework.

I checked my phone to make sure it wasn't broken or disconnected or muted or something.

Nope, working fine.

I went downstairs to heat up some dinner for myself. All that studying and fretting had made me hungry. Mom and Dad weren't home, having gone to Grandma's house earlier in the afternoon. But my mom had left me some lasagna in the fridge.

After wolfing down my food, I popped the dishes in the dishwasher, then trudged back upstairs to finish the rest of my homework and make some more love matches to help correct the Derek mess. What a lively evening I had planned for myself.

I cracked open my American history book and read the assigned chapter, taking notes as I went along. Mr. Schrupe had said he would be testing us tomorrow, and I had a bad habit of not paying attention in his class when he talked. I couldn't help it, though—the man was as dry as yesterday's toast. But I needed to pay attention to the chapter and do a good job so I wouldn't feel so guilty about my slackerly ways.

My phone rang, jarring me out of my reading. I grabbed it—the caller ID said Andy's number.

"Hello?" I said cautiously, wondering what excuse I was going to hear. If she said she was too busy playing tonsil hockey with Tyler to come study with me and Maya, I was going to throw up all over my phone.

"Heyyyy," she said, sighing heavily. "How did the study session go? I'm so sorry I couldn't make it. I had to fill in for one of the other servers at The Burger Butler. I just got home a few minutes ago. I'm exhausted."

My heart thudded in surprise. And guilt.

So she didn't ditch us for Tyler. Whoops. Maybe it would do me some good to stop jumping to conclusions so quickly.

"Oh, don't worry about it at all," I said, overenthusiasm pouring into my voice and making me blabber on and on. "We just discussed the book we're reading in English. *The Scarlet Letter.* Are you guys reading that one too? Anyway, sorry you had to work. I bet that sucked."

"Actually, we're reading *The Hobbit* right now. I think I like the movie better." She chuckled. "So, you said you had some news. What's going on?"

I briefly filled her in on Derek sort-of-not-really asking me out.

She squealed. "Really? That's so cool. I knew he'd come around to it one day."

"Thanks, but it's not like that. We're just friends."

"But after this date, that'll change. You know, Tyler says Derek is a really cool guy. And he's a good judge of character."

I didn't necessarily need the Tyler Seal of Approval, but I could be amenable.

"Well, speaking of," I said, "I was hoping you and Tyler would come with us. Maya already said she and Scott would come. Wouldn't that be fun?"

Not being a fifth wheel for once would be a miniblessing. And making it a group date instead of one-on-one would remove some of the pressure, and distract me from spending the entire time just wishing Derek saw me the way I saw him. I didn't think I could handle a whole evening of that.

"Definitely! I know Tyler will love that. Hold on a sec." She cupped her hand over the receiver and shouted, "Yes, Mom, I'm coming!" She uncapped the phone. "Sorry, gotta run. Mom's nagging me again. I swear, she can't do anything by herself. I wish she'd just hire a pool boy to entertain her for a while."

I laughed. "Maybe you could save up your extra money from working and buy one for her. Oh, and let me and Maya know when you do so we can come by. Um, for moral support, of course."

"Hah. You know it."

We hung up. I placed the phone back in its cradle, feeling worlds better. Andy, Maya, and I were going out on a triple date (okay, it's a date in the loosest sense of the word, but whatever). Once Derek and I had a chance to talk outside of school in a group date, where I could relax and be myself, he could see how charming and fun I am—not just how love struck and tongue-tied I tended to be around him.

With a jaunty hum, I whipped out my handy LoveLine 3000 and started making some matches. After all, since I was on the edge of something marvelous, it was time to pass that on to my fellow students.

chapter seven

T minus twelve minutes until Derek showed up for our nondate date.

I sat on the couch in the living room, trying not to stare at the clock. My shaky fingers kept fidgeting with my freshly done hair. It was styled, but not too much so.

I wore my favorite jeans and a hot-pink T-shirt with cute little cherries on the front. An overall look of hotness without trying to look hot.

At least, that's the effect I was going for. Since it wasn't a real date, I didn't want to look like I was making more effort than necessary, or he'd be turned off. But I still needed to look hot enough to make him notice me in a nonfriendly way.

Being a girl was enough to drive me crazy sometimes.

Andy, beside me on the couch, patted me on the back. Tyler was going to meet us at my house too, and we would all ride in his car to dinner and a movie, where Maya and Scott would be waiting for us. After the movie the girls and I would crash at my house for our weekly TGIF sleepover, where we could blab all night about how the evening went.

"Chillax, Felicity. It'll be fine."

I nodded solemnly. "Does my outfit look okay?"

"Stand up."

I did so, slowly turning around.

Andy scrutinized my outfit with the utmost seriousness. She totally got how important this was to me. "Looks good to me," she finally said. "Hot, without looking like you put in too much effort trying to be hot."

I sighed in relief. "Oh, thank you! That's exactly the look I was going for."

The doorbell rang. Heart thudding painfully, I glanced at the clock—Derek was several minutes early. At least he wasn't going to keep me waiting.

Andy quickly squeezed my hand. "Keep your cool. You're sexy, and you own it."

"Thanks." I shook my head to clear the cobwebs, sucked in a deep breath, and pasted on a smile as I opened the door.

It was Tyler.

My shoulders slumped, but I fought to keep the smile on my face and the disappointment out of my voice. "Oh, hey, Tyler. Glad you made it. Andy's in there." I hitched my thumb behind me.

"Felicity, who's that?" my mom hollered from upstairs.

"Just Tyler. We're waiting on Derek, and then we'll be taking off."

"Well, be careful. Take my cell with you, just in case. I expect you home by ten."

I rolled my eyes and tried to smile at Andy and Tyler, who were now cuddled on the couch. "Sorry," I whispered, closing the door. "You know how moms are."

The door stopped right before closing. "Um, hello?" came a voice from outside.

It was *him*.

I tugged the door back open, cheeks flaming because I'd tried to close it in his face. "Oh, sorry, I didn't see you there."

Derek looked . . . well, he looked great. A soft, gray, long-sleeved T-shirt accentuated his muscled shoulders. He wore faded jeans with a pair of dark gray Skechers.

He looked at me, a small smile on his face. "So, can I come in?"

Duh. "Oh, yes, sorry. I spaced out there for a second." I held the door wider so he could pass.

Andy, Tyler, and Derek said their hellos. I hurriedly grabbed the cell phone from the kitchen table, then ran back to the living room and grabbed my purse. "We're taking off, Mom," I hollered. "Bye." I hoped we could get out of there before she—

"Hold on a second," she yelled back, coming down the stairs. "Let me say hi to your friends first."

Crap. Here it comes.

Mom headed into the living room, tucking a strand of loose hair behind her ear. "Hi," she said, sticking out her hand to Tyler, then Derek. "Where are you guys headed tonight, and who's driving?"

"This is my boyfriend, Tyler," Andy said, sidling up to Tyler and pressing her chest against his back. She wrapped her arms around him tightly, then gave him a small kiss on the back of his neck. "He's driving. We're just going out to dinner and a movie."

Mom eyeballed them. I could tell exactly what she was thinking. Should she say something about Andy, whom she's known for years, inappropriately close to *a boy*? Or should she let it go, since she wasn't Andy's mom?

Fortunately for me, she chose the latter.

"That sounds fun," she replied, then turned her hawk-eyed stare to Derek. "So, Derek, I expect you to be responsible tonight too."

Oh, dear God. Like he was going to try to jump my bones or touch my naughty bits. The boy didn't even know I was alive, other than as a buddy.

"Mom," I growled through my teeth, "we're just friends." *Unfortunately.* "We're just hanging out as a group, okay?"

Derek nodded, his face serious. "I promise I'll watch over her and make sure she gets in on time."

Mom smiled broadly. "Thanks. I'd appreciate it. Felicity here," she said, giving me a knowing look, "thinks she's too much of a big shot to be watched over by her mom."

Fabulous. I was like a freaking preschooler being nagged not to eat paste.

"Mo-o-ommmm," I groaned, "pleeeeease. We gotta go. Maya and Scott are waiting for us at the restaurant."

Derek, trying to keep a serious face, bit his lower lip.

Mom laughed and chucked me on the arm. "Oka-a-aaaaay. Go. Have fun. I'll see you back here at ten."

I practically ran out of the house, sucking in deep breaths to calm down. She really was a piece of work sometimes. I'm sure she meant well, but seriously. Not cool.

We piled into Tyler's Ford Focus and took off—Tyler and Andy in the front, Derek and me in the back. Since Derek had long legs, he had to sit behind Andy, who pulled her seat up closer to the dashboard to make room.

Derek's left hand absently traced patterns on the middle seat. I tried to keep my cool, my brain whirring to figure out a way to get closer to him. Maybe I could lean extra hard into a curve, and oops—I'd fall right on top of him.

Nah, too obvious.

"—supposed to be pretty good, actually," Andy said, her hand caressing the back of Tyler's neck. "Right, Felicity?"

"Huh? Uh, yeah," I said, having no idea what she was talking about.

She didn't seem to notice, or care. "I can't wait to try their food." She perked up and looked at Tyler. "Oh, honey—this is our first Friday date out! I should have gotten you a card for it ... I'm sorry."

"Don't be sorry, babe," he replied, glancing over at her. He stroked a hand across the back of her head. "I didn't think about it, either. So *I'm* sorry too."

I shook my head and glanced at Derek, who jokingly rolled his eyes. We shared a small chuckle at the gagginess known as Andy and Tyler's TRU. ULTIMATE. LURVE.

Things weren't much different in the restaurant. Derek had chosen a new, casual burger place with great atmosphere to give us all a chance to talk. However, there wasn't too much talk happening among the whole group. Instead, Andy and Tyler sat across from each other, hands linked and eyes locked. They were murmuring back and forth to each other, totally excluding anyone else from the conversation.

Maya and Scott were at least a little more social. They kept dropping all these couple-y inside jokes, but they did make a point of drawing everyone else into conversation.

Meanwhile, Derek and I pored over the menu, trying not to feel like the fifth and sixth wheels.

"Um," I finally said to him, "I'm thinking of trying the El Rancho Burger. What about you?"

"That sounds good." Derek pondered the menu. "Actually, I was thinking about the Sacre Bleu Cheese Burger with Le Crunchy Frenchy Fries."

I giggled. "Well, if that doesn't do it for you, you could always try the Leaning Platter of Pizza. Actually, that sounds ginormous. If you got that, you'd have to change into your fat pants."

Maya jerked her head over, jaw dropped and eyes wide.

When I realized what I'd said, I flinched. Oh man, that totally came out wrong.

I tried to backpedal. "Um, not that you'd have any. 'Cause we all know you're totally not—"

Derek held up a hand, chuckling. "It's okay. I know what you meant."

The waiter arrived, and Andy and Tyler stopped gazing at each other long enough to pick out something to eat from the menu.

After he left, Andy grabbed my hand and tugged me and Maya out of our seats. "I have to pee," she said. "And Felicity and Maya have to pee too."

We laughed.

"Well, okay then," I said.

"Go ahead," Scott said, waving us off. "We know girls can't go to the bathroom by themselves."

The three of us headed straight for the sink to scrutinize our reflections.

"I swear, I must be chewing my lipstick off," Maya said,

grabbing dark pink gloss from her purse and gliding it across her lips. "I just put this on right before we got here."

Andy glanced around the stalls, then looked back at the mirror, widening her eyes as she reapplied her mascara. "You guys, I think I'm head over heels in love," she breathed. The mirror fogged in a small circle in front of her mouth.

I froze in place, jerking my eyes to look at her. "In love? Don't you mean 'in crush'?" I choked out. She'd just started dating him, like, two seconds ago . . . and that was because of *my* matchmaking. Yes, part of me was glad to see Andy so happy, but the rest of me was shocked by how fast things were progressing.

"He's perfect," Andy said with a soft sigh. "Simply perfect in every way."

"He *is* a sweetie," Maya said, popping her lipstick back in her purse and turning to lean her backside against the bathroom sink.

"Yeah," I hesitantly began, fixing a smudge on my lower lip, "he's a great guy. Even though he tends to do the 'seafood' thing a bit too much."

Now that I thought about it, I hoped he didn't show us his half-digested food tonight. That would be nasty.

Andy laughed, fluffing her hair. "Oh, I know. But it's cute.

Anyway," she leaned in closer, "I think I'm ready to do it."

"Do what?" Maya asked.

"Go all the way with him." She widened her eyes again to apply mascara on the outer corners of her upper eyelashes.

I ripped my gaze from the mirror and stared at her in shock. "What?"

"Andy, that's a big step," Maya said, her brow furrowed. "You guys haven't been together a long time. It's only been a few days. Are you sure you're ready for that? Scott and I have been together for a month now, and we haven't even talked about that yet."

"Tyler's the guy of my dreams. It's never gonna get more perfect than this." Dropping her mascara in her purse, Andy stepped away from the mirror and headed to the door. "Come on, you two. Our dates are waiting."

Oh God, what have I done?

chapter eight

I hardly knew what to do with myself the rest of dinner. I tried to keep my attention focused on whatever conversation was going around, but all I could think about was what Andy had said in the bathroom.

She was ready to give it up ... to Tyler? After only one date? I mean, he was a nice guy and all, but having sex was no small thing.

I shuddered.

Derek glanced at me, concern written in his eyes. "You okay?"

"Yeah," I mumbled, "just a chill. I'm fine now, thanks."

We paid our bill and headed back to our cars, dashing across town in time to catch the movie. It was some kind of psychological thriller Andy wanted to see. We headed into the theater, grabbed our tickets, and got seats.

Derek sat on my left side, his elbow rubbing lightly against mine on the shared armrest. Even as my skin got tingly from the closeness, I tried to remain relaxed and cool. *This is not a real date*, I chanted to myself.

Scott left to grab drinks and popcorn for him and Maya, who were sitting on the very end of our row. Tyler and Andy were already cuddling in the middle seats.

I chuckled under my breath, remembering the last time the three of us girls were here. That was when Maya was juggling simultaneous movie dates with two of the three guys I'd matched her with. What a nightmare that had been—I'd had to run into the men's bathroom to distract the guys so they wouldn't talk to each other and discover they were both out with Maya at the same time.

I think I was still scarred from what I'd seen in that men's room.

With a low laugh, I leaned to my right and said to Andy and Maya, "This should be better than the *last* time we were here, right?"

Maya shook her head, squinting at me. "Very funny. I don't even want to think about that."

Andy looked blankly at us. "Huh?"

"Remember the last time we were here?" I said carefully, trying not to give too much detail, since there were boys present.

She stared at me for another couple of seconds, then nodded lightly. "Oh, right. I forgot all about that." She stood up. "I'm craving some popcorn. I'll be right back."

Tyler immediately hopped up. "Me too, babe. Let's go together."

Fingers intertwined, the two headed back down the aisle.

Yowch. Andy's disinterest stung. I leaned back into my seat and sighed deeply, watching them go.

"Hey," Derek said, "you okay? You seem like something's on your mind."

"Well," I said, "I'm just nervous that Andy's over her head with Tyler. They seem to be getting into this awfully fast." There. That was the truth, without giving too much away.

"I understand. They seem . . ."

"Attached at the lips?"

"Yeah." He laughed.

"I know it." I turned in the chair to face him. "See, we used to make fun of girls who clung to guys like that. And now—"

"And now, she's one of them."

I shrugged, suddenly feeling guilty for griping on my best friend.

Derek nodded, catching my eyes. "People do weird things when they think they're in love."

"Yeah, that's true."

"Give her time. She'll get over the 'love glow' and come to her senses."

Oh my God, he was right. Why didn't I think of that? Once the love spell wore off, she would be more aware of what was going on and could make a clear-headed decision. It had worked for Maya— she was obviously more levelheaded and not so absorbed in her relationship now.

I perked up, suddenly feeling better. "Hey, thanks. You know, you're pretty good at giving advice."

"You would be too, if you constantly had younger brothers and sisters hounding you. 'He stole my Barbie!'" Derek mimicked in a high-pitched voice. "'No, I didn't! But if I did, it's because she took my G.I. Joe!'" He rolled his eyes.

"I'm sure it's been a blast for you," I said with a chuckle.

He nodded in agreement.

We sat in comfortable silence for a few minutes watching the previews. Scott returned, taking his seat beside Maya. Andy and

Tyler made it back to the seats just before the movie started.

The film was weird, but it went fast. It was one of those thrillers that gets a ton of ad hype. My brother would love it. I can't say I was totally into it, but I don't think I was the target audience. Everyone else seemed to dig it, though.

We left the theater and got back to the cars. Andy and I gave Maya a quick hug, since Maya needed to run home and get her clothes before coming to my house for the TGIF sleepover. We got in Tyler's car and headed back home.

As we rode, I couldn't help but steal little glances at Derek. And a couple of times, I caught him looking at me, too. My heart fluttered with each catch of the eye, but I was too chicken to say anything to him.

It's a good thing it was dark, because I could feel my cheeks burning.

Before I knew it, Tyler was pulling back into my driveway to drop all of us off. It was just before ten o'clock—Derek sure kept his promise to my mom.

Trying to push down the disappointment in my gut at the end of our nondate date, I pasted on a big smile. "Well, guys, it's been a blast."

Tyler planted a huge kiss on Andy's lips. "See you later, babe."

Inwardly I cringed at his frequent use of the word "babe." I don't know why, but I hated that word with a passion. It sounded so . . . cheesy.

Derek smiled at me. "It's been fun."

We stared at each other. For a moment I got the impression that he wanted to say more. But he didn't.

Seconds ticked by in silence, except for the sounds of Andy and Tyler making out.

Okay, then. I guess it was time to go. I got out and closed the door.

"Bye!" I said as perkily as possible, then crossed in front of the car, opened the front passenger car door, and tugged Andy out.

Andy and I stood in the driveway and watched both guys take off in their respective cars. Then we headed into my house.

Once I closed the front door, I flung my purse and body onto the couch, desperate to start analyzing the entire evening with Andy, and then rehashing it again when Maya arrived so I could get her perspective too. We needed to run through every conversation with a fine-tooth comb to see if I'd missed anything important . . . or if I'd done something stupid without realizing it.

"Oh man, that was too interesting," I started. "I don't know what to—"

Andy jumped a little, then dug into her pocket and pulled out her phone. "Oh, hold on a sec. My cell's on vibrate." She flipped it open. "Hello?"

Okayyyy.

I headed into the kitchen and grabbed the requisite rocky road ice cream and three spoons in anticipation of Maya's pending arrival. A staple of our post-guy encounters.

Andy followed me. "Oh, hey, sweetie," she said in a quiet voice into the cell. Probably trying to not disturb my folks, sleeping upstairs. "Aw, I miss you too."

Good grief. They just saw each other, like, two minutes ago.

"Is that Tyler?" I asked in disbelief.

She shushed me.

"Sorry, baby," she said into the phone. "What was that?" Pause. "Okay, sounds good. I'll see you tomorrow. Good night." She made kissing sounds into the phone.

I grabbed three bowls and started scooping ice cream into two of them, then glanced up at her. She still had the cell open and up to her ear.

"Hey, you didn't hang up," Andy said. She giggled. "Okay, let's hang up together. Ready? One . . . two . . . three." Pause. "Well, you didn't hang up, either!"

Oh, for God's sake.

I grabbed the phone from her hand. "Hey, Tyler. She misses you, but she'll see you tomorrow, okay? Bye." I closed it.

Andy snatched the cell out of my hand, fire blazing in her eyes. "How dare you! That was unbelievably rude."

"Oh, come on," I huffed, the irritation and frustration I'd been burying down in my gut over the last few days boiling right to the surface. "You two are getting downright disgusting with the lovey-dovey crap. 'I love you,'" I mock crooned. "'I love you more.' 'No, I love *you* more.' Blah, blah, blah." I pointed at her. "You're not acting like yourself."

And even more importantly, why was Andy doing this when she was *supposed* to be spending quality time with her BFF?

Andy stared at me in disbelief, her jaw dropped open. She crammed her cell into her pocket. "I don't wanna stay here tonight. I gotta go. Later." Andy grabbed her overnight bag from the living room and stormed out of my house.

I stared in shock at her retreating form. I couldn't believe she'd backed out of our TGIF sleepover. I mean, it was our tradition. A hallmark of our friendship.

She had to be furious with me.

Well, you know what? She was acting stupid. Just because she was in love—and not even *real* love, thank you very much—she had to go act all psycho now. Who wanted to be around that? She'd become the kind of person we always mocked.

Even my crazy crush on Derek never deteriorated into what she was doing now. Ditching your girlfriends for a guy is the ultimate betrayal.

I ate my ice cream and Andy's, stomped into the living room, and waited for Maya, willing myself to push the argument out of my mind. No way was this fight with Andy going to keep me down tonight. I was still going to have a good time with my *real* friend.

But I knew there was no way I was going to be able to let this go.

"Felicity, pay attention," Mrs. Cahill, my health teacher, said on Monday, her tone snippy.

A couple of people snickered.

My head jerked up from the doodle in my notebook. Mornings stunk, and this one was no different.

"Sorry. I'm trying," I grumbled.

Someone notably *not* here today was Andy, who usually sat on the other side of me. I wondered if she was absent because of our fight.

Mrs. Cahill flitted to the corner of the chalkboard. "Instead of making you take a final exam this year, I'm going to try something different."

Cheers filled the room.

"I figured you'd like that," she said, laughing. She turned and wrote on the chalkboard, SPECIAL CREATIVE PROJECT.

The cheers quickly died into groans.

She threw us a look. "Basically, you're going to pair up with someone else in the class and do a creative project about something we've discussed. It can be a videotape about how pregnancy, or bulimia, or drugs can affect a teen's life. It can be a story about eating the right foods. The more creative, the better. Have fun with it!"

This was going to be so. Awful. We had a couple of weeks to come up with some stupid project about health, of all topics. Yeah, tons o' fun.

Mrs. Cahill grabbed a piece of paper off her desk. "I've already paired you up with your partners, so no griping."

As she read down the list, a sense of panic welled in me. *Please don't let me be with someone lame.* Maybe praying would help. There was nothing worse than being stuck with a dud for a class project.

God, I promise I'll be a good girl, and I'll stop judging my brother for the tramps he dates, and—

"Felicity Walker and Bobby Loward."

I heard Bobby say, "Yessssss," in a soft tone under his breath.

Yup, it was official. My life was over.

chapter nine

"So," Bobby said after class ended, hot on my heels, "when should we get together for our project? I already have some ideas...."

I dodged left out of the classroom, trying to shake him. "I'll have to let you know," I mumbled over my shoulder.

I couldn't believe my bad luck. But really, why was I surprised? After all, it seemed lately like everything I touched turned to crap. The reverse Midas touch.

"Okay, sounds good," he said.

I stopped suddenly, remembering I needed to swing by my locker since I didn't have my lunch with me. Bobby thudded right into my back, causing my books to fly across the freshly waxed tile floor.

Peals of laughter echoed through the hallway.

"Geez, Bobby!" I hunched over, scrambling to grab my stuff.

He helped gather the rest. "Sorry," he muttered, a dark blush working its way across his cheeks. "I didn't mean to run into you."

I sighed deeply, taking the papers out of his hand. It wasn't his fault I was fighting with Andy, and I shouldn't be taking it out on him.

"It's okay. Thanks for helping." I ripped a corner off my notes and scribbled my home phone number down. "You can call me here later tonight. We'll figure out what we're going to do."

Bobby shot me a huge smile. "Sounds good." He spun around and took off, then quickly turned around to wave. "Bye!"

I headed to my locker, scouring the hallways for any sign of Andy. This was probably the worst fight we'd ever had in the history of our friendship. She hadn't called me all weekend— something we've never done before. Going that long without talking was starting to make me feel a bit unnerved.

This was bad.

While I knew I was right in being so pissed off at her annoying behavior, a part of me felt guilty. Maybe I should have talked rationally to her instead of alienating her. Well, the love spell would be wearing off soon enough in any case—only one more week to go—so maybe I'd be better off playing it by ear. After Andy snapped out of her funk, she'd more than likely want to talk.

I loaded my books into the locker and grabbed my lunch bag, my head swirling with all these thoughts.

I hadn't heard from Derek all weekend either (not that I'd truly expected to), and I wondered what he thought about our Friday non-date date. Did he decide I was too lame to hang out with anymore? Was he going to meet me at the library today after school?

Only one more week until the spell wore off the entire student body. Would Derek still want to hang out with me after that?

Maya, who was sitting alone in the cafeteria, was already chomping into her sandwich.

"Hey," I mumbled, plopping into the seat beside her. I opened my bag and took out my stuff, but my stomach was twisted into a pretzel. There was no way I was going to be able to hold anything down.

She glanced up. "Oh, hey. I take it you didn't hear from her?"

I shook my head, the backs of my eyes burning. No way was I going to cry over this. With an angry swipe, I rubbed my hand over my eyes.

"Sorry. I didn't, either. Maybe she's sick or something," she offered, her eyes sad. I could tell she didn't believe it, though.

"Yeah, maybe she's sick. Or working late. Or maybe she forgot. She always has an excuse for everything," I pointed out.

Maya sighed, then took a sip of her Coke. "This sucks. I hate when everyone fights. I just can't get away from it."

"Who's fighting?" Scott asked, coming up from behind us. He moved into the other available seat beside Maya, placed his lunch tray on the table, then leaned over and kissed her on the cheek.

I stood and gathered my stuff, suddenly not feeling like being social.

"Oh, no one. It's no biggie," I said. "You two have a good lunch, okay? I'm gonna head to anthropology class a little early and ask the teacher a question."

It was a total lie, of course, but they didn't seem to notice.

"Okay, talk to you later!" Maya said. She slipped her hand into Scott's, and I left them in happy-couple bliss.

I sludged throughout the rest of my day until art class. Most of the students were still all over Derek, but the buzz about him seemed to have hit a plateau, which was good. And the students

I'd paired up with each other this past weekend were ignoring Derek completely.

However, as usual by now, my art table was almost deserted as at least half the class crowded around Derek's table.

I glanced at him from across the room. When I caught his eye, he gave me a heart-stopping smile and a small wink.

So he didn't think I was a total loser at all. My shoulders relaxed. I attempted to focus my attention on the floral arrangement we had to sketch.

"Pssst." Kristy, a bleach-blond girl who usually spent most of the class time socializing, wiggled her fingers at Derek as a cutesy kind of hello.

He glanced up and gave her a polite smile, then tucked his head back down to focus on his drawing.

She giggled and picked up her chair, squeezing it beside him.

Mr. Bunch glared at her. "Kristy, what are you doing?"

"I needed a better perspective," she said, blinking her eyes rapidly in a pseudo-innocent look.

"Don't bother Derek—he's concentrating on his art," Mr. Bunch grumbled, but went back to his grading book.

"Derek," Kristy whispered, "I have a question for you."

"Yes?"

My ears perked. I tried to pretend I wasn't eavesdropping by faking a deep fascination with my art project, but I was so being nosy.

"I was wondering, who are you going to prom with?"

I swallowed hard and jerked my head up, my hand suddenly shaking. I put my pencil down, afraid I was going to drop it.

"'Cause if you don't have a date, I thought we could go together," she finished, beaming at him.

His face pinched up. "Well, actually . . ." He stalled off, his eyes glancing around the room, looking desperate for help.

"He's going with me," I blurted out.

His jaw dropped, as did mine. I closed my eyes and licked my lips, struggling with what to say next. "I mean, well, he's going—"

"Yup," Derek said. "I'm going with Felicity. Sorry."

Kristy pouted again, this time at Derek. "Oh. I see."

For the rest of the period she sulked in her seat as several students in the classroom griped about Derek's prom date. With me. I've never had so many people glare in my direction before.

I don't think I actually breathed the entire time. Once the bell rang I darted out of the classroom and went straight to the library, anxious to talk to Derek in private so I could apologize.

Long minutes passed before he finally made it. I sagged in relief. Even if he was mad at me for my blurting faux pas, I could at least get this chance to make things right. I'd put him in a situation where he had to agree with my wild, hare-brained idea so I wouldn't be publicly embarrassed.

"Look, about what I said in there—"

"About the prom thing—" he started, then stopped when he realized we were talking at the same time.

I chuckled nervously. "Go ahead."

If I let him speak first, maybe I could try to save face, based on whatever he said. I could even say I was buying him some time to figure out who he really wanted to ask. Yeah, that would work. I'd look like I was being helpful, instead of desperate.

"Well," Derek started again, "I'm glad you volunteered to be my date, because I was going to ask you anyway."

I stared at him. Was I hearing him right? "Eh?"

He grinned. "I was going to ask you if you wanted to go with me. I had a blast hanging out with you on Friday, and I figured a no-pressure prom would be a lot of fun. What do you say?"

This was, like, the best and worst day of my life.

What could I say but yes?

"Of course I'll go with you," I answered, hoping the big faketastic smile on my face looked enthusiastic enough, but not *too* enthusiastic. Just-friends enthusiastic. "It'll be a lot of fun."

"Great!" Derek unloaded his anatomy textbook and notebook from his backpack. "Let's start studying."

I chuckled weakly, cracking open my anthropology book. "Oh, absolutely."

Liar. Like I was going to be able to concentrate on anything but wondering how I was going to fake my way through prom as Derek's friend.

At my Monday night work meeting, I filled Janet in on the status of my love matches. Of course, I conveniently left out the part about how half the school was still in love with Derek, and that the others I'd paired so far were matched up in desperation and would probably regret their kisses in a week's time. And, just as fun, that the match for Andy was going so well that I'd now lost my best friend—who, by the way, was about to give up the V for a guy she barely knew and was basically drugged into thinking she was head over heels for.

All in all, an eventful week, none of which I admitted to.

After she synched my PDA and paid me for the week, I went

home and returned Bobby's call. Actually, *four* calls. Mom had written the messages on a purple Post-it note.

Bobby and I came up with a tentative date a few days from now to plan out our health project. That settled, he tried asking me if I wanted to play some poker afterward, but I managed to avoid setting a date for that and got off the phone as quickly as I could.

Then, I popped over to my PC and logged on to my blog, setting it to diary entry so Andy and Maya could not read it.

> *This has been such a weird day. Andy still isn't talking to me. I don't think it's fair that she's turned into a total flake and has totally abandoned herself to love, but she's mad at me for staying true to how I am.*

I chewed one of my fingernails, my stomach twitching a little. That was a bit harsh.

> *Okay, maybe it's not fair for me to blame her this much. I just hope things will get better when the spell wears off. I've made such a mess of this, but at least the matches I made are going strong.*

Oh, and the most important news: Derek asked me to prom!

Yeah, it was only as a "friend" thing, but still . . .

I posted the entry, closed the browser, and shut off the monitor, a sudden wave of depression hitting me. The best thing in the world had happened to me, and I couldn't share it with one of my best friends.

I picked up my phone and dialed Maya.

"Howdy," she said upon answering. "I was gonna call you later tonight when I finished all my homework. Did you read the assigned chapter in *The Scarlet Letter* yet?"

"Actually, I have way more important things to discuss," I said, pausing dramatically. "Something big happened to me today."

"Ooooh, what? Do tell. I'm intrigued."

"I. Have a date. For prom."

"Shut up!" She gasped. "Who are you going with?"

"Derek," I breathed.

"Omigod, are you two dating now? When did this happen? I guess Friday's date made a bigger impression than we realized, huh?"

I shifted the phone to rest between my ear and shoulder. "Well, unfortunately, we're going as 'friends.' He's looking forward to a no-pressure event."

"But after you have the perfect prom date with him, the day where he sees you as the girl of his dreams, you'll be dating him for sure. I just know it."

"You think so?"

"I *know* so."

Maya always knew what to say to make someone feel better. "Thank you. It means a lot to me that you believe in me. Especially with . . . well, you know what's going on."

She sighed. "Yeah, I know. I hope everything will straighten out soon. I'd love for all three of us to go to prom together as a group. Wouldn't that be awesome?"

"That's what I want too."

We said our good-byes, and I hung up. I slouched my way downstairs into the kitchen, where my mom was drying the dinner dishes. "Hey, Mom."

She glanced at me over her shoulder. "Oh, hi. What's up? How did your work meeting go tonight?"

"It was fine." I paused, trying to lend importance to my next words. "By the way, I've got a date for prom."

"Oh, are you going with Derek?"

How did she know? She never failed to surprise me.

"Actually, yes. I thought you'd be more . . . surprised."

"Why should I be?" She hung the dish towel up to dry. "He's a nice boy. You're a nice girl. I'm not surprised he likes you."

"It's not even like that, though. We're going as friends. We're just buds, you know." For some reason I had the impulse to wipe away her know-it-all tone.

She raised one eyebrow at me. "Hmm. If you say so."

I sighed. "I'm going to take a shower. I need to hit the hay."

"Sounds good." Out of nowhere, she kissed me on the cheek, a gesture she hasn't done in years, and tucked a strand of hair behind my ear. "We'll talk tomorrow about your prom dress."

My prom dress! I hadn't even thought of that. As I headed back up the stairs, I bit back a squeal and did a little boogie.

chapter ten

On Tuesday I came out of my trig class, starving for lunch. It was pizza day—luckily, not quadrangle school pizza, but real pepperoni pizza. Papa John's. I was practically drooling thinking about it.

When I got into the cafeteria, I grabbed a couple of slices and glanced around. Andy was sitting in the back corner with Tyler. They were whispering in each other's ears, and she had a huge smile across her face. Tyler grabbed the pair of drumsticks from behind him and started pounding out a rhythm on the lunch table.

My stomach clenched up. What should I do? Maya wasn't here to dole out any advice, since she had some kind of band practice she had to attend. Should I go over and speak to Andy, or wait for her BFF radar to pick up on my existence and signal me to come over?

Andy looked up, and our eyes connected. Her face looked sad at first. Then fire blazed in her gaze. She turned away from me and looked back at Tyler, pasting an overly fake smile on her face.

My mind quickly flashed back to Friday's bathroom conversation, and I worried if she and Tyler had had sex yet. I couldn't tell just by looking at her.

Tyler crammed a piece of pizza in his mouth and did the seafood stunt, and Andy laughed.

"Oh, Tyler!" she exclaimed loudly, swatting him on the arm. "You're such a goof!"

Fine. She wanted to be like that? Then I didn't care.

I parked it at a nearby table by myself, scarfing my pizza down fast. I didn't want to sit in there any longer than I had to.

Once I finished my food, I bolted to my locker. In the classroom to my right, I heard some hushed voices arguing.

"—don't think that's a good idea," a male voice said. "I have a game that Saturday. Plus, my parents would probably say no."

"Come on," a girl replied. "It's just one weekend. Can't you tell your parents you're staying with our family? And maybe miss just one game? For me?"

"But I haven't missed a game yet," he hedged.

Of course, by now I was dying of curiosity. With as much casualness as I could muster, I peeked into the room.

It was Jon and Megan, two seniors I'd matchmade a couple of weeks ago. I'd met Megan when I did a round of volunteering in the front office last year—she and I spent the whole time filing paperwork and giggling about the missed-day excuses people brought in.

I hadn't seen the two of them around since I sent the love e-mails. Maybe I should have been spending more time scoping their relationship out, though—by the sound of it, things weren't going well. I made a mental note to watch my other couples as well.

Megan leaned her back against the chalkboard, arms crossed as she stared at Jon.

He sighed heavily, rubbing a hand over his hair. "I have to think about it."

"Come on," she said, sidling up to him. "It'll be fun. My folks will leave us alone for practically the whole weekend."

Jon huffed, pushing away from the chalkboard. "I can't deal with this right now." He walked toward the door.

I jerked back toward the lockers, trying to make it look like I was searching for a friend in the hallway. Jon didn't even notice me as he stomped past.

After he left, I heard sniffling in the classroom. Megan was obviously distraught. Should I try to talk to her?

Tentatively, I tiptoed in.

Megan jerked her head over to look at me, then glanced away, wiping the tears off her cheeks.

"Sorry if I'm being nosy," I said to her, "but I heard you crying. Just wanted to make sure you were okay."

"Oh, hey, Felicity. I'm fine." Megan paused. "Except that he's such a jerk sometimes!" she blurted out.

"What's going on?"

"I tried to set up a weekend for us to get some alone time, but Jon doesn't want to go. He'd rather play golf than go with me on a getaway. I think he's just not into me anymore." She swallowed hard, then looked up at me with tear-rimmed eyes. "I don't know what to do! I'm trying to do something nice with him, but he won't see my side of things."

I wracked my brain for advice. "Maybe . . . you two just need a third party to help translate things."

"You mean, like a counselor?"

"Yes, exactly!" I latched on to the idea, which was growing bigger in my mind by the second. "Guys talk a different language than girls. You two just need someone to help you understand each other. Actually, I could even do it if you want." I lowered my voice. "I've helped a few of my friends out with love problems."

She sniffled. "That might work. But what if Jon doesn't go along with it?"

"I'm sure he will, if you ask him nicely."

After a moment Megan nodded resolutely. "Okay, I'll do it." She gave me a watery smile. "Thanks, Felicity."

"Great! Just call or e-mail me when you two are ready to talk."

We left the classroom, both of us in higher spirits than before. I drifted through the rest of my day, pleased as punch about how I helped Megan and Jon. Doing for others even helped me get my mind off my own personal drama with Andy. What dedication I had to this job, and to love! To helping my fellow teens!

Maybe they'd name a humanitarian award after me. The Felicity Walker Award for Caring Teens. Yeah, I liked the sound of that.

In the library I made a quick list of resources. After all, if I was going to give love advice, I should at least catch up on the latest trends.

1. TiVo the following shows: *Maury, Dr. Phil, Oprah,* and *Judge Judy.*

Yeah, I know *Judge Judy* isn't a counseling show, but she keeps a tight rein on her courtroom. I could learn a thing or two from her.

2. Check out some books from the library on dating and communication.
3. Ask a guy for advice on a guy's perspective of life?

Speaking of guys . . . Derek popped up in the library.

I gave him my biggest, most charming smile. "Well, you're here just in time. I need some help."

His eyebrow rose. "Oh, really? With what?"

"I need a crash course on how to think like a guy, and you're just the one to do it."

Derek smirked. "Oh, is that right? You need my help?"

"Yup. I'm trying to help a young couple in love save their relationship."

"How very selfless of you." His eyes sparkled as he shook his head at me.

"Yeah, it's my way of giving a little back." I laughed, trying to calm the flutter in my stomach. He was just so. Freaking. Hot.

"Seriously, though, it's not that huge a deal. They're just having problems understanding each other. I can help him understand girls, but it's the whole 'guy' thing I'm not fully up on." I gave him a meaningful look. "Yet."

Derek leaned back in his seat. "So, what do you need to know?"

"Oh God, where to begin? There are so many things confusing about your gender," I said. "For starters, what's with guys' fascination with boobs?"

His jaw dropped.

My stomach clenched in response when I realized what I'd blurted out. Oh. My. God. *What is wrong with me?*

"Bad place to start, huh?" A flush rose over my cheeks.

"Just . . . surprising," he said, blinking. "I wasn't expecting that."

I shrugged as casually as I could muster, trying to brush off my embarrassment. Bravely trying to rescue the conversation, I continued on. "Okay, scratch that question," I said. "Here's a new one. Why do guys get obsessive about certain things, then mad if a girl isn't on the same level as him?"

"Like what?"

I studied him, trying to figure out a good example without

giving away too much of the situation between Jon and Megan. My eyes caught hold of his football jersey.

"Let's say . . . a guy loves football with all his heart," I started. "He watches every game of his favorite team, signs up to play fantasy football, even sleeps with the ball—"

Derek rolled his eyes, holding his hands up for me to stop. "Okay, I get your point."

I laughed. "Anyway, why does he get ticked off if the girl doesn't care about it as much as he does?"

Derek thought for a moment. "Well, some guys find their identities through activities. It makes us who we are, so if a girl doesn't 'get' these activities, we think she doesn't 'get' us." He shrugged. "I like football, but not to the point of obsession. Now boobs, on the other hand . . ." He leaned forward, then waggled his eyebrows exaggeratedly.

I reached across the table and smacked his arm, then crossed my arms over my chest and swallowed hard. I was suddenly very aware of my own rather small girl parts.

"Ha, ha. Very funny."

"Come on," he said, "I'm just teasing. You brought it up. I only said that to make you laugh." His mouth curled into a very sexy smile.

I stared at his lower lip. What I'd give to kiss him, just once. A real, honest-to-God kiss, where he didn't want to be "just friends" with me.

Maybe it could happen at prom.

Right. And maybe I'd suddenly grow a C-cup overnight.

"So," I said, desperate to get my mind off my small chest, "what else do you think I should know about guys?"

"Well, let me see." Derek scratched his chin. "We do care about how we look, regardless of what we say."

"Mm-hmm."

He looked me straight in the eyes. "And we're often too shy to tell a girl what we're feeling."

My heart jumped to my throat. "Oh?" I croaked out. Was he trying to tell me something? *Pleasepleasepleaseplease?*

He nodded. "And sometimes—"

"Oh, Derek!" a loud voice said with a giggle. "What a surprise. I didn't know you were here."

He whipped around, and I groaned at the sight of Mallory, my nemesis. Great. Way to ruin a magic moment.

She sidled up to the table and thunked down in the seat beside him. "This is *such* a coincidence. I just came here to study. Imagine meeting you here."

He smiled. "Yeah, I come here to study too."

Was that smile for real? He looked real. Could Derek possibly like *Mallory*?

I squinted, studying her too-shocked face. Wait, she *knew* he was here, the liar! She must have been following him. I felt like our own private sanctuary was now violated. Was no place sacred anymore?

"Mallory," I said, suddenly feeling quite catty, "it *is* quite a shock. I didn't know you even knew where the library was."

She shot me a sugary smile. "I can see why you'd think that. But *I* usually do well enough in my classes that I don't need to come here."

Ouch. Touché.

I gathered up my stuff. I'd had enough of her face and attitude to last me for a lifetime. "I'll see you later, Derek."

"Oh, okay. Bye!" He gave me a big grin.

I walked away from him, back straight and head held high, like I didn't have a care in the world. Yeah, who was the liar now?

chapter eleven

Later that night I held a large, neon blue satin monstrosity against my figure and stared at my reflection in the store mirror, groaning.

"It has a butt bow. For God's sakes, Mom, a butt bow!"

Was she really so clueless that she didn't realize the heinousness of this dress?

Mom laughed. "Fine. Go put it back and find something else. But no high leg slits or too much cleavage showing."

I caught her eye in the mirror. "Right. As if I need to worry about that."

I returned the dress to the rack, wishing I could run out back and burn it, just to save some other girl from having to see it.

"Felicity?" a familiar voice asked from behind me.

I spun around to find Andy's mom at the next rack over.

"Oh, it *is* you," she said. "Hi!" She came over and gave me a big hug. At least she was still cool with me.

Andy watched us from behind the rack a few feet away, a deep frown on her face. "What are you here for?"

I swallowed, feeling nervous for some reason. I hadn't gotten a chance to tell her I was going to prom with Derek.

Well, it wasn't like she'd tried to talk to me, either. I wondered if she was here picking out a prom dress.

"I'm getting a dress," I finally said.

"Oh. Yeah, me too." Andy tucked her head back down and continued flipping through the rack.

Andy's mom looked back and forth between us. "Is something going on here?"

God, this was terrible. I felt like I was going to puke. Maybe I should just apologize. Was it really worth it for us to be so distant because of a guy?

She might even appreciate me making the first move.

I opened my mouth to speak.

"Mom, we need to get going," Andy said, turning away from

me. "I don't see any dresses here I like." She moved toward the front of the store.

Her mom shot me a sympathetic glance. "Bye, Felicity. See you later." She followed Andy out.

I sighed, all enthusiasm for prom dress hunting suddenly gone. Conflicting emotions poured over me—anger at Andy's continued stubbornness, guilt because I'd pissed her off to the point where we weren't speaking, loneliness because I wasn't close to one of my best friends anymore.

Would we ever be close again?

Mom popped up beside me, holding a long black dress covered in sequins. "How about this?"

I laughed. I couldn't help myself. "I'd look like Grandma in that."

She raised an eyebrow at me, about to say something, then glanced back at the dress. "Hmm. Yeah, I guess the shoulder pads are a bit excessive, huh?"

I nodded, my eyes sweeping the boutique. A sleek red gown caught my eye. I ran to it and held it up for scrutiny. It had two thin spaghetti straps on one side and a sophisticated side slit.

"Oh, Mom," I breathed. "I love it."

She studied it, her eyebrows pinched together in the middle of her forehead. "That slit looks a little high."

"Can I try it on? Please?"

After a long moment, she nodded. I dashed to the dressing room, then tugged my clothes off and slipped into it.

It fit like a dream.

I glanced at myself in the mirror. The dress was *made* for me. There was no way Derek could stay "just friends" if he saw it. It screamed sexy and glamorous.

"Well, come out!" Mom hollered. "I want to see it."

I stepped outside, holding my breath.

"Oh, it's gorgeous," she breathed. Tears welled in her eyes. "Honey, I can't believe how beautiful you look."

My throat closed up. As crazy as my mom could be, she sometimes knew just the right thing to say.

"Thanks."

"How much is it?" she asked.

Crap. I'd gotten so excited about it, I forgot to look at the price.

I glanced at the tag, the wind whooshing out of my lungs. "Two hundred and fifty dollars."

Mom coughed delicately. "Well, that may be outside your budget. Maybe we can find one like it for cheaper."

That was so not going to happen, and we both knew it.

I sagged my way back to the dressing room and changed into my boring clothes. Disappointment oozed from every pore of my skin. I wanted that dress so badly—and I wanted Derek to see me looking better than I've ever looked before.

I wanted him to see me as beautiful. Because if he thought of me as more than just a friend, I could be one step closer to winning his heart.

"So," Bobby said, eyeballing me, "do you have a date for prom?" He shifted in the chair at my kitchen table.

We'd decided to get together after school on Wednesday to work on our health class project. I figured it was easier to just have him meet me at home. I certainly wasn't going to meet him at the library, where Derek might see us and get the wrong idea. And I didn't really want to go over to his house, either.

I nodded enthusiastically in response to Bobby's question, thankful I wasn't available. What an awkward spot that would have been. Another minor crisis averted, thanks to my quick thinking. "Yup. I'm going with Derek Peterson."

His shoulders slumped. "Oh, I see." He chewed on the end of his pencil, staring at his notebook. "Just curious. I haven't gotten around to asking anyone yet."

"I'm sure you'll find someone."

"Yeah."

He looked so dejected, I felt a bit bad for him.

"Hey," I said in a cheerful voice, "let's figure out something really funny to do for our project. Have any ideas?"

He flipped to a page. "I already started thinking about it. Here are a few things I came up with."

I scanned the paper. Most of the ideas on the list were dumb, like making an instructional video or a health pamphlet, but one caught my eye.

"A game. That could be really fun."

Bobby perked up. "You think so?"

"Sure." My brain was going now. "We could do something to mimic the board game Life. Or like Monopoly. It could be really, really funny."

We worked hard for the next hour, bouncing ideas off each other. I had to admit, Bobby Blowhard wasn't actually that bad. He came off as a total dork in school, but when he wasn't around other people and trying too hard to impress everyone, he was actually pretty decent to be around.

After he left I threw my books upstairs and came down to help Mom with dinner. She was making meatloaf, my absolute favorite. My lovely brother was coming over for a midweek dinner, probably so he could filch some leftovers to take home.

"So," Mom said, cracking two eggs into the bowl of thawed meat, "I haven't seen Andy around lately. Everything okay?"

I shrugged, rinsing some potatoes off in the sink. "I guess. We're just fighting. No biggie."

"Well, I'm sorry to hear that." Mom ground the mixture in the bowl, then poured in some milk. "I saw her at the store last night with her mom. She seemed pretty mad, so I didn't say anything."

My throat clogged up. I grabbed a knife, parked myself at the table, and focused on skinning the potatoes.

"We haven't talked in days," I said, trying to keep my tone even. "She's gone boy crazy, and it's come between us." I sucked in a quick breath. "It's just not fair. She and I are supposed to be closer than that."

"It's hard when people start getting serious with a guy. It can make the other person feel left out. Maybe Andy felt a bit left out because of your attention to your new job, so she turned to her boyfriend."

I paused. I hadn't really thought of that before, but it was true. Since taking the job, I'd been obsessed with matchmaking . . . and repairing the effects of it.

And that included the Derek disaster.

Maybe Andy wasn't just mad about the cell phone incident, but about my distance as well. How odd that we could possibly be feeling the same emotions and not realize it.

I grinned. "You're a pretty smart cookie, Mom."

"Well, your dad seems to think so," she said, chuckling. She scooped the meatloaf into two glass pans, then popped them in the oven.

When I finished skinning the potatoes, I ran upstairs to my computer and turned on my monitor. I hopped into e-mail and composed a new message.

To: burgergirl@speedymail.com

From: dramaqueenie@emailmama.com

Subject: Sorry

Hey, it's me. Sry things R weird. Job's been stressful, and I know UR tight with Tyler. Also sry 4 hanging up UR cell.

That was not cool. :(

Hope we can talk soon. Miss you!

♥

Fel

There. I sent the e-mail and shut down my PC, feeling better than I had in days. At least I'd tried.

I studied for my trig test for an hour or so. Needing a break, I grabbed my PDA and scoured through my profiles so I could get more people out of love with Derek and in love with each other. I found another ten or so matches, so I made them and closed out of the profile document.

After that, I headed downstairs. It was finally dinnertime, and I was starving. The delicious scent of meatloaf had wafted up to my room.

I glanced around the kitchen, which was empty except for my mom. "Where's Rob?"

"He called my cell while you were upstairs. He can't make it tonight. Something about having to hang at the police station while some other officers are out."

"Well, I guess that's more meatloaf for me," I joked.

"I don't think so. I'm starving," my dad said, coming up behind me. I was surprised to see him home so early in the evening on a weekday. Workaholic and all that.

I gave him a hug. "Dad, I found the most gorgeous prom dress at the mall, but it was so expensive."

Mom swatted my butt with the hand towel. "Well, you're a working woman now. Save up that money! You can get it in no time."

"But I don't know if I'll be able to save that much in time," I said, my voice veering on the edge of whiny. "Prom's only a few weeks away."

"Your mom's right," Dad replied. "You can squirrel away enough money if you try. Or, if not that one, another that's just as nice."

Ugh. No sympathy from the parents at all. What a hard life I led.

Thursday morning before English class I searched for Andy in the hall and at her locker, but didn't see her. Nor had I heard back from her yesterday. Maybe she'd blocked me from her address book and wouldn't respond to my e-mails anymore. Great.

In a surly mood, I shuffled to my locker and dumped my backpack inside, grabbing whatever crap I needed for my next class.

"I heard the funniest rumor," a shrill voice said from behind me.

I whipped around to see Mallory talking to her friends Jordan and Carrie. They were all staring at me.

Double great. What a way to make a day even better—being taunted by the biggest jerk in school.

Jordan, chomping on a big wad of gum, replied to Mallory, "What did you hear? I wanna know!"

Mallory tucked a strand of golden blond hair behind her ear and said dramatically, "I heard Derek and Felicity are going to prom together. I never would have imagined it."

"Gee," I said, blinking as innocently as possible. "You know what *I* can't imagine? Why you're so concerned with what's going on in my life. Is yours just a little too boring right now? Or maybe you just don't have a date of your own for prom?"

She sneered. "Of course I have a date. I just wondered what the full story is. The only reason a guy would take *you* to prom is because he felt sorry for you, or because he was trapped into doing it." She tilted her head sideways and pursed her lips at me.

I felt a thud in my chest as my heart slammed hard. She didn't know how accurate that barb was.

"So," Mallory continued in a singsong voice, "I wonder which option applies here. Because you and I both know you're definitely not in his crowd."

"And again," I ground out through gritted teeth, "I wonder why you care so much."

My stomach lurched with irritation at being caught in yet another catfight with her. I was tired of her and her big mouth.

Mallory leaned in close to her friends and whispered, their loud giggles drifting.

Geez. Could she be more rude?

I shook my head in disgust, then darted away from my locker, glad to take the opportunity to escape. I tucked my head down and stared at the floor, slamming right into a huge back.

"Watch it," the guy snapped. I recognized him, though I didn't know his name. A football jock, hanging with the other cool guys.

"Sorry," I mumbled.

His friends stopped talking and stared at me.

"She almost knocked you over, puss," one guy said to the jock, his voice echoing down the hallway. Not an easy feat, given how many people were talking as they were walking to class.

Another guy with spiky brown hair eyed me. "Maybe you should try out for the team next year. You're pretty thick."

The guys started laughing hard.

A surge of heat flooded my cheeks. What an ass. This was quickly turning into one of those days I wished I could undo. Or go back to bed and stay there forever.

Derek came from behind them and slipped into the group. He looked superhot today in a dark blue shirt and jeans that fit him perfectly.

Please don't let them humiliate me in front of him, I silently prayed.

"Hey," he said, slapping one guy on the back. "How ya doing?"

Everyone's attention snapped to Derek, and the guys beamed at him, inching closer. I bit back a laugh. I hadn't thought about it, but even Derek's friends were affected by my matchmaking error. For a few more days, anyway.

"Hey, man," the spiky-haired guy said. "We waited for you so we could walk with you to class."

"Cool," Derek said. He noticed me standing in the group and shot me a smile. "Hey, Felicity. What's going on?"

My heart raced, and I swallowed.

"Nothing," I blurted out.

After all, what could I say? *Hey, Derek, I think you're a great guy, but your so-called friends made me feel like a fat, clumsy pig.*

"Oh, *hi*, Derek," Mallory said from behind me, sliding up to Derek's side in her teeny, tiny skirt.

My cue to leave. No way did I want to get into yet another fight with her when I was still recouping from the earlier one.

"Talk to you later," I said to Derek.

"Oh, okay. See ya!" He waved at me, then turned his attention back to Mallory and the rest of the group.

I took off down the hall to my next class, aware of how awkward I was, especially next to Mallory. Maybe she was right. As much as I was madly in love with him, as nice as he was to me, I didn't fit in with his group.

Not that I was a social outcast or anything. I had friends, and I got along with most everybody. But the jocks—and Mallory's fluffball friends, who usually hung all over those guys like a bad case of herpes—totally excluded me.

What bitter irony that Derek was in with them. Especially since he never treated me like an outsider.

I felt like he and I were Romeo and Juliet—destined to be kept apart because of awful circumstances and even more awful people.

It was just like Shakespeare. Well, other than the fact that Romeo actually loved Juliet back.

I stepped into English class and sat down, waiting for Maya to show up. I wished I could drown my sorrows in a pint of Ben and Jerry's. If ever an ice cream fix was needed, it was right now. Never had rocky road seemed more applicable to my life.

chapter twelve

"Hey," Andy said to me later that morning, nudging me in the back with her arm.

Startled, I spun around, slamming my locker closed.

"Oh, hi," I said as casually as possible, heart thudding in nervousness. I'd been starting to think she was going to ignore me forever.

"I got your e-mail," she said. "Thanks."

I nodded slowly, relief seeping through my limbs. It seemed we were making up, finally.

"Well, I feel bad things are so awful between us." I fixed my eyes on the hallway's speckled white tile floor. "I'm really sorry about what I did, Andy. I didn't mean to piss you off so badly." I glanced up at her.

"It's okay." She shrugged, giving a half smile. "Anyway, Tyler's busy during lunch. Maybe we can sit together and catch up."

Not the friendliest offer in the world, but at this point, I'd take it. "Sure."

We headed to health class together, carrying our stuff.

"You ready for our quiz?" I asked.

Andy nodded, twiddling a strand of hair with her free hand.

"It took me forever to get through that last chapter. It was massive, and so gross." I shuddered. "Those STD photos are nasty. So, what did you think about it?"

"Hmm? Oh, yeah, definitely a hard one to read." Andy glanced away and stepped into the classroom.

I got the distinct feeling she hadn't read the material. I parked myself in the seat beside her, then leaned over. "You sure you're all ready? Did you study last night?"

She pursed her lips. "Of course. Everything's fine."

Yup. She was so lying.

Andy is quite possibly the worst liar in the world, other than me. If they wrote a book on how to tell if someone is lying, it could be filled with the two of us. Andy always twitches her eyes funny and purses her lips in the same way when she's telling a big fat whopper.

I don't know what my giveaway tics are, but I'm sure I have them too.

I shook my head. "Okay, then." If she wasn't up for talking about it, I guess I wasn't going to force the issue.

Besides, if Tyler was at the root of the problem, I could see why she was hesitant to talk to me. I bet she'd spent every waking moment with him since our fight and hadn't studied at all. That was so not like her.

My stomach sank. This wouldn't have happened if I'd insisted we study together, like we normally do.

Or if I hadn't matched her with "babe" in the first place.

The quiz went by fast. Well, at least for me. Luckily, I'd squeezed in some study time in between staring at Derek under my eyelashes in the library.

As I wrote my answers, I kept sneaking peeks at Andy, watching her struggle. A part of me was tempted to help her, but I knew better. My luck, I'd get busted and thrown out of school for cheating.

The class bell rang. It was time to eat, thank God.

After telling Andy I'd meet her in the cafeteria in a few minutes, I grabbed my brown paper bag from my locker, then ran to the cafeteria as casually and coolly as possible. I'm sure I looked like a total dork who couldn't *wait* to eat her PB&J sandwich, but I didn't care. I needed to talk to Andy.

She was sitting at the corner table, our usual spot, with her iPod in her hand and her earbuds in her ears. No Tyler, just as she promised. Maya and Scott were already there, digging into their food.

I waved eagerly at the three of them and wove my way through scads of hungry freshmen to get to our table.

"Hey," I said, sitting on Andy's left side.

Maya gave me a quick, encouraging smile, then turned to talk to Scott. She knew Andy and I needed to have some talk time. I made a mental note to give her a big thank-you hug later.

Andy turned off her iPod and jammed it into her jeans pocket. "Hey, how's it been going, anyway?"

"Oh, fine." *Act casual.* "I've just been crazy busy the last few days, with work and school and all. You?"

"I've been busy too. Tyler and I are going to prom together, of course, so we're trying to figure out what to wear. I found a gorgeous gown, but it's pink, and Tyler doesn't want to wear a pink tie and cummerbund. But we're together, so of course we have to match, so I didn't buy that one. Anyway, the dress saga continues." She sighed dramatically, her eyes sliding to mine. "Soooo, when I saw you at the store a couple of nights ago . . . what's going on?"

I shot her a casual smile. "Oh, not much. I'm just going to prom. With Derek."

Her jaw dropped open, and she squealed. "Omigod, seriously?"

I nodded like an idiot, wearing a big doofy grin. "Yeah. But don't get too excited. We're only going as friends." I dropped my voice. "I just need to wear the absolute perfect dress."

That red one I saw in the store would be fabulous, if I could find a way to afford it. I'd only been a cupid for a couple of months, so I wasn't exactly rolling in the dough. Maybe I could put my paychecks aside and hold off on getting a cell phone, which I still hadn't managed to buy yet.

Andy squinted and tilted her head to the side, rubbing her chin. "Yeah, you need to look so hot that Derek can't resist you. He'll fall head over heels when he sees you."

"That's what Maya said. Obviously, I agree with that plan." My heart warmed as I shot Andy a big smile. Things felt like normal again, thank God. Even those few days of not being close were way too many.

I cleared my throat. "I just wanted to say, I'm sorry again about everything that happened."

"I know. It's fine. Let's just drop it, 'kay?"

"Sure thing." At this point I was so relieved to be on talking terms with her again, I would have promised just about anything. It didn't even matter that she never apologized to me.

"So, you wanna come over Friday night for a TGIF sleepover?" Andy asked. "I already asked Maya, and she's in. Ohhhh," she said in a breathy tone, "I can tell you the latest about Tyler and me."

"Sounds good." Not that I wanted to hear how much the two of them loved each other and probably wished upon a star every night for eternal happiness, but I could give a little. After all, people in love do bizarre things, right?

Like going to prom with someone just as a friend, in the small, desperate chance of making a romantic connection.

I guess I couldn't really be irritated with Andy. After all, at least Tyler returned her feelings.

"So," I said to Derek as casually as possible at our usual after-school meeting spot in the library, "what colors are you wearing to prom? I figured we could coordinate." I chewed more bite marks on the end of my pencil.

Desperate to push down my noninnocent thoughts about

how utterly attractive Derek looked today in his jersey and jeans, I figured I'd distract myself with my new favorite topic. Prom madness.

He looked at me with wide eyes, faking confusion. "I thought I'd wear black and white. You know, regular tux colors."

"Hardy har." I pointed my pencil at him. "You just don't understand girls. We put a lot of thought into this."

"Guys don't care about junk like that. So, Little Miss Prom Planner, what do *you* think?" He tapped his lower lip with his index finger. "Should I wear my azure blue vest? Oh, but what if I can't find the right shade of socks to match? The horror!"

I squinted at him in a mock glare. "Oh, a funny guy, eh? How'd you get so smart?"

"With a family as big as mine, you got to get attention somehow."

Oh, he'd never have to worry about that with me. I hung on his every word. During the past almost two weeks of hanging out, I'd gotten to know him better. Derek wasn't just a supreme hottie—he was smart and funny too. The ultimate combination.

I shook my head, amazed at how drooly I sounded to myself. *Loser.* No wonder Mallory thought I was a total dork.

I needed to stop feeling so desperate. Keeping cool was the best strategy. Derek was trying to avoid crazy people, which was why he'd been meeting me in the library in between school and practice.

This was probably the last time we'd hang out like this. Because starting on Monday, he wouldn't need to hide out in the library anymore. The spell would be over, so Derek could stop having to find peace of mind in here with me. Great.

I tried to ignore the sinking feeling in my stomach. "Anyway, it's not a big deal about the prom colors. We can figure it out later." I glanced at my watch. "Oh, crap, I gotta go. I'm meeting Andy and Maya in a half hour."

The three of us, sans guys, were going to eat Chinese buffet at The Paper Lantern. I couldn't wait to pig out on General Tso's chicken, my absolute fave. But I still had to swing by my house to pack my clothes for tonight's sleepover, which meant I had to cut my library time with Derek short.

"Have fun! I'm gonna stay and finish my homework." Derek smiled, melting me into a little puddle of longing.

God, what I'd give to have him smile at me like that with more than just friendship on his mind.

The longer this whole saga went on, the more my heart ached.

Wanting to be in a relationship and being sooooooo close, but no cigar, totally sucked.

I hightailed it out of the library, ran home to pack, and met Andy and Maya in the nick of time, pulling into The Paper Lantern's parking lot with two minutes to spare. I ruled.

"Hey, girls," I said after I got inside the building. I slid into the red leather booth.

Maya gave me a big hug, whispering in my ear, "I think everything's okay now with Andy."

I squeezed her back. "Thank you so much," I replied, tears stinging the back of my eyes. She'd truly been a rock during all this drama.

Over the next two hours Andy, Maya, and I yapped like everything was back to normal. Andy talked about her dates with Tyler, but to her credit, she asked how things were going with Maya and Scott and about what was going on with me, too.

I dished about my overwhelming feelings for Derek, desperate to pick their collective brain about how to handle it.

"You need to play it cool," Andy said after chewing a mouthful of pork fried rice. She waved the chopsticks in the air as she talked. "You don't wanna freak him out like the school has with that superweird obsession going on."

"You are so right. Luckily, that'll go away on Monday," I said, nodding in agreement.

Maya, in the middle of drinking her Pepsi, stopped mid-sip, her eyes pinning me. "What do you mean? What's happening on Monday?"

Oh, crap.

Me and my big mouth.

chapter thirteen

Ever tried to will your brain to think fast on command? Doesn't work.

I stared at Maya, trying to come up with something clever to cover my tracks. "Um, well . . ."

Yeah, great start, Felicity.

Andy raised an eyebrow. "Is there something you know that you're not telling us?"

"No. It's just that . . . I'm planning to let more people at school know Derek and I are going to prom on Monday, so they'll stop hounding him." Whew. Close call.

"Oh, okay," Maya said, nodding her head. "Good idea."

"Yeah, I guess that makes sense. I'll try to help with that too." Andy chomped down on another bite of rice.

I dragged in several slow, deep breaths to calm my heart rate. I really needed to be more careful about the cupid thing. One little slipup like this could cost me my job. And maybe next time I wouldn't be able to come up with a cover-up at all.

Conversation diverted, we finished up our food and headed to Andy's house, parking ourselves inside her room.

I was dying of curiosity and couldn't wait anymore. "So," I said as carefully as possible, "are you and Tyler getting any ... closer?"

"He's so great," she gushed, grabbing a comb from her dresser and raking it through her hair. "We cut class the other day just to sit and talk in his car. He said he loves me so much."

Maya shot me a quick look of concern, then neutralized her face. "That's sweet that he cares so much about you," she said, plopping down on the floor and tucking her feet under her legs. "You two look adorable together."

"Yeah, that's really nice." I knew I sounded awkward, but I wasn't too thrilled to hear her admit to cutting classes. But calling her out on it would have been the worst thing to do. She and I were finally getting our friendship back, and I didn't need to blow it by telling her she was acting stupid.

"We're definitely ready to take our love to the next level," she said, braiding her hair into two thick plaits and wrapping a ponytail holder around the ends. "Tyler's band is playing at a party tomorrow night. I think it'll happen right after that."

"*It?*" I asked, afraid to have her clarify, but wanting to make sure I understood. I fiddled with the ends of my own hair, trying to appear calm and rational and totally nonjudgmental so Andy wouldn't get mad at me.

"*It.* You know. Sex." She dug into her drawer, pulling out her pajama pants.

Maya sucked in a quick breath. "Wow."

"Well, I hope everything works out the way it's supposed to," I said. "And that you two are . . . safe and careful." There, that was generic and supportive sounding. I mentally patted my own back.

"Thanks, you guys. And don't worry, we'll use condoms." Andy beamed at me. "I'm glad we're not fighting anymore, Felicity."

For once I could tell her the straight-out truth. "Me too. So, whose party is it?"

"Jenny's. Hey, do you two wanna come with me? She told me to bring some friends."

I weighed the options. Sit at home and worry about Andy making hasty, spell-induced choices, or go and have the chance to maybe talk her out of it. Plus, I could do some matchmaking research while I was there. A total no-brainer.

"I'm there," I answered.

"Want a beer?" a wasted jock said from behind me. His words slurred as he sloshed a red plastic cup toward my face. He smiled as he looked me over, his eyes watery and unfocused. "You look thirsty."

As he moved, light amber liquid jumped over the side of the cup, splashing onto the carpet.

Luckily, I dodged out of the way, preventing the beer from splashing onto my clothes. My mom would kill me if she thought I was at a drinking party, and coming home smelling like a brewery was a surefire way to get locked up in my room forever.

"Um, no thanks." I held up the full cup of soda in my hand. "I'm good."

I turned away from him and rolled my eyes in disgust. If anyone needed a health class list of nondrinking activities to do at a party, that guy did.

Maybe I should recommend a few ideas to him. Mrs. Cahill would be so proud.

"Whatever." The drunk guy ambled across the living room, squeezing through the crowds, presumably headed out back to where Tyler's band was playing.

I mean "playing" in the loosest sense of the word, of course. Now that I'd actually had a chance to hear them, I quickly realized how much I disliked being subjected to cover after cover of whiny emo songs.

Andy, of course, ate it up. She'd insisted on all of us grabbing lawn chairs and parking right in front of the band. But after hearing five songs of Tyler's overenthusiastic drumming, I'd taken a break from the music to grab another soda.

I think Maya and Scott were happy I did so, because they'd hightailed it after me. We'd been people-watching in the house for the last several minutes, checking out the hookups . . . and giggling at the guys who were being denied.

"Okay, that guy's totally going to be ditched by that girl he's talking to in less than five minutes," I said, pointing toward a couple in the corner of the room. "Just watch."

Scott laughed. "You're probably right. He already spilled his beer all over her pants. That's a great way to win a girl over."

"Yeah, you know that would work for me," Maya said with a snort. She took a sip of her soda.

The guy in question, a sophomore at our school who apparently did not know how to hold his alcohol, was gawking with bleary eyes at his date's chest, like he wanted to grab hold and never let go. He was a good six inches shorter than she was, so his gaze hadn't risen above her chest more than once or twice as he'd rambled on and on.

Poor girl. That had to be no fun. Not that I'd ever had anyone leer at me like that, but I could just imagine the awkwardness. Bobby was bad enough with the hard-core flirting, but at least he'd never blatantly stared at my boobs.

"So," the guy said in a loud voice that carried to our side of the room, "what're you doin' later tonight?" He pressed the palm of his free hand on the living room wall behind her, pinning her in.

The girl noticed where he was staring and glared at him, crossing her arms in front of her. She mumbled something, glancing around the room.

"Aw, come on," I heard him groan. "Who cares where they are? I'm right here."

"Aaaaand here's where she makes her grand exit," I said, sitting back triumphantly. "She's looking for an escape right now."

"Good call," Maya said, snickering. "She's desperate to get away."

The girl gestured as she talked, then ducked under his arm and took off running up the stairs.

Now alone, the guy sulked off toward the kitchen. Likely, to refill his beer cup . . . again. Because that was a great idea.

I did not envy the hangover he was going to have tomorrow.

"Well, that was fun. I'm gonna go find Andy," I said to Maya.

She nodded, slipping her hand into Scott's. "I think we're gonna stay in here," she said. "It's much nicer."

I gave her a quick hug, then stepped outside. Dusk was starting to fall, so I wanted to find her before it got too dark to see. I didn't recognize some of the people here, but most were from our school.

Jenny had a huuuuuge house. One of the most popular girls in our school, she was always throwing parties when her parents were out of town—not that I'd been invited before, but I'd heard all about them. Her backyard stretched on for over an acre. Which was good . . . and bad, considering how many red plastic cups littered the lawn. She was gonna have a fun time cleaning up the mess tomorrow.

I just hoped her parents, who weren't due back from their vacay in Aruba until tomorrow night, didn't decide to return home early.

I noticed Mike, a guy in my American history class, sitting all by himself on a lawn chair. He was busy pulling handfuls of grass out of the ground. Maybe I needed to give him something else to occupy his time. Like . . . a new love match!

I looked through the crowd until I found a candidate for him. Wendy, a girl I knew from anthropology, was standing against the fence with a couple of her friends, checking her watch every minute or so and gripping her cup in her other hand. She looked utterly bored too. That was one thing they had in common, anyway.

I grabbed my PDA and sent them love messages. Not ten seconds later, both of them grabbed their cell phones and flipped them open, nearly simultaneously. Then their eyes glazed over and they rubbed their chests.

Wendy handed her cup to her friend and wove through the crowd to Mike.

"Hey," she said, licking her upper lip. She gave him a wink.

"Hey yourself," he answered back, staring at her mouth. "Whatcha up to?"

"Not much."

Next thing I knew, she was perched on his lap in his chair, running her fingers through his hair as they kissed.

Ah, another blissful match made. Hopefully, they wouldn't go too crazy with the public displays of affection . . . or private. The last thing I needed was to be responsible for a wave of teen pregnancies during the next nine months.

On that sobering note I put my LoveLine 3000 away. Time to do what I'd come outside for—find Andy.

I spotted her near the front, still in her lawn chair where I'd left her, and made my way to her side.

"Hey," I said loudly.

"Oh, hi!" she yelled back over the sound of the music. "I'm glad you made it back. Did you bring me a Cherry Coke?"

I smacked my forehead. "I'm sorry. I completely forgot—some idiot was getting on my nerves and almost spilled beer on me. I'll go grab it."

She rose from the lawn chair. "Nah, it's okay. I'll get it. Here, save my seat."

I sank into the chair, watching Tyler spin his drumsticks as he jammed into another drum flourish. I didn't remember this particular song having a percussion solo, but hey, what did I know?

"Tyler's rockin' that drum set, huh," a husky voice said in my ear, sending goosebumps across my skin.

I glanced up to see Derek beaming at me.

"I didn't know you were going to be here," I said, standing up. My eyes soaked in the sight of him.

"I didn't, either. Just decided to come at the last minute. I couldn't miss Tyler's big gig, you know."

I laughed, glancing at the band. "So, what do you think of them?"

He shrugged. "Not too bad."

"Not too good, either," I joked.

His teeth sparkled in the dusky light. "I wasn't going to be the one to say that."

Someone pushed by and jostled Derek into me. He grabbed my arm to steady himself, and before I realized what I was doing, I boldly pressed up against him, taking advantage of the moment.

We froze, me staring up into those beautiful eyes of his. I felt like I was drowning.

I saw him swallow, and he leaned his face closer down to mine, his mouth mere inches away. "Felicity, do you—"

"Derek!" some guy said, popping up from nowhere. "Hey, man, want a drink?"

I groaned as Derek pulled away and turned his attention to the intruder. Why was it we couldn't get more than a few sentences into a conversation without someone interrupting us?

Derek nodded. "Um, sure." When the guy took off, Derek shrugged at me. "Who am I to pass up a free butler, right?"

I laughed. "If I'd known you would be here, I would have loaned you mine. Jeeves does so love to serve."

He raised an eyebrow at me, chuckling. "How thoughtful of you."

The song ended. Tyler's voice rang through the speakers. "Thank you! We're gonna take a quick break."

The lead guitarist added, "We'll be back in a little bit, after the groupies get drunk."

The crowd laughed.

Jenny darted to her stereo, pulling up a playlist on her iPod to keep the music going, then headed toward the band. When she passed us and saw Derek, her face broke out into a broad grin.

"Oh, I didn't know you'd be here!" She hugged Derek tightly.

Jealousy clutched my stomach, and I tried to push the feeling down. He wasn't mine to be green-eyed over.

"Can I get you something to drink?" she asked him.

"Actually—" Derek started.

"No, I insist. You stay here. Don't move." She took off toward her house, sashaying her curvy figure.

Derek laughed. "I guess I'll just stay here, then."

Andy returned and chatted with us for a minute. Then Tyler appeared out of nowhere by her side, and she shot him a loving glance.

"Hey, baby," she said, winding her arm through his. "I was hoping to have some time with you." She dropped her voice and gave him a meaningful look. "Alone."

Crap! I ordered my brain to think of a stalling tactic, glancing desperately around the backyard for inspiration. If I could keep her outside until Tyler had to play his next set, maybe she wouldn't do . . . *it*.

"Hey, did you hear the news about . . . Wendy and Mike?" I said, referencing the couple I'd paired up a few minutes ago, who were currently still going at it on his lawn chair.

She paused, her interest obviously piqued. Andy loved a good story and always was the first to know about anything, but since being with Tyler had eaten up a lot of her recent time, she wasn't as current.

Even Derek looked curious, his eyes fixed on me.

"No, what about them?" Andy asked.

"They're all over each other like white on rice," I said to them, pointing in the couple's direction. "Looks like one wild and crazy hookup." I paused, an idea formulating in the back of my brain. "And I bet there will be more tonight, if we all hang out together and watch for them." Hell, I'd make matches all night, if that's what it took.

Andy cast her eyes between me and Tyler a couple of times. She chewed on her lip, considering her options, then said, "You and Derek have fun. I'm gonna hang with my baby for a little bit."

Before I could say anything else, she and Tyler took off inside the house. I watched them go, hoping against hope they weren't ducking up into a bedroom to do the nasty. As tempted as I was to stay right on her heels, I didn't think it was the best idea for me to follow them. Now that would be *really* nasty.

"I'm sure it's fine," Derek said to me, his low voice warm and comforting. "The house is packed with people."

I looked back up at his eyes. "How did you know what I was thinking?"

"Your face is pretty easy to read." He gave me a crooked grin. "I can tell you're worried about Andy. She's smart. It'll be okay."

I swallowed. If he could read my thoughts that well, who knows what else he'd read on my face? Did he know how deeply in love I was with him?

I felt heat crawl up my throat and sneak across my cheeks. I was grateful for the darkening sky, which hopefully hid my embarrassment.

Derek's "butler" came back, thrusting a cup into Derek's hand. "Here ya go," he said, grinning toothily. "Hey, wanna go shoot some hoops? Jenny's brother has a basketball net set up in front of the garage."

"Thanks, but—" Derek started to say, but was interrupted by Jenny, who jumped between the two of us.

"Derek, here's your . . ." She trailed off when she saw the drink in Derek's hand. Her mouth turned down in the corners. "Oh. You already have one." She paused. "Well, do you want to see the kitchen? I can show you where it is." Her eyes raked over Derek, and she smiled, running a finger across her lower lip. "Or I could always give you a tour of the house."

"*Or*, we could play some hoops," the guy said, shooting Jenny a glare.

She glared back at him. Then both turned expectant faces toward Derek.

He coughed, shuffling from one foot to the other. "Well, actually, I need to find the bathroom. Where—"

"Here, let me show you," Jenny said, grabbing his arm. "Follow me."

Jealousy reared its ugly head again, this time stabbing me in the stomach. I sighed. This worship over Derek was getting to be a bit too much. I needed to break away before I did something really stupid.

"Okay, you guys have fun. I'm gonna head out." I glanced at my watch. "Gotta be home early anyway, or my mom will kill me."

Derek nodded, but he didn't look too happy. I wished it was because I was going. "Okay then."

Jenny tugged on his arm, pulling him toward the house.

Well, I wasn't happy, either. I was getting damn sick of watching people fawn all over him. And it's not like I had any right to say anything.

I was only a friend, after all.

"See ya," I said, heading back through the house to the car, stopping only to say good-bye to Maya and Scott. While I loved Derek, I wasn't going to be just another groupie.

At least I had my dignity. Cold comfort that it was.

chapter fourteen

I spent the earlier part of Sunday fretting obsessively about Andy.
I tried calling her cell several times, but got no answer. No doubt
she was too busy—*ick*—to call me back. I didn't even want to think
about what she and Tyler were doing together.

Tyler was an okay guy, but after getting to know him these past
two weeks, I wasn't as fond of him as I was at the start (unlike
Maya's guy Scott, whom I'd grown to like more and more, especially
since he and Maya were so good together). And I definitely didn't
like the side of Andy that Tyler was bringing out.

Tyler was way too immature for Andy, and his clinginess only
made Andy superclingy too. Not exactly what I had in mind for
my BFF when I made the match. Yes, if Andy really loved him,

of course I'd be supportive of her choice, but there was no way to tell if it was true love until after the spell wore off. I wished Andy wouldn't make this huge decision before then—it was just one more day!

I closed my anthropology book, unable to focus on the reading. *Please still be a virgin,* I prayed silently about Andy. It was my fault things were like this, and I couldn't let that feeling go.

I mean, what if she was too love-blind for condoms, and she got pregnant, or got an STD? She'd end up one of those single moms on a cheesy made-for-TV movie, and I'd be the "best" friend who led her astray by introducing her to love.

I logged on to my PC and set a blog entry for private.

> *I'm so worried about Andy right now. She hasn't called me back. She's dropping everything for Tyler. It's almost like an obsession.*
>
> *How could the love spell make her this crazy, that she's rushing to do . . . it, after two weeks?*
>
> *Should I keep trying to call her? Should I go over to her house and see what she's doing?*

I stared at my fingers resting on the keyboard, realization hitting me square in the face. This was totally not what friendship was about. I was trying too hard to control her relationship—which wasn't mine to control.

And even more, my "help" wasn't wanted.

Andy needed my support and friendship, not me trying to enforce what I felt was best for her. After all, if Derek returned my feelings the way I wanted him to, I'd probably be wrapped up in dating him, just like Andy was with Tyler. Was it fair for me to be so high and mighty about everything, when I didn't know how I'd be in the same situation?

Maybe it was time to get back to the heart of the matter—that friends support one another, no matter what.

I erased what I'd written and replaced it with new text:

I solemnly vow to support my friends, regardless of whatever choices they make. Because friends do that for each other, and I'd want them to support me.

I saved the entry, feeling worlds better about my decision. Of course, it didn't take away all of my anxiety. But it was a good first step.

• • •

Monday morning I scanned the courtyard in front of the school, looking for Andy. She was there, waving frantically at me.

I darted over, pulse galloping like mad. *Stay cool,* I told myself. *Remember, you're here to support, not control.*

"So . . . how are things going?" I asked her. "Have you been busy? I didn't hear back from you yesterday."

"Things are fine. Sorry, I was swamped." She leaned in closer. "Tyler's grandma got sick while we were at the party on Saturday, so we didn't get a chance to . . . well, you know. Cement the deal."

"Oh, for real?" I struggled to keep the excitement out of my voice, even as I mentally vomited at the awful image she painted in my mind. "Well, I'm sorry to hear that about his grandma."

The bell rang. We headed down the pathway, where Maya joined us just inside the front doors. We moved to a less trafficked area of the hall and stopped to talk.

"You look tired," Andy said to Maya. "You been sleeping okay lately? Or are you too busy with Scott to sleep?"

Maya gave a small smile, swatting Andy on the arm. "Things have been a bit crazy lately around the house. You know how it goes."

Hmm. Now that Andy mentioned it, Maya did look a little different. She still pretty much acted the same, but I'd noticed her face was more . . . drawn lately. I remembered her heated comments about *The Scarlet Letter* from before.

"What's going on?" I asked Maya. "You *have* been off lately."

She sighed. "My parents have been a bit hard on me because I'm spending time with Scott. All they do is gripe—with me, and with each other. They want me to study instead of go on dates."

"That sucks. I'm sure they want you to do your best, but it's not like your grades are a problem or anything," I offered.

Andy nodded sagely to Maya. "I feel your pain. It's hard when you're trying to make a relationship work, and you don't feel support from your family."

I swallowed, guilt washing over me. "Or friends," I said meekly.

Andy hugged me. "It's all in the past now. Things are looking better." She paused. "Besides, now we all have dates for prom and can go together. How cool is that?"

The three of us yapped about prom for a couple of minutes, with Maya telling us all about the gorgeous black prom dress she'd snagged this past weekend. I'd pretty much given up on my dreamy red gown, so it was time to look elsewhere for something a little cheaper. I only had a hundred bucks or so saved from my job, and even if I got bonuses from all my latest matches for lasting, I'd still not be able to buy both the dress and shoes in time for prom. Plus, there were other expenses that went along with it: dinner, boutonniere, and so on.

As we talked, I glanced around the hall, sensing a distinct mood change in the air. No longer was everyone gushing about Derek.

In fact it was unusually quiet, only whispers flitting through the air. People didn't scour the halls looking for him, but pushed through with heads down, as if embarrassed to be seen loitering around.

I heard one guy at his locker mutter, "Derek's cool, but he's not as amazing as I thought."

Caren, a brunette I knew from last year's English class, nodded thoughtfully at his words. She looked at him offhandedly, then gazed at the guy's face again, like she was really seeing him for the first time.

Sucking in a deep breath, she twirled a lock of hair around her finger, pushing out her chest a bit to catch his attention.

Oh my God, she was totally flirting with him. And I hadn't even gotten to pairing her up with someone else yet. She'd gotten over Derek on her own.

It worked! The spell was gone.

I glanced over at Andy, who didn't seem any different, given how much she'd talked about Tyler this morning. So she still had the hots for him, regardless of their spell wearing off. Her relationship with Tyler was here to stay, then.

I bit back the disappointment. If I wanted her to be a friend to me, I'd have to be a friend to her and support her, even if she continued to be annoyingly in love.

Maya and I parted ways with Andy and headed into English class. We slid into our seats, busting out our copies of *The Scarlet Letter* for today's discussion.

"Settle down," Mrs. Kendel barked to the class, shooting all of us a glare. She closed the door with a heavy thud.

Everyone zipped their lips fast. She was obviously in a mood, and when Mrs. Kendel was mad, it was a good idea to stay quiet.

"Okay, let's finish up our discussion on *The Scarlet Letter*. There's a part in the book," Mrs. Kendel said, flipping through her well-worn copy, "where Hester's daughter Pearl asks if she will be getting a scarlet letter of her own when she's older. What do you think is the reason she asks? What's the main purpose of this scene?"

Everyone stared silently at Mrs. Kendel. Yeah, it was totally Monday in here.

Maya raised her hand.

"Miss Takahashi," Mrs. Kendel said, "go ahead."

Maya cleared her throat. "Um, I think since the letter represents sin, that maybe Pearl wonders if she's going to sin as a grown-up, like her mom has?"

Mrs. Kendel blinked rapidly, obviously surprised. "That's exactly it."

"Though . . . Pearl could also be making a point about judging others," Maya continued, getting more impassioned as she spoke. "And that really, no one person is better than anyone else. And holding people to standards *you* think they should be achieving is totally unfair to that person."

I glanced at Maya, whose cheeks flamed red. She clamped her mouth shut, leaning back into her seat.

This stuff with her parents must be bothering her more than she's let on. I'd never seen Maya rant like that before.

"That's absolutely true," Mrs. Kendel said, not noticing how upset Maya looked. "In reality we all sin, so we all bear a scarlet letter."

I scrawled out some notes on what Mrs. Kendel was saying,

but I had a hard time focusing. I definitely needed to talk to Maya about what was going on with her.

And soon.

Later that morning Andy and I strolled through the hallway to health class.

"So anyway, I didn't get a chance to tell you earlier, but I finally bought *the* perfect prom dress," Andy said, bouncing in excitement. "It matches the dark purple of Tyler's cummerbund perfectly."

"Awesome. Derek teased me when I tried having the conversation about matching outfits," I said.

Out of nowhere Tyler appeared in front of us, stopping us in our tracks.

"Hey!" Andy gasped, then leaned over to kiss him on the cheek. "I was just talking about you. I hadn't heard from you at all this morning—what's going on?" Deep lines etched in her brow. "Is your grandma doing any better? She didn't have to go to the hospital, did she?"

He glanced away and dug into his back pocket, handing her a note. "Uh, look, Andy. I need to run, but I wanted you to read this."

"Sure."

He turned and left. Andy's eyes followed his rapidly retreating figure down the hallway.

"Well, that was weird," I said, trying to cover up the uncomfortable moment. "Maybe he was just in a hurry."

She nodded, opening the note and scanning its contents. Her face fell, and tears welled in her eyes. "Oh my God," she said, pressing her free hand to her mouth.

"Are you okay?"

Wordlessly, she handed me the note.

I scanned its contents, biting my lower lip as I read. "I'm so sorry," I whispered to her.

She sniffled. "I can't believe he broke up with me, Felicity. And in a stupid note! How could he do this?"

Startled by her raised voice, students turned and glanced at Andy's burning cheeks.

"Come over here." I pulled her aside. "We have a couple of minutes before class starts."

Hands shaking, Andy squinted away the fresh tears in her eyes and began to read the note out loud. "'Babe, I've been thinking about this a lot.'" Andy looked up, scoffing. "Right. Breaking up with his girlfriend though a freaking note? Sounds like he put a *lot* of thought into this. And he sure didn't sound like he was thinking about dumping me last night when we were talking on the phone."

I rubbed her back, my stomach lurching from Andy's pain and my own guilt. I couldn't tell her that last night, he'd still been under Cupid's spell. "It's okay. I know you're pissed."

"Believe me, I am. And hurt." She glanced back at the note, continuing where she left off. "'I don't think this is gonna work between us. It's going too fast. I need some more space. Let's just be friends.'" She scoffed. "But this part is the most unbelievable: 'I hope you'll still come see our band perform on Friday. Tyler.'"

I shook my head in disbelief. "What a total jerk. He obviously didn't deserve you."

The whole scenario floored me. I hadn't even thought of the possibility that the spell could wear off Tyler but not Andy, since Andy was clearly more amazing and Tyler didn't deserve her in the first place.

I felt like such a heel. I'd tried to help her find love, but all I did was set her up to get hurt, and in such a callous manner.

Andy crumpled up the note, fire flashing in her eyes. She dumped it in a nearby garbage can.

"We'll get through this," I said. "Don't sweat him. You're too good for him anyway."

We headed back down the hall to health class, Andy alternating between being supremely pissed off and supremely hurt. In one moment she cussed him up and down, then cried in the next about how she'd been wrong to let herself be vulnerable with him.

She stopped suddenly outside of the classroom door, her mouth flying open in shock. "Oh my God, I just realized I don't have a prom date now. What am I going to do? I already bought a dress."

Crap, crap, crap. The suckiness of the situation just kept piling up. With the drama about him breaking up with her, I'd forgotten all about prom.

"We'll figure something out," I said. "I promise."

The idea of pairing Andy up with someone else came to mind, but I pushed it away just as quickly. It was way too soon. Besides, I didn't want her to just go through this heartbreak again.

I had to do something to make this better, though at the moment, I was fresh out of plans.

chapter fifteen

Bobby, who never had good timing, accosted me right before the bell rang for health class to start. Today he had on a shirt that showed his midriff, but at least it wasn't see-through.

I guess that could be counted as progress. Baby steps, right?

"Hey," he said. "Thought about which board game we want to mimic? That needs to be turned in next Monday, right?"

I stepped around him and headed to my seat, knowing he'd be following me closely. "Yup. We should figure that out."

He slid into the seat beside me, nodding eagerly. "How about tonight?"

"Well, I have a work meeting, but maybe we can meet afterward."

Andy slumped into her chair, swiping a hand across her red-rimmed eyes. My heart broke for her. "Hey, Bobby," she muttered.

Bobby waved at her. "Hey. I was just talking to Felicity about our health project. We're working together. As a team. Just the two of us."

I bit back a groan. God, could he be any louder about it? Why didn't he take out an ad in the school paper while he was at it?

"Let's definitely get together tonight, Bobby, okay?" I needed to shut him up, so maybe placating him would do the trick.

A few minutes into class Andy slipped me a folded scrap of paper. I furtively opened it, pretending to take notes.

Fel,

Haven't worked on project yet. Maybe Cahill will let the 4 of us work together? My partner's James.

Actually, that could work. It would save me from more alone time with Bobby, at least. And maybe James would mention how things were going with him and Mitzi. It had been a couple of weeks since I'd paired them, but I'd barely had a chance to observe them together, seeing as how Mrs. Cahill wouldn't let them change seats and sit beside each other in class.

Plus, I could help Andy make up some of the schoolwork she'd missed while salivating over Tyler.

I scrawled an answer:

Sure. We'll ask after class. Lgr!

We approached Mrs. Cahill after the bell, ready to beg, if necessary. But she was surprisingly receptive to the idea, though she specified we were all to pitch in and help with the project.

Art class at the end of the day confirmed that things were basically back to normal. Students weren't hovering around Derek's table. In fact, a few people—including the teacher—completely ignored him. But Derek seemed relieved to have breathing room.

I tried to act casual, but couldn't keep my eyes off him. What if he decided he didn't want to go to prom now that he could find another person to go with as a friend . . . or something more? I was torn between asking him outright and just letting it slide.

After the final bell of the day rang, I scooped up my stuff and headed to the library to study.

Okay, I went to wait for Derek, even though I suspected he wouldn't show up. After all, for him, the library sessions were about hiding from the adoring crowds, and now he didn't need to do that.

But by now, I had to be honest and at least admit to myself that *I* didn't care about studying. It was really about spending time with him. Seeing his face at the end of school always made my day. I was just as in love as ever, but that love was deepened by a closeness we didn't have before.

Not that I could fess up to him about any of it. I still had to play the "best buds" role to keep from scaring him off.

Derek came in just a minute after me, a huge smile on his face.

"Did you see?" he asked as he slapped his backpack on the table. "Things are back to normal."

I nodded. "I'm sure you're happy about that."

"Absolutely. Now, I don't have to keep hiding out in here. What a relief."

And just like that my world came crashing down. What a kick in the gut. Who was I kidding? Only myself, apparently.

I was nothing to him. Never would be.

Throat tight, I gave him the biggest fake smile I could muster, gathering my books and cramming them in my backpack. "That's great. I guess we can stop hanging out now. I'm sure you're ready to have your afternoon back."

Derek gave me a funny look. "I guess."

I needed to leave before I started crying in front of him. "Well, I'd better run. I'll see you around, okay?"

I swept past him and, once I'd fled the library, let the tears spill freely down my cheeks.

As soon as I got home from school, I grabbed a pint of Ben and Jerry's ice cream from the freezer, then dug around in the silverware drawer and snagged a spoon. This was no ordinary depression. This was full-fledged, I'm-in-love-with-a-guy-who-only-wants-to-be-a-friend-or-maybe-just-a-friendly-acquaintance depression.

The worst kind, if you ask me.

Maybe there was no sense in trying with Derek. All this time, I'd thought getting closer to him would show him how good we'd be together. And all he was thinking about was how he didn't want to be in hiding anymore.

Great job, Felicity.

Over the course of my cupid employment, I'd managed to butcher nearly every match I'd made, including the ones for both of my best friends, as well as my own pathetic attempts to endear myself to Derek. I sucked at my job. I sucked at my life. Yeah, I'd pretty much hit the ultimate low.

The only thing that could make things worse would be to find out I was really born a boy or something.

A few minutes into feasting on my comfort food, I heard Mom's key in the front door. She strolled into the house, whistling a little tune.

"Oh, hey," she said, then stopped midstride, eyeing me chowing down on Chunky Monkey. She hung her keys on a hook, put her purse on the table, and sat across from me. "Bad day, huh?"

I nodded and swallowed hard, my throat closing up. "Things just aren't going right for me at all anymore."

She stared at me for a moment, then got out of her seat and went upstairs. A minute later, she came back down, a long bag in her hands. The curve of a clothing hanger peeked out the top.

"What's that?" I asked.

"Just open it and see." Mom had a mysterious smile on her face.

I slid the bag off, gasping when I realized I was holding a red dress. My dream prom dress! Mom had gotten it for me.

My eyes blurred, and tears slipped down my cheeks. "Oh my God. Thanks, Mom. This means a lot to me."

She smiled bigger. "We were going to wait and give it to you later, but you looked like you needed a pick-me-up today."

I squeezed her in a tight hug. "Yeah, that sure did it."

She hugged me back. "You still have to get your own shoes and accessories," she said, "but your father and I wanted to do something special for you. We know you've been working hard at your job and school lately. And you really did look gorgeous in it."

I slipped the bag back over the dress. Was this fate's way of telling me not to give up? Maybe the dress was a sign that I still had a chance of winning Derek over.

I dashed upstairs and hung up the gown in my closet, then grabbed the phone and started punching in Andy's number. I paused. She probably wasn't in the mood to talk about prom stuff, seeing as how she and Tyler just broke up. It was tempting to call Maya's cell, but I knew she was at band practice.

Well, it was time to go to my meeting with Janet anyway, and then hurry home so I could help plan the health project with Andy,

James, and Bobby, who were all coming to my house tonight.

I borrowed Mom's car and drove to Cupid's Hollow head-quarters. Once I got inside, I darted into Janet's office, breathless as I plunked myself down in the seat.

"Sorry," I said, trying to relax and look professional. "It's been a crazy day."

Janet raised a perfectly arched eyebrow. "I see. So, how go your matches? If I remember right, the big spell should have worn off by now."

I nodded, slightly awed at Janet's incredible recollection powers. I wasn't sure how many cupids were out there, but she must have had hundreds, or even thousands, of matches to keep track of. And I could barely keep on top of the ones I'd matched myself. "You're good. Yeah, the spell ended last night, and fortunately, it seems like everything's back to normal."

"That's good. Be sure to watch your other matches closely, though," she said, eyes fixed on mine in a warning stare. "You don't want them to go down the drain while you're focusing on repairing the damage from this accident. It's too easy to lose control."

I swallowed and handed her my PDA. "Yeah, I made a lot of couples over the last two weeks." I paused. "I did have a . . . person who was still in love after the spell wore off, but the other person fell out of love."

Janet sighed. "That's a real risk of the job." She plugged my LoveLine 3000 into her computer, synching it with the master program. "It's unfortunate when that happens. The best you can do is try again."

Yeah, I *could* try again in the near future. With Andy, I mean, not with Tyler—I was so pissed at him, it wasn't funny. No way could I make an objective match for him right now. But when would Andy be ready?

"How do you know when someone's ready to be matchmade after they've broken up?" I asked Janet. Maybe she could help give me tips.

She pursed her lips. "I wish there was an easy answer, but each person's different. Some are ready to jump right back into love, while others need to heal for a while. That's why it's good to take your time and make the best quality matches you can."

I nodded solemnly, trying to ignore the light, nervous fluttering in my stomach. The rapid matches I'd made weren't exactly the highest quality . . . but they sort of mostly met the minimum compatability requirements and the initial chemistry seemed pretty strong, so surely the odds of them working out were on my side. Right?

Janet handed me back my PDA, as well as my paycheck. "Next week we'll see how your other couples are doing. Meanwhile, check and double-check your e-mails before you send them, just in case."

I stood. "Thanks again for your help."

"Anytime."

"That's dumb." James crossed his arms and sulked. "Games are stupid."

For the two hundredth time in the past five minutes I clamped my teeth down on my lower lip to keep from yelling at him. Next to me at the table Andy was about to have convulsions from rolling her eyes so much, and I didn't blame her. James was being a total pain in the ass to deal with.

"Well, unless you have a better idea, that's what we're doing," I said.

One eyebrow raised, I waited for a minute while James glared at me.

"No?" I asked. "Great."

Bobby shuffled through some papers on the table until he found the one he was looking for. "Here's a rough sketch of what I thought we could do." He handed me the paper, a dark blush working its way over his cheeks.

Aw, he was embarrassed over offering his ideas. Probably not too comfortable being around Jerky James, knowing anything and everything was fodder for mockery.

I glanced over the paper Bobby had given me, then paused in surprise. It was actually quite clever.

"Hey, this isn't bad!" I exclaimed. "I like how you made our game look like a Monopoly board."

Andy eyeballed it over my shoulder. "Oh my God, this is too funny. Look, you made 'jail' into a VD clinic!"

We both giggled.

Bobby shrugged, a shy smile on his face. "Just trying to help."

"Don't be so modest." I looked him over, suddenly seeing him in a new light. He was much smarter than I'd given him credit for. "This is really good."

Andy whipped out a pencil and started marking on his paper. "We can set up each of the squares to be hot dating spots, or different places around the city."

James kept pouting.

"Well, if we're having a VD clinic, a pharmacy should go on here too," Bobby said. "Maybe the pharmacy can be the 'free parking' space for the game."

"I like that idea," I said to Bobby. "You did a great job with planning this out." He'd taken the brainstorming ideas from our last session and followed through with them in an effective way.

Maybe he wasn't so horrid and obnoxious after all. He just needed to be in his element, which was apparently a small group setting.

Bobby glowed under the praise. "Well, thanks!" He tucked his head near Andy's, and they pored over the paper as she wrote.

By the end of the session we'd split up the duties for who would work on what. James was going to create the figurine pieces, Andy would make the money and property cards, Bobby would handle creating the board, and I'd craft the outer box.

The only thing left was to vote on the name.

"I vote for my idea of Crabble," Andy asserted, leaning back in her chair and crossing her arms in satisfaction. "That one makes me giggle every time I think about it."

"But that's dumb. It makes you think of Scrabble," James pointed out, "which isn't the kind of game we made. This is a Monopoly board."

"Who cares?" Bobby said. "I think it works too."

I glanced at him in shock. I'd never seen him stand up to other guys like that before. Bobby usually asserted his masculinity through severe fitness workouts, not by running his mouth or standing up for himself.

Or for anyone else, for that matter.

"I like Crabble too," I said to James. "That makes it the majority vote. Besides, I didn't see you coming up with anything. If you're going to keep shooting down all of our ideas, at least come up with something else."

Man, he was totally annoying. One of those guys who didn't like anyone else having funny ideas, because he couldn't get the glory for it. Thank God we were now far enough along to not have to work with him as closely anymore.

Honestly, I couldn't tell what Mallory had seen in him when they'd dated freshman year. But that reminded me—I wanted to ask him how the love was going with Mitzi.

I quickly thought up a way to ask about her as slyly as possibly. "Hey, James, who is Mitzi paired up with in health class? Do you know what she's doing for the project?"

Instantly his demeanor softened. I'd never seen anything like it—especially considering the love magic was already gone. This was genuine emotion I was seeing in him, possibly for the first time ever.

A soft smile played on his lips. "She's working with Mary. They decided to do a poster. Speaking of which, I gotta run." He flipped open his cell phone to check the time. "We're studying together tonight."

Andy, Bobby, and I watched him go.

My chest ached with the bittersweet irony that I'd actually made a decent match for a guy I couldn't stand, but Andy, one of my best friends in the world, had gotten messed over because of my poor matchmaking on her behalf.

And not only that, I'd screwed things up for myself as well. Surely I'd end up alone, in an old Victorian house with eight hundred black cats all named Mittens, hosing down kids who walked across my lawn. And when I died, they'd find my bones propped up in a rickety rocking chair, wearing my red prom dress—

"Hello, earth to Felicity." Andy waved her hand in front of my face. "You still here with us?"

I blinked rapidly, shaking away my morbid thoughts. "Yeah, sorry. Zoned out there for a minute."

Andy and Bobby glanced at each other, a knowing look passing between them. I guess they were both used to dealing with me by now. I offered them a chagrined smile.

"Actually, I gotta run too," Andy said, packing her stuff in her bag. "I need to study." She sighed deeply, the corners of her mouth turning down, and I knew she was thinking about Tyler and missing him.

"It'll be okay," I said, giving her a big hug. "You're better off now."

Tears pooled in her eyes, and one slid down her cheek. "I know. But I just miss him. I can't believe it went like this."

Bobby nodded. "Breaking up is hard. That was lame of him to dump you in a note."

Andy and I stared at him, jaws dropped.

"How did you know what happened?" I asked.

He shrugged. "Everyone at school knows. Sorry."

Andy started sobbing, fat tears plopping onto her shirt. "Great. And I'm a laughingstock now too!"

"No, you're not. They're all saying what an ass Tyler was." He awkwardly patted her on the shoulder.

She sniffled and swiped her hand across her eyes, glancing at him. "Really?"

"Yup. Everyone knew you were too good for him anyway."

Wow, Bobby was proving to be a pretty decent guy. I appreciated the way he was trying to comfort Andy. I think it helped her to hear these things from other people, not just me.

"Thanks," I said to him.

He gave me a small smile, then turned his eyes back to Andy. "No problem. No problem at all."

chapter sixteen

"Okay, Jon. Why don't you start? Tell us what's going on from your point of view." I shifted in the booth and took a sip of my iced mocha latte.

It was Tuesday, and we'd decided earlier this morning that Starbucks was safe, neutral ground for Jon and Megan's after-school couple's therapy session.

He drew in a slow breath and kept his eyes on his coffee. "Well, I think Megan's great, but she's a little too . . . gung ho about this weekend trip to the cabin. To the point where she's—"

"Gung ho?" Megan yelped. "If you love me, I should be more important than golf."

"I don't think going to one golf game means I don't care about you," he rebutted.

"Okay," I said. The last thing we needed was for things to get too heated. "So, you guys are afraid your ... values don't align with each other's. Good start." I paused, considering my next words carefully. "Is it possible to find a compromise you can be happy with?"

Megan sniffled, then took a drink of her chai tea. "I just can't compromise on this. I need all of him, not just whenever it suits his needs."

Jon blinked. "I want to play golf. It doesn't mean I don't care. I just don't want to be pushed."

Poor guy. I could kind of see his point. Megan was being surprisingly stubborn about this. I'd never known her to act in this way. Of course, I'd never dated her, so maybe her attitude with guys was way different.

Megan glanced at Jon, then looked away, her eyes following a guy with his arm wrapped around a girl. The guy kissed the girl on the top of her head, drawing her closer.

"See that guy?" Megan asked, nodding her head in that direction. "Look how he's nurturing her. You can tell she's important to him."

Jon's jaw clenched. "Well, if I'm so terrible, go find a guy like that."

"Fine." Megan stood, swiping her chai tea off the table. "This is ridiculous anyway. You're obviously wrong for me. I need someone who puts me first every time. We are over."

My mouth flew open in shock. I instantly regretted matching Jon up with her. And the shock on his face as she walked out the door was like a kick in the nuts—or would be if I had any.

Jon gripped his cup so tightly I was afraid it would crush beneath his hands.

I struggled for a moment with what to say. Then, an epiphany hit me. Actually, Megan was right. Trying to counsel them to stay together *was* ridiculous. If the match wasn't right in the first place, I couldn't and shouldn't force them to work things out with each other.

"Well," I finally said, "I think you're better off. She's on crack if she thinks any guy in his right mind will deal with that attitude for long."

Jon stood, giving a pinched smile. "No kidding. I'm outta here."

I wanted to hug him, but I didn't think it would be a good idea. So I nodded my head and said, "I don't blame you. And for what it's worth, I'm sorry."

Jon smiled in earnest this time. "Hey, thanks for trying."

. . .

The rest of the week flew by rapidly, and before I knew it, it was already Friday. I sat in art class, unable to tear my eyes away from Derek, who was studiously working on a paper mosaic. He'd been friendly as usual toward me since Monday, but without our after-school library sessions, things weren't the same, and I basically tried to avoid him. I was feeling the bitter sting of his absence and missing him terribly.

Junior prom was a month away. I needed to find a way to get closer to him before then. But how?

Luck, it seemed, brought the answer to me. After the bell rang Derek popped over to my desk.

"Hey," he said. "How are you?"

My heart thudded in my chest. "Fine. You?"

"Not bad." He gave me a crooked smile. "Just working and stuff. So, how's your job going? Have you done any matchmaking yet?"

We strolled out of the classroom and down the hall at a casual pace. "Well . . . ," I stalled, weighing my words carefully. One slip could do me in. "I'm just keeping busy right now in the accounting department."

In a way it was true—I'd been counting nothing but unhappy couples all over the place.

Yes, it seemed I was quite possibly the worst matchmaker in the world. My best effort hadn't helped squat with hardly anything. My pairs were splitting up left and right. That morning, on the way into school, I'd seen two couples break up right in front of me.

It was a class-A disaster.

But I didn't want to focus on that right now. It was time to change the subject. "So, prom's coming up soon," I said in a shaky voice, staring at my feet as we walked.

"Sure is. Did you find your pumpernickel dress or whatever? I don't remember what color we'd decided on."

I laughed. "Lucky for you, it's plain red."

"Works nicely. I have black and white everything. The downside is, I look like a waiter at The Burger Butler." He shifted his backpack higher on his shoulder as we passed through the school's front doors.

"I'm sure you'll look great. Probably better than poor Andy looks in one. She's a server there." An image popped up in my head of Derek wearing a tux, his broad shoulders accentuated by the cut of the suit jacket.

Oh, God, he was going to look so. Freaking. Hot. It would take all of my willpower not to throw myself on him and beg him to love me.

"What's on your mind?" he asked.

"Um, nothing." Nothing I could repeat anyway.

I glanced around in front of the school and saw Andy just a few feet away. She waved at us and dashed over.

"Hey, Felicity. Oh, *hi*, Derek," she said, a sly smile on her face.

Oh, God. Please don't let her spill the beans about my mad love for him. I sent her a message through my brain waves: *Don't you dare embarrass me!*

She waved me off with a small hand movement, as if my concerns weren't valid.

"So, I hear you're taking Felicity to prom." She squinted at him. "Getting to be good friends, aren't you two?"

"We sure are," I butted in, trying to nip the conversation before it could get under way. I couldn't sit there and listen to Derek talk about what a great bud I was, or how I was probably like one of the guys to him. "So, Andy, you ready to head out to my house? We need to wrap up our health class game."

That was actually true—the projects were due on Monday, so we were going to finalize our presentation plans before our TGIF sleepover tonight and make sure all of our elements were completed in time.

Derek snickered. "I remember doing that. Have fun." He waved and strolled off around the corner, like he didn't have a care in the world. Especially not a care about me.

I groaned, wishing I could bang my head through the school's brick walls.

"This is pure torture, Andy!" I cried out. "I'm never going to get him to see me romantically."

"Hey, at least you get the chance to be in a romantic environment with him. Prom's your opportunity for love. My date ditched me." Andy's shoulders sagged, and her smile slid off her face. "This sucks."

My gut twisted. I felt like such a heel. Here I was, going on and on about my problems, when Andy had a truly crummy situation.

"I'm sorry. If you want, I'll hang with you that night instead of going to prom. We can rent a few bad movies and pig out on Chinese."

She looked at me, tears in her eyes. "You'd do that for me? You'd give up your one romantic moment with Derek?"

I nodded rapidly. I truly meant it. Andy and I had had our ups and downs lately, but she was still my best friend.

"Absolutely," I said. "Friends come first. Always."

She hugged me tightly, and I heard her sniffle. "I should have put my friends first while dating Tyler. I'm sorry."

"It's okay," I replied. And it was. "Sometimes, falling in love is like . . . being under a spell."

"It sure is," she said, pulling back and swiping a hand across her damp eyes. "Anyway, I don't want you to give up your prom date."

"Thank God," I laughed, "because my dress is so hot. I don't think you could appreciate it in the same way a guy would."

She laughed and slugged me in the arm. "Hardy har. Funny one."

A brilliant idea hit me.

"Hey, you should still go with all of us. Derek and I are just going as friends, anyway. Unfortunately." I gave her a mock grimace. "Seriously, though, we could all hang out. It would be a blast. You could be Derek's other date. He'd feel like a total pimp, having two hot mamas on his arm. I wouldn't want you to waste your prom dress, either."

"Thanks, but that's okay. I don't need to be a third wheel. Maybe I can find another use for my prom dress, like mopping the floor or something."

I saw her bite back a sigh and paste on a big smile. I couldn't believe she wasn't going to go. Prom wouldn't be the same without Andy.

chapter seventeen

"So, like, chlamydia would be terrible to catch. As would pretty much any sexually transmitted disease. They're totally gross." Mitzi opened up her huge trifold poster for everyone to see. "Just to reinforce this, I pasted in lots of pictures to show you guys."

The dozen or so images she'd glued onto the poster board were horrific. Fortunately, several of them were bad photocopies, so I couldn't make them out. But the ones I could see were just wretched.

The whole class gagged in near unison. I had to look down at my paper for a moment to keep from ralphing on the desk. I could hear Bobby retching slightly from right behind me. It was weird that he wasn't sitting on my other side for once, but he probably just wanted to keep our group closer together. With Andy to his left and James behind her, we could have almost passed for a unified team.

Even Mrs. Cahill blanched and gave a slight shudder. "Um, nice job, Mitzi and Mary. That was very . . . informative."

Mitzi beamed, folding up the dreaded poster board and tucking it under her arm. She slid back into her seat. "Thanks!"

Most of the presentations had been pretty clever so far. One group made an instructional video of dating scenarios on how to tell your potential partner if you had herpes, complete with what worked and what didn't.

We all busted up into fits of laughter for nearly five minutes over the film—especially the part where the girl was explaining to her "date" in a posh restaurant downtown that you didn't catch herpes by sitting on a toilet.

Even better, in the background of the restaurant you could see all the patrons who were trying to eat dinner, eyes wide with shock over the subject matter. I couldn't believe they'd actually filmed on location.

Mrs. Cahill actually had to smother a laugh behind her hand at that one. You know, she wasn't too bad, actually. Considering the subject matter she was teaching, I guess she made the best of a crappy situation.

"Next up are . . ." Mrs. Cahill looked at her list. "Bobby, Felicity, Andy, and James. They all worked together on their project. Come on up, guys."

Stomach twisting in nervousness, I grabbed my piece of paper. My job was to explain our project, while the other three would "model" the pieces.

"Well," I said, exhaling slowly and trying to keep my hands from shaking, "we decided to create a board game about STDs called Crabble."

The class interrupted my speech with fresh peals of laughter.

I gave it a moment, then continued. "We made ours like Monopoly, though you'll probably never see a game like this in stores. And that's too bad, because it's both fun *and* informative."

For the next ten minutes we explained the ins and outs of Crabble, with Andy and Bobby doing a great job of showing the workings. James pretty much sat there and did nothing except trade flirtatious looks with Mitzi. Of course.

Oh, well—I didn't care. He'd helped make the game, so he technically did carry his own weight. I was just ecstatic to be done dealing with him. And thrilled that he and Mitzi were still going strong. At least *that* match hadn't ended in heartache and disaster. And if they stayed together long enough, I'd get a nice bonus in my paycheck that I could put toward the perfect boutonniere for Derek, and new makeup to complement my dress.

When the presentation was over, we got some great applause. I went back to my desk feeling good about how that went.

I slid a note to Andy:

Nice job! Glad that's over.

She wrote back:

Srsly. Total relief! Another stress off our plates.

After she handed the note to me, I saw her turn back to another piece of paper, scribble something on it, then fold it up and hand it to Bobby.

What the . . . ?

I heard him snicker from behind me, then the scratching of a pencil as he replied to her note.

During the rest of the class period, I pondered the note-passing. What was going on with that? I'd never seen the two of them talk before. It was great to see Andy in a good mood again, though she'd gotten a little weepy when the subject of Tyler came up during our TGIF sleepover. But Maya and I had both been relieved and impressed by how well Andy held up for most of the weekend. I knew she was still sad about what happened with him, but she seemed more like her old self by the minute.

Suddenly, I had an epiphany: Bobby realized how important Andy was to me. In order to help me see what a great guy he was, he was talking to her and helping her feel better after the Tyler fiasco.

Not that it was going to make me date him, but I could totally appreciate the new side of Bobby. He was growing less obnoxious and more tolerable to be around. In fact, he was rather thoughtful.

Feeling like I'd reached a new peak of enlightenment, I strolled to my locker after class to fetch my lunch, then headed to the cafeteria.

Andy and Bobby were already there, the board game in front of them. They were pointing and laughing at some of the places on the cover.

I had to give myself kudos too—I really outdid myself with the box design. It was sheer genius.

Okay, the genius was Bobby's with his brilliant idea, but I totally came through on my part.

Andy waved me over. "Hey, girl! We were just talking about how great you did with the box. It's hilarious."

Bobby nodded enthusiastically. "It's one of the best parts of the whole project. You rock."

I shrugged modestly and slipped into the seat across from them. Good old Bobby—he could always be counted on for an ego boost. Guess he was just that kind of guy. It was tragic, really, that I didn't like him more. I could see how he was pretty cool, if you looked past the mesh shirts.

Actually, he wasn't even wearing a mesh shirt today. In fact, his top didn't show any part of his abdomen or muscles at all. Interesting. Either Bobby was working harder to impress me, or he was "dressing up" for the presentation.

Well, whatever the reason, it was a refreshing change. It made me not embarrassed to be around him.

"Thanks. That was fun," I answered.

I dug out my requisite PB&J sandwich from my lunch bag and started chowing down. All that hard work and thinking had sure made my appetite spike.

• • •

After lunch I told Andy I'd see her in class, then darted to my locker. I'd completely blanked on bringing my anthropology notebook with me.

I opened the lock and rifled through my backpack.

"Hey, Felicity," a low voice said from behind me.

I spun around. It was Derek. Of course, my heart did its typical jump-into-my-throat action.

I forced myself to relax. "Oh, hi, Derek. How are you?"

If looks were an indicator, I'd say he was doing mighty fine. Yowza, he looked extra hot today in a green T-shirt that made his eyes seem piercing.

Or was it the look he was giving me? I'd never seen Derek staring at me so intently before.

He swallowed, then shot me a crooked smile. "I'm on my way to lunch, but I wanted to ask you a quick question. What are you doing tonight?"

"Uh, nothing. I don't have anything going on this evening," I blurted out in a rush. I hoped that didn't make me sound like a total loser, but it was true. No study date tonight, and my meeting with Janet had been postponed until Wednesday because she had to go out of town unexpectedly. "Why, what's up?"

"Well, I was wondering . . ." He paused, clearing his throat. "I wanted to know if you'd like to come over for dinner tonight."

"Who, me? At your house?"

"Absolutely," he said, chuckling. "My mom wants to meet you, since we're going to prom together."

Oh my God. Meeting Derek's parents?

That was kind of a big deal, wasn't it? I mean, even though Derek and I were going as friends, it still was a good idea for me to make a favorable impression on his family.

"Sure, that'd be great," I said.

He paused, looking like he was going to say something else, then glanced at his watch. "Oh, gotta go. I'll pick you up at six thirty, okay?"

I nodded mutely, watching as Derek's fine figure strolled away. What a crazy, crazy day it had been so far, and I had a feeling tonight was going to be just as interesting.

The rest of the school day went torturously slow. But once I got home Mom kept me busy cleaning around the house, so evening came surprisingly fast.

In my bedroom I finished dressing and stared at my reflection in the full-length mirror. My hair was softly pulled up on my head, with small tendrils curled around my face, and my dress was flattering to my figure, but provided full coverage for modesty. I needed to make a good impression on his family, and looking like one of my brother Rob's hoochie dates wasn't going to do that.

As I glanced at my feet, clad in cute sandals, it hit me that Derek would finally have a chance to see my painted toenails. At that moment, staring at my toes, the full impact of going to dinner at Derek's house hit me.

Oh my God. I was getting ready to embark on the most important moment of my love life with the guy of my dreams.

The breath whooshed out of my lungs, and I dragged in a deep gulp of air, trying to calm myself down. *Chill,* I ordered myself. This was not the time to put pressure on myself. *Remember your mantra of cool and casual.*

I grabbed my purse and headed downstairs, stepping carefully so I wouldn't take a header and break my neck. Because that would totally be my luck.

Mom and Dad were reading on the living room couch. Mom glanced over and gave me an approving nod. "Oh, honey, you look lovely. I wish you'd dress up more."

"Thanks, Mom," I said, giving her a wobbly smile.

"He's going to be bowled over, I just know it," she said. "Remember your manners, because his family will be watching every move you make."

Crap, she was right. They would be watching me, sizing me up.

As I continued to think about it, it started to seem that my entire life and possible future happiness was riding on tonight.

Oh God, oh God, oh God. I was going to be sick.

Mom eyed me, a deep frown line between her eyebrows. "You okay, Felicity?"

I nodded slowly, sucking in air. I needed to stop psyching myself out, stat. This was ridiculous. It was just dinner, not a meeting with the Pope.

"I'm okay," I said, ordering my pulse to steady itself. "Just nervous."

"Don't be," Mom replied. "You're gorgeous. Derek would have to be blind to not see that."

The doorbell rang, and Dad got up to answer it.

Derek strolled through the door, and my knees buckled. He shook my dad's hand, said hello to my mom, then looked at me.

"You look great, Felicity." He shook his head with a smile.

"I mean, you always look nice, but you look great today." A light flush swept up his throat and across his cheeks.

Was he nervous too? My heart rate sped up again. I managed to thank him, though my throat was closed so tightly, I don't know how I got the words out.

"You ready to head to my house?" he asked.

I nodded. "Absolutely."

We zipped down the road in his car about a mile, ducking through side streets and making small talk, until we pulled into the driveway of a nice-size house. Well, it would have to be with that many kids.

Derek got out of the car and came to my side, opening the passenger door for me. What a gentleman!

I hoped against hope my body wasn't shaking visibly, because my insides felt like boiling butter.

He opened the front door and ushered me in. Giggles echoed throughout the living room, and I heard scrambling sounds. A stuffed animal flew through the air and smacked against my stomach.

Derek's jaw dropped. "Hey! Who did that?"

The sounds stopped. A blond boy, who had to be in kindergarten, stepped out. "Sorry," the boy said to me, his eyes cast down. "I was aiming for Derek."

I ruffled his hair. "It's okay. There's no internal bleeding or anything."

A woman's voice came from another room. "Derek? Is that you?"

Another wave of nervousness came over me. It was time to meet Derek's folks.

chapter eighteen

A blond woman with delicate features rounded the corner and stopped, patting a hand to her chest. Her stomach was huge and round, so I guessed she had another bun in the oven. I remembered what Derek had said about his parents loving kids. Obviously, he wasn't kidding.

"Oh!" she exclaimed, her eyes sweeping over my face and figure. "You're even prettier than Derek said!"

Derek talked to his mom about me? And he'd told her I was pretty?

In shock, I turned to look at him.

"Mom, *please* stop it," he said.

"It's okay," I replied, trying to make him feel better. "After seeing you, my mom told me what a hunk she thinks you are and how cute we are together."

His cheeks turned red. When I realized what I'd said, I could feel mine burning too.

Hey, way to keep digging that grave for yourself, Felicity. Maybe next time I could just show him my top secret blog posts and save myself the trouble.

Luckily, his mom intervened. "Felicity, we're having fried chicken and baked potatoes. I hope that's okay." She glanced at Derek, then looked back at me, a twinkle in her eye. "Derek loves my chicken, so I made a few extra just for him. He has a hearty appetite."

"Mom," Derek said in a low voice, swiping a hand through his hair. I don't think I'd ever seen him so flustered.

"Sorry, honey." She hugged him, then hugged me. "I'm glad to finally meet you," she whispered in my ear.

"I'm glad to meet you too," I whispered back, smiling. She was a really nice lady. I could see why Derek was so cool, with a mom like that.

"Okay, you guys get the kids settled in the dining room. We'll bring the food in," Mrs. Peterson said.

Derek escorted me toward the dining room, his hand on the

small of my back. I could feel his warm fingers through the fabric of my dress and fought the urge to turn around and lean against him.

I took the free seat across from Derek, between two of his siblings. They all looked the same, including Derek, just with varying ages. It was so cute.

"Mommy, I'm staaaarving!" the teddy bear thrower, Sam, cried out. He grabbed his fork and thumped it on the table in beat with his words. "Chic-ken legs! Chic-ken legs!"

Derek shot him a stern look. "Stop that, or I won't let you watch the robot movie tonight."

That did the job. The boy stopped midcry and put his fork down, folding his hands in his lap and giving an angelic smile. "Look, I'm being good now, okay?"

"And you're doing a great job at it," I told him, deadpan. "My brother's four years older than me, and he doesn't behave *nearly* as well as you do. He's a bad boy who gets in trouble all the time."

"Really?" he asked, eyes wide. "Does his mommy spank him?"

"Not nearly enough," I answered, giggling.

Mrs. Peterson entered the room, holding a big glass pan of chicken in her gloved hands. Derek's dad followed her closely, carrying the baked potatoes.

"That smells great," I told them. "Thanks again for inviting me over."

I looked over at Derek to find him looking at me, his face unreadable. A hot flush swept over my cheeks, and I prayed I hadn't sounded dumb.

Dinner was a louder affair than I was used to, but lots of fun. I managed to get through the entire meal without any nervous vomiting, so that was good. After talking to Derek's parents, I could totally see where he got his wit, and his warmth. They had plenty of both.

The only thing that made me feel a little nervous, actually, was Derek himself. I'd catch him staring at me sometimes, like he had something on his mind, but he never said anything. He kept the conversation light and fun.

Was I hallucinating things, or maybe reading into his looks because I wanted to believe he was interested in me? It wouldn't be the first time I'd misread a situation.

After dessert, I thanked Derek's parents for the great meal, hugging his mom and then shaking his dad's hand. Derek ushered me into his car, and we rode back to my house in mostly silence.

"My parents really like you," he finally said as he pulled his car into the driveway. "They wanted me to let you know you're invited over to our house anytime. And Sam wants you to come back over and watch the robot movie with him."

I grinned, bending over to grab my purse from the floorboard. "That's nice of them."

I sat up, and our eyes connected for a long moment. I glanced at Derek's full lips. Would he try to kiss me?

I jerked my eyes away. This wasn't a date. We were just friends. Having these fantasies about him was just going to ruin a good evening. I didn't need to put myself in a position to make things awkward between us . . . or even worse, embarrass myself.

"Thanks again for having me over," I said. "I had a great time."

His lips slid into a smile. "It was my pleasure."

I walked to school Tuesday morning, eager to dish to Andy and Maya about how dinner went yesterday. I'd spent the rest of the evening lying on my bed and staring at the ceiling, replaying the dinner through my head over and over. I'd been tempted to call them, but I knew Maya was on a date with Scott. And Andy was helping her mom with her mom's latest woo-woo obsession.

In some ways I couldn't believe how well the night had gone.

As I walked down the sidewalk, I replayed all the information I'd gained, ready to dissect it with the girls.

One, Derek had touched me several times on the hand and lower back. Definitely a good sign.

Two, he'd told his mom that I was pretty . . . unless she was saying that just to be nice. No, she didn't seem like that kind of person.

Three, dinner was great. No awkward silences. Just casual, fun conversation. And even better, his family liked me.

But four, no signs of a kiss or irrefutable signals that I was anything more than a friend in Derek's eyes. One through three meant I *could* be—but he might also just be an affectionate pal. I needed Maya's and Andy's advice on how to find out for sure.

I came through the school's front doors and stopped dead in my tracks. Almost a quarter of the students in the hallway had a sullen mood that permeated the atmosphere. People were moping down the hallway with deep frowns on their faces. I even saw a few girls crying.

I spotted Maya near her locker, kissing Scott on the cheek. He left, and she waved me over.

"Hey!" she said, then glanced around. "Actually, I probably shouldn't be so perky on a day like today. It seems like the whole school is in a bad mood."

"I wonder why." I paused, then said in a low voice, "Oh, no, did someone die?"

"—such a jerk," I heard one girl say as she walked by, her voice wobbly. "He just dumped me out of the blue, saying he couldn't understand what he'd seen in me for these past two weeks."

Oh, crap. The picture suddenly cleared up, and I realized what was wrong—and whose fault it was.

A massive chunk of the love matches that I'd made two weeks ago in a fit of matchmaking fury had worn off . . . and apparently, for the worse.

My stomach sank clear into my feet, and I groaned out loud.

"What's wrong?" Maya said, concern etched in her face. "Did something bad happen between you and Derek too? It seems like everyone is griping about love lately. It must be something about prom season."

I shook my head. "No, Derek and I are fine. Confusing, but fine." I grabbed her elbow. "We'd better head to English. I'm betting Mrs. Kendel won't be in a good mood if we make her wait."

Besides, I'd paired Mrs. Kendel up with a fellow teacher, and considering the way so many people looked horrible and depressed, odds were she would be too.

Class seemed to drag on forever. Almost everyone kept quiet, their downturned faces reflecting their bad moods. Mrs. Kendel seemed crabbier than usual, doling out an essay assignment for us to work on in silence during the class period. She sat behind her desk, a perpetual frown on her face as she glared at all of us.

I felt sick to my stomach, knowing I'd wreaked more havoc.

Perhaps I shouldn't have made those hasty matches after all. If I had just waited for my original love spell to wear off the whole school, there might have been a lot less heartache all around.

Well, give yourself another brownie point, Felicity, I grumbled to myself. *You screwed up. Again.*

I finished writing the world's worst essay and handed it up to the front of the aisle. Well, that was a fun waste of time. I'd been so distracted trying to figure out how to fix the matchmaking problem that I knew I totally blew the assignment.

The rest of my morning classes were more of the same—mopey students everywhere. Fortunately, it wasn't everyone. There were a few couples I saw who actually looked in love still—a few that I'd matched, and several that must have found love on their own. At least I hadn't messed up everyone's lives.

Maybe I needed to stay out of the business of love, both in my professional and personal life. I should just give up on Derek, give up on being a cupid, and go back to being plain old Felicity. No pressure, no stress. No risk of hurting people . . . or being hurt.

I made my way through the hall toward health class and got an unexpected glimpse of Derek. He was with a group of his friends.

"Hey, man," one of his football friends said, thumping him hard on the back. "Did you see that game last night?"

"Nope, missed it," Derek replied, slugging him in the arm.

Guys. If I lived a million years, I'd never understand the draw to pain.

"There was this amazing shot you should have seen," the guy said. "I'll tell ya later about it."

His friends took off in one direction, and Derek kept heading toward me. We locked eyes, and he smiled, the dimple deepening in his cheek.

I melted, and all the embarrassment of my mismatched matches faded away. I was so, so crazy for this guy. Who was I kidding? I couldn't stop loving him any more than the sun could stop rising in the east, or the moon could stop causing the tides.

Hell, I couldn't even stop myself from making sappy metaphors about how much I loved him.

"Hey," I said, hoping my feelings weren't all over my face. "I had a great time at dinner last night. Tell your mom—"

"—and the cashmere sweater was on clearance, since they're getting rid of their winter stock," a loud voice said from behind me. But not just any voice.

Of *course.*

I bit my lower lip and rolled my eyes, willing myself to relax. I could get through this.

Mallory and three of her giggle-box friends moved beside me. "Hey, Derek," she said, her eyes raking over him, then me. "Oh. Felicity. What are you doing?" The question itself was innocent, but her tone implied I didn't have the right to be around him. God, you'd think I was hanging out with Derek just to torture her or something.

"I'm heading to class," I said, my tone snippier than I wanted it to be. I hated letting Mallory know she got the better of me.

Her jaw tightened for a quick moment. Then she relaxed her face into a smarmy smile and glanced at her friends.

The four of them continued down the hallway.

"See ya," Mallory said to me over her shoulder.

As they walked off, I saw their heads close together. One of the girls peeked back at me, shaking her head.

Great. I just loved being talked about by stupid, snotty girls. I hoped Andy would show up soon. She'd know what to say to make me feel better.

"I'd better go," Derek said, shifting a book higher between his arm and side. "We'll talk more in art, okay?"

"Yeah, that'll be good."

I waved bye to him and made it to health class. Andy arrived right as the bell rang, so I didn't get a chance to talk to her about the dinner date at Derek's house. And Mrs. Cahill kept us busy.

I swear, everyone was conspiring against me today.

When the bell rang, Andy grabbed my arm. "I gotta talk to you," she said.

"Oh my God, me too," I said, happy I'd finally have some uninterrupted time to talk to my BFFs at lunch.

"Felicity," Mrs. Cahill said. "Can you come here a second?"

I closed my eyes and breathed in deeply. "I'll be right there," I answered Mrs. Cahill. I told Andy, "Go ahead and wait for me in the cafeteria," then went to talk to the teacher.

"Felicity," she said, perching on the edge of her desk, "it's about your project."

"Yes?" I asked, trying not to sound too nervous.

She smiled. "Nothing bad, I promise. Your group board game was really, really clever. I'd like to bring it to a continuing education class I'm participating in, as an example of good health class activities."

"Really?" I was floored. She actually thought it had merit.

"Absolutely. It was creative and fun, and made a dull topic more interesting."

So she knew we were all bored to tears. Well, at least she was trying to spread the love and help other health class teachers keep from boring *their* students.

"Sure thing," I said. "I'll bring it back to school tomorrow."

She dismissed me. I flew to my locker and grabbed my brown bag. Carrying my lunch, I went into the cafeteria, spying Andy at a table, her back facing me. She was leaning over and whispering in a guy's ear.

She laughed, and he turned to face her, a huge smile on his face.

Holy crap. Andy was talking that closely with . . . Bobby Blowhard?

chapter nineteen

I walked as calmly as possible over to Andy, tapping her on the shoulder. "Andy? What's . . . going on?"

She whipped around in her seat, gasping when she saw me. "Oh, Felicity!" She stood up and hugged me, then sat back down, her face beaming. "I was trying to talk to you earlier. I wanted to surprise you. Bobby and I are going to prom together!"

The oxygen rushed out of my lungs. Whoa, I was certainly not expecting that.

"Well, you sure did surprise me," I said slowly, taking a seat beside her. I glanced at Bobby's beaming face, then looked the rest of him over, taking in his nice, completely non-see-through shirt.

Bobby saw me evaluating him. A flush spilled over his cheeks, and he dropped his gaze to his twiddling fingers.

"I knew Andy was depressed about prom," he explained. "And I already had a tux in my closet from my older sister's wedding last summer, so I asked if she would go with me."

"Wasn't that sweet?" Andy's eyes flitted back and forth between me and Bobby. "He didn't want my dress to go to waste. And since we had fun working together on the Crabble game, we figured it would be fun to hang out. Plus, we were each gonna sit at home alone anyway. Now we can triple-date with you and Maya!"

I squinted and stared at Andy, who was babbling like crazy. She seemed edgy, her fingers playing with the strap of her purse. Why would she be so nervous, unless—

I mentally smacked myself on the forehead. How could I have missed the signs?

1. the notes passed back and forth

2. sitting together at lunch

3. Bobby taking a sudden interest in Andy, which

   I'd always thought was because of his interest in *me*

God, how vain was I? I was a class-A idiot. Bobby and Andy were crushing on each other. I didn't know when he got over me, but he sure did, with full force.

Some matchmaker I was—apparently, my love radar must be permanently broken.

The irony of the situation struck my funny bone, and I started laughing hard until tears streaked down my cheeks.

Andy stared at me with a weird look on her face. "Did I say something funny?"

I wiped the tears away. "No, no. Sorry. I just realized some stuff. I guess I've had my head stuck up my own butt for a while now." I looked at him, then her. "I didn't see you two getting . . . closer."

Andy bit her lower lip. "So, you're not mad at me?"

"Are you kidding?" I smiled. "I'm just glad to see you happy."

"Well," Bobby said, "I'm sure you guessed that I used to have a small crush on you." He slipped his hand into Andy's. "But then I realized Andy is the one for me. I hope I didn't hurt you or anything. Don't give up on those dreams of finding someone special just because of me, Felicity."

I almost started laughing again, until I realized he was dead serious.

Keeping my face as straight as possible, I said, "Thanks. I'm a pretty strong girl. I think I'll make it."

Bobby tugged Andy out of her seat. "Come on, I'll buy you some lunch."

"We'll talk in a few," Andy said to me, heading with Bobby into the lunch line.

Unbelievable.

I propped my elbows up on the table and plunked my face in my hands, stunned at the unexpected turn of events. This was turning out to be one craaaazy day.

And what was even weirder is that no one was paying Andy and Bobby one bit of attention. They were too busy moaning and groaning over their loss of love to notice the overly happy new couple.

Maya showed up at the table, plopping her lunch on the surface. "Hey, how's it going?"

"Not bad. How are you? Are things getting better at home?"

She shrugged. "I guess so. I finally talked to my parents yesterday and told them they have to back off. I can juggle school and a boyfriend without my grades suffering."

"Good for you!" I was thrilled Maya had finally put her foot down. She did her best to obey her parents' wishes. It wasn't fair for them to treat her this way. "And what did they say?"

"They didn't seem too thrilled, but they let it go. I'm glad they did, because I am *not* giving up on Scott. I'd just sneak out and see him if I needed to." She glanced around. "Hey, where's Andy?"

"She's in line," I said, then paused dramatically. "With Bobby Loward."

"What?" she said, confusion written across her face.

"They're dating now. And they're also going to prom together."

"Whoa, whoa, whoa," she said, holding her hands up. "Back up. When did they start dating?"

I laughed. "I think, like, five minutes ago."

Andy and Bobby returned, carrying their lunch trays.

I let Andy fill Maya in on all the juicy details as I sat back and stayed quiet. Maya squealed and cooed with Andy over her new relationship. This was Andy's time to shine, and I didn't want to butt in.

Besides, I hadn't even matched them up. I guess love was still going on around school, whether I had a hand in it or not. That thought should have been comforting, but it just reminded me of what a bad job I was doing as a cupid.

The lunch bell rang.

I gathered my stuff and went to anthropology class, where more cranky students were griping about the woes of lost love.

By now I was wearing thin. My nerves were raw from hearing so much complaining. I didn't think I could sit through another class like this. I needed a moment to myself in peace and quiet, even if just for a bathroom break.

I borrowed the hall pass from the teacher, claiming I wasn't feeling well and needed to see the nurse, and practically ran to the bathroom. The shuffle-sprint I was doing probably looked ultrastupid, but I needed a quiet moment to collect myself.

I ducked into a stall and sat on the lidded toilet, forcing myself to breathe in calmly through my nose and out my mouth. Maybe it was time to practice some Zen-like relaxation techniques I'd learned from Andy's mom. I closed my eyes and pretended I was on some Tibetan mountain, looking at the sunrise.

A couple of minutes later I felt remarkably calm. There was something to this meditation stuff. I should try it more often. Maybe Andy's mom wasn't so wacky after all.

Okay, I could totally handle this situation. What was important was to keep my focus and come up with a way to repair the matchmaking damage I'd done. Maybe I could take my time and do fewer matches in a day, but make them higher quality. I could stay home in the evenings instead of going out until I'd paired everyone who was unhappy.

Yeah, that part sucked, but this was my job, so there was no sense griping about it. After all, it certainly wasn't going to fix itself. Only one person could make things right—me.

With that in mind, I stood and grabbed the door handle to exit the stall. Then I heard a few voices come into the bathroom . . . one being Mallory's.

I bit back a groan of misery and parked myself back down on the seat. No way did I want yet another confrontation with Her Royal Snottiness.

"Omigod, did you see Mitzi's dress today? Totally tacky," one of the girls said.

"Ew, I know!" another chimed in. I heard lip-smacking sounds— one of them must have been fixing lipstick. "Who wears shoulder pads anymore? That's so eighties."

"Yeah, I guess," Mallory said, her voice sounding a bit flat.

"Well, I'm superhot now. I'm ready to head back out," the first girl said.

"Go ahead, you guys. I'll meet you in a sec. I gotta . . . go to the bathroom," Mallory replied.

I heard the door close.

Great. Trapped in the bathroom with my archenemy, a.k.a. Satan's Future Bride. Just how I wanted to spend my serenity break time.

Suddenly, I heard a sniffling sound. Then a few choked-back sobs that echoed off the tiled walls.

Wow, was she *crying*? I didn't know Mallory had a soul, much less emotions.

It hit me—she must be really upset about James and Mitzi being together. Seeing them around, happy with each other, must be getting under her skin.

Crap, what should I do?

If I came out, she might be embarrassed to be busted crying. But I'd never seen her like this before, and a part of me felt bad for her. Especially since I was the one who'd caused this misery for her through my matchmaking. It didn't matter if she was my nemesis— helping her was my professional obligation.

Well, it was now or never.

I opened the door slowly and peeked my head around the corner. Mallory was slumped over on the edge of the sink, dabbing at her tears with a tissue. I shuffled to the far end of the row of sinks. My movement caught her eye and she gasped, straightening up instantly.

"Geez, you scared me," she said, her lip automatically curling up at the sight of me. "Wait—were you eavesdropping on us?"

I rolled my eyes. "Like I want to listen in on your conversations. There *are* other reasons to go in the bathroom, you know." Not that I was actually using it for that purpose, but she didn't need to know that.

Mallory stood, heading to the door. "Whatever."

Okay, this wasn't going well so far. Maybe not one of my better ideas.

"Look, I'm sorry if you're upset," I said.

She stopped and turned to me slowly. "I'm. Fine," she bit out through ground teeth. "And even if I weren't, I don't need *your* pity."

"You know what?" I retorted, sick of her crap and unable to stop myself. "I never did anything to deserve you treating me like this. I know you think I had a thing for James, but I didn't. I don't need to steal friends' guys."

Especially if that guy was James. Ew.

Her jaw dropped open, and she stared at me for a moment. Then she lifted her chin and glared at me over her nose.

"Whatever," she huffed. "Once you got tired of trying to take my boyfriend, you decided to move on to someone else." She paused and tilted her head, tapping a finger to her chin. "Gee, I wonder if Derek knows how strongly you feel about him. I know you've been crushing on him since freshman year. He's in the cafeteria right now. Maybe he should find out."

Mallory grabbed the door handle and jerked it open, stalking out of the bathroom. Her tall heels clacked across the tiled floor in the hallway.

Heart about to pound out of my chest, I followed right on her heels, my brain desperately clawing around for what to do.

"Stop," I said, my throat choked up. She kept moving.

We burst through the cafeteria doors and reached Derek's table, where he was surrounded by his jock friends and a couple of girls in Mallory's group.

Mallory slid into an open seat. I stopped right beside her. This could *not* be happening.

"Hey, everyone," she said, her eyes wide as she glanced around and caught Derek's attention, "I learned some interesting info about our good friend Felicity. She's in love. And you'll never guess who the guy is."

chapter twenty

Hearing Mallory spill things out like that, so freaking rudely, totally pushed me past my limit. No way was she going to get glory from outing me.

Um, so to speak.

Nope, I'd just have to "out" myself.

Digging my nails into my palms, I said in a loud voice, "Let me spare you the boring story, Mallory." I turned to Derek, who stared at me. "It's you, Derek. I've had a crush on you since freshman year. What can I say? You're a great guy. Who wouldn't want to be with you?"

The whole cafeteria went silent. It seemed everyone was shocked that I'd actually confessed my feelings, out loud, in public.

Even Mallory blinked rapidly, unsure of what to do.

Derek's eyes went wide, and his jaw dropped.

Before he could speak, I charged on, tears welling in my eyes. "But don't worry—I won't throw myself on you."

I dragged in a deep, ragged breath. With blurry vision, I faced Mallory. "You know, I may not be the smartest girl, or the prettiest girl, but at least I can go to bed every night grateful I'm not like you."

With that, I whirled around and fled the cafeteria, not even stopping to apologize to the people I bumped into. I charged down the hallway and ducked into the library—back to the empty room where Derek and I used to meet—then let the tears flow freely.

I cried for a couple of minutes with my back pressed against a bookshelf, my chest aching in embarrassment. God, what an idiot I was! No way could it have worked. He was so out of my league.

And now I was a joke. I'd never hear the end of this, and I was sure news would be all over school within an hour about my dramatic declaration of love. In fact, they were probably laughing their asses off in the cafeteria right now about me.

Well, maybe not Derek—he didn't seem like that kind of guy—but I probably shocked him in a bad, bad way. No way would he still take me to prom, now that our "just friends" agreement was shot.

At any rate, after my little confession, I was going to have to join a convent now. I sniffled loudly and tried to imagine what life as a nun would be like. It would be happy and fun, like the musical *The Sound of Music*. Those nuns were always dancing around on hilltops and singing.

Maybe there was actually something to that idea. No evil people trying to make you look bad. No worries about dating.

But no chance of finding love at all.

No, I'd just have to suck it up out here in the real world and try to make it. Once I got to college, I wouldn't be seeing most of these people anyway.

But I *would* have to see them when I left the sanctuary of the library, and for the rest of this year.

And all of next.

Ugh. I wondered if there was a way to transfer to another school. Or maybe Mom could homeschool me from now on.

I heard a light cough in the room and looked up. Derek stood in the doorway.

I glanced away and swiped at the tears in my eyes, trying

to pretend like I wasn't crying. Like I hadn't spilled my guts in front of everyone in the most mortifying way possible. What had seemed courageous at the time looked really, really stupid in retrospect.

Derek scratched the back of his neck, his eyes intense as they locked with mine. "I need to talk to you."

He looked almost angry. Was he mad because I'd embarrassed him? I hadn't even thought he might be ticked from my public confessional.

We stared at each other for a long, uncomfortable moment. I dropped my gaze. I didn't know what else to say, especially since I'd pretty much laid it all out in the cafeteria.

Then Derek was suddenly right in front of me, touching under my chin to tilt my face up toward him. He brushed my lips with his and then deepened the kiss, his hands stroking my neck and back.

Oh God, is this really happening? Is Derek really kissing me?

Yeah, screw the nun idea—*this* was the stuff I wanted.

I breathed in his light cologne as we continued to kiss. I had no idea how long it lasted, nor did I care. It was everything I'd ever dreamed it would be. His mouth tasted warm and slightly sweet.

He tugged me closer to his body. I wrapped my arms around his neck, falling into this amazing moment.

Derek pulled away, and I fought the urge to drag his head back down to kiss me more.

I bit my lower lip and looked up into his eyes, only inches from mine. "Does this mean you're not pissed at me for the way I . . . blabbed my feelings?"

He cupped my face. "Felicity, I am totally, utterly crazy about you. But I'm also mad that you left like that. You didn't give me a chance to respond."

Shame swirled in my chest. Derek was right—I hadn't even considered that he could possibly match my feelings. I hadn't let him say anything, too afraid he was going to break my heart, right there in front of Mallory and the others.

I squeaked out through a tight throat, "I was embarrassed."

He dropped one hand and pressed it against my back, creating delicious sensations. "I practically did everything I could to show you I fell for you. And you still didn't get it."

Wait—he'd liked me, even before my confession? Wow, I was totally clueless.

No wonder I was such a bad matchmaker. I hadn't seen what

was right in front of my nose. First, Andy and Bobby. And now, this. It was high time I opened my eyes and really looked at what was going on around me.

"Sorry. Apparently, I'm pretty bad at things like this."

Derek laughed. "Yeah, I figured that much out." He pulled back, grabbed my hand, and sat with me at one of the nearby tables. "Look, I have something else to confess to you."

"What's that? You like to collect American Girl dolls or something?" I chuckled.

"Not quite." Derek's eyes darted away from mine, and he swallowed hard, suddenly looking nervous. "Look, I know what you are."

This time, my throat completely closed. I knew beyond a shadow of a doubt that he was talking about the cupid thing.

I stared at him in horror, wondering what to do. I must have given myself away somehow. I was so going to get canned. Janet was going to pitch a fit.

I drew in a deep, calming breath. "What are you talking about?" Yeah, maybe denial was the route to go. I could plead the fifth.

He raised an eyebrow, then dug into his pants pocket and whipped out a hot-pink LoveLine 3000.

Just like mine.

I stared at the PDA for a good thirty seconds, trying to figure out what to say. Pieces fell into place—Derek's hesitation to talk about his job. His continued questions about *my* job. The starry-eyed couples that *I* didn't match up.

He shifted on his chair. "Aren't you going to say anything?"

I opened my mouth, then closed it. Then burst out laughing.

"What a pair we are," I said, wiping more tears off my face. "I never would have guessed you were a cupid. So, why didn't Janet tell me I wasn't the only one here?"

"Well, she'd suddenly decided she wanted a guy and a girl to work each school, since she figured it would be more balanced. So I was hired just a few weeks ago to be our school's other match-maker."

"Then you knew I was a cupid here."

Derek shook his head, a small smile on his face. "Actually, Janet didn't tell me who the other cupid was. She wanted to wait until she'd had a chance to meet with both of us together. But I figured it out when you made the whole school fall for me."

I blushed. "Oh, that."

"When I realized you were one of the only people not touched by the cupid magic, I started watching you closely. I didn't say anything at first because I was trying to find the right way to approach you on how we could fix the . . . hasty matches you made."

"Yeah, that didn't go so hot," I groaned.

He grabbed my hand and rubbed his fingers across the tops of mine. "Don't sweat it. We'll get it fixed, together."

I had a hard time thinking with his warm hands touching me, but I made a valiant attempt anyway. "So no one else knows about us, then?"

"Are you kidding?" Derek scoffed. "Can you imagine the hazing the football team would give me?"

"That's true."

Wow, he was in an even worse spot than I was. And here I kept feeling sorry for myself about keeping it a secret. Poor Derek had to keep looking macho while making his love matches in secret.

With a hot-pink PDA, to top it off.

He snuggled closer to me, his warm side pressing against mine. "Wanna get out of here? You have a class to get back to, and I'd better finish my lunch." He paused. "But we could hang out after art class. Study or grab some coffee or something."

"That sounds great," I said. It would be good to have his help and advice in fixing up the matchmaking disaster. It would be even better to have him to kiss and hang out with as way more than just friends.

Hand in hand, Derek and I strolled out of the library. For the first time in weeks I felt a sense of contentment with life. Andy had found a great match in the unlikely Bobby. Maya had stood up to her parents and was still doing wonderfully with Scott. And I'd finally gotten the guy of my dreams.

Love was all around. What more could a cupid want?

PUCKER UP

chapter one

Could a person die of happiness overload? Because if that were possible, I was so going to keel over any second.

But what a way to go.

My brand-new boyfriend Derek's strong, lean fingers threaded tightly through mine as we strolled through the door of Starbucks. It was our first official date since we'd begun going out yesterday afternoon. We'd decided to grab some coffee after school to discuss how to help all the broken-hearted single people I'd hastily matched with each other when I was trying to reverse the effects of me accidentally making them all fall in love with him.

Yeah, not one of the better ideas I've had in the couple of months since being hired by my boss, Janet, at Cupid's Hollow.

But fortunately for me, I also found out yesterday that Derek was a fellow cupid, and he'd promised to help me out. And I just knew that we were going to make things right—together.

"Hey, Felicity, what kind of drink do you want?" he asked, turning those piercing green eyes to me.

I swallowed, wanting to pinch myself in über-glee. I was on an honest-to-God date with the guy I'd been crushing on since freshman year, something I'd fantasized about for*ever*.

"Felicity?" he asked, one eyebrow raised.

Hey, dork! He asked you a question! I mentally chided myself, trying to snap out of my love haze.

"Um, how about a Mocha Frappuccino?" I suggested. "Those are supergood." And super laden with caffeine. Yum!

He smiled, his cheek dimpling slightly. "Sure. Why don't you find us a private spot to sit?"

I nodded, picking out a booth in the back corner where no one was around and settling into one side of the table. Plenty of isolation for us to discuss our top secret cupid business matters.

Digging through my purse, I pulled out my hot-pink LoveLine 3000, the handheld technology we cupids use to send matchmaking e-mails to our targets. I put it on my lap, turning it on. While I waited for Derek to return, I kept myself occupied by staring at his absolutely perfect butt.

After a couple of minutes Derek sauntered over to the table, drinks in hand, and slid into the booth seat across from me. I accepted my drink gratefully and forced myself to take a slow sip through the straw, not wanting to give myself brain freeze. That crap *hurt*.

"Okay, I'm dying to ask you a question," I finally said, leaning over the table toward Derek in excitement. "When Janet hired you, did she take you to the bow-and-arrow room and give you a . . . demonstration?"

I rubbed the middle of my chest, remembering how it had felt at my interview to have the gold arrow hit me and disappear, leaving only a tingle. Janet, our boss, sure didn't mess around . . . she'd wanted to make sure I knew the cupid powers were real. Not that I'd doubted her after she shot me, but over time I'd learned the reality of matchmaking all too well . . . both the ups and downs.

Derek laughed. "So she shot you with an arrow also. Glad I wasn't the only doubter she'd hired."

God, it was so awesome to be able to work with my new boyfriend. I'd finally have someone I could talk about my cupid woes with! Not that I wasn't desperate to dish it all to my two best friends, Andy and Maya . . . but my contract specifically stipulated I wasn't allowed to tell anyone the specifics of my job, upon pain of death.

Okay, the contract terms weren't *that* drastic, but I just knew something awful *would* happen to me. I sure didn't want to find out what, though.

"Janet's kind of scary," I whispered, almost afraid that by some weird voodoo she could overhear me talking about her.

"No kidding. She's intimidating." He took the lid off his cup, releasing a puff of steam into the air, and took a drink.

"So, how many matches have you made so far?" I asked him. We each had a weekly quota to meet, and I was eager for tips and motivation.

"Only a few." He shrugged. "I'm trying to take my time and still perfect my profiles. It's hard work, studying everyone and making sure I represent them accurately."

I nodded in sympathy. "Yeah, it took me a while to do those too."

A souring thought hit me, and I pinched my lips together. If I'd taken more time to add greater details to my profiles, like Derek was doing, maybe I wouldn't have made so many bad matches since I'd started working as a cupid. And thus, there wouldn't be so many desolate people grumping their way through school when their love spells had worn off.

Shaking my head resolutely, I pushed the thought out of my brain. All I'd been trying to do was get my classmates' attention off Derek and back on one another, where it belonged. Besides, there were now two matchmakers on the job at Greenville High, ready and eager to get things fixed up before prom, which would be in just over three weeks.

And I couldn't focus on my own prom happiness with Derek until I got these disaster matches resolved, once and for all.

I took my LoveLine 3000 out of my lap and put it on the tabletop, ready to get down to business. "Did you bring yours?"

"Sure did." Derek tugged his out of his back pocket and turned it on. "Last night I made a list of everyone in school who is currently single and in need of a match. I'll e-mail you half of the list." He bent his head over the PDA, typing on the little keyboard.

Weird, I'd never thought about e-mailing another cupid. I wonder what would happen when he sent me the document. Would it make us fall even more in love? Maybe we would be like my parents were when I'd had a "brilliant" idea and decided to matchmake the two of them for their anniversary a few weeks ago.

I shuddered, remembering their feet sticking out of their bedroom doorway as they went at it on their floor. Time to push that gross little memory into the dark recesses of my brain, back where it belonged.

"Hey, you still here?" Derek asked, a crooked grin on his face. He reached over and brushed my hand, causing my skin to tingle.

"Yeah, sorry, had a bad flashback," I said, drinking some of my Frappuccino with my free hand. I'd tell him about matchmaking my parents later, after I'd done another mental scrub or two or twenty.

My PDA vibrated. I opened my new e-mail from Derek, half expecting my chest to tingle—the surefire identifier of a love match.

Nothing happened.

After staring dumbly at the screen for several long seconds, I almost smacked my own forehead. *Duh, Felicity.* I'd forgotten that cupids can't matchmake themselves, so Derek sending me an e-mail wouldn't have any power over me, anyway.

I focused my attention on the list, scrolling down to check out the names. "Okay, I need to make matches for everyone on here, right?"

"Yeah. I think if we take our time and do some quality matches, they should hold together with better odds."

My stomach twitched. He was right, of course, but I was embarrassed that Derek, who had been a cupid for only a few weeks, had managed to figure out more about matchmaking than I had.

He reached back into his pocket and pulled out his cupid manual. "Each person can be matched with someone else on the list, just to keep things simple. I prepared the two lists according to the manual. There was one formula that seemed overly complicated, but the one on page"—he drawled off, flipping through the book—"fifty-two seemed like it would do the job."

Derek turned the manual facing toward me and pointed at a tiny chart filled with wavy lines and arrows.

Yeahhhhh . . . I'd completely forgotten about that book. Whoops. The writing was so dry and boring, I'd almost fallen asleep reading it. I think I'd stuffed it in my bookshelf a few days after becoming a cupid and never opened it up again, preferring to wing it my own way.

I nodded sagely, pretending I could interpret the chart. "Good thinking. That one should work out great." Right, like I knew what the crap he was talking about.

I made a mental note to dig my manual out again and make a more valiant effort to read the damn thing. Geez, we'd only been here a short time, and already Derek was schooling me in the art and science of matchmaking. How mortifying.

My cheeks burned.

Well, it was my own fault. This wasn't the time for embarrassment or shame. I had to do what the situation called for, and none of my ideas had worked out well so far. Time to try Derek's plan now.

"Let's run this by Janet first," I said, "just to be safe." I knew from experience that our boss liked to be kept in the loop. Plus, she'd probably like to see us working together. And anything that made Janet happy was good in my book.

"Sure, that's a good idea." He took a sip of his drink and smiled at me. "I'm looking forward to working with you."

"Me too," I replied with a happy sigh, a warm glow spreading through my chest and limbs.

I didn't need a love arrow shot at me to make me get tingles—being in Derek's presence was more than enough.

"Well," Janet said to me and Derek, leaning back in her plush executive chair, "I think that's a great plan. And I like even more how you two are working together on this. I was hoping you'd get along." She gave us a nod of approval.

I beamed, happy that Janet could not only squeeze in a meeting with us on such short notice but also approved of our idea on how to fix the matchmaking mess at school. That way we could get started on it ASAP.

"Thanks," I replied, excitement bubbling in my voice. "Derek's great to work with." With all the strength I could muster, I resisted the urge to cast a lovey-dovey gaze at Derek, who was sitting in the chair beside me, across from Janet's desk. But out of the corner of my eye, I saw him smile at my words.

After solidifying our matchmaking plan at Starbucks earlier today, Derek and I had also decided we'd lie low with the boyfriend/girlfriend stuff around work until we'd scoped the situation out first. Janet didn't know we were dating, and we didn't want to make anything more complicated than necessary right now.

"Okay, let me see your PDAs," she said, reaching her hands out toward us. "I'll download a copy of your lists for reference."

We handed them over to her, and she synced them, one by one, to her main computer. After she was done, she laid them on the desk. "I'll review the documents later, but it seems like you're on the right track." She paused. "Actually, Derek, since you're here, there's another guy cupid I'd like to introduce you to. He's in the office next door. Felicity, we'll be back in a few minutes—just wait right here."

"Sure thing," I said, trying not to give Derek any inappropriately slutty looks as he filed past me and followed Janet out the door.

I crossed my legs and fidgeted for a couple of minutes. Then I stood up and plucked my PDA off her desk so I could put it back in my purse. As I lifted the LoveLine 3000, I saw my name at the top of a list on the left page of her daily planner. My heart pounded, and I swallowed hard.

Was I in trouble? Maybe she was on to me and Derek and was upset about us dating. Or maybe she'd found out some of my other cupid secrets, like that I'd previously matchmade my friend Maya with three guys . . . or that I'd paired up my parents for their anniversary. I'd deleted those e-mails from my LoveLine 3000, but maybe she'd gotten the info somehow.

I had to know. With a furtive glance at the door, I quickly jerked the planner off the desk, scanning its contents. It was a to-do list, and there was a checkbox beside me. And after my name was Derek's name. Under us were other pairs of names. What was this?

Then it hit me.

Janet must have matchmade me and Derek.

chapter two

My jaw dropped in shock. Janet had paired us up? But I didn't remember getting a love e-mail or anything else yesterday. In fact, I didn't remember any sort of weird tingling feeling at all.

I shook my head, staring at the words. How had she done it?

Well, cupids *have* been around for thousands of years. Maybe there were many other methods of matchmaking that I hadn't even imagined.

The doorknob turned. I dropped the planner, deftly plopping back in my seat. Something told me I probably wasn't supposed to know about being matchmade, so I decided to keep my mouth shut about what I'd seen.

"You can call him anytime," Janet said to Derek as they walked into the room. "Okay, we're all done here, you two." She moved behind her desk and handed Derek his PDA back. "I'll see you in your individual meetings next week."

He turned and smiled at me, his eyes lighting up as they crinkled in the corners. I melted a little, like ooey-gooey butter. If he and I were together a hundred years, I'd never get enough of him.

Then a startling thought flew into my mind. Did this new discovery of mine mean the only reason Derek was in love with me was because we'd been paired together by Janet? Was his love genuine or just a result of a magically induced spell? I knew mine was sincere because I'd been in love with him for years. But it wasn't the same story for Derek.

With suddenly shaky legs I stood, offering Janet a weak smile. "Well, I'd better get home before my mom wonders where her car is."

We headed back to the parking lot. I tucked my hand into Derek's, but on the inside I was almost dizzy from the new worry that swirled in my head. I knew I should be more understanding of Janet's actions. After all, that's what *I* did for a living—find people who belong together and give them a chance at love. But I had to admit, I'd never considered the idea that Derek and I could have been paired up too.

I guess I'd just figured that he and I were destined to be together and that my bold confession to him in the cafeteria yesterday about my true feelings had set our destiny into motion. I still couldn't believe I'd found the courage to spill my guts in front of Derek, his friends, and a crapload of people eating lunch, me loudly proclaiming that I'd been crushing on him since freshman year. Even now my stomach flipped over itself when I thought of it.

We stopped at Derek's car. He tugged me close to him, and I reveled in the sensation of his warm body against mine.

He pressed his lips on the top of my head. "I'll give you a call tonight," he whispered against my hair.

I nodded, not trusting myself to speak. He got into his car and waved as he drove away from me.

After slipping into my own driver's seat, I navigated out of the parking lot and through the back ways to get home, unable to enjoy the usual pleasure I got from seeing the springtime blossoms erupting on the trees lining the streets of the neighborhoods. As I drove, I wrestled back and forth with the idea of letting Derek know we'd been paired up, then decided against it. I didn't want to plant any seeds of doubt in Derek's mind about what I now perceived as our fragile relationship.

Now I almost wished I *hadn't* seen Janet's planner because I was going to be superparanoid and would scrutinize every aspect of our relationship for the next two weeks. Especially since I knew from professional experience that, unfortunately, pairing two people didn't mean they'd stay together after the love spell wore off.

I pulled the car into the driveway and ambled into my house. Though I was tempted to run straight to the freezer and grab a carton of Chunky Monkey ice cream for insta-therapy, I was better off trying to push my worried thoughts out of my head and make some love matches instead.

If I continued eating ice cream every time I was upset, I was gonna have to wear a muumuu to prom. And there was no way I was going to eat myself right out of my fabulously hot red dress.

"Mom, I'm home from my work meeting," I said, dropping the borrowed keys back on top of her purse on the hall table. I gazed at the logo on the car key chain and sighed. How many lasting love matches would I have to make to save up for a car of my own? It sure would be nice to start getting more bonuses in my paycheck.

"Hey, Felicity," she said from the kitchen table. "Did you put the car keys back in my purse?"

I resisted the urge to roll my eyes at the House Nazi. "Yes, *Mom,* I did."

I flew up the stairs toward my room.

"Make sure you clean up that mess in your room," Mom yelled up to me.

Sheesh. I closed my door and grabbed my phone off my side table. I was desperate to call someone and talk about Derek, but I didn't want to be one of those obnoxious chicks who did nothing but blab on and on and on about her boyfriend. Ick. That got old fast.

Instead, I dialed one of my BFFs, Andy, to see what she was up to.

"Hey, Felicity," she said when she picked up. "Long time, no talkee. I'm still cracking up about your cafeteria love confession yesterday. I only wish I'd been there to witness it."

"Yeah, I think I'm a legend at school now," I said, giggling. I thought school today would have been a nightmare of one embarrassment after another, given the way I'd practically screamed my love for Derek out loud. But instead, I'd had several girls come up to me and congratulate me on being so ballsy, wishing they had the guts to do the same thing with the guys they liked.

And Mallory, the über-jerk who had started the whole incident by threatening to rat my feelings out to Derek in front of everyone, had stayed away from me all day today. Talk about an unexpected bonus!

On the other end of the phone I heard Andy's mom hollering something at her.

"Okay!" Andy said to her, her voice piercing my eardrums. "Sorry, I gotta go," she mumbled to me. "Mom asked me to run up to the store and pick her up another container of soy milk." She sighed. "I'm so, soooo glad I got my license. I always wanted to be her personal errand girl."

"You're not the only one," I commiserated. "Mom seems to think I'll jump at the chance to borrow the car, even if it's picking up her crap." After saying that, I peeked toward the door, half-afraid the House Nazi had somehow overheard my griping. She had a way of knowing everything that happened in this house.

"We'll catch up tomorrow, 'kay?"

"Sure thing," I said. "Have fun."

We hung up.

I sludged over to my bookshelf. Guilt over my lazy cupidness forced me to pull out the manual Janet had given me when I was hired. Draping across my bed, I tucked a pillow under my upper body and flipped the book open to the description of the chart Derek had pointed out. Surely the guidebook wasn't as bad as I remembered.

After all, if Derek could get it, so could I, right?

I'd heard in my health class that after childbirth women somehow mentally block how painful the whole birthing process was. My teacher had explained that was nature's way of making sure people continued to have kids instead of just popping out one and then never having another baby again because of all the pain.

Maybe being a cupid came with the same kind of mystical amnesia because after staring at that stupid chart in the manual, I'd quickly realized that I'd forgotten how wretched that book was. And how painful it was to be going through it again, especially when the material read like this:

> To facilitate the highest-quality compatibility between
> two parties, refer to chart 412B, above. Note: The
> applied elements contained within the chart, combined
> with a timely and accurate profile for each party, will
> ensure a higher ratio of matchmaking accuracy,
> provided all conditions are met.

I'd studied that one page for a full half hour, finally succumbing to my impulse to close the book and throw it back onto my bookshelf, where it would meet its final resting place.

Maybe I was better off just talking to Derek if I had questions. That way I would encourage conversation between us . . . which would allow me to take some notes as I shamelessly picked his brain. Plus, it would help get my mind off the whole love-spell thing between us, which was now constantly lurking in the back of my consciousness.

The evening had passed fast. I'd made a few matches from my list and had gone to bed early, eager to start seeing the results. Especially since I'd noticed, as I headed toward school this morning, that many students were still sour and depressed. People shuffled quietly through the hallways, grousing under their breaths.

It would be so easy to sink back into a deep funk and let it get me down too, but I was determined to float above it.

"Hey," Maya called out to me, waving with her free hand. In the other hand she clutched her ever-present trumpet case.

I gave her a quick hug. "How's it going?"

She shrugged. "Not bad. Except—"

Before she could finish, Scott, her supercutie boyfriend, came up and gave her a big hug from behind, kissing the top of her head.

I smiled, warmed by my friend's romantic happiness . . . and, to be honest, by the fact that this was a match I'd made that had actually lasted.

Maya turned to face him, hugging tightly. "Hey, you."

The first bell rang. I glanced around but didn't see Andy. I wasn't alarmed, though—she sometimes ran on her own schedule, and I knew she'd check in with us soon enough.

Maya and I said good-bye to Scott, then went to our first period English class. Mrs. Kendel was at her usual station by the door.

"Miss Takahashi, Miss Walker, come in," she said gruffly, waving us in with her thick hand. She closed the door after we entered and went to the chalkboard, writing some terms on the board.

I slid into my seat and, with as much subtlety as I could, glanced over at Mike, a quiet guy in the back corner of our classroom. He was one of the people I'd matchmade last night after studying the list carefully to find the perfect person for him.

I'd finally settled on Adele, the girl who was assigned the seat in front of him. She was usually a quiet person as well, and they seemed to be nicely suited for each other. I'd even used more than my usual three compatibility factors, just to make sure they had enough in common to make the match last.

Plus, I had no doubt that Mike was already crushing on her. Throughout the year I'd seen him look at Adele when he thought she wasn't looking. I hadn't paired them up before because she'd had a boyfriend, but they'd broken up recently.

And no, that *wasn't* my fault, thank you very much—they had been together before I'd become a cupid.

Now that she was single, and happened to be on my list, she was fair game.

Adele hadn't arrived in class yet, and I couldn't read Mike's face to see if he'd opened the love e-mail I'd sent him. He was as calm and serene as ever.

I chewed on my lower lip, hoping I hadn't messed up. He wasn't exuding any kind of romantic aura around him, and most guys by now were practically—

Right then Adele slipped into the room, instantly casting her gaze onto Mike.

He rose from his seat, going right to her.

"Mr. Jones," Mrs. Kendel said, her wrinkled face scrunched up in irritation. "Please take your seat."

Ignoring the teacher, he and Adele leaped into each other's arms, boldly kissing right there in class.

My eyes about popped out of my head, and I cupped my hand over my mouth in surprise. I guess it was the quiet ones you had to watch out for. Well, at least I had solid confirmation that the matchmaking had worked.

The class erupted in equal parts applause and giggles. Even in a negative mood, no one could resist people publicly proclaiming their horniness in the middle of class. Some things never change.

"You go, girl!" one girl cried out.

"Get it on!" a guy in the back of class said, chortling wildly.

"Mr. Jones! Miss Mossinger!" Mrs. Kendel snapped, stepping over to the two of them and tugging them apart with a hefty jerk.

Mike's and Adele's lips made a popping sound from being separated so quickly, and they stared at each other with glazed eyes. Mike's mouth was smeared all over with Adele's pastel-pink lipstick.

"Need I remind you that this is *not* appropriate behavior in class?" Mrs. Kendel sniffed in disdain, anger making her body shake. "Go to the principal's office, *now!*"

A few students snickered as Mike and Adele walked out of the classroom hand in hand, oblivious to Mrs. Kendel's blast. She stared in shock at their retreating figures and gripped the end of the door, forgetting for the moment that she was supposed to be teaching us about whatever crap she'd been in the middle of writing on the board.

"You know they're going to the bleachers," some smart-ass guy behind me said quietly. "They're so gonna make a baby."

Maya snorted. "Holy crap, was that crazy," she said.

"Just as crazy as when that one photography guy came in here and read you that poem," a girl on the other side of her whispered, loud enough for everyone to hear. "Remember that? God, that was awesome," she said wistfully.

Maya's cheeks flamed red, and she cast her gaze onto her desk.

I'd completely forgotten about Quentin, one of the three guys I'd initially paired Maya with in my fiasco-fest back in March. He'd burst into the classroom and had begged Mrs. Kendel to let him ask Maya out on a date via his lame poem. And I was willing to bet Maya had probably blocked that little memory as well.

"Anyway," I said, trying to change the subject and save Maya the embarrassment of dates from the past, "aren't you glad we're finally done with reading novels in here and are moving on to something different?"

At my words, Mrs. Kendel finally shook herself out of her shock and shuffled over to the chalkboard. I guess I couldn't blame her— she'd been a teacher here forever and a day and probably had never had things like this happen until I became a cupid. The poor woman was going to be driven to early retirement if her students didn't knock it off with the crazy makey-outey stuff.

It also didn't help things that pairing her up with the chemistry teacher last month during my frantic rematching had ended disastrously. I'd seen last night that she was on my list of people to fix, but I had *no* idea what kind of a man was right for her. Which meant I needed to watch her closely and get to know her better.

A fun prospect for me. This one would require all the magic I could scrounge up in my PDA.

Mrs. Kendel shook her head rapidly and blinked. Then she turned a beady eye toward the class, clearing her throat. "Class," she said in a crisp, professional voice, as if the last couple of minutes never happened, "we're going to be discussing narratives for the next couple of weeks. We'll start by reading examples of stellar narratives and then follow the lesson up by writing a narrative of our own." Before anyone could respond, she continued, "And, yes, before you ask, it will be graded."

I groaned inwardly, rolling my eyes in Maya's direction. She suppressed a giggle in response.

We both knew what this meant. What should probably have been a relatively fun project would most likely have all the life sucked out of it by Mrs. Kendel, in the quest to write the perfect narrative. She didn't have a fun bone in her pruny body.

With a heavy sigh, I tugged out my notebook and started jotting down whatever Mrs. Kendel was talking about. I couldn't wait to talk to Derek and see if his matchmaking had gone as well as mine.

chapter three

"Your mosaic is awesome," I whispered to Derek, who was sitting beside me in art class at the end of the school day.

He gave me a huge smile, putting down a tiny scrap of red paper he was about to glue onto his artwork. It was an image of a football player about to catch a ball. I wasn't a big sports person or anything, but his mosaic was good enough to draw even me in.

"I'd kiss you in thanks," Derek replied, "but I heard the teachers are cracking down on that."

I chuckled, putting down my scissors and trying to ignore the tingly feeling spreading across my lips at the thought of kissing Derek again. The last bell of the day couldn't ring fast enough for me.

"Tell me about it. That incident was in my class!" I dropped my voice even lower. "I'd paired up the two makeout bandits last night."

"You did good work," he said, admiration in his voice. "I heard it was quite a scene. Wish I could have been there."

Our art teacher, Mr. Bunch, who was leaning back in the chair at his desk, shot us a dirty look for talking when we should have been focusing on perfecting our craft. I tried to return my attention to my own crapola mosaic. It was supposed to be a woman playing a violin but instead looked like Picasso had vomited on my paper.

Oh, well. I had to accept there were some things in life I just wasn't good at. And art was apparently one of them.

Derek continued gluing the little squares of paper on his masterpiece, concentrating with the seriousness of a professional artist on his work.

As I glanced at the mosaic, a heavy lump of jealousy settled squarely in my chest. It was a good thing Derek was so cute and sweet because it would be easy to feel threatened by him and his multitude of talents. Everything he touched turned out perfectly.

Finally the gods of school took mercy on me and rang the last bell of the day. I cleaned up my art station and waited for Derek to be done so we could go to the library, where we'd be able to talk in privacy.

As he walked toward me, a bright smile on his face, I couldn't help the feeling of pride. He was looking at *me*, his girlfriend!

But is it magic induced, or real? a cruel little voice in my head taunted.

Shut up, I ordered myself.

But I couldn't help looking at the sparkle in his green eyes a little differently, with a little less pleasure than I'd had before. After all, hadn't I seen that exact same look on the guys I'd paired Maya up with? And on Andy's former boyfriend Tyler, when he'd been under the love spell too?

And on Mike this morning in English class, the moment he'd laid eyes on his love match Adele?

Derek linked his fingers with mine and gave me a warm kiss. We paced down the hallway, my gaze focused on the ground. I stared at my feet as we walked, unsure of what to say. Was I being paranoid, or was there a grain of truth in my worry?

Once in the library, we headed to our table in the back. Derek flung his backpack onto the desk and dug out his cupid manual, his PDA, and a notepad, putting them on the tabletop. He dropped into the seat across from me and shot me a devilish grin.

My heart thudded painfully in my chest in spite of my sudden mood change. God, he was so. Hot. I tried to shake off my funky mood and focus on the task at hand, taking out my PDA so we could get down to business.

"How many matches did you make last night?" I asked him.

He raised one eyebrow at me. "How many did *you* make?"

"I'll tell if you tell," I joked.

"I made eight," he admitted, shrugging his broad shoulders. "I was going to make more, but I wanted to pace myself."

"I made ten," I said with a smirk.

His other eyebrow shot up. "Ten? Sounds like someone's trying to up me."

"Hey, we never designated a set amount," I pointed out, crossing my arms in mock irritation. "So I didn't know I was upping you."

"How many people are still on your list to be paired up?" he asked.

I opened the document and scrolled down numbered names. Wow, I still had so many people to go. How would I get through them all before prom?

"I have almost a hundred and fifty," I stated, "excluding the ten matches I made last night."

Derek scratched his chin, deep in thought. "If we each average eleven good, quality matches a day, we should be able to get through our lists in two weeks . . . which is more than enough time to mend all those broken hearts before prom for the juniors and seniors."

Eleven matches a day. I could totally do that. And how sweet of Derek not to rub in that it was my fault there were so many broken hearts in the first place.

Could I ever live that down?

I thrust out a hand to him across the table. "You're on," I said with more bravado than I felt, shooting him a teasing smirk. "But you're gonna need to bring your A-game. I've had over a month on you as a cupid, you know."

Derek's mouth opened slightly in surprise from my assertive words, but then he clamped it shut and grabbed my hand, shaking it enthusiastically. "How about a little challenge to sweeten the deal, then?"

I swallowed. Who knew Derek was so competitive? It was a little intimidating, going up against the guy who was perfect at everything. But no way was I gonna walk away from a competition.

"What's the challenge?" I asked.

He stopped shaking my hand and turned my palm over to run his fingers across the tips of mine. I shuddered from the delicious swirls he painted on my skin. He had to know what he was doing to me, making it hard to focus!

"Let's see who has the most couples still together at prom time," Derek suggested. "The loser takes the winner out on a victory dinner wherever he—or she—wants to go."

A little healthy bet between the two of us wouldn't hurt anything, right?

"I hope you don't mind losing," I bluffed. "Because I'm totally going to order lobster for my meal."

Derek smirked. "We'll see about that."

Mallory Robinson: the two most evil words in the whole world.

I should have put a 666 beside her name because she was certainly the bane of my very existence.

I belatedly wished Derek would have put her on his list and matched her up without ever telling me because I didn't want anything to do with her.

That evening, up in my bedroom, I shifted in my computer chair and sighed, staring woefully at Mallory's name on my LoveLine 3000. Our friendship had dissolved freshman year because she'd thought I was crushing on her then-boyfriend James (who, by the way, has since been one of the most surprisingly successful cupid matches I've made—and not with Mallory, of course). And since that fight, things had only gone downhill.

How was I going to make a quality match for her? I was *so* not subjective when it came to Little Miss Prissy Pants.

Maybe I could work on someone else instead. Mallory was near the bottom of the list, so I'd start at the top and work my way down.

I cracked open the profile of the girl on the top of my list to see what I'd written from my observations of her in the hallways at school:

Name: Marie Sherry

Age: 14

Interests: Manga, anime, drawing. Seems to crush on every guy she sees (always stares at boys in the hall). Nose stuck in a book. Likes Hello Kitty (all over backpack and notebooks).

Style: Shy Loner

Ah, now I remembered her. Marie's the tiny freshman who always wears anime-covered stuff. She'd perch all by herself at a table in the corner of the cafeteria, scribbling in her notebook and chewing on her huge Hello Kitty pencil.

For a few minutes I scoured my profiles to find a suitable match for her and landed on a person who seemed perfect:

Name: Alec Marshall

Age: 14

Interests: Likes film critique and appreciation, and foreign/indie music. Likes to bust out a beret sometimes. Possibly into guyliner.

Style: Quiet Nerd

Perfect—could two people be more suited for each other? Both were into the arts and foreign TV, so surely Alec would be able to hold lengthy conversations with Marie about the marvels of Japan. And they were both quiet people, so one wouldn't bug the other with constant conversation.

I composed a blank e-mail, adding Alec's and Marie's addresses in, and sent it. One high-quality match from my nightly quota down, ten more to go. I was already kicking ass and taking names.

But first an Internet break—time to connect to the mother ship.

I booted up my PC and deleted the insane amount of spam e-mail I'd gotten, then checked out Andy's latest locked blog entry for Maya's and my eyes only. In it, Andy dished about her date earlier this evening with Bobby Blowhard—er, Loward. I guess since they're dating now, I shouldn't call him by his nickname.

Bobby took me out to Hoggy's. You guys know how much I love that place—how sweet is he? Their corn chowder is KILLER good!

Anyway, while we were eating, we saw a guy propose to a girl.

I was stunned! I'd never seen a proposal before. Besides, it's not like we were at a fancy restaurant. But I figured maybe that was "their place" or something special for them.

I guess not, though. The girl blinked rapidly and said no, she just couldn't do it. Then she grabbed her purse and ran out of the restaurant, crying.

The whole place got really quiet and just watched the dumped guy in awkward silence. After a minute of sitting quietly in his seat, he dropped a wad of cash on the table and left.

I felt so, so bad for him. It reminded me how awful it is when you love someone who doesn't love you (aHEM, remember Tyler, anyone?). Thank God I'm not in that situation anymore, right?

Well, that was my night out. Hah—beat THAT, Fel and Maya!

I shook my head, baffled. How in the world do you get over the shock of a public humiliation like that? I guess you just pick up and move on . . . poor Andy did, after Tyler (the guy I'd originally matched her with) dumped her via a lame-ass note in the middle of the hallway. And look at her now, happier and more relaxed than I'd seen her in ages.

I left a quick comment, saying I was glad she'd had fun and that I certainly couldn't top her night, then shut off my PC, feeling strangely deflated. Hearing stories like that about heartbreak not only made me feel bad for the people involved but also reminded me of my own precarious situation with Derek.

Tomorrow night was my weekly TGIF sleepover with Andy and Maya. Maybe some chat time with my BFFs would help take my mind off the situation.

• • •

"Omigod, I have to crank this song!" Andy hollered on Friday night, bouncing off my bed and running over to my iPod speakers. She turned up the volume, and the thumping bass filled my bedroom.

Good thing my parents were out to dinner, or else the House Nazi would surely be thumping *her* way up to my room to ground me. She was really picky about how loud the noise in my room could be.

Maya, who had been lying silently across my bed for a good half hour, stood and stretched. "I'm gonna go raid the fridge for snacks," she said. "I'll be back with supplies in a few minutes."

I nodded, then stretched out on my plush rug, trying to snap out of my funk. I was desperate to spill my guts to Andy and Maya about my worries, but how could I get it across without revealing the cupid stuff, too? It seemed impossible.

And so I kept my mouth shut.

But perceptive Andy seemed to pick up on my worries, anyway. She sat down beside me, crossing her long legs as gracefully as a ballerina.

"Okay, what's wrong, Felicity?" she asked me point blank. "You finally got the guy of your dreams. The school year's almost over. You're gonna be a knockout in your prom dress. You should be doing the happy dance in your undies right now, not moping around like the world ends tomorrow."

I shrugged, staring at my ceiling. "You're right." I chewed on my lower lip. "But I can't help—" I stopped myself.

"Help what?" she asked, craning her head to look down at me. Her eyes were filled with worry. "Is something wrong?" She paused, and her voice took on a low, but teasing tone. "Derek didn't pop the question to you in Hoggy's and then you turned him down, right? I mean, what could be as bad as that?"

Knowing that Derek and I were only together because of a spell seemed like a pretty good one to add to the list of "crappy things that happen to couples."

I shrugged.

She leaned back against the foot of my bed. "He's absolutely crazy about you, you know. I've seen the way he looks at you, like you're his world. He seeks you out when you're not around. He talks about you to everyone. Derek is so in love, honey. So don't doubt your relationship."

I sat up, blinking rapidly. I shouldn't have been surprised that she'd pick up on what was bugging me; Andy was always intuitive about problems. But while I wanted to take comfort in her words, I knew the truth.

Maya swung my bedroom door open, bearing a large carton of ice cream and three spoons. She plopped down beside us on the floor and put the ice cream container in the middle, handing out spoons.

"I'm serious," Andy said to me, wagging the tip of the spoon in my direction. "You'll drive yourself crazy and analyze the life out of your relationship. Trust me. Just relax and let it be."

I took my spoon and dug into the vanilla bean ice cream, relishing the creamy taste. At least something always stayed constant for me, and that was ice cream.

"Don't you agree?" Andy asked Maya, who had been staring aimlessly to the side of the room.

Surprised, she jerked her head over to look at Andy, then shrugged wanly. "Yeah, I guess."

Wow, surprisingly nonwarm words. Maya was usually the first one to offer comfort to someone in need.

"I'm kinda tired," she continued, standing up and resting her spoon on the ice-cream carton's lid. She glanced at her watch, then turned the music down. "I think I'm gonna go to sleep."

Andy's brows scrunched, but she didn't say anything.

"Sure, do whatever you want," I said, trying to push down my reaction to Maya's apathy. But the stinging disappointment made it hard for me to keep my tone normal. "Make yourself comfortable."

Was she having problems? Or was discussing *my* love life just a little too boring for Maya?

chapter four

You know, if I thought *my* relationship issues were crazy, it was nothing compared to my brother Rob's. His flavor-of-the-week date for Sunday dinner somehow managed to surpass any other he'd brought home. And *not* in a good way.

When I opened the front door to let in Rob and his date, who was digging into her purse, she didn't instantly set off my radar—I couldn't see through any of her clothes, and all of her body parts looked real.

And then she lifted her face and made eye contact with me.

I blinked, stunned speechless.

Holy crap, she had to be several years older than my parents, not to mention at least a couple of decades on Rob, who was only twenty-one. She was almost old enough to be our grandma, actually. His date was still quite attractive, with a head of glossy, platinum-blond hair, but I could see gray roots where she was in need of a touch-up. The lines around her eyes and mouth were deep set, and she shot me a wide-mouthed smile.

"Well, hello," she said in a deep, throaty voice, patting me on the head. "You must be Felicity. You're just adorable."

Oh my God, she even talked and acted like a grandma. Seriously, did Rob have some kind of oedipal issue going on here?

Mom was going to Freak. The crap. Out. I almost couldn't wait to see it, if I wasn't so horrified myself.

Speak of the devil, Mom darted past me to the door to greet Rob and his date. When Mom saw his date, she froze in place, her face a stiff mask of shock.

"Guys, this is Mary," Rob said, smiling like nothing in the world was wrong. "Mary, this is my mom, Becky."

Wait. I'd heard of women like this before, on a talk show I'd watched when I was home sick. They're called cougars, known for prowling around bars for much-younger men to seduce. What in the world had made her pick my brother up, of all people?

Actually, an even better question was, what made him pick

her up? Did Grandma not show him enough love or give him enough Hot Wheels when he was growing up?

A surge of giggles bubbled in the back of my throat, and I forced myself to swallow it back down. Laughing was sooo not the appropriate response right now.

Mary took off her light jacket, revealing a purple dress shirt and black pants, and handed the coat to Rob. She cleared her throat, a raspy, grating sound that instantly pegged her as a pack-a-day smoker. Extra nice. "Hello, Becky," she said to Mom, thrusting out her hand. "Pleased to meet you."

"Welcome . . . Mary," Mom said, and moved aside to let them in, clearly trying to be as warm as she could. Her voice sounded like a frozen frog trying to talk. "You two can go . . . sit on the couch. Dinner will be ready shortly—we're finishing it up right now."

Mary gave a tight-lipped smile in response.

My mom went into the kitchen, and I followed Rob and Mary into the living room. They took a seat on the couch, and I sat on the recliner beside them.

"So," I asked Mary politely, "what do you do?" Other than hunt for younger guys to date, I meant.

She glanced at me for the briefest of moments, then looked

away, turning her attention to Rob like I hadn't spoken at all. "Sweetie," she purred, batting her lashes and running an arm down Rob's forearm, "I'm really thirsty. Can you get me a drink, please?"

Rob jumped up at Mary's words. "Sure," he said eagerly, then headed to the kitchen.

I leaned back in my chair and rolled my eyes. Great. This was going to be yet another superfun evening. And now I was left alone with the stuck-up Grandma Mary, who was spending her time glancing in disdain around the living room.

"God, this couch is so uncomfortable," I heard her mumble, shifting on the cushion.

My jaw dropped. "Excuse me—"

Mom's call for dinner interrupted me midsentence. Probably for the best, as I was about to say something rather biyotchy.

I followed Mary as she rose and went into the dining room, almost running into my mom, who was carrying a large baking dish of lasagna. Mary reached out a hand to steady herself on my mom's arm.

"Oh, dear," she said, eyes wide, and reached out for the lasagna dish. "Here, let me take that for you, Becky."

My mom's face twitched wildly. She looked confused about

whether or not she should accept help from Rob's cougar date. "Thanks," Mom finally said, handing the dish over. "That'd be great."

My dad came in from the kitchen, bearing a full tray of bread. He glanced at Rob's date, then looked away just as quickly. I bet Mom had already warned him about her, given the way he didn't freak out.

Dad took his place at the head of the table and passed the platter of lasagna around to Mary, who was on his left. "Hi. I'm Stephen, by the way," he said awkwardly.

"Helloooo," Mary said slowly, her eyes raking Dad up and down. She took the platter from him and sniffed it, smiling. "Oh, this lasagna smells just fantastic, Stephen. Did you make it yourself?"

The compliment seemed to relax him a bit. He smiled. "I did, thanks. It's an old family recipe passed down on my mother's side for generations. The bottom layer has sausage we buy fresh from a farmer's market. It gives it just the right kick."

Mary scooped an extra-large helping, then passed the tray over to Rob, not taking her eyes off my father. "Well, I can't wait to feast upon it," she said to him, her red-lipsticked mouth exaggerating her words as she blatantly flirted with my dad.

Dad flushed at her words and looked down at his food.

Ewwww! My jaw dropped, and I stared in horror. Grandma Cougar was unbelievable. What a pair of brass balls this lady had. Yeah, my dad wasn't a bad-looking guy, but she was sitting right beside my brother . . . her date!

Mom, who was on Dad's right, cleared her throat loudly. "Let's eat," she said through pressed lips.

Awkward silence continued on and off throughout dinner, interrupted by requests to hand down salad or rolls or salt.

Mary wolfed down her first helping of lasagna, then went back for seconds, making sure to lick her fork clean after each bite. It was like she'd forgotten Rob existed and was focusing solely on making sure my dad knew she was into him—batting her eyelashes, laughing at all his jokes, the works.

Mom's cheeks burned with anger the entire time, but she was too polite to make a scene in front of everyone. Especially since Rob seemed oblivious to how crazy-talk whacko his date was. He continued to chomp away on his serving of lasagna.

Then Grandma Cougar's hand dropped into her lap, and she slid her gaze toward Dad. A moment later Dad flinched, then jumped up, shooting Mary an angry look.

"Excuse me," he said, dropping his napkin onto his plate. "I need to use the restroom." He left the dining room quickly.

The cow! I bet she'd tried to feel my dad's knee or something. Please, let it have only been his knee. Gross, gross, *gross!*

It was time for her to go, now.

"That was so tasty, Mom," I said, pushing my half-eaten plate of lasagna away from me. Normally I wouldn't have left any on the plate, since it was one of my favorite meals, but I could tell we were all ready to end this disaster of a dinner. And I was willing to do my part to help the cause.

Mom, who had spent the entire meal glaring at Mary and chewing her lower lip raw, grabbed my plate as soon as I moved my hands away from it. "Thanks, Felicity. Well, I hope dinner was enjoyable for everyone else, too."

Mary seemed to realize her welcome was long worn out. She glanced at her watch, sighing. "Rob, can we go now? I have somewhere to be shortly, and I'm dying for a smoke."

I saw my mom swallow back whatever words were on the tip of her tongue. Instead, she gathered up a few more dirty plates and headed into the kitchen. "Rob, Felicity, help me clear the table," she called out over her shoulder.

I gathered up the rest of the plates, while Rob snagged the cups. We made our way into the kitchen.

As I scraped off the excess food and loaded the plates into the dishwasher, Mom clutched Rob's upper arm in a death grip.

"Let me tell you something," she said quietly, but I heard the fire simmering in her voice. "If you ever bring another date like that into my home again, I will disown you."

I could tell she wanted to talk more about how flirtatious Grandma Cougar had been with Dad, but she also didn't want to hurt Rob's feelings. So she left it at that.

Rob chuckled, trying to wiggle out of Mom's grasp. "Okay."

Mom, obviously realizing Rob wasn't taking her seriously yet again, busted out The Evil Eye—the one look my brother and I had seen throughout our lives that had scared the living pee out of us. Our mother had a way of squinting her eyes in a wrathful, angry look that made you want to run upstairs and pray for divine intervention so she wouldn't beat the living crap out of you.

When Rob saw The Eye, he paused. "You're . . . serious."

"As a heart attack."

He swallowed, then nodded. "I'll try to find someone better," he said. "It's just hard finding nice girls."

She leaned in closer, still pinning him in her gaze. "Try. Harder."

My cupid radar went off, in a sudden brilliant plan. I closed the dishwasher and started the cycle.

It was time to help my brother find love. He'd been a student at my school recently, so couldn't I stretch the rules to make him count? Okay, he'd graduated four years ago, but still.

Finding Rob the perfect girlfriend wasn't going to be easy. In fact, it was going to suck a lot. Because Rob was a total weenie, and ever since he became a cop, he'd gotten even harder to deal with.

But I was a cupid, and it was my job to make love happen. I would make it a priority to follow him around and learn all I could about him to make his profile as accurate as possible. Surely there was someone out there who would both love my brother *and* not drive our family insane.

Mom hugged Rob. "Okay, go take her home. Please, for the love of God."

"Hey, Rob," I interjected as casually as I could, "how's your upcoming week looking?"

He looked at me suspiciously, and with good reason. I didn't normally ask him questions like that. "Why?"

Crap. *Think fast, brain!* "Um . . . because . . . I'm interested in . . .

learning more about cops. I was hoping I could follow you and maybe see what you do." Wow, that was a killer save. Go, me!

"I think that's a great idea, honey!" Mom said, beaming. "Rob, set something up so your sister can shadow you at work, okay?"

He shrugged. "I'll e-mail you with my work schedule later. You can tell me when you want to come by the station."

Awesome! Once I had his schedule, I'd be able to pick the optimal time to spy on him. Plus, if I needed to ask anyone at his work questions, I could use meeting him there as an excuse. It was the perfect plan.

"Okay, thanks!" I said to him.

He and Mary left, with her surprisingly quiet. Maybe, somewhere inside, she realized she'd pushed it tonight. Probably not, though. Most people like that never think they do anything wrong.

But Mary would bother us no more. Because next Sunday Rob would be bringing a new date to dinner—a girl I'd picked out for him myself.

Monday morning at school I slipped behind my desk in English class right before the bell rang. I'd waited with Andy out in front of school for Maya as long as I could, but she hadn't shown up. She'd acted really bizarrely at my sleepover, and I was not only hurt by her distance but also worried that something was wrong. I'd even e-mailed her about it last night but never got a reply.

Mrs. Kendel shut the door to start class, then plodded over to her desk to pick up a big stack of papers. Gee, that looked promising. Not.

"Take out your notebooks," she ordered as she passed the packets down the aisles. "I want you to read the short narratives I'm handing out."

A few students grumbled under their breaths.

She stopped to glare at them, then continued, "Here's a list of things you need to identify when reading a narrative. Number one, who is our speaker? Number two, what is the tone of the story? Number three, what is the setting? And number four, what is the purpose of the story?" She glanced at her watch. "Okay, begin now."

I groaned inwardly, trying to focus whatever Monday-morning attention I could muster on the first narrative. Unfortunately, it was the most awful, dull story ever. Of course we couldn't get a story that would keep our interest.

No, the narrator of this enchanting piece of work was

some older guy reminiscing about how he didn't get the dog he desperately wanted when he was a kid. Then his younger brother made him a pet rock that looked like a dog . . . but, of course, the narrator didn't want it because it wasn't a *real* dog, and he threw the rock out a window in a fit of anger. Eventually, though, the narrator came to appreciate that precious pet rock, as well as his family.

And now he keeps the pet rock on his desk.

What a *heart*warming story of love amongst brothers—I was moved beyond words. Okay, seriously, who wrote this crap? And even more important, why in the world would anyone publish it?

I picked up my pencil and started to write my less-than-flattering viewpoint of the story, when Maya came into the class-room.

Instantly I noticed her red-rimmed eyes and pale face as she scuffled over to Mrs. Kendel's desk. The teacher saw Maya's face also, and though Mrs. Kendel didn't comment on it, she had a worried look.

I heard Mrs. Kendel whisper the assignment to Maya, who nodded slowly in response, then made her way to her desk beside me.

"Hey, are you okay?" I whispered to her, having decided this was worth facing Mrs. Kendel's wrath.

Maya sighed and shook her head. She ripped a piece of paper out of her notebook and began writing furiously on it.

After a minute she folded it up and slid it over to me.

I clutched the note and shot a look around the room. Mrs. Kendel was flipping through some huge-ass novel on her desk. The coast clear, I furtively opened Maya's note and read it:

Sorry about our sleepover. I feel really bad. I know I wasn't acting like myself.

Things suck at home, and I just can't take it anymore. My parents told me yesterday that my dad's moving out and they're getting divorced.

I had a bad feeling on Friday that it was coming. :-(

I've been out of it all weekend.

I pressed a hand to my mouth in shock, blinking rapidly and rereading the paper. Maya's parents, splitting up?

No wonder she'd been so distracted on Friday. I'd be too, if I'd sensed that impending news like this was coming.

I wrote underneath her message:

I am so, so, soooo sorry. Let's talk more after class, okay?

We'll get through this, I promise.

After another glance at the front of the room to confirm I wasn't being watched, I gave the note back to Maya.

My stomach turned over itself in guilt. Maybe I hadn't been the best friend to Maya that I could have been because of my focus on work and Derek. But she needed me right now, and I was determined to help her in any way I could.

chapter five

The bell ending English class finally rang. I was desperate to talk to Maya about her parents' divorce. Plus, I didn't think I'd survive class if I had to read one more stupid narrative. Someone needed to have a serious heart-to-heart with Mrs. Kendel about her choice of reading matter, and soon.

"What's going on?" I asked Maya as soon as we exited the classroom door.

With a firm grip, I held her by the elbow and eased her to the side of the hallway, where we'd have a minute or two to talk.

Her eyes welled up, and she choked out in short bursts, "Dad . . . he decided he didn't . . . want to stay anymore. He moved out last night."

I hugged her tightly, wishing I could say the perfect words to take away her pain. "I'm sorry."

She sniffled against my shoulder. "And what's worse is that my mom still loves him. So this is breaking her heart—" She paused, drawing in a ragged breath. "Because I think she wants it to work out, you know?"

We pulled apart, silent for a moment. I had to say, I wasn't surprised her dad was the one leaving. I never saw him at their house—it was always her mom who was around. He, on the other hand, was always working. And I thought *my* dad was a workaholic.

"We'd better go to class," Maya mumbled. "We'll talk more at lunch, okay? If you talk to Andy before I do, you can fill her in. I'm sure she's wondering what's up."

"Okay. Hang in there."

After we separated, I got through my morning classes and finally made it to health, where I shared class with Andy. Unfortunately, I didn't get a chance to talk to her beforehand, so I tried to be patient and wait until lunch. In the meantime, when our teacher's back was turned to the class, I scrawled on a piece of paper:

Must talk after class. Private, please!

I slipped it to Andy. She opened it, then nodded in agreement.

Mrs. Cahill, our teacher, rambled on for the entire period about something or other. I think she was talking about making healthy food choices and cutting back on sugar intake . . . not that I was paying much attention to her. I pretended to studiously take notes while my mind was occupied with heavy thoughts.

There had to be something I could do to fix this divorce situation, or to help Maya take action somehow. I was a cupid—love was my business! I knew, however, that it would be pushing the limits of my cupid job too far to simply send a love e-mail to her folks. I wasn't supposed to matchmake anyone outside of school. I could kinda sorta justify matchmaking my brother, since he was a former student at Greenville High. But it was way too risky to attempt it with Maya's parents. If I got caught, surely I'd be canned.

Besides, when the e-mail's spell wore off in two weeks, there'd be no guarantee her parents' feelings would last. And that would just make the situation even worse.

Finally health class was over. Andy told her boyfriend, Bobby, she'd meet him at lunch in a few minutes. She and I headed to the cafeteria, during which time I filled her in on the situation.

Maya was already at the table with Scott, her boyfriend. He had his arm behind her, rubbing her back.

"Hey," Andy said in a soothing voice. She hugged Maya, then took the seat beside her. "You okay?"

Maya shrugged halfheartedly.

"This sucks," Scott said. He leaned over and kissed Maya's temple.

Out of nowhere a brilliant idea came straight from the heavens into my head. "Guys," I said, slipping into the seat on Scott's free side, "I think part of the problem is that Maya's dad and mom need a chance to reconnect."

"It's kind of hard to connect if you're not around each other," Maya said, bitterness creeping into her voice.

"But what if your mom was irresistible enough to make your dad want to be around her?" I said, warming to my idea.

After all, even though I couldn't risk sending love e-mails, that didn't mean Maya's mom couldn't do a cool makeover or something. And then Maya, Andy, and I could come up with some ideas to throw her mom in her dad's path. Surely, once he saw her looking her best, he would be drawn to her again.

Maya wiped a tear out of the corner of her eyes, looking over at me. "Maybe that could work. My mom does need a wardrobe update desperately. And this might be enough to help her feel happier, too."

"Well, I like it," Andy announced. "And I think we should do it." She saw Bobby entering the cafeteria and waved for him to come over.

I nodded enthusiastically at Maya. "Okay, let's take the rest of the day to think it over. We'll get together again and map out our plan. Operation Hook Up Mama Takahashi."

Maya gave a watery smile, sniffling again. "Thanks, guys. You're the best."

Andy squeezed Maya again. "Hey, that's what friends are for."

All through art class I couldn't stop staring at Derek's lips. We hadn't kissed all day—I swear, it should be illegal to go that long without it.

In between bouts of admiring my guy's mouth, I turned my attention back to my crappy mosaic. Maybe I should just scrap this one and start over, crafting the perfect image of Derek's mouth. Not that I'd do it justice or anything, but at least I'd have a vested interest in the project.

Derek must have read my mind. He glanced over at me, seeing

my eyes on him again, and shot me a sly wink, puckering up and blowing me a couple of air kisses.

A hot flush swept over my cheeks. I could totally understand now why so many couples I'd matchmade couldn't stay apart from each other. Every moment we weren't together, he lingered in my mind. Because I'd had these feelings long before we'd started dating, I knew my love wasn't magic induced. But his could be.

Mr. Bunch stood in front of our tables, gesturing toward several large paintings in the back. "I need a student or two to carry these oil paintings for the art show to the teacher's lounge. Please be careful with them."

Derek and I looked at each other, then shot our hands up in the air.

The teacher nodded, heading over to his desk to write us a permission slip. "Okay, Derek and Felicity."

Yay! Time alone with Derek during class—what a rarity!

We gathered our slips and the artwork, promising not to dawdle in the hallway (yeah, *right*), and walked as slowly as we could toward the teacher's lounge. I tried to think of something intelligent and interesting to talk about.

Out of nowhere, Derek reached an arm over and pressed a warm palm against my stomach, stopping me in my tracks, then propped his paintings against the wall. He wrapped his arms around me and slid his lips over mine. I moaned softly and let my paintings lie against my leg, twining my fingers through his hair.

Oh, this was *so* much better than talking. We stole a few moments kissing, enjoying the sensation and heat, then regretfully stepped apart.

"Whew," I said, grinning wildly. My lips were puffy, and I knew my face had to be red all over from nervousness and excitement. I could have stood there and kissed him all day, if it weren't for the whole I'd-be-grounded-for-life-if-I-were-busted-by-a-teacher thing.

"That was great," he stated, his smile as big as mine. "I've been waiting all day to do that." He picked up his paintings again and brushed another quick kiss on my lips.

We walked in a warm silence to the teacher's lounge, where Derek opened the door for me. I stepped forward, then promptly stopped in the doorway, the air swooshing out of my lungs in a rush of surprise.

Mr. Wiley, my anthropology teacher, had Brenda, one of the front office secretaries, pinned underneath him on the couch. Given their heavy making out, they obviously had gotten the love e-mails I'd sent them last night.

Derek, who couldn't see the scene, nudged me forward. "Hey, these paintings are getting heavy," he teased as he stood beside me, then sucked in a quick breath when he saw the scene in front of us.

At Derek's words Mr. Wiley jumped off the couch, his back stiff as a board. Brenda gasped and straightened her mussed clothes.

"Oh, Felicity," Mr. Wiley said, trying to affect an air of calm control. He pushed the knot of his necktie further up. "You surprised us. We were . . ." He paused, swallowing, and I could almost hear the gears in his brain cranking hard to come up with an excuse.

"You were . . . showing her how to do CPR?" I filled in helpfully, trying my hardest to bite back the laugh that threatened to come out.

Brenda nodded wildly, smoothing her hair. "That's right. Mack—I mean, Mr. Wiley was showing me the proper CPR technique." She paused, sliding her gaze over to him, and her lips parted. "He's really, really skilled at it."

"I happen to think you're a natural," he replied, inching closer to her.

Derek elbowed me in the side, confusion on his face.

"They were on my list," I whispered out of the corner of my mouth. To Mr. Wiley, I said, "Mr. Bunch asked us to drop off these paintings."

He nodded abstractly, his eyes back on his love match and hers on him.

Derek and I ditched the artwork and booked it out of there, closing the door behind us. We heard the door lock.

The laughter I'd been holding in bubbled out of me, and I cupped a hand over my mouth. "Oh my God, that was way too hilarious," I said. "They were all over each other . . . and during school hours!"

Derek shook his head, chuckling. He grabbed my hand, and we strolled back down the hallway toward art class. "You did a great job matching them up, Felicity."

"Thanks," I said, glowing from his praise. "They seemed like they'd be good together. I just paired them up yesterday."

"It always amazes me how hard the love spell hits some people. Mr. Wiley's always been a quiet teacher. He never struck me as someone who would be caught kissing someone, much less during school hours." Derek paused, mulling it over. "The love spell can change people from their natural impulses, can't it?"

The smile wiped off my face. How quickly I'd forgotten about the love spell cast on my own relationship. But Derek was right—look at how different people were when they were entranced.

I resisted the urge to look at him, forcing my voice to sound calm and even. "Why do you think that is? Is it because we have these impulses in us, and the spell brings it out?" Because that would be the optimal answer, and I was desperate to hear him agree with me.

Instead, he shrugged. "Who knows? Well, other than Janet."

"But the spell can't make you love someone who is absolutely wrong for you, right?" I pressed. "After all, that's why we have to do the compatibility charts."

"I don't know, actually. I haven't paired up people who are bad matches, so I can't answer that."

We got back to class, me feeling decidedly much less enthused than I did before.

"Everything go okay?" Mr. Bunch asked us.

I nodded, pushing down the bleakness that threatened to take over me. "Yup. Just fine."

chapter six

My Monday night meeting with Janet went well. She didn't mention the love spell she'd cast on Derek and me, so I didn't ask her about it. Besides, I felt uncomfortable whining to my boss about her doing her job, especially when sending love e-mails to two compatible people was the very same thing I'd done to my own friends.

I also didn't want to be a glutton for punishment. And obsessing over the genuine nature of Derek's love wasn't going to get me anywhere, not until I could figure out how I wanted to handle my worries.

So I decided to push the situation out of my mind and focus on one of the projects on my plate: finding a girlfriend for Rob. It was time to get that rolling.

As I drove out of Cupid's Hollow's headquarters that evening, I dug into my backpack and took out a notebook, where I'd plotted out my plan in great detail the previous night. It was sheer genius, and my only regret was that I couldn't share it with anyone else. I was tempted to run it by Derek, but I hadn't told him about matchmaking people outside of school, and I wasn't sure what his reaction would be. Maybe it was better to keep this to myself, then.

Rob was off work tonight, so I would spend an hour or so studying him and his behavior. This was the best way to complete his profile accurately, since I'd kind of lost track of his hobbies and habits now that he lived on his own. Then, per our agreement, I would go to the station and ask lots of questions of him and his co-workers, both to help round out my profile and possibly find any female colleagues who might be suitable for him.

After all, who better to be his potential girlfriend than a woman who understood the ins and outs of being a cop?

I pulled my car into a parking spot on the far end of the parking lot of The Dive, a bar I'd recently learned that my brother liked to visit (one of his former dates had blabbed on and on about how they met there—classy). When scheduling our meeting, Rob had told me he was going to meet some friends there.

He was probably going to pound down a few beers on the bar's massive back patio and then find his new flavor of the week.

Well, not if *I* could help it.

Hidden by the dark night shadows, I cast a furtive glance around me to make sure no one was coming, then grabbed my black long-sleeve shirt, to match my black dress pants, out of my backpack to throw over my shirt. I pulled my hair back into a ponytail and covered my head in a black baseball cap, then draped my binoculars over my neck, just in case I needed them for better observation.

There. Now no one would see me when I peeked through the fence slots of the bar's patio. It was the perfect way to spy on my brother in his natural element without actually sneaking into the bar and getting in megatrouble with the law.

When I noticed no one was around, I slipped my LoveLine 3000 into my pocket and got out of my car. Not that anyone would have heard me, anyway—the bass from the music on the patio thumped loudly enough to cover an elephant stomping through the parking lot.

Trying to look like it was absolutely normal for a seventeen-year-old girl to be hanging around outside of a bar, I maneuvered my way to a corner of the patio fence that was covered with bushes and waited for Rob to appear. As I hung out, I studied the patio, which was supposed to look like a tropical paradise.

Yeahhhh, the fake palm trees with neon-green paper fronds made the setting *so* authentic. There was also a giant tiki-themed counter near the door, where two female bartenders waited on customers.

Hey, wait . . . the one on the left, with the orange-colored tan and fried blond hair, seemed familiar. I think Rob had brought her over to the house for Sunday dinner a few weeks ago. I distinctly remembered this girl because she laughed like a hyena . . . which she was doing right now.

This totally confirmed my suspicions that Rob just dated any girl who happened to cross his path—he'd probably come here the night before dinner and, not having a date, asked the bartender if she was free on Sunday. Nice.

After a few minutes Rob and his work partner barreled through the bar's back doors onto the patio. They were laughing loudly and clapping people on the back as they made their way to the bar. Wow, my brother seemed to know, like, every person here. Party hard much, Rob?

I made a mental note to make sure whatever female I paired

him up with had other hobbies that Rob could be introduced to. He obviously needed to expand his horizons a bit more, and soon.

Rob didn't even have to order something to drink. The other bartender chick, some hoochie in the tiniest white T-shirt I'd ever seen, winked at my brother and said in a piercing voice that somehow managed to be even louder than the music, "Officer Rob, here's your beer, hon."

She slid a bottle down the bar's smooth wooden surface, and he caught it.

"Thanks, Maggie," he replied, giving her a smarmy grin. "Maybe I'll leave the handcuffs in the car tonight."

Ew, gag.

My brother and his attempts to flirt were vomit-tacular. I tried not to hurl as I peered through the fence slots, watching him make his way to a table. Crap, now I couldn't see him from my position.

With as much stealth as I could muster, I slowly made my way to my brother's table, using the fence as cover. He and his partner were alone, talking about the Cleveland Indians' latest baseball game.

I whipped out my handy-dandy LoveLine 3000 and began entering in my brother's profile:

Name: Rob Walker

Age: 21

Interests: Drinking/socializing. Sports. Cop equipment (including handcuffs, ick). Available women.

Style: Confident Player

Okay, obviously I needed more to add to his interests. I turned my attention back to Rob. Three women had joined him and his partner at the table in the few minutes it'd taken me to create his profile. I guess I shouldn't have been surprised.

"You're a cop?" the brunette asked Rob.

"Sure am."

She giggled, her overly red lips flying open as she breathed in deeply. "Hey, have you ever shot someone?"

Actually, that was a good question. I realized I didn't even know the answer.

Rob puffed his chest out. "Well, I drew my gun on a couple of thugs during a B and E last month." He paused, then leaned toward her in a conspiratorial manner. "That's 'breaking and entering,' in cop terms."

Unlike me, the woman seemed awed. "But did you actually *shoot* them?" she pressed him.

"Didn't need to. Just seeing my gun was enough to scare them straight."

I stifled a groan. Good grief, his ego was impossibly huge. He'd have to get over himself before I could find him the perfect—

"Excuse me," a deep voice said behind me, just as a hand clamped down on my shoulder. I was spun around, finding myself face-to-face with an on-duty cop. Crap!

"What are you doing, ma'am?" he continued, eyeing the binoculars dangling around my neck. He grabbed a flashlight out of his belt and flashed the beam directly in my face.

My heart thundered to about three hundred beats per minute. A flush stole over my face, bathed in the bright light.

This was bad. Really, really bad. I was in huuuuge trouble now, unless I could somehow charm him into letting me go.

"Oh, hello, Officer . . . ," I drawled, then smiled as confidently as I could, waiting for him to tell me his name.

"Banks," he said in a monotone, continuing to stare at me.

Okay, so maybe charm wasn't the way to go. Maybe connections would work better. After all, cops knew each other, right?

"My name's Felicity Walker," I said, consciously aware of the LoveLine 3000 currently hiding in my sweat-laden palm. It didn't seem like he'd noticed it yet, and I intended to keep it that way. "My brother's an officer in this city—Rob Walker. Do you know him? He's here in the bar, having some drinks. Off duty, of course," I hastened to add to the drivel I was spewing out.

The cop continued to stare at me expectantly, his face blank.

I kept rushing to talk, feeling the urge to unburden myself to this officer of the law. No wonder those people on the show COPS always blabbed on and on—the cops never spoke! "Well, anyway, I'm watching him. I'm ... doing a report for class on police officers and trying to see if I want to be a policewoman myself. That's all."

Officer Banks's eyebrow rose. "Why are you watching your brother, dressed head to toe in black, without him knowing you're there?" He lifted his walkie-talkie off his belt. "Do you have a license or other form of identification?" he asked me.

"Uh, yeah." I opened my backpack, hands shaking, and carefully placed my LoveLine 3000 inside before taking out my license. "Here you go."

The officer studied the license. Then, over the walkie-talkie, he radioed in my identifying information.

A tense moment passed. I was thankful that at least the music was so loud, no one would notice what was going on on the back side of the fence . . . for example, my brother. If he knew, he'd rat me out to Mom for sure—and this was assuming I'd get out of this situation without needing to call her, anyway.

I prayed fervently in my head that Mom would remain blissfully unaware of whatever happened tonight. There would be a *serious* grounding or possible fatality in store for me. And with prom soooo close, I didn't want to do anything to incite her wrath.

Maybe spying on Rob hadn't been the best idea, after all. I could have found other ways to observe him instead of making myself look like a psycho stalker. I should take more time to thoroughly plan out my ideas from now on so I wouldn't get stuck in situations like this. No wonder things always went wonky for me.

The walkie-talkie clicked back on, and the person on the other end said some stuff to the officer, who then ended the conversation. Dropping the walkie-talkie back in his belt, he looked at me and handed back my license.

My heart thudded painfully in my chest, and all the air in my lungs froze in fear as I waited for him to tell me my fate.

"I'd highly recommend you get yourself home, Felicity. It's not safe for people to be out in the dark, and it looks suspicious. And it's not a good idea for a minor to be hanging around establishments that serve alcohol." He gave me a meaningful look.

I exhaled through my nose, forcing myself to stay calm. "You're absolutely right, Officer," I said, my voice buoyant with relief. "That was dumb of me. I'll make sure to observe my brother in a much more public manner from now on." I was so happy to not be arrested or ratted out to my mom, I almost went to hug the officer in gratitude, but he didn't look overly friendly.

Slinging my backpack over my shoulder, I made my way to my car. Officer Banks followed me, probably to make sure I wouldn't try to continue lurking in the bushes.

I mentally slapped myself on the forehead. *Stupid idea, Felicity!* I'd never thought about the possibility of the bar being patrolled.

He watched me as I turned on my car and drove out of the bar's parking lot. I pulled on to the main street, careful to go slowly and use my turn signal—I didn't need to give him a reason to follow me—and headed home.

Step One of Operation Hook Up Mama Takahashi: Get rid of all sweat suits. Unfortunately, it didn't seem like Mrs. Takahashi was taking too kindly to our suggestions.

She sighed heavily, crossing her arms over her chest. "I'm not sure I want to do this," she hedged, the crease between her brows deepening. "I know you're trying to do something nice for me, girls, but I feel comfortable in these clothes."

Andy, Maya, and I were standing beside Mrs. Takahashi in her bedroom after school the next day, ready to implement our plan to help her win back her husband. But I don't think any of us were prepared for Mrs. Takahashi's closet. How in the world could one person have accumulated so many pairs of gray sweatshirts and sweatpants?

"Mom, the first step in reinventing yourself is finding clothes that are comfortable *and* stylish. Please," Maya said, her eyes begging as she took her mom's hand, "let us help you. I promise, we won't make you wear anything that's itchy or awful."

Maya's mom gave her a weak smile. "Okay, I'm willing to give it a try. But no hot pink or other crazy neon colors."

We laughed. Andy took Mrs. Takahashi's other hand. "I think the first step here is to purge yourself of all these sweatpants."

I stepped forward and gathered them in my arms.

Maya cheered. "See how much room you have in your closet to add all those new clothes we're going to buy? We'll go ahead and take care of these sweat suits for you, okay?"

If by "take care of," she meant "burn," then I was totally game. "Before you know it," I said to Mrs. Takahashi, "you'll forget all about those sweat suits. I promise."

She smiled. I was glad to see she was going along with our plan. And now that the hard part was done, it was time for Step Two—taking her to the mall.

chapter seven

All was going well with Mrs. Takahashi's superhottie makeover for the first hour or so. We found several outfits that flattered her figure. She even bought some honest-to-God makeup. Maya pulled me and Andy aside in the store Sephora and told us that her mom hadn't worn even so much as ChapStick in probably a dozen years.

Not that I was a makeup freak or anything, but wow. I couldn't imagine living with dry lips for that long.

Mrs. Takahashi walked out of Sephora, beaming as she bore two huge bags of clothes and makeup. Her face glowed from the skin-care samples the saleslady had put on her. She looked a good five years younger.

Maya followed closely behind her mom, bearing three more

bags. Andy and I, just behind, each carried other miscellaneous items that Mrs. Takahashi had purchased.

Andy suddenly sped up in her tracks and moved beside Maya's mom. "You need to go in there," she proclaimed, pointing to a store on her left.

Victoria's Secret.

Mrs. Takahashi shook her head, her cheeks flaming red. "No, really, I'm fine."

Maya blanched. "No. Way. Come on, guys, I'm sure she's already got plenty of . . ." She stalled on her words, trying to find a way to talk about her mom's underclothes in a public arena without freaking herself out.

Good luck with that. Having busted my parents midcopulation, I completely felt her pain. No teen wanted to think of her parents as sexual beings. Ick.

Andy handed me her bags, then grabbed Mrs. Takahashi's hand. "Trust me. You don't have to get anything trampy, I promise."

At her words, some older man, who was doing walking laps in the mall, slowed his pace and stared with interest at our conversation. Geez, guys were such perverts, no matter how old they were.

I shot him a glare, mentally shooing him away, then turned my attention back to Andy. "I don't think—"

"Aw, come on," Andy said, sighing with impatience. She tugged an uncertain, blushing Mrs. Takahashi across the mall's hallway toward Victoria's Secret. "Look, I'll take her inside, okay? You and Maya go grab an Orange Julius or something. Meet us in the food court in twenty minutes."

With that, they disappeared inside.

"I think I need something to drink," Maya said, looking like she was going to be sick. "I do *not* want to think about my mom buying teeny-tiny panties. I don't care if it *is* for Dad."

"Let's go to Orange Julius, then. And, hey, it's on me," I said, trying to be jovial.

Once there, we ordered a couple of fruit juices. I love their strawberry-banana drinks. So tasty.

To be honest, I was glad Andy was brave enough to take Mrs. Takahashi in Victoria's Secret. Great outfits didn't count for anything if you were wearing a grandma bra and big white bloomers underneath.

Maya and I grabbed a seat in the food court, waiting quietly for a minute for her mom and Andy to return.

"So, your mom got a lot of great stuff," I offered. "She's going to look fabulous. Your dad will hardly recognize her."

"Once she goes to her hair appointment tomorrow, she'll be a new woman," she agreed, tucking a strand of hair behind her ear. "She really needed to pamper herself. I'm glad you guys helped me talk her into it."

"No problem. Everyone deserves a chance to fight for the person they love," I said. "And maybe having an air of mysteriousness and newness around her will help draw him in."

Whoa, wait. My mind spun with a new possibility I hadn't considered. If reinventing herself would work for Mrs. Takahashi, why couldn't it work for *me*? I could reinvent myself, update my looks, learn how to be mysterious.

And Derek wouldn't be able to help wanting to be around me after the love spell ended next week because he'd be so intrigued by me.

Maya and I made small talk while we waited. In the back of my mind, though, I compiled a mental list of things I needed to do:

1. *New looks.* This required spending some of my hard-earned cupid money, but an investment in love is always a good thing.

2. *New attitude.* The best way to learn how to be alluring was to study

those who were good at it, like all the popular girls. In fact, I could also make sure to imitate their fashion sense, too, before going out and splurging on new clothes.

Andy, grinning from ear to ear, returned about half an hour later with a much more sober Mrs. Takahashi in tow. She was holding a V's Secret bag pinched tightly in one hand. Maya glanced at it in horror, probably hoping that the bag only contained a couple of pairs of full-coverage underwear rather than lots of tiny thongs.

"Okay, I'm ready to go home now, girls," Maya's mom said tiredly. "It's been a long day."

We left the mall and headed back to Maya's house, where Andy and I told the two of them good-bye, then walked home.

As soon as we rounded the corner, Andy busted up laughing. "Oh my God, I'm so glad Maya wasn't in there," she said, gasping for air. "You should have seen the underwear her mom picked out at first—it was the ugliest pair of granny panties ever. And they were, like, three sizes too big for her. Who knew Victoria's Secret even carried those?"

"Really?" I asked, giggling. "We should have known she'd go for those first."

"I swear, it took everything I had to convince her to try boy-cut panties. But once the saleslady got hold of her, Mrs. Takahashi had two new bras, and even a thong!"

"Yeah, I'm really glad Maya didn't witness that," I said, then gave Andy a hug when we reached my house. "Okay, I'll see you later!"

"Okey dokey!" Andy wandered off in the direction of her house.

I headed inside mine, still chuckling. No one was home, which was good. It gave me time to plan out how best to implement my latest and greatest idea.

I went right upstairs to my closet, flinging open the doors. First things first, it was time to get rid of the old so I could make room for the new, which I would be buying based on tomorrow's ultrascientific study of the popular girls.

Good-bye, old Felicity! Hello, hotness!

The next morning at school I did what I never thought I'd do . . . I studied my archnemesis, Mallory.

As she talked with one of the senior football team members in the hallway before first period started, I took stock of her clothes so I'd know what to get when I went on my shopping spree tomorrow night: flats, tight jeans, and an Ed Hardy V-neck T-shirt covered in old-timey-looking tattoo pictures.

Then I noted her gestures and body language, making sure I was out of sight, of course—being busted for watching Mallory was *not* on the list of things I wanted to do today. She had her shoulder blades pressed against a locker, her back arched just enough to push her chest out and show off her cleavage.

Yeah, that one was going to get me nowhere, as I had none to show off. Oh, well. I'd just work with what I had, right?

Mallory nodded at something the jock said, licking her lips and tilting her head. "Really?" I heard her say. "God, you're so smart. I never knew that!"

He shrugged casually, leaning in toward her and pressing a palm against the locker right beside her head. "Not a lot of people do."

Oh, so she was stroking his ego, eh? *Good tactic, Mallory.* I grudgingly had to give her credit—her technique was clever when done with just the right amount of flirting, and Mallory seemed to intuitively know how to do it.

The bell rang, warning us to get to class. I headed into Mrs. Kendel's room. I noticed there was hushed whispering going on, and several people stopped talking when I got inside. Mrs. Kendel was nowhere to be seen.

What was going on?

Then I saw it. On top of my desk was a blood-red rose, a small note tied around the stem.

My heart pounded in my chest. Was that for me, or was it put on the wrong desk by accident? I was almost afraid to move closer in case it wasn't and I'd gotten my stupid hopes up for nothing.

"Go get it!" Maya whispered, waving me over. Her cheeks were flushed, and her eyes sparkled at me. "Oh my God, this is so cool! It was already here when we all got in the room."

I shuffled over, throat constricted, and plucked the flower off the desk. With a shaky hand, I flipped the note open and read the handwritten contents:

You're on my mind—all day, every day. Derek

I pressed the petals against my lips, sighing happily as I slid into my chair. I'd never gotten flowers before, ever.

Other girls were still staring in my direction. Even Adele and Mike unplugged their lips from each other long enough to shoot me a curious glance.

"Derek is sweet," Tessa, the girl behind me, said.

I nodded in agreement, still unable to speak.

Mrs. Kendel came into the room then, closing the door hard behind her. I dropped the flower onto my lap so she wouldn't see—I didn't want to get flack for introducing yet another romantic incident in class. "Okay, ladies and gents. Let's get to work."

As if I could concentrate. All period long I stroked the soft petals with the tips of my fingers. I don't think I heard two words she said. Nor did I really care. I just kept thinking, *Oh my God, he bought me a flower!*

When the bell rang, I darted out of the room, clutching the rose in my hand (I'd actually forgotten my books, so I had to run back in and get them), and waited in the hallway for Maya.

She popped out, then grabbed my upper arm and squealed. "Felicity! I can't believe Derek surprised you like this!" She sighed dramatically, pressing her hand over her chest. "This is so freaking romantic. You have to tell him he made my day."

I snorted. "You're telling me! I wasn't expecting this at all." After all, things like this didn't happen to me. They happened to Maya, or Andy, or other people who had been matchmade.

A sick thud hit my stomach. Derek had only given me the flower because he was under a love spell. I pushed the depressing thought aside just as quickly as it had hit me. Well, so what? Even if it was only spell induced, it was still a sweet gesture. And I wanted to focus on that, if just for a day.

"Okay, I gotta run," Maya said. "We'll talk at lunch." She beamed at me again, gave me a quick hug, then ran down the hall.

I made my way toward my second-period class, still holding the rose. I probably should have put it in my locker, but I didn't want to part with it, for fear that I'd hallucinated what was probably the most romantic gesture I'd ever gotten in my life.

Superpathetic? Yes. But I didn't care.

Mr. Shrupe's American history class was buzzing quietly, and the teacher was writing something on the board. When I stepped inside, a couple of girls pointed to my desk.

"Felicity, look!" Mandy said. "This was sitting here waiting for you."

No. Way. There was another rose, laid across my desk. Was this for real? I practically dove into my desk and whipped the note open:

If this rose could talk, it would tell you how special you are to me. Derek

"Please open your books to page two hundred and fifty-two," Mr. Shrupe said, oblivious as usual to anything going on in class.

I kept the roses on my desk this time, unable to stop looking at them all period. Two roses? This was insane. This was romantic.

This was unbelievable.

Every class period that day was the same. I came in, and some giddy person guided me to my desk, where there was a rose with a romantic note waiting for me. No one had seen Derek put the flowers on my desk. By lunch I had a good handful, which I of course carried with me to show a superexcited Maya and Andy.

I hustled through the rest of the periods, collecting roses along the way and eager to see Derek in art class. I was anxious to thank him for the incredible gift he'd given me today. Though I knew his gesture was clearly love-spell-induced, it was sheer magic for me to walk into each classroom and find a flower on my desk.

When I got into art, I settled into the seat beside him and put the big pile of roses on my desk, giving him a quick hug and kiss when the teacher wasn't looking.

"I missed seeing you today," he said, giving me that heartbreakingly adorable smile. "But I see you got my messages."

It equally thrilled and pained me, knowing his feelings for me, that beaming grin of his, these flowers, everything about our relationship was under false pretenses. My mood sank a little, but I forced myself to keep the smile on my face. After all, I already had a makeover plan in place to make things last after the spell wore off. It had to work.

"They are beautiful. Thank you so much. I'm sorry I missed you this morning." I glanced around, then whispered, "I had some cupid stuff to do." In a way, it was true—I'm a cupid, and I had some self-improvement to work on.

He nodded. "Gotcha. How go your matches?"

"Not bad," I replied. "I'm getting through my list every day and making fantastic progress." Before I could ask him how his were going, class started.

Mr. Bunch, who was fiddling with the projector in the back of the room, moved forward and dimmed the lights. "Today, instead of working on our art projects, we're going to watch a short film about one of my favorite artists, Jackson Pollock."

Oooh, a movie day! Another great surprise. It meant a chance to sit quietly beside Derek in the dark, where we could hold hands and spend a little bit of quality time together. Especially since I would have to leave right after school to run to the mall and get some new clothes and also interview my brother.

Sure enough, Derek slipped his warm, strong hand into mine. I squeezed it tightly and pretended to pay attention to the movie. But all I could think about was how to implement my makeover and knock his socks off.

I would prove to him I was worth this effort. It was time for Derek to see the new me!

chapter eight

"And here's where we eat," Rob said to me later that afternoon as he led me into the little lunchroom in his police station, which consisted of a beat-up table and a microwave. "We'll do our interview in here."

I sat down across from him and whipped out my notebook, prepared with some questions to make our meeting look like an authentic interview. "Okay, what's a typical day like for you?" I asked him, pen hovering above paper and ready to write. "Where do you normally go?"

Rob leaned back in his chair, the front two chair feet rising off the ground. "Well, I like hanging out at The Burger Butler, but I also dig the lattes at Dunkin' Donuts." He paused, as if realizing I'd meant his job. "Um, that is, when I'm not out patrolling. I'm a beat cop, so I'm usually in my car pulling over drivers for moving-traffic violations."

I nodded intently, scrawling down that he liked coffee and burgers. Gee, how promising to know that life wasn't just about booze and chicks for him. It actually included other kinds of drink and flesh. "Okay, great. What do you think has been your greatest success as a police officer?"

After several seconds of silence, he said in a quiet tone, "Honestly? I don't think I've had one yet. I haven't really saved a life or jumped in the way of a bullet."

I froze, startled. It was rare for Rob to be serious.

"Maybe the things you think are small are actually big to someone else," I answered slowly. "Sometimes those little things mean a lot more to people. Remember that time at dinner when you told us you stopped a man from beating his wife again by throwing him in jail? I'm sure that meant the world to her."

He shrugged and leaned his front chair legs back on the floor, the badge on his chest glinting in the glaring fluorescent light overhead. "I guess you're right. But I'd like to experience those big moments sometime."

I chewed on my pen cap, then wrote *ambitious* and *awkward* on my list. It was good to see this side of him because it helped me understand that he could be vulnerable. Good traits for a guy.

For my last question, I'd asked him what was the worst thing he'd ever seen.

I swear, his eyes got a little watery when he described finding a near-dead homeless man in the alley a few months ago during a particularly nasty January storm. Fortunately, he and his partner had gotten the man to the hospital before hypothermia had caused irreversible damage.

When our time was up, I lingered in my chair, almost not wanting the moment to end. I couldn't remember a time when I'd felt this close to my brother. It made me feel good to be finding him a worthwhile girlfriend.

Speaking of . . . time to work on the next phase of Operation No More Hoochies in the Home.

"Rob," I said, "I think it would be great to talk to some female officers, if that's okay. I'd love to know what it's like to be a woman on the police force."

He nodded. "Sure. We have a couple of people in the station right now." He led me down the hall and through various rooms to get back toward the front of the station.

On my right I recognized Officer Banks, the cop who had busted me outside the bar.

Crap!

My heart rate sped up rapidly, and my palms began to sweat like a waterslide. Fortunately, Officer Banks hadn't seen me yet. I lifted my notebook and pretended to be fascinated by whatever I'd written in there as we walked by him.

It wasn't until after we'd turned the corner that I exhaled the lungful of air I didn't even know I was holding in. Another minicrisis averted, thanks to my ninja–like reflexes.

We finally reached the front of the station, where several officers milled around, chatting. There was a bench where a few people sat waiting—one guy had a massive black eye, and the other was missing a few teeth. The officer standing close by was glaring at them both.

Whoops, guess fighting wasn't the right way to solve whatever problem you two had. I rolled my eyes and headed toward the two female cops, a brunette with a ponytail and a short-haired redhead, who were talking behind the desk.

"Heyyyy," my brother said, his bad-boy cop persona firmly back in place. "This is my sister, Felicity. She'd like to talk to you lay-dees about what it's like being a female cop. And I figured you two were the finest cops here, so you could answer her questions."

"For you, hon? Anything," the brunette said flirtatiously, winking.

"This is Officer Annette Lars," Rob said, pointing to the brunette. "And this is Officer Randi McPherson," he continued, indicating the redhead. "I'll be back in a few minutes to wrap up our interview." He took off.

Okay, two candidates for me to interview. Maybe luck would continue to be with me, and one of them would be the ideal match for Rob.

We found a few available seats in the corner of the room. I whipped out my notebook and wrote their names down.

"So, how do you get along with the men on the police force?" I asked them, hoping to discover how personable they were. "Have they ever had a problem dealing with you because you're women?"

Officer McPherson shrugged, smiling. "No issues. The men are usually respectful toward us, though you do have guys like your brother, who are a little flirty. But I've been here five years and never had a complaint against any of them."

"I agree," Officer Lars interjected. She leaned back in her seat, propping an ankle up on her thigh. "But it's sure nice having eye candy around, if you know what I mean."

She was *obviously* the saucy girl here, no bones about it. Whereas that might be bad for some people, it seemed like my brother responded to it with no problems whatsoever. I jotted that down underneath her name.

I cast a furtive glance to their hands. No wedding bands or engagement rings on either of the two candidates. Another good sign. However, that didn't mean they didn't have boyfriends . . . or husbands.

"How do your . . . families or significant others feel about you being an officer?" I asked, priding myself on the cleverness of the question.

Officer Lars grinned. "I don't have anyone at home except a cat, and she doesn't seem to be bothered by my job."

I chuckled. "Fair enough."

"Well, my boyfriend seems supportive of my job, though I'm sure he wouldn't like me being in harm's way," Officer McPherson said, giving me a knowing grin and a shrug.

Bingo. Looks like we just narrowed down the playing field. Time to home in and make sure Officer Lars would suit my brother.

After writing more notes in my journal, I asked, "What do you two like to do when you're not working? I'm sure it's good to relax after a busy day."

"My boyfriend and I go out to dinner, or I go shopping when I'm off," Officer McPherson said.

"I usually hang with my girlfriends," Officer Lars said. She tucked a loose strand of hair back into her ponytail. "We go out to dinner and a movie, or occasionally to a bar." She paused, then looked at me. "But I never, never drive drunk," she said. "We always have a designated driver. Having a cop busted for a DWI is very, very bad."

So she liked to party but was smart about it? Definitely a bonus.

Rob came back into the room and headed over to us. "You all done?" he asked. "These ladies probably need to get back to work."

They both beamed at him.

"It was a pleasure," Officer Lars said to him, her eyes sparkling.

"Is it okay if I get your e-mail addresses, in case I have further questions?" I asked them both.

They quickly scribbled their e-mails down on a clean piece of paper.

"Please feel free to talk to me anytime," Officer McPherson

said. "It's been a pleasure. I like seeing young girls take interest in typically male careers."

She was totally awesome. Even if she already had a boyfriend. I decided her guy was one lucky man.

"Thank you," I told her, shaking her hand. Then I shook Officer Lars's hand. "I'll be in touch," I promised her.

And I would. Because I was totally going to send love e-mails to her and my brother. Tonight.

chapter nine

I should have realized the fake eyelashes would be a bad idea.

"You okay?" Derek asked me from across the table, his brows knit together.

We were on our official "second week together" date at Starbucks on Thursday night, where I was carefully sipping a delicious Green Tea Frappuccino through a straw to keep from wearing off too much of my brand-new pale pink lipstick.

As part of my makeover plan, I'd realized that most of the popular girls played up only one feature of their faces. So I'd decided on making my eyes pop even more than usual by gluing on some fake eyelashes I'd found in the drugstore. To balance it all out and keep from looking like a mini-hooker, I also wore natural-toned makeup on my cheeks and lips.

"Yeah, I'm fine," I answered Derek, tossing my hair and giving what I hoped was a flirtatious smile. "Why?"

He squinted and leaned over, studying my face closer. "Your right eye seems . . . off. Do you have something in it? Need a napkin?" He held one toward me.

I waved it away and blinked rapidly for the four-thousandth time, casually slipping my finger along the edge of my eyelid to press the lash back on. In my head, I prayed to the makeup gods that it wouldn't fall off. It seemed I hadn't put enough glue on (nor had I been smart enough to bring that glue in my purse for emergencies), so I was in constant peril of ruining the date and embarrassing myself through the loss of my fake eyelashes. Lovely.

Well, no time to worry about that. I needed to get my flirt on. Good makeup was only going to get me so far, after all. Right now I needed to tease him, draw him in with my masterful allure.

"Oh, I'm just winking at you, you hottie," I answered him coyly. "You look so good today."

And he did. It was a good thing Derek was sitting across the table from me because he'd need to wear a rain jacket from all the drool I'd get on him. His broad shoulders were well defined in a jersey-style shirt. And I'd seen earlier that his butt looked better than usual in a pair of nicely fitted jeans.

Taaaaasty. I was one lucky girl.

He took a bite of the superfudgy brownie he'd bought. "Thanks. So, how are your matches going? I'm almost through my list, with around twenty-five couples left to make. I should be done by the end of this weekend."

I swirled the straw for my drink between my index finger and thumb, then mimicked a trick I'd seen one of Mallory's friends do at lunch yesterday—she'd rubbed the end of the straw across her lower lip, then had taken a sexy little sip.

Except no drink was coming out.

I took a bigger sip through my straw, and a surge of icy cold, thick drink flooded my mouth and slid down my throat.

"My—matches—" I hacked out, trying to push away the impending brain freeze, "are fine—thanks."

Yeah, this was going well. How come I never saw Mallory lose an eyelash or get brain freeze?

"Might wanna take a bit smaller sips," Derek pointed out.

"Yeah, I kind of figured that out," I snapped, unable to keep the aggravated tone out of my voice.

"Just trying to help," he mumbled, looking down at his mug.

Crap. Okay, I wasn't supposed to alienate him or make him feel bad. This night was about giving him a good impression of me that would last past the spell wearing off.

I glanced at my chest, tugging down my V-neck shirt just a wee bit more. Not that it made me suddenly grow cleavage or anything, but the action seemed a little more in line with my makeover plan.

"I'm sorry, honey," I finally purred, leaning forward. I would have winked at him, had I not been afraid of my eyelashes flying off. Now that would have been a disaster I could never fix. "Brain freeze gets me every time. I should have listened to you, though, because you're sooooo smart."

I almost ralphed with how hard I was laying it on, but if I'd learned anything from watching Mallory, it was that flattery got you everywhere, especially with guys.

Derek shot me an odd look. "Um, okay. Anyway," he continued, pulling out his LoveLine 3000 from his back pocket, "I was thinking we could work on making this evening's matches. I haven't gotten to mine tonight, and it's fun getting your opinion on things."

I didn't want to work; I wanted to seduce! But maybe this would give me an unexpected opportunity. Grabbing my purse and drink, I slid out of my seat and over to the available space beside Derek.

Why didn't I think of this before? I could "accidentally" press up against him. Surely that would drive him wild!

I pulled out my LoveLine 3000 and turned it on, bringing up my list. "I still have . . . thirty couples to match up," I said, leaning toward him with an arched back.

He scrolled down through my names, paying absolutely no attention to my chest. "This looks great," he said, smiling at me. "You've got some good people still on here. I'm sure it'll be easy to pair them up."

Dude, what gives? Was I doing this wrong?

Then awareness struck me. I was forcing it too much on him. If I wanted to win his attention, I needed to draw *him* to *me*, not press him. I would be the spider with the pot of honey, sitting pretty in my parlor, luring in the unsuspecting fly. Or something like that.

After all, guys liked what they couldn't get, right?

I sucked my chest back in, drawing my LoveLine 3000 back

toward me. "Yup, and I have a strategy in place to get these matches done fast and accurately."

I had no such thing, of course, and was bluffing through my phony eyelashes, but I needed to appear like I had some mysterious smarts that he didn't know about.

"Oh, really?" Derek asked, curiosity written on his face. He raised one eyebrow. "So what are you going to do?"

Crap. Maybe I should have thought this through better.

"Ummmmmm," I stalled, then finally said in what I hoped was a husky voice, "that's for me to know."

Yeah, not the most mysterious thing I could have said, but it worked. He stopped pressing me about the subject.

"So, I was thinking of pairing up Sam from the soccer team, but I wasn't sure if this girl would be right for him, or this one," Derek said as he leaned closer to me, pointing at some names on his list. "What do you think?"

Yarrrrr. I could smell the clean scent of his cologne, and it took all my willpower to maintain my new mysterious persona and not jump on top of him. I hadn't thought to wear perfume for our date, so I made a mental note to snake some of my mom's to wear to school tomorrow. Something told me that the baby powder lotion I usually wore wasn't quite as alluring as I wanted.

"Well, I happen to know that Ellen," I said, pointing to the first girl on his list, "is big-time into acting. She was the star of the senior play."

"And Sam was in it too. I forgot about that," Derek admitted, a slow grin spreading across his face. "Very clever, Felicity."

"Thanks. I've heard I have good ideas every once in a while," I joked, then stopped myself.

I was supposed to be mysterious, not my usual goofy self. *Concentrate!* My love was on the line, and no way was I going to lose him.

"And I've learned a thing or two while being a cupid," I added, hoping I sounded wise and all-knowing.

Derek's eyes connected with mine, and I stared back. It was an intense moment; all the background noise of the café faded away.

We leaned toward each other, our mouths mere inches apart. His eyes became dark, hooded, and I closed mine, mentally drawing him into my spidey parlor.

"Hey, man!" I heard a guy say.

My eyes flew open. A few of Derek's jock friends surrounded our table. Right behind them Mallory and two other girls who didn't go to our school were gathered in a small circle, staring boldly at me as they whispered under their breaths.

Of *course* they were here. When we were by ourselves, it was easy to forget that Derek was superpopular.

I turned back toward the table and steepled my fingers like I was deep in thought, using the gesture to cover up smoothing down my eyelashes in the inner corners. They were starting to peel off my eyelids again.

Okay, no way was I going to have one of my fake lashes fly off while Mallory was around. Time to ditch them. I would play around with how much glue to use later at home, but for now they were more of a liability than an asset.

"Dude, what's up?" Jay asked, thumping Derek hard on his back.

He stood to face them, deftly slipping his LoveLine 3000 into his back pocket before anyone could see. "Hey, man, not much. We're just having some coffee."

The girls squeezed into the booth seat across from us, plunking their drinks down on the table and sighing heavily.

"God, I'm so bored," one of the blond chicks whined to the other. She blew a huge pink bubble and let it pop. "Why are we here? I thought we were going to a movie."

"I don't want to see a movie," the other girl replied. She took a sip of her drink. "Everything in the theater is utter crap right now."

The guys kept talking, oblivious to what the girls were doing.

Taking advantage of the fact that none of them paid me any attention, I leaned over like I had to fix my shoelace. Then I slipped my compact mirror out of my purse. Under the table I ripped off my eyelashes and crammed them in my mirror, snapping it shut.

One problem solved. Now, how could I get rid of my other problem, currently sitting across from me?

"Ew, what's in that?" Mallory asked me, sneering at my drink. "It's *green*."

"It's a Green Tea Frappuccino," I explained, trying not to sound defensive. "They're actually really good."

"Oh. Well, I hate tea." She blanched. "Give me an espresso any day of the week."

Gee, color me surprised. My temples started to throb. I had to think fast. It was torture to sit here and let her and her stupid friends ruin my evening.

I turned toward Derek and tugged gently on his sleeve. "I'm sorry, honey," I said, grimacing, "but I have a bad headache."

He studied my face in concern. "Okay, let's get you out of here.

Do you want to stop at the store on the way home and pick up some pain pills?"

I shook my head. "Nah, I have some in my cabinet."

We left, with me not paying one bit of attention to Mallory, her friends, and the jocks, who quickly took over our table and started yapping amongst themselves. Buh-bye!

I had to admit, it was wonderful being nurtured by Derek, who insisted once we'd reached my front porch that I needed to take some aspirin and go right upstairs.

"And call me if you need anything," he insisted, opening my front door for me. "I mean it."

"I will, I promise."

God, he was so sweet and thoughtful. I gave him a big bear hug. A sensation of fear tickled my chest over the panic of possibly losing him, and I tried to fight it down. Granted, I'd sucked big-time at my attempted seduction-slash-makeover, but I'd get another chance to try again tomorrow.

After all, I still had six whole days until the love spell wore off. More than enough time to make true love happen, right?

chapter ten

Thank God it was Friday . . . and lunchtime! I was starving and ready to nosh on my sandwich.

All this acting-mysterious stuff was way harder work than I'd realized. If I'd actually liked and respected Mallory, I'd have to give her props for keeping the gig up all day, every day. How tiring to constantly perform, to keep up a persona.

Not to mention the high makeup maintenance. Good grief, I must have reapplied my lipstick about forty times so far today.

Dropping into the seat beside Maya, I pulled out my PB&J sandwich and started digging in.

"Oh man, I'm totally dying of hunger," I proclaimed between bites. Right then I didn't care about taking dainty nibbles.

Maya, who was eating a slice of pizza, giggled and shook her head at me. "I can see that."

"Most guys can appreciate a girl who's not afraid to throw down," her boyfriend, Scott, added.

"That must be why you like sitting at our table," I offered. "Because Maya and I know how to eat heartily."

Andy and Bobby, bearing lunch trays, showed up at our table and sat down.

"Oh my God, could you believe what Mrs. Cahill said in health class today?" Andy asked us all, picking up her pizza slice as she talked. "She totally—"

When her eyes hit me, Andy stopped midsentence.

I frowned under her scrutiny, squirming slightly in my seat. "What?"

Everyone else stopped eating and stared at me too.

Oh, goodie. Did I look like a total freak or something? Was there food on my face? Had my boobs fallen out of my low-cut shirt?

I sneaked a quick peek down at my chest—everything was still in place, thankfully. Then I patted a napkin on my cheeks and mouth to make sure there wasn't anything weird on there and ran my fingers along my eyelids as subtly as possible. Whew, the lashes were still glued on just fine.

Andy tilted her head, chewing on her lower lip. "Something's different about you. I can't figure it out—"

"Well, I got some clothes. And I'm playing around with different makeup styles," I interjected, not wanting to point out my fake eyelashes for obvious reasons. I was hoping I'd just look more appealing to everyone without people being fully aware of why.

After playing around with my lashes last night, I'd finally figured out the perfect amount of glue to use. Presto change-o, I was a newly made goddess. It did bother me a bit, though, that Derek hadn't said anything about my new appearance. But maybe he was waiting until we were alone to tell me if he liked it.

Or maybe he doesn't like it, the evil whisper inside my head said.

Shut up, I ordered myself. Wallowing in self-pity and fear wasn't going to keep Derek's love. "By the way, does my lipstick still look okay?" I asked Andy, trying to distract myself from my woes. "I'm trying out a new shade of pink."

"Yeah, your lips look fine," Andy said, raising one eyebrow at me but saying nothing else.

I sat in silence and picked at the rest of my lunch, my appetite soured because of my secret doubts and the less-than-warm reception I'd gotten from everyone so far about my makeover. Maya and Andy talked for several minutes about Ms. Chan, who had told her class today that she was going on sabbatical next year to live in India. Talk about out-of-the-blue surprises . . . especially since we'd heard that a male freshman English teacher was going to do the exact same thing.

What a coincidence.

Something told me those two had been paired up with each other by Derek.

Lunch ended, and Andy and I headed to anthropology together.

"Okay, we're alone now," she said in a low voice as we paced through the hallway. "You have to tell me what's going on, because you look very different, and you're acting really weird."

The longing to open up to my best friend caused an avalanche of words to spill forth from my lips. "I'm worried that Derek may not really love me like I want him to love me so I was hoping if I dressed exotically and seemed interesting and different that he'd be drawn to me and wouldn't want to leave."

I stopped and sucked in a few deep breaths. Whew, it felt so good to unload that off my chest.

Andy grabbed my elbow and tugged me to the side of the hallway. "Okay, all of this makes sense now. I wondered why you were suddenly concerned with your makeup and clothes. And why your eyelashes suddenly looked thick and luxurious," she added in a dry voice, giving me a knowing look.

A flush crept up my neck and cheeks. "Yeah, well, it works for other girls around here," I mumbled. "They keep guys wrapped around their fingers."

Her face softened. "Look, I know Derek is an awesome guy and that you're crazy about him, but is he worth changing yourself like this?"

"To me, he's definitely worth fighting for," I said quietly. "I love him, and I need to keep him attracted to me."

The second bell rang, letting us know we were late for class.

"Let's go. But we're gonna finish this conversation later," Andy said as we started walking again. "Mr. Wiley's really uptight and hates when people are late."

I snickered, remembering the way he'd looked when I'd busted him making out with the school secretary Brenda in the teacher's lounge.

"Well, I'm willing to bet he won't yell at us," I casually replied, knowing I was about to drop some interesting info on Andy. "He's been . . . occupied the last few days with his own romance."

Her jaw dropped. "Wait, you know gossip that I don't? Oh, man, I cannot *wait* to hear all about this."

Okay, only thirty couples left to make. Just thirty, and then I'd be all done with my list. I could do this.

From my corner of the library, I saw two couples cuddling at nearby tables. One was a pair of seniors who must have been on Derek's list. I instantly recognized the Hello Kitty backpack beside the other girl—it was Marie, the freshman I'd matchmaded with Alec. Finally, a chance to see how these two were doing! I hardly ever saw them around school.

"Oh my God, I can't wait to see that series," Marie was saying to him, clapping her hands in excitement. "It's huge in Japan. They should have brought it to the U.S. long before now." She dropped her voice. "I heard they're hiring American actors to do the voice-overs."

Alec shook his head, his face filled with disgust. "I know. It sucks that we get these horrible voice-overs for the series they release here. Because America is obviously too stupid to understand or appreciate original Japanese casts. But whatever. When I move to Japan, I'll see the originals for everything."

Marie sighed. "I desperately want to go to the Hello Kitty store in Japan. They have everything you could possibly want. I could die happy in that place."

"Hey, wanna go watch something at my house?" Alec asked. "I just got the newest season of *Bleach*."

"Yeah, that sounds great!" Marie stood and slipped her backpack on.

The two of them left.

I grinned. Watching them together, speaking their nerd language so happily with each other, made me feel pretty good. It was probably a good thing my friends weren't here with me. Andy would have seriously ripped on them had she overheard that conversation.

I whipped out my LoveLine 3000, wishing Derek were with me. His dad needed him to help out at the sports shop after school today, though, so I was going to chill out here in the reference section for a couple of hours until I met Andy and Maya for our TGIF sleepover. And the best way to be productive, since I'd already finished most of my homework, was to make more couples.

But for some reason I couldn't concentrate. An image of Andy's smiling face popped in my head. Boy, watching people fall in love always surprised me. I never would have expected her to hook up with Bobby, not in a million years. She was gorgeous and fun, and he was short and eccentric, to say the least. It was so weird that the two of them were somehow drawn together, all because of working on our health class project as a group.

Or . . . was that the real cause?

Letting the LoveLine 3000 rest in my lap, I mentally replayed last Wednesday, when I'd finally found out that Andy and Bobby were going out. I'd shown up at the cafeteria to find the two of them cuddling close. And later I'd realized they'd been talking to each other even when I wasn't around.

Was it possible that Derek had matchmade Andy and Bobby? After all, he'd become a cupid by then and obviously had his own quotas to make.

The idea drew out conflicting emotions in me. I was glad to see Derek was intuitively good as a cupid—he was pairing up couples who, upon first glance, might not look like they belonged together. And from the way Andy and Bobby shared jokes and hobbies, it seemed quite possible that they wouldn't break up even after their spell wore off.

But on the flip side of the coin, what did that mean about *me*, as a cupid? Because I was obviously missing something big by not seeing these potential couples.

I lifted my PDA and stared at the names on the list that I'd already matched up. My heart started to race as I scrutinized each name and the person I'd paired them up with. What couples had I messed up because I hadn't made their profiles detailed enough, or thought "outside the box" in my matchmaking?

Fear bubbled below the surface of my skin, and I looked again at the people I still had to match. Sixty individuals, waiting for me to find them the perfect love match. But could I do the job justice? What had once seemed like such a cakewalk now felt almost impossible.

As my thoughts entered a spin cycle, the couple near me that Derek had matched walked out of the library, fingers linked, leaving me alone.

Okay, let's not be ridiculous, I told myself. *Focus*. No sense freaking out right now. I could do this.

Besides, just because Derek was a good matchmaker didn't mean I was bad. We could both be good at our jobs. I'd made some high-quality couples that were still going strong, like James and Mitzi, or DeShawn and Marisa. I mean, for all our teasing and bravado, it wasn't *really* a competition between me and him . . . right?

Well if it was, I was never one to back down from a challenge.

I picked the next guy on my list, a sports nut named Dale who I'd seen at most of our school's basketball games, then scrolled down to find the perfect match for him from the remaining people on the list. Hmmm, Deanna, a girl in my American history class, might be a good one, since she was a huge hockey fan.

I composed the e-mail, adding their two names, and went to hit send but then paused. Just because two people liked sports didn't mean they'd be a great couple. Did they have enough in common with each other to make them ideal matches? Or was there someone else who might be better for him?

A sudden sick feeling hit my stomach. I wasn't ready to send this e-mail yet. I needed to do more research to make sure these two were actually right for each other. Maybe I could enrich their profiles first.

My course of action decided, I turned off my LoveLine 3000 and tugged out my American history book and notebook to study for a test next week. Not that it was a faboo alternative, but at least there I knew what I was supposed to do.

• • •

"Guys, I need your help," Andy said to Maya and me at our TGIF sleepover. She wrung her hands and swallowed. "But you have to promise not to tell anyone. Because I am totally. Screwed. Unless I get this fixed."

Crossing my pajama-clad legs, I sat up on Andy's bed. "Well, color me intrigued."

Maya perked up too, pulling her attention away from the *Cosmo* she was reading. "Yeah, what's going on?"

Andy pressed her index finger against her lips and went over to her door. "Just follow me and be superquiet, please. My mom is in bed, and I don't want to wake her up."

Silent as the grave, Maya and I followed Andy down through her house and into the three-car garage. And yes, they actually had three cars to fit in there. Andy flipped on the light switch and led us to the covered car at the far end, tugging back the black cover.

The first thing I noticed was the smashed-up corner of Andy's dad's fire-red Porsche. The headlight was broken, and the hubcap was missing. Ouch, that was bad.

I exhaled loudly. "Whoa, what did you do?" I asked.

Maya grimaced, squatting down to check out the damage. "Yeah, that is so not good. How are you going to get it fixed?"

Andy dropped the tarp and sighed. "That's what I wanted your help with. My dad's on a business trip, so he hasn't seen it yet. But when he gets back, he's gonna want to drive it." She paused, tilting her head. "I think I hear something. Let's go back upstairs and finish talking."

We crept back up to Andy's bedroom and closed the door behind us, taking our spots on her bed again.

"Okay," Andy said. "This was really, really stupid of me, and I've learned my lesson. And I'll never do it again, I promise." She held up her fingers in the Boy Scout's–promise kind of way. "So earlier today I decided to treat Bobby to dinner. I wanted to do it in style, so I—" She stopped. "Well, I'm sure you can figure it out. Home alone, with the keys to the most awesome car ever." She grimaced, shaking her head. "I had no problems driving to pick him up or going to the restaurant, but after I dropped him off and was heading home, I got into a . . . minor accident."

Andy's parents were usually pretty chill, but if they found out what she'd done, they'd ground her forever. That car was her dad's baby, and everyone knew it.

"Oh, no!" Maya exclaimed. "Did the police come?"

She bit her lip. "Well . . . I didn't exactly report it. I was digging through my purse to find my cell phone and accidentally hit a mailbox. I was so freaked out, I panicked and just drove home. Then I threw the tarp on over the car and decided to see if you guys could help me figure out what to do."

Maya twiddled her feet off the edge of the bed. "What if you . . . told them the car had been temporarily stolen?"

"And then brought back into their garage? I don't think they'd buy that," I said.

We sat in silence for a moment, trying to think of the perfect solution.

Andy sucked in a quick breath. "There has to be something I can do. And I figured three heads were better than one." Tears welled up in her eyes, and she sniffled. "I'm afraid if I tell my dad what I did, he'll ground me from going to prom."

"We'll make everything better," I said, hugging her. "Don't cry."

Maya rubbed her chin. "I heard if you divert your attention to something else, the solution to problems will come from your unconscious mind when you least expect it." She glanced around the bedroom and snagged the *Cosmo* she'd been reading. "Okay, let's take a quiz to distract ourselves. I bet afterward we'll know what to do."

Andy shrugged halfheartedly. "I guess so."

"Okay." Maya thumbed through a few thousand pages of stinky perfume ads, then stopped. "Aha, here we go. *Are you made for each other? Take this quiz to find out.*"

I groaned. I didn't need something else to remind me of my woes with Derek. "Can we do another quiz, instead?"

Maya's eyes studied me with concern, but she nodded silently, then flipped through *Cosmo.* "How about . . . *What's Your Ideal Career?*"

Now, that was more like it. I couldn't wait to see what this quiz would reveal about me and my best buds.

chapter eleven

"A therapist? Really?" I asked. I didn't know why I was surprised, though—it's not like the quiz would have cupid listed as one of the choices or anything. But I guess I wasn't expecting to hear I'd be a good shrink.

Maya, who had tallied up my answers first, nodded, the corners of her mouth curving up. "I totally believe it. Everyone comes to you when they have problems. And you love helping people out."

Andy nodded. "You're always trying to make things better for your friends and family. That's a good thing, though. Remember how hard you worked to help Maya figure out which guy was the right boyfriend for her?"

"But she ended up going with a totally different one," I pointed out.

"So what? At least you tried," Andy said. "That's what counts."

"Yeah, I guess you're right. Okay, so what did it say for you?" I asked Maya, wanting to take the focus off me.

She crunched the numbers for a minute, then read the entry and started to giggle. "It said I'd be ideal working in an analytical but artistic environment. Like maybe as an architect or designer."

"I believe that. You'd do a great job designing things," I said to her. "And maybe in the future you can design a car that automatically fixes itself so teenagers won't be killed by their parents for minor accidents."

Andy jumped up, grabbing me by the shoulders. "Wait a minute. I can't believe I didn't think about this before, but I think Bobby's older brother fixes up cars. I bet he could help me out, or at least find someone who can!"

"Yay! See, I told you the answer would come to us if we were patient," Maya said sagely. "Always trust me, young one."

Andy slugged her in the upper arm, causing Maya to grimace in mock pain. "Thanks a lot for the tip, sensei."

"Are we there yet?" I teased Derek in a mock whiny voice. I stepped over a fallen tree limb on the walking path through the park's wooded trail, clinging to his hand as I lagged behind him.

Derek turned back to look at me, shaking his head lightly. "Patience. We're almost there. Just a few more minutes." He slung his mysterious duffel bag over his shoulder and continued forward.

I was glad he'd at least told me we were going to be outside on this Saturday afternoon mystery date he'd planned for us. I was originally planning to wear another one of my new hoochie outfits, but I certainly didn't need bugs or leaves or other outdoor crap falling down my shirt or into my hair. So instead, I had on my favorite jeans, a green T-shirt with a picture of the Beatles on it, and a black baseball cap.

In the back of my mind I kept repeating my secret mantra: *Derek isn't himself right now because of the love spell, so don't be too excited by whatever he does, or you may set yourself up for heartbreak later once the spell wears off.* The worst thing I could do for myself was to start believing this was all real. I could and should be appreciative, but until I'd won him over for good, I had to stay on my guard and not mess anything up.

We walked for what seemed like forever until we stepped into a clearing. The trees opened up, and there was a large field of grass and multicolored flowers in front of us. The sun peeked out from behind the clouds, warming us instantly.

"Derek, this is so pretty!" I exclaimed, squeezing his hand in excitement. My face turned up to the sun as I soaked in the moment.

He tugged me forward. "Come on, we're not done yet."

We walked into the middle of the field, where Derek dropped his duffel bag and started digging through it. After a moment he whipped out a small blanket, just big enough for two to fit on, and spread it over the grass.

"Have a seat," he said. He turned back to the bag and pulled out two food containers, cans of soda, silverware, and a stereo. After plugging his iPod into the stereo, he pressed play. A romantic song by Coldplay came through the speakers.

I swallowed, taking off my hat and sitting down. "I love this song," I whispered. Damn, he was making it hard for me to maintain an impersonal distance. Today's date might be the biggest challenge of my life.

Derek nodded, locking eyes with me. "Yeah, I know."

"How?"

He shrugged casually. "I have my ways. Anyway," he continued, pressing one of the food containers into my hand, "let's eat. I'm starving."

I peeled the lid back, and a waft of deliciousness hit my nose.

"Oh man, meat loaf!" I exclaimed. "I can't believe you can cook, too!"

Derek blushed. "Didn't make it. I enlisted my mom's help. Ya know, 'cause I wanted the food to be edible."

"Well, be sure to thank her for me." I grabbed a fork and began to dig in. My stomach was rumbling, especially after all that walking we did. It was delicious and tender and juicy. I could probably have eaten his plate, too, but decided not to look like a superpig.

Needless to say, we polished off the food in record time. After tossing the containers and silverware back in the duffel bag, we lounged back on the blanket and stared at the sky. Another of my favorite songs came on, this one by The Fray.

My heart sped up. Had he made a mix playlist for me? Geez, Derek didn't believe in doing anything halfway. He sure was pulling out all the stops.

He reached his arm out and tugged me close to his side. I could feel his chest rising and falling. The heat from his muscular body poured into mine, warming me. We kissed for several intense minutes. I stroked his back and shoulders as he rubbed my waist and pressed me against him.

Finally, I pressed one last kiss on the corner of his cheek, then closed my eyes, laying my head on his shoulder. We lay in perfect silence, me cuddled in the crook of his side and my arm flung over his chest. I wanted to relax and fully enjoy the moment, but my mind wouldn't stop spinning. It was so, so tempting to flat-out ask him how he was feeling, if he really liked me for me or if it was the spell. But I already knew the answer, even if he didn't.

I opened my eyes, turned on to my back, and stared at the thick mass of clouds as they slid back in front of the sun.

"You okay?" he asked, turning his head to look at me.

"I'm fine," I said. "I'm just . . . digesting my food." Ugh. Yeah, that was supersexy of me to say, especially after we'd just been making out. Good grief. Talking like that wasn't going to keep him in love with me. It was time to change the subject. "So . . . how about you tell me more about yourself?"

Brilliant idea! If I could find out those little details about his likes and dislikes, maybe I could do some well-tailored wooing of my own. Surely he'd be flattered by whatever I did, right?

"What do you want to know?" he asked me, giving me a crooked grin.

"How about this: We'll do a quick question and answer. Don't think, just answer the questions, okay?"

"Sure, but you have to do it too."

I nodded. "You got it. Okay, favorite movie?"

"*Kill Bill* one and two. Favorite color?"

"Blue," I said. The wind picked up and rustled my hair around. I tucked it behind my ear. "Worst thing you've ever done?"

"Whew," he said, blinking. "Hitting the hard stuff, aren't we?" He paused, thinking. "Okay, I'll be honest. I stole a used CD from one of those exchange stores a few years ago. Not my finest hour, and I regret doing it. Most embarrassing moment?"

God, like I could pick just one. I decided to not admit the whole fiasco when Derek had seen me trying on bikinis in Target, and my mom had shouted to the entire store about my small chest size.

"Maybe seeing my folks getting it on, right there on their bedroom floor? Or how about the time last year I had a rip on the back of my jeans and didn't know it, and my ass cheek hung out for the whole world to see? Or perhaps the time I face-planted while diving for a volleyball in gym," I said, grimacing.

Derek shook his head, chuckling. "You could write a book on disasters."

He had no idea. "Okay," I said, "worst date ever."

"Well," Derek said, turning his face back toward the sky, "I took a girl out last year, and all she did was complain about everything:

She didn't like the restaurant. She thought the movie was awful. She spent the entire evening telling me how terrible her life was and how much she hated most people at school, including my friends."

I cringed. Actually, I didn't like his friends, either. They were snobby and rude. But I decided to keep my mouth shut.

Derek continued, "As you can imagine, that was our first and last date. Anyway, tell me your biggest regret."

The oxygen froze in my lungs. I knew without a doubt what was my biggest regret—knowing that my relationship with Derek would forever be tainted. Not that I could tell him that, though.

I sat up and stared at my feet stretched out in front of me. My good mood had slipped away, again. How could I keep going through this? Having him do these sweet, romantic gestures and not being able to enjoy them properly?

In a low voice I simply said, "Cupid issues." There, that was generic enough. He'd probably think I was talking about the job, not us.

"What do you mean?" he asked, his brows scrunched up.

"I don't want to get into it right now," I hedged.

He sat up and fixed a hard stare on my face. "I thought that was the point of the game. To be honest."

The sky grew dark. I glanced up.

"I think it's going to rain," I said quietly.

Right at that moment the clouds opened up and raindrops began pouring down. We jumped up off the blanket, piling our belongings and all of our trash into the duffel bag as quickly as we could. I crammed the hat back on my head and shivered as big splotches of rain smacked me on the shoulders.

Derek held out the blanket to me. "Wrap up in this to keep you dry," he said. The rain smashed his hair against his head as it beat down harder. Drops of water slid down the angles of his face and plopped onto his shirt.

"But you'll get wet!" I protested. I handed it back to him. "Here, take it."

"Just use it," he said with a sigh, tugging the bag over his shoulder. He moved toward the path. "Let's get back to the car."

I wrapped the blanket around my upper body and hustled after him. We plunged into the woods, brusquely walking along the path. Mud sloshed our feet and peppered my pants legs. I stared at his back, the wet shirt clinging to his broad shoulders. Always the gentleman, he'd sacrificed his own comfort for mine.

It would have been easy to blame the end of the date on the rain. But, deep down, I knew it was my fault, my inability to take him at face value and my discomfort with the secret knowledge I had about him.

And my unwillingness to illuminate that, for fear it meant I would lose him for good.

"Would you like another bowl of chili?" my dad asked Annette, the cop I'd paired Rob up with, at Sunday dinner.

She smiled, rubbing a hand over her stomach as she leaned back in her chair. "Oh my God, I'm stuffed," she said with a laugh. "But thank you! That was killer chili. . . . What did you put in it? Mine never turns out that good."

"Well," Dad said, leaning across the table toward her in a conspiratorial manner, "my secret ingredient is Jack Daniel's. The alcohol cooks out, but it adds a rich flavor that can't be beat."

Whoa.

My dad had never told anyone outside the family what was in his chili. And I mean *never*. He guarded the recipe as if it were a Fort Knox–worthy secret. In fact, according to my mom, he didn't even tell *her* until after he'd proposed. So, Annette must have really made a good impression on him.

Of course, given the kind of women Rob had brought home, it

wasn't too hard for her to stand out above the rest. But even so, she was the best date he'd ever brought around. From the time Annette came through the door, she was smiling, friendly, and responsive to us and, most notably, to Rob.

Plus, she'd helped set the dinner table and complimented my mom on our house.

And not only that, but my brother seemed genuinely smitten with her. I'd never seen him like this before—affectionate and sincere in his attention. Every time she told a joke, he laughed like she was the funniest person he'd ever heard. He'd even jumped up to get a paper towel when she'd spilled a little bit of her drink, insisting on no one else helping.

It would almost be a little gaggy if I hadn't been reveling in the glorious sensation of another happy love match. I fervently hoped they would make it past the two weeks.

Mom carried the empty chili bowls into the kitchen. "Felicity, can you help me clean up?" she hollered into the dining room.

"Sure." I grabbed the rest of the dirty dishes and went into the kitchen after her, loading up the dishwasher. "So, Annette seems nice," I offered, wanting to see Mom's opinion of my love match for Rob. I knew I could count on her to be honest.

Mom, who was putting the leftover chili into the fridge, nodded in agreement. "I like her. This girl seems quite different from others he's brought home."

"Well, it helps that she's fully dressed. And that she's not trying to date Dad," I said, laughing.

She closed the fridge door. "Yeah, that's always a relief. I'm tired of having to fight for him," she joked. "Truthfully, though, I've never seen your brother fall this hard for a girl before. She'd better treat him right."

Peals of laughter from Dad, Rob, and Annette came from the dining room.

"Mr. Walker, you're hilarious!" I heard Annette say. "Rob, you didn't tell me your dad was so funny. I can see where you get your great sense of humor from."

"So, does she get your official seal of approval?" I asked Mom.

Head cocked toward the dining room, she nodded. "Absolutely."

"She gets mine, too," I said quietly, with a smile. I didn't always like my brother, but he deserved to be with someone who made him happy. And it made me feel good to find a girl like that for him.

chapter twelve

Riding high on my brilliant matchmaking, I ran upstairs once Rob and Annette had left and grabbed my LoveLine 3000. I fired it up, randomly picking one of the names on my list: Randall Schlemming.

I pulled up his profile:

Name: Randall Schlemming

Age: 18

Interests: Filmmaking. Quirky postmodern art galleries. Loves to talk about hot topics to people in class.

Smart guy.

Style: Artsy Individualist

I heard him say that after graduation he was hoping to move to California and become a movie director. He needed to be matched to someone who was ambitious and outgoing to match his strong personality.

I scrolled through my list, finding two different girls who seemed like they might work well. Janie was a writer who had won some regional writing contests. The fact that she was competitive and believed in perfecting her craft would certainly appeal to someone like Randall.

On the other hand, Laura was truly an artiste, into action painting and performance art. She, too, wanted to move to California and be a part of some artistic movement when she graduated.

So, which girl was the right choice?

I studied them both for a few seconds, overwhelmed and unable to select. My heart rate sped up, and my lips started to tingle as a wave of dizziness swept over me. What if neither one of these girls was right for Randall—was I being too superficial in my matchmaking again?

Maybe I should just pick one and give it a try. I chose Janie and added her and Randall to my love-matching e-mail.

Press send, I told myself.

But I couldn't do it.

There was definitely something wrong with me. Where was my enthusiasm, my courage from ten minutes ago? Why had it vanished on me?

I laid my PDA on my nightstand and draped myself across my bed, burying my face in my pillow. This was so, so not good. How could I be a cupid if I couldn't even make any matches? I mean, hello—that was the purpose of my job.

What was I going to do?

Hey, maybe I could talk to Derek about it.

I reached over to grab my phone, then stopped. Things were a little awkward with us right now after our date yesterday afternoon, and this wasn't going to help me look appealing to him. Besides, after boasting so hard that I was kicking butt with my list, it would be lame to say, "Hey, I take it back. I suck at this, and I'm stuck."

Just as I went to pull my hand away from the receiver, the phone rang. A startled shiver ran across my skin. Was Derek calling me?

I lifted the phone and checked the caller ID—nope, it was Maya.

"Can you come over?" she whispered after we said our hellos.

"My dad's on his way here to meet with my mom, and I need some moral support."

I sat up, sucking in a quick, nervous breath. "Absolutely. I'm on my way."

After we hung up, I threw on my tennis shoes and headed to Maya's house, fretting the whole way as I paced the sidewalk. Would our attempt at helping Mrs. Takahashi make herself over work?

Finally I got to the front door. Before I could even knock, the door was flung open, and Maya tugged me inside without saying a word, leading me up to her room.

"Thanks for coming," she finally said, hugging me quickly. When we reached her room at the top of the stairs, we left her bedroom door open so we could hear what was going on down in the living room, then perched on the edge of her bed. "I just got really nervous and started to feel sick, and I figured this would be easier if you were here."

"I wouldn't be anywhere else," I said. "Is Andy coming, too?"

She shook her head. "She's at work right now, and I didn't want to bother her there. Anyway—"

Maya stopped when we heard the front door open. She gripped

my hand tightly. "Oh God, he's here!" she whispered, her eyes wide. "He hasn't seen my mom yet. I hope he's surprised!"

"Me too," I said, trying to ignore the shooting pain going up my arm from her death grip. "I'm sure he'll be floored."

Mrs. Takahashi, who I guess had been in the kitchen, came into the living room. "Come on in," she said, her voice soft and warm. "I'm glad you could make it. Here, let me take your coat."

I saw Maya swallow and lean toward the door, her body tense.

The warm, delicious smell of Japanese food wafted up to the room. As part of our plan, Maya's mom had made her husband a traditional dinner, knowing he had a soft spot for her cooking.

"I'm sorry; I can't stay long," Maya's dad said in his typical low, rumbling voice.

Silence.

"But I thought you were staying for dinner," Mrs. Takahashi said. "I thought we were going to talk."

Maya sucked in a quick breath, turning her frantic eyes to me. "He's not staying? That wasn't part of the plan. And he hasn't commented on my mom's looks at all."

I shrugged helplessly, my heart sinking. This wasn't going well, and I had a bad feeling that they weren't going to make amends tonight, regardless of how nice she looked or how confident she tried to seem.

"I'm sorry," Mr. Takahashi repeated.

We heard some papers rustling. Then more silence.

"What's going on?" Maya whispered to me, the line between her brows deep. "Why aren't they talking?"

"I didn't realize . . . you were actually going to go through with this." Mrs. Takahashi's voice was quiet, unemotional. "You already have papers drawn up?"

Mr. Takahashi cleared his throat. "I need to go. I'll have my attorney contact you tomorrow, okay?"

The door closed.

Maya and I stared at each other in horror. I mean, what could I possibly say to make anyone feel better?

"I should . . . go downstairs." Maya rose from the bed and went out of her room, me following right behind.

Mrs. Takahashi stood in the living room, staring at the front door. Her back was ramrod straight, and she clutched the divorce papers in her hand.

I opened my mouth to speak, then decided to stay silent.

Maya, though, ran over and hugged her mom tightly, tears

springing to her eyes. "I'm sorry, Mom," she said. "I'm sorry we let you down."

"You didn't do anything wrong," Mrs. Takahashi said, her voice choked. She patted Maya's back. "It just wasn't meant to be, I guess."

"Maybe we can try something else," I offered.

She shook her head sadly. "No, I think I'm done. I'm better off accepting the reality of this situation than chasing a dream."

After a moment of silence I decided to let the two of them have some private time together.

"I'll catch you at school, okay, Maya?" I said, easing toward the front door.

She gave a slow nod, too choked up to speak.

Once I'd closed the door behind me, I let the tears I'd been fighting slide down my cheeks.

How awful! I couldn't believe the dinner had gone that badly. None of us had expected it to end that way.

Mrs. Takahashi's words haunted me, echoing round and round in my head. Was she right? Was true love just a dream?

As I sludged my way back home, I thought of all the failed couples I'd paired since I'd become a matchmaker, and of all the love-spelled pairs that could so easily break up when their spells wore off.

And then I thought of my own tentative match with Derek, a spell that would end in three days. Would we make it past then?

We had to. We just *had* to. Or I didn't know what I was going to do.

I opened the front door.

"Oh, Felicity," Mom hollered from the kitchen, "is that you? Can you help me with the laundry?"

"Sure," I replied, trying not to groan.

Oh, well . . . maybe sorting lights and darks would help get my mind off all the bad stuff going on right now.

In the basement I got the first load of laundry started, then went up to my room as quietly as I could before Mom could assign me another task. I locked my door behind me, booted up my computer, and logged on to my blog, setting the entry to private diary. I needed to spill all of these crazy emotions out of me.

Everything is just chaos. Why can't I seem to make love go right for anyone—including myself?

Being matched up with Derek should probably have been a good thing. Instead, I'm paranoid and studying his every move . . . and my own, wondering if I'm going to accidentally do something to push him away from me. Every time I'm around him, I'm awkward and end up making things a little crappier than before.

And just as bad, I seem to have lost my matchmaking mojo. What's the deal with that? I try to pair people up, but I freeze. I just can't make myself send the e-mails.

My phone rang. The caller ID showed it was Derek.

Heart racing, I picked it up. "Hello?"

"Hey," he said. "I tried to call earlier, but your mom said you were out. How was your day?"

"Well . . . things are going kind of bad for Maya right now, so I went over to hang out with her," I answered slowly. I didn't feel like trying to be Miss Mysterious, so I let the act go for the night.

"You're a good friend to her. I'm sure she appreciated it."

His voice sounded so warm, I almost wanted to cry. After what had happened with Mr. and Mrs. Takahashi, I was beyond glad to talk to him. And to see that he wasn't being supercold because of the way yesterday afternoon's date ended.

"So, how are things going at your house?" I asked, hoping my voice didn't give away my angst.

"Not bad. My mom's stomach is getting bigger every day. She says she can tell this baby's gonna be a soccer player because he's kicking her constantly. You can even see his foot pressing against her stomach. It's weird." He laughed. "Just what we need—another sports nut in the house."

"Felicity!" Mom's voice echoed all the way into my room. "I need your help straightening the pantry and shelves in the kitchen."

I groaned. "Gotta go. The House Nazi strikes again, and she's beckoning me to do more slave work."

"Okay, I'll see ya tomorrow morning outside of school," Derek said. I could hear the grin in his voice.

We hung up, and I logged off my PC as well, trying to hold on to a bit of Derek's warmth. Surely I wasn't just chasing a dream ... right?

chapter thirteen

T minus two days and counting until the cupid spell would wear off of me and Derek.

I stood on the front steps of school and scoured the grounds with my eyes, waiting for him to show up. I'd dressed to kill today, wearing another of the new outfits I'd bought with my cupid earnings: a pair of low-rise jeans, ballet flats, and a fabulous red top.

Confidence. Self-assurance. Those were my mantras for the day, the subtle messages I'd replayed in my brain over and over to remind myself of the ultimate goal: keeping Derek past Wednesday. Bonus: This might also help me with my other goal, which was to get my sorry hiney back into matchmaking.

After lying awake for hours in bed last night, I'd finally gotten up and sneaked downstairs to watch a movie, hoping to take my mind off all the turmoil. There wasn't much on the boob tube at the time except for a bad infomercial, about some "magical" exercise product that could flatten your abs in ten seconds a day, and a black-and-white Katharine Hepburn movie. I opted for the latter.

Surprisingly, I found myself giggling at her antics, as well as admiring her. She was tall, sassy, and confident, and she owned it. No wonder she'd drawn the male lead to her . . . how could he resist?

So, I'd decided to not dwell on my panic and fears for the next couple of days, but to make a genuine attempt to enjoy the time I had with Derek. I'd give him good memories of me instead of acting like a total insecure freakshow, and surely that would make it hard for him to walk away.

I hoped.

"Hi, Felicity," Derek whispered in my ear from behind me, his soft breath tickling my neck.

I spun around, heart leaping into my throat. "Hi, yourself," I answered, giving him as big of a smile as I could manage. He needed to see how much I loved his company. His laughter. *Him.*

"Sorry I'm a little late." The sunlight hit his hair, bathing it in a bright gold. He looked like a Greek god.

Trying not to swoon at his feet, I said, "No big deal at all. I was happy to wait for you." Crap, I didn't mean to sound so needy or desperate.

Back off, Felicity, I ordered myself. *Remember the plan.*

I threaded my fingers through his and walked through the school's front doors, trying to figure out my next move. What witty thing could I say to show him I was the most confident, self-assured girl at Greenville High?

"So, how did your evening go?" Derek asked before I could bring up a discussion topic, his face eager as he peered over at me. His thumb slowly swirled against my skin of my palm. "I got the last chunk of my matches done last night. Those tables and charts in the manual were invaluable."

Aw man, it looked like I was totally going to lose the bet. I should have known he'd want to talk about this. And I couldn't believe he'd actually finished his whole list.

The guy was determined, for sure.

"Oh, that's fantastic!" I said. Maybe my praise and enthusiasm about his accomplishments would deter him from pressing me further about my own performance. I squeezed his hand, hoping some of his matchmaking mojo would rub off on me. "You're doing so well at this. Janet's going to be impressed."

"Thanks. So did you finish—" He stopped himself midsentence and turned his attention to his football-jock friend Toby Brown, who was barreling down the hallway toward us. "Hey, man!"

"Derek!" Toby hollered as he slapped him on the back. Everything Toby said was at maximum volume, which got to be really annoying about five seconds into him talking. Maybe he should get his ears checked or something. "Dude, you gotta come to my locker. I have the funniest picture in there—it's so gross." He grabbed Derek's upper arm and tugged him away, totally ignoring me.

Derek paused, turning to look at me. "You coming?"

Toby stopped, his upper lip curling as he turned my way. Yeah, he totally didn't want me there—it was written all over his face.

"What are you guys going to look at?" I asked.

"You probably wouldn't be interested. It's a guy thing," Toby answered, then turned his attention back to Derek.

Suck. I'd been looking forward to having some extra time with Derek this morning, but it was apparent he wanted to go hang with his friends, too. No way, though, did I want to spend more than point-five seconds in their company. I'd had enough of that at Starbucks a few nights ago, thank you very much.

Besides, secure girlfriends didn't cling to their guys like they knew they were going to up and leave any second, right? And just as important, they didn't come between a guy and his friends. Derek never did that to me, and I wanted to give him the same respect.

I gave a casual wave to them both. Trying to sound like my heart wasn't slamming in my chest, I said, "Nah, you two go on. I gotta run to class early, anyway."

"Okay, I'll catch you later!" Derek said with a big smile, then turned and left.

Hmmm. Though I'd wanted to show him how self-confident I could be, pretending like being dissed by his friends didn't hurt my feelings wasn't what I'd intended. But lately that kind of thing was happening more and more. Was it possible they were trying to lure him away from me?

It's not like that was unheard of. I distinctly remembered how often the friends of Marisa, a girl I'd matchmade, tried to get her to dump her boyfriend DeShawn. She'd stuck by her guns, though, and had refused to give him up.

Would Derek do the same for me?

I headed toward English class, running the concept through my head. As much as I wanted to be indignant, I understood how influential friends could be in each other's lives. I weighed the opinions of Andy and Maya very heavily. If they'd told me to stay away from Derek, would I have listened to them?

Well, anyway, it was a moot point. My friends would only say that if he were a jerk. And he wasn't.

But did Derek's friends have a problem with *me*?

Maybe I'd done something accidentally to insult them, and now they didn't think I was good enough for him. Or maybe they were just big jerks. Who knew? I'd just have to be extra careful around them and not give them any new reason to dislike me.

Fortunately, the bell to start the day interrupted my thoughts. I made my way to my desk and sat down beside Maya, who was already in class.

Mrs. Kendel lingered by the door for a minute or so, then closed it, thumping her way to the front of class. "I graded your papers," she said, her lips pursed. "Not. Good. I was very disappointed in the quality of your narratives."

My stomach sank. Was she talking about mine? Granted, I'd been working my butt off with matchmaking and trying to keep

Derek . . . but something told me Mrs. Kendel wouldn't understand that, or care.

Well, so much for oozing self-confidence. With each passing second, I got more and more insecure.

Come on! I ordered myself. My fluctuating feelings were getting out of control. I felt like everything was spiraling away from me— could that be part of the reason I was having a hard time making matches?

Mrs. Kendel wandered up and down the aisles, handing back our papers. She put them facedown on our desks. When she got to me, she plopped the paper down and moved on.

I stared at the back of it, almost afraid to flip it over.

Maya nudged me in the side. "What did you get?" she asked, her voice low.

With a quick movement I turned the paper faceup. And then groaned, wanting to thunk my head on the desktop.

"A C-minus," I whispered back.

Oh joy, Mrs. Kendel had even written a note at the top: *Come see me after class.* Gee, that sounded promising. Maybe she wanted to praise me for having the best C-minus paper she'd ever graded. Yeah, I'm sure.

Somehow I managed to fake my way through the rest of class like I was listening to everything she said. In reality, I wanted to run back home, jump in bed, and pretend like this day hadn't started yet.

But one good thing did come out of the period—when thinking about my plans for the evening, I'd realized that Janet was the perfect person for me to talk to about my cupid matchmaking problems in my meeting with her tonight. While I wasn't crazy about 'fessing up, I knew as soon as she saw my PDA that my lack of matches would be obvious.

Therefore, I figured I could approach her and ask for some advice. A little proactivity on my part couldn't hurt.

The bell rang. I told Maya I'd meet her at lunch and then slowly made my way to the front of the classroom, feeling like I was walking to my own funeral.

And, in a way, I was. Mom was going to kill me for getting a C-minus on my paper. I just hoped she didn't take her wrath out on me in a way that would affect prom.

"Miss Walker," Mrs. Kendel said, staring up at me from her chair with arms crossed over her ample chest. "I'm very disappointed in the quality of your paper. I expected better from you. You're one of my best students in class."

Yowch. Mrs. Kendel didn't beat around the bush or anything, did she?

Then the second part of her words hit me like a brick in the face—she considered *me* one of her best students?

"R-Really?" I sputtered. Color me floored. Praise from Mrs. Kendel was a rare occurrence, indeed.

"You always give smart, thoughtful answers on the assignments, but this narrative isn't quite up to your standards. It lacks the focus and depth I'd have expected. But I think you knew that already, didn't you?" She gave me a pointed look with her small, steely eyes, one eyebrow lifted.

I swallowed hard and gave a small nod.

Ziiiing. Mrs. Kendel had no idea how accurately she'd nailed the problem I'd been struggling with for almost two weeks . . . and my relationship woes weren't even what she was addressing! Too weird.

"Do you have any ideas about how I can make sure my papers have focus and depth?" I asked.

She scratched her chin, leaning back in her chair. "Well, I recommend outlining exactly whatever it is you want to achieve in your paper. Break it down in simple language so you stay on track, but don't get overwhelmed by whatever you're facing."

"Okay, I can do that."

"Slow and steady works well. And stick close to your main purpose—that's the important part." She flipped through a big-ass pile of papers on the corner. "Here," she said, thrusting a handout at me. "This'll give you tips on how to outline and draft a paper."

Actually, the idea had merit not only in my English class but also in real life. Maybe instead of wandering around and grasping at straws trying to come up with a billion different plans regarding Derek and my matchmaking woes, I should focus on one solid idea and follow it through.

"I'll give that a try—on the next paper, I mean," I said awkwardly, clutching the outline handout.

"Luckily, this shouldn't affect your grade too much. But don't start sliding downhill," she warned, wagging a finger at me. "It's much easier to drop a grade level than it is to raise it, you know."

"Okay." I made the "cross my heart" gesture.

She scrawled a note out for me, permitting me to be late to American history since we'd talked past the bell, and then sent me on my way.

• • •

That evening at work, during my regular meeting with Janet, I sat in the chair across from her desk and unloaded my matchmaking problems. To her credit, she didn't make a sound, letting me spill the beans about my worries and panic for several minutes.

"And I just don't know how to get my matchmaking mojo back," I said in summary. "Do you know what I can do?"

Janet nodded her head knowingly, folding her hands on the smooth surface of her desk. "Oh, so you got cupid's block."

"Huh?"

"Cupid's block. Like writer's block, but instead of being blocked while writing a novel, you're blocked while making matches. It's very common among first-year cupids," Janet said, her voice smooth and even. "Happens to most of us."

A small, sullen part of me bet that Derek would be among the small percentage of those who were never afflicted. But since that was uncharitable and totally jealous of me, I quieted that part down.

"Have you ever gotten it?" I asked.

"I did, yes." She paused. "I'd only been a cupid for six months at the time. I quit the company for a full year because of it."

"Whoa, really? What happened?" Maybe hearing her experience would help me unblock myself—er, so to speak.

She sighed, rubbing a hand along the back of her neck. "Oh, it was a long time ago, and I was very insecure and nervous. I'd made several matches that had fallen apart—very publicly—and I was mortified when those celebrity couples split up. One of the relationships ended in a tragedy. I don't want to go into details, but needless to say, it wasn't good."

Wow. I guess matchmaking teens wasn't nearly as bad or pressure-filled as what Janet had gone through. At least I wasn't making celebrity matches!

"After that, I couldn't seem to make any more couples," she went on. "No matter how hard I tried, I was petrified that they'd end up hating each other and breaking up after the spell wore off. So, I turned in my bow and arrow and gave up the business." She propped her chin up with her hands, a small, wistful smile on her face. "I actually went to beauty school, thinking I'd change careers and leave matchmaking behind me."

"But you didn't. You came back."

"Yes, I came back. It was in my blood, you see." She placed her hands in her lap. "I just had to take time to learn some tricks for getting over my cupid's block."

"Such as?" I leaned forward, eager to take mental notes.

"The first thing I had to do was relax."

I drooped my upper body against the back of my chair. "Okay, I'm there."

She chuckled. "I mean, relax my attitude, though I guess relaxing your physical self can help too. It's so easy to get caught up in the madness of matchmaking and blow it out of proportion, but remember that love is only one aspect of someone's life. Not everyone is going to fall in love with each other. And even if they do, that doesn't mean that they'll stay in love forever."

I nodded in agreement, thinking about poor Mrs. Takahashi's broken marriage. And about my own precarious match with Derek. "No kidding. It's so scary thinking that love can end at any time."

"Well, if I kept my purpose in mind," she continued, "then I was golden. My job was to help people find the opportunity for love as best as I could."

I listened to her words, replaying them in my head a couple of times. The opportunity for love. Okay, I could do that. After all, it sounded like a lot less pressure than my current motto, which was more like, *Don't screw up and matchmake the wrong people together, idiot!*

"I'm afraid to make mistakes," I admitted sheepishly.

"And that's part of the reason why you have cupid's block.

Being a matchmaker is 'divine work,' if you will. Don't forget that you're human, though, just like everyone else. Nothing we do is going to be perfect. Love certainly isn't perfect—it's messy and crazy and fun and scary. But would we have it any other way?"

The tension in my shoulders seeped away for real this time, and I let her soothing words wash over me. Janet was surprisingly easy to talk to about this. I only wish I'd come to her sooner.

"It'll also help if you try to keep from getting personally involved with your subjects," she continued, her eyes suddenly squinting and staring at me. "I'm guessing this is the other issue affecting you, am I right?"

"Well, it's hard not to," I replied, fighting the edge of defensiveness that slowly crept into my voice. "A lot of them are my friends. I go to school with them. It's natural to want to make the best matches I possibly can."

"Of course you do. That's why I chose you and Derek to work at your school, because you two best understand what your fellow students need in a relationship. But when you're matchmaking, you need to put on your business face, not your friend face." She paused. "Understand what I mean? You have to learn how to create a wall within yourself, so to speak, to be an effective matchmaker."

Ugh. Janet had a good point. It was hard to stay objective when matchmaking people you knew—or who were your best friends. That's why I'd chosen someone I didn't know as my very first match. Maybe I'd gotten too far away from this principle over time, and it was causing me trouble now.

I sighed, squirming in my seat. Man, I wished this job was easier sometimes. "Okay, I'll try."

"If you need help, I'm sure Derek would be more than happy to split the rest of your matches with you," Janet said, her lips parting in a sly smile.

He probably would. There was no way I was going to ask him that, though. I had some scraps of pride left, and handing over my workload to him wasn't going to help me feel better. But I *could* work with him tonight to encourage me to get back on track, and to get his opinion on matches. "Thanks, but I'd rather finish it myself."

"I understand. Okay, why don't you hand over your PDA so I can sync it with the computer? Then we can get you out of here and back to making matches."

At that moment I felt the sudden urge to blurt out that I knew she'd matchmade me and Derek—partly to see if she had any advice on how I could handle it, and partly to see what she'd say about it.

I started to open my mouth but then closed it again. She might get pissed that I was looking through stuff on her desk. And I didn't want to get on her bad side, especially since I'd been screwing up a lot lately. Something told me not to push it with her.

No, this was something I was going to have to deal with myself, just like any other paired-up person who had been hit by Cupid's dart. Or e-mail. Or whatever crazy method she'd used on us.

I wordlessly handed over my PDA. She synced it, and I left, focusing on Janet's advice on the drive home. She was absolutely right about what my problem was and how I could get myself back on the right track for matchmaking.

Now I needed to muster the courage to take her counsel and push past my cupid's block, once and for all.

chapter fourteen

"Your room isn't quite what I'd expected it to be," I said to Derek later that evening. I glanced around, a little in shock. Actually, I wasn't sure what I'd thought it would look like, but it wasn't as nice as this.

There were a couple of framed sports posters hanging on the wall in addition to the classic art pieces, like a print of Salvador Dali's melting clocks. The bed was immaculately made and covered with a dark brown comforter. Actually, the whole room was spotless—not an errant sock in sight. Even underneath his bed was clean.

"My mom would kill to have a child like you," I continued with a laugh.

He shook his head, then gestured toward the bed. "Yeah, I like a clean room. That's my type A coming out. So, have a seat." He walked to his door and swung it wide open. "House rules," he said with a chagrined smile.

"No problem. I'm not even allowed to have guys in my room," I explained as I sat down. I pulled my LoveLine 3000 out of my purse and placed it on my lap. "So, you're a step ahead of me." The House Nazi seemed to think if I were left alone with a boy in my bedroom, his sperm would magically travel through his pants and impregnate me, even if we weren't doing anything sexual.

Derek sat down beside me. "So, what's going on? Did your cupid meeting with Janet go okay? You didn't say too much in your phone call."

It took me a moment to answer him. Mostly because I was very, very aware of the fact that Derek and I were alone in his bedroom, and I suddenly didn't want to talk about work crap, which was my original plan for meeting with him. Instead, I wanted for him to grab me and plant a whopper of a kiss right on my lips. And maybe a few on my neck too.

Oy. If I were honest with myself, I guess I could kinda understand now why my mom was trying to avoid this very scenario at our house. Not that I was gonna rip my clothes off and throw myself at him (no babies for me, thank you very much), but the feelings were still quite potent.

I shook off these thoughts and tried to focus on the conversation. "Um, the meeting went fine." I paused, realizing I was about to concede utter defeat in the cupid arena and therefore acknowledge that Derek was better than me. Sigh. "I still have a bunch of matches to make, though, and I'm having problems getting them done."

"And you need me to do them for you? Sure!" Derek went to grab my PDA.

"No!" I shouted.

He froze, eyes wide in shock.

Idiot! I realized how badly that had to sound, both to him and to his family in the rest of the house.

"I, uh, think the answer to that question is five point two," I continued in a loud voice. Then I whispered, "Sorry. I didn't want your parents thinking something bad was happening up here." I paused. "I didn't meant to blurt that out like that. All I need is some advice on pairing up the rest of my couples. I can totally still do them myself."

He chuckled lightly and moved his hand away. "Okay. So what's going on?"

Briefly, I filled him in on my cupid's block, making sure to mention how Janet said it was very common. As I talked, Derek listened intently.

"So, now I still have these couples left, but I'm a little scared to do it. I can't afford to mess up any more lives."

He nodded. "Okay, I think I get it. Let's take it slowly and focus on one person at a time. When I feel overwhelmed, it helps if I look at things in smaller chunks."

"I can do that," I said. Yeah, it sucked that I probably looked really doofy to Derek right now because of this cupid's block, but this wasn't just about me. I had to get these people paired up, so I was checking my ego at the door for the greater good. I turned on my PDA and found my list. "Here's the original list of people, showing who I've paired up so far and who is left," I said.

He took it from my hands, scrolling down. "Hmmm. I see. Okay. I'm a little surprised you paired Tina with Martin. I figured she'd be perfect for Riley, who is still on your list. What compatibilities did you have for Tina and Martin?"

My cheeks flamed. I forced myself to bite my tongue. *He's trying to help. He's trying to help*, I told myself in my head over and over again.

"Actually, I'd rather focus on the couples I haven't worked on yet," I said, my voice shaky. I cleared my throat. "Besides, I've seen Tina and Martin flirting with each other before, in addition to other things."

My tone must have been edgier than I intended because his lips pinched for the quickest of seconds. "Got it." He turned his attention back to the PDA. "Okay, so let's start with Riley then, since he's still single."

I dug into my purse and whipped out the small notebook I'd brought with me, ready to jot down our ideas. "Sounds like a plan. I had a hard time figuring out who would work well with him, because he's kind of . . ." I paused, trying to find a gentle way to say he was a loudmouth who loved attention.

"He's very outgoing," Derek suggested, ever tactful as usual.

I grinned. "Nice way to word it. Anyway, most of the girls left on the list don't feel to me like they'd be the right match for him."

"So, what results did you get from the charts?"

I knew he'd eventually ask that, so I gave a noncommittal shrug and stated my preplanned answer (read: lie). "Well, the results were inconclusive," I said. I already felt stupid enough needing Derek's help, and I sure didn't want to go down the "charts" road again. "That's why I'm here, talking to you."

He blinked. "Huh? How can they be inconclusive? I've never had that happen before—is that even possible?"

I gritted my teeth. "Derek, why do you always bring up the charts? Not everything in this job can be done through mathematical formulas. At least, not for us lowly cupids who can't seem to make them work right." I swallowed, more than a little surprised at the strength of words that came out of me.

Evidently he was too. His back stiffened. "And what does that mean?"

"It means I want help, not to be referred to the stupid manual. I want to talk to you about this and bounce ideas." My breath was coming out fast, and I struggled to keep my voice low.

"Fine," Derek said, his voice strangely flat. "But I don't see the point in outright ignoring the charts and graphs. Have you even given them a fair try?"

God, did I have to spell it out? Was he going to make me state out loud that I was a grade-A moron?

I stood and started pacing his room. "Yes, okay? I did try them.

They just don't work for me. There's no one right or wrong way to do the matches, you know."

"Maybe if you'd tried to use them a little bit more, things wouldn't be so crazy right now at school," he said quietly.

Ouch.

I reeled back, almost like I'd been physically hit. I turned to face him, staring into his hooded eyes and perfect face. "Maybe *you* should get off your high horse. You don't know everything." All of the dark words that had been building up in me over the past couple of weeks spilled out, and I couldn't stop myself from speaking. "You have to be the best at everything you do. The most wonderful son. The most gifted at art. The smartest guy in school. The best football player we've ever had. The most thoughtful boyfriend a girl could ask for. The prime example of a high school matchmaker. No one else can even come close to your achievements because you've already beaten them to it."

He rose and stood in front of me, his face coldly staring into mine. "Is that really how you feel? Be honest with me. For once."

I nodded, because it was true. And yet it wasn't. I knew Derek wasn't doing all of those things to spite me or anything. But I was angry and hurt and tired of feeling like a moron around him. Why did he have to be the best at everything? Why was I always lagging behind?

Derek crossed his arms. "Wait a minute. I see what's going on here. This isn't about me. It's about you and your feelings of insecurity."

I swallowed. He'd nailed it. Of course. "Oh, and now you're the best amateur psychologist around, too. Gosh, Derek, however do you find time to do it all?" I grabbed my stuff off his bed, crammed them into my purse, and turned toward the door. "I'm just gonna go home and think about how unworthy I am to be with you."

With those parting words, I left.

I woke up the next morning feeling like my face had been smashed with a mallet. My eyes were so puffy from crying all night that I could barely see. How did everything go so horribly wrong? What was it about Derek that brought out the absolute worst parts of me? I hated feeling like a loser all the time around him, knowing he was so talented and smart and special. It was hard to feel like I deserved him.

All the mean words I said to him echoed in my head. God, I was so nasty. He'd wanted me to speak the truth. And boy, had I given it to him, in spades.

I sighed and sat up, shuffling my way to the bathroom. Once

there, I splashed about a million gallons of water on my face, trying to reduce the swelling. I was going to look like a train wreck at school today, but hopefully I could reduce the damage through some strategic makeup application.

My stomach lurched as I thought about Derek. What should I say to him at school? What would he say to me? Today was our last day of being under the spell, and I highly suspected that I'd blown it last night. He probably wouldn't speak to me now, and our relationship would fizzle out before it even could have for-real begun.

I dressed quickly, skipped breakfast, and headed right to school. My heart raced the entire time. Would he be waiting for me outside? Would he want to talk? Would I be the first person in the world to be dumped before the spell even wore off?

This was ridiculous. I forced those questions out of my head. He most likely would not be waiting for me this morning. But I could take time today to talk to Maya and Andy to see what they thought I could do. I had to be generic, of course, and not mention the cupid angle. But I could still give them the gist of the situation. I'd been too stressed and tearful to even call them last night, wanting to get some perspective before I dumped everything on them. So I was eager to see them today.

I headed to the front of the school, staring at the steps. The makeup had covered some of my blotchiness, but not all. So the less eye contact I made with people, the better.

A hand reached out and tapped me on the shoulder. It was Adele, the girl in my English class I'd matchmaded who had made out with her new boyfriend in front of all of us. "Have you seen it?" she asked me.

"Seen what?"

"Oh my God, you haven't seen it yet," she whispered. A huge grin broke out on her face. "Just wait. Eeh! I'm going to come inside with you."

I blinked, offering her a watery grin. "I have no idea what you're talking about, but okay." She and I weren't BFFs or anything, but we were on friendly terms. I was a little surprised to see her come up and talk to me, though. Maybe the love spell I'd done on her had made her more outgoing.

"Felicity!" Maya said in front of me, running down the top half of the stairs toward me. "Wow, you have to come inside. Come in!"

"What's going on?" Things were Twilight-Zone crazy here this morning. Why did everyone want so badly for me go into the building?

"Just come and see," Maya said, her eyes wide.

As I ascended the stairs, I noticed people were staring at me, whispering fervently. I felt like I was going to throw up. What was all this? Was I in trouble? No, that couldn't be it—Maya wouldn't let me walk into the lion's den unprepared.

The doors were pulled open for me, and I stepped inside the front lobby. Right away I saw pillars set up with various sculptures. Paintings and drawings of all shapes and sizes adorned the wall.

Duh, the art show. With all the drama in my life lately, I'd completely forgotten. I'd even carried a couple of the paintings to the teacher's lounge with Derek—that was when we'd busted Mr. Wiley and Brenda going at it on the couch.

Then I froze. On the left wall there was a huge framed mosaic that had to be almost five feet tall.

It was an image of me.

The sounds of the hallway faded away from me, and the only thing I could hear was a rushing sound in my ears. I stepped toward the mosaic, staring in shock and disbelief. It was me, sitting outside of school on a bench, staring off into space. The sunlight poured onto my hair, and my eyes sparkled. There was a slightly mysterious smile curving my lips.

I looked . . . beautiful.

The bottom-right corner signature confirmed my suspicions. Derek had created this picture and entered it in the art show.

"Felicity! Felicity!" Maya's voice penetrated my fog. "Oh my God, isn't it amazing? He must have worked forever on this piece."

"I can't stop staring at it," Adele said, sighing happily.

"It's amazing," I replied, my tongue thick. "He's really gifted."

The most gifted at art. My words to Derek last night echoed back to me. I felt like a huge, huge ass.

What was wrong with me? Why had I lashed out at him so harshly over my own personal issues? I knew before I dated him that he was supertalented. It was one of the things about him that I'd fallen in love with. He wasn't just a meathead like other guys at school—he had depth, substance, real talent. Which was why he was so freaking popular at school and so many people loved him.

And I'd rubbed all of that in his face as if it were a flaw instead of something to be proud of.

I sighed. Still, that didn't take away the fact that this had obviously been a love-spell-induced portrait. It was too perfect, too stunning, too carefully crafted to be otherwise.

God, why couldn't things be normal in my life, just for once? A beautiful image of me was here in the hallway, proclaiming Derek's love for all to see. But could I enjoy it? No. I knew our relationship was a sham. Plus, we'd had that horrible fight last night, which made things all the worse.

Maya snapped a pic of the mosaic with her cell phone. "This way we can enjoy it whenever we're not near this hallway to see it in person."

Adele, Maya, and I headed to first period. Mike jumped out of his seat and gave Adele a big hug, which was a bittersweet sort of feeling for me. I was happy to see their relationship going well but wishing mine would get some breaks.

Of course, I didn't focus on a single word Mrs. Kendel said the entire time. Instead, I thought about what I'd say when I saw Derek in art class . . . or if I happened to see him in the hallways earlier.

First, I'd apologize for our fight last night. And Derek being Derek, he'd probably apologize, too. He was too much of a gentleman not to. Then I'd thank him for the mosaic and ask if I could keep it when the art show was over. That way, even if he and I ended up splitting up (my throat closed up every time I thought this), I could have something to remember him by.

My stomach was a total mess all day. I didn't even eat lunch, just picked at my sandwich like a bird. Instead, Maya and Andy kept looking at Maya's cell pic of the mosaic and gushing over how great of a job Derek did in rendering me. I nodded and smiled in all the right places, but on the inside I felt hollow and tired. This wasn't the time to ruin everyone's good mood and go on and on about how he and I had fought last night. I'd just talk to them later.

It didn't help that I hadn't heard a word about Derek, and no one else had seen him at all today.

Art class finally came and went. Unfortunately, Derek was nowhere to be found—he'd called in sick. I should have known he wouldn't come. Of course. He was obviously fully aware the art show was going on and didn't want to see me.

But I could call him later today from Bobby's house, since I was going with Andy as moral support while she met with Bobby's car-mechanic brother. I knew Andy would let me borrow her cell for a few minutes.

Yes, I resolved to make things right. I'd apologize to him for the harsh words I'd said and thank him profusely for the mosaic. It was the least I could do.

What would happen after that was anyone's guess.

chapter fifteen

"Can you fix it?" Andy's eyes were small and filled with fear as she watched George, Bobby's car-fixer-upper brother who was currently crouched in front of the Porsche's bumper, studying the damage.

I rubbed her back, trying to give her a little comfort, and mentally crossed my fingers that George could repair the damage.

He stood and, with a thick hand covered in dirt and grime, scratched his chin that bristled with short, coarse, black hairs. Surprisingly, he looked a good fifteen years older than Bobby, which made me suspect their parents were a lot older than mine.

In fact, he could almost be Bobby's dad, especially since the two of them looked just alike, down to the thin black muscle shirt George was currently wearing and had obviously cut the sleeves off of long ago.

Maybe muscle shirts were a family trait. I briefly wondered if his dad and mom wore the same sort of clothes to their jobs.

"Bumper's junk," George said slowly, not taking his eyes off the car, "but there's no structural damage elsewhere."

"And that's a good thing," Bobby offered as a translation. He was instantly rewarded by Andy's smile.

"Well," George continued, "I know where we can get a bumper. And we can replace the headlight as well."

"Oh, thank God!" Andy proclaimed, clapping her hands in glee. "I am so, so happy to hear you say that. I don't care what it costs. I just have to get this fixed immediately."

"Andy!" I gasped, then dropped my voice to whisper. "You probably shouldn't say things like that."

Bobby, who had obviously overheard me from his position on the other side of Andy, shot me a hurt look and took Andy's hand. "George won't take advantage of her."

"Sorry," I said, a heated flush covering my face and throat. "I just saw a news report a few months ago that said girls were more likely to get ripped off by servicemen than guys were. I wasn't trying to insult your brother."

I chewed on my lower lip and forced myself to shut up. Maybe I should just stay quiet, eh? Creating bad blood with the guy who was going to fix Andy's car and thus save her from a lifelong grounding was not the best idea.

"Head inside," George said. "I'll pull the car out back to work on it. I'll call a buddy to help me get it done faster."

Andy nodded in relief, dropping the car key into his open hand. "Please take care of this," she said to him quietly.

We went inside Bobby's house, which was immaculately clean. And decorated to the T with feminine frills. Okayyyyy, definitely not what I was expecting to see in his house. I'd figured it would be wall-to-wall exercise equipment.

Bobby led us to the living room couch, which was covered in a deep-red rose pattern. "Would you two like something to drink?"

"Coke for me, please," Andy said, her butt perched on the edge of the couch.

"I'll have water," I answered, sitting beside her.

Bobby left.

Andy and I exchanged glances as we checked out the decor.

There were more doilies in here than I'd even known could possibly exist in one location. They were on the side tables, the coffee table . . . even draped over the arms of the couch—every piece of furniture was covered by at least two pristine white doilies.

It was like being in grandma hell. I briefly wondered if Grandma Cougar Mary's house looked like this.

"Bobby's mom crochets," Andy offered, grinning sheepishly. "She sells some of her stuff on the weekends at craft fairs." She dropped her voice and leaned toward me. "I've been here a few times, and it still surprises me."

"Yeah, you wouldn't think his house would be this . . ." I faltered, trying to find the right word.

"Girly?" Andy gave me a wry smile.

"Exactly. Hey, can I borrow your cell?" I asked. "Derek was out of school today, and I want to thank him for the mosaic."

She whipped it out of her pocket. "Have at it."

I slipped into the bathroom for some privacy, closed the door, and dialed his cell. It went right to voice mail. Crap.

"Um, it's Felicity. I noticed you weren't in school today. I hope you're not sick. Anyway, I wanted to . . ." I stalled. Actually, I didn't want to go into this in a voice mail. Especially while standing in

Bobby's bathroom. It just didn't feel right. "I wanted to talk to you. Can you give me a call at home tonight? Okay, I'll talk to you soon."

After I hung up, I went back into the living room and gave Andy her cell back. "Thanks so much."

Bobby returned, handing us our drinks in gold-rimmed glasses. "Here you go," he said, sitting on the other side of Andy. "Soooooo," he said, glancing at me, then Andy. "Can you believe the school year is almost over? I'll be glad for summer."

"Are you planning to work any?" I asked him.

He nodded. "My dad has me work at his landscaping company every summer. It's a good way to keep in shape." I saw him start to lift his arm to show his muscles, but he stopped, giving Andy a crooked grin and dropping his hand onto hers. "And to earn a little extra money so I can take Andy out, too."

She swatted him lightly. "Oh, come on. You know you don't need to do anything like that for me."

Wow, so Bobby was even getting over the self-bravado act and not feeling the need to flash his muscles to everyone around him. I never thought that would happen, but love does crazy things. Maybe Andy was a good influence on him and was helping him realize he didn't need to boast to make people like him.

He held his arm out, showing me a leather bracelet. "Check this out, Felicity. Andy bought this for me. Isn't it great?"

Andy blushed. "Come on now," she said, looking up into his eyes.

He leaned toward her.

"Well, I'm gonna go outside and watch them work on the car," I said, standing and stretching my arms over my head. A good cupid knows when to make a graceful exit and let a couple have time alone. "I'll be back in a little bit."

I slipped through the kitchen and through the back doors, settling into a seat on the patio. God, it felt good to be outside in actual warm sunshine. The winter had seemed to last for*ever*. I turned my face toward the sun and soaked up the rays for a couple of minutes.

I could hear George and his friend working on the car already. Well, that sounded promising.

Bobby's glee about the leather bracelet stuck in my head. It was a simple gift Andy had bought, but personal and from the heart. Maybe I could make something like that for Derek? That is, if we stayed together. God, I hope we weren't going to split up over all of this drama. I'd be so miserable without him. If he still wanted to be with me, I'd do my best to show him I cared about him. And if that meant making handicrafts and stuff like that, then I was willing to try.

Feeling a little better, I opened my eyes and glanced around. No one could see me. Maybe this was a good opportunity to matchmake some of those names on my list. It was time to end this cupid's block for good.

Whipping out my handy-dandy, ever-present LoveLine 3000, I pulled up some of the pending e-mails I'd created but had been too afraid to send. Janet had said I needed to build some kind of internal wall and distance myself when working. And boy, was she right. I knew instinctively that it was so much easier to matchmake couples if I didn't feel too personally vested in the results.

Drumming up all my courage, I sucked in a deep breath and forced myself to hit send on the love e-mail. There. The match was all done now . . . and if I'd made one match, surely I could make a few more.

I could totally do this.

After what felt like a thousand years but was in actuality only a couple of hours, the Porsche was finally finished. Fortunately, I'd managed to make six matches while we were waiting, including finding a person for Mrs. Kendel, so I was riding on a cupid high and feeling pretty damn good about it. If I could resolve this crap with Derek tonight, life would be completely perfect.

I'd only been sitting with Bobby and Andy again for a few minutes when George came into the living room.

"Whew," he said, wiping sweat off his rather large brow. A streak of dirt remained behind. "Okay, we're done."

Andy jumped off the couch. "Awesome. Let's go check it out!"

We ran out the back of the house toward the car, passing around the driver's side to check out the bumper. When I saw it, I swallowed hard and turned a quick eye toward Andy, hoping I was mistaken.

She stopped dead in her tracks, her eyes fixed on the front of the car. "That's not . . . how it's supposed to look."

Crap. I'd been right. I wasn't exactly a car expert or anything, but the color of the bumper he'd used wasn't even close to matching the original one. They were two different shades of red. Andy's dad would notice this for sure.

George's brow furrowed, and he said in a low voice, "I replaced the bumper and the headlight, as you requested."

"But the color of the bumper is completely wrong," she said, crossing her arms over her chest. "It isn't the same as what's on the car. My dad's going to know when he gets home. He's crazy about his car. He'll know it's been wrecked!"

"Maybe we're not looking at it right," Bobby said, two bright spots of color high on his cheeks. He stepped between George and Andy and tried to smile. "Let's just look closer." He leaned down and studied the two shades, not speaking for a long moment. He seemed to be trying to find something to help ease the tension, his mouth opening and closing several times in a row.

I came over to Andy's side. "Hey, the important thing is, he found a bumper that works. We can always go to the dealer and buy the paint. Or we could even ask if they'll paint it for us ... don't they blend the color in with the rest of the car or something? And then your dad will never know."

That seemed to calm her a bit. "That could work," she said, turning her attention to me. "Let's go put this back under the tarp before my dad gets home."

"It'll be okay," Bobby said, his breath short and rapid. His eyes darted between Andy and George, as if he was unsure of where to place his loyalties.

Andy silently whipped out some cash from her back pocket and handed it over to George. He dropped the key into her open palm, and she mumbled, "Thanks."

The ride back to Andy's house was pretty quiet. We rode in her dad's car, going almost ten miles under the speed limit the whole way. I think she was petrified to get in another accident . . . not that I could blame her.

I heard her suck in a shaky breath when we turned onto her street.

"God, I hope my mom is still out," she whispered. "Because all of this would be for nothing if she knew I had the car."

"It'll be okay," I said, feeling my own heart race with nervousness.

She pulled into the driveway and, using her dad's remote control, opened the garage door. It slid up easily, revealing an empty garage. Whew.

Andy navigated the Porsche in there and turned it off.

We hopped out quickly and threw the tarp back over the top, per our plan. As soon as possible, we would venture over to the dealer and see if we could find the paint we needed. But for now, in the dim garage light, the car looked just fine.

Andy patted down the back of the cover, then made her way

along the passenger's side and crossed in front of the car. "Thank God that's done. I—" At that moment she accidentally knocked her hip against the front of the car, causing the entire bumper to crash to the ground in a thunderous clang.

Standing in the garage doorway to the house, I froze, staring at the car in horror. I cupped my hand over my mouth. Dude, the bumper just fell off? What the hell did George use to affix it, a Band-Aid?

"Did that. Just. Happen?" Andy ground out through gritted teeth, staring at the bumper that peeked out of the bottom of the car cover.

My heart slammed in my chest. Poor Andy—she just couldn't get a break with this stupid car!

"Okay, okay, we can fix this," I said, rushing to her side. My hands gripped one side of the bumper. "Grab the other side. Maybe it just needs to be snugged in there a little tighter. Or maybe a bolt fell off or something." I had no idea what I was talking about, since I knew nothing about cars, but I tried to sound confident and strong for Andy's sake.

She flipped back the front of the tarp, then grabbed the other end. We heaved it back on the front, trying to see if it would fit in anywhere, but it just wouldn't stay on.

"OmigodwhatamIgoingtodoFelicity?" Her words came out in a breathless rush, and tears streaked down her cheeks.

It broke my heart to see her so upset. "Let's hide the bumper for now. We'll figure out an answer, I promise."

She lowered her bumper down, pushing it under the car against the front tires. I did the same. "I can't believe he didn't fix this right," she spat out, her eyes flaring in anger. "Now I'm stuck with a crappy bumper that doesn't even stay on!" Andy paused, and her voice got shaky. "Why would Bobby let him butcher the car like this?"

I covered the back of the car and took Andy's arm, leading her inside the house. "It's not Bobby's fault," I said gently. Yeah, I wasn't his biggest fan ever at the moment, but I could tell that Andy meant the world to him. "He'd be crushed if he knew this happened."

She sighed, plopping down onto her couch. "Yeah, you're right. I should have taken it to the dealer in the first place, I guess."

"Well, we'll definitely do that now. They can fix it, I bet."

They just had to, for poor Andy's sake.

chapter sixteen

"So, where were you this morning?" I asked Derek in as calm a voice as I could muster, trying not to fiddle with my drawing pencil and give away my nervousness.

The spell Janet had cast over the two of us had worn off earlier today, Wednesday. Plus, our art class was the first I'd seen of him since our fight. He'd called me back last night at home, but my mom made me immediately get off the phone and do a pantload of laundry, so we didn't get a chance to say anything other than hi and bye.

Which, of course, had me massively paranoid that we didn't talk any today. Was Derek avoiding me? Was he trying to find a kind way to break up with me? Was I simply overreacting?

I just had to know, one way or the other.

"Sorry, I had to get the younger kids ready for school this morning," he said, his eyes still on his picture. "Mom asked me to help her out again because her feet are badly swollen."

Drawing in a deep breath, I stared at my drawing paper and whispered, "Look, I owe you some serious apologies. I'm truly sorry we got into that fight on Monday. I feel awful. And I feel even worse since I saw that gorgeous mosaic you made for me. It took my breath away."

I dared to glance up at his face. He was studying me quietly. His eyes weren't angry or cold, which I took to be a good sign. But he wasn't saying anything in response, so I continued to nervously babble.

"So anyway, I'm an ass, and I was totally rude when you were just trying to help me out. And—"

He reached a hand over and touched my arm. "I get too focused on trying to solve every problem. It wasn't right for me to take over when you just wanted some help." He paused, and his voice dropped down so quietly I could barely hear. "And I don't think I'm better than other people. Far from it."

His body was turned slightly toward me as we talked. During my last TGIF sleepover, I'd read in *Cosmo* that this was definitely a plus. Maybe he still wanted to be with me.

"I know, and I'm sorry," I said again, trying to curb my increasing desire to cling to him and brashly ask if he was still into me.

Back off, I chided myself. I could scope him out without being a total spazz. Pushing him would just make things worse right now.

"So, how are your matches going?" he asked, tilting his paper to pencil in some darker shade lines around the edges of his still life drawing. "Did you finish them all?"

"Actually," I said, "I still have a few left to matchmake, but I think I got past my—"

"Shhhh," Mr. Bunch interrupted me, his eyes turning toward the two of us. "Quiet while you're working, please."

Whoops. I swallowed and nodded in assent.

Derek turned his attention back to his project. I tried to follow his lead. We worked in silence for a few more minutes. Not that I actually got any *work* done, of course. I was way too busy analyzing the situation in as professional a manner as I could.

Derek's thigh had just brushed against my leg ever so slightly. Somewhere, probably on *Oprah* or one of those kinds of shows, I'd heard that maintaining physical contact was important in relationships. So, signs like that could definitely be a positive.

Then again ... Derek's contact with me seemed more accidental than purposeful. Even if he could feel it and wasn't pulling away, he didn't seem to be trying to increase it.

And, even worse, he hadn't talked to me very much today. This worried me the most. When the cupid spell was still going on, he'd told me many times a day how often I was on his mind and how eager he was to see me.

But he hadn't told me this at all today. That could be the result of the spell wearing off. Or it could be residual issues from our fight. Or a combo of both.

My heart thudded painfully in my chest. What should I do? I fervently wished I could talk to someone about my problem.

I tried to imagine what advice Maya and Andy would give me. Maya would likely hug me and tell me I was overreacting. Andy would tell me that too but would then say I should try to remind Derek why he and I belonged together.

Good advice, Andy-in-my-brain! I could do that.

I perked up and leaned over toward Derek. "Are you looking forward to prom?"

He glanced up at me, his forehead creased. "Hey, about that—" he started but was cut off.

"Derek, Felicity, I'm not going to tell you again," Mr. Bunch said, openly glaring at us this time. "Zip it."

"Sorry," I mumbled. God, was he crabby or what? Who peed in his oatmeal this morning?

I turned my attention back toward my crappy drawing, but on the inside I was crumbling. What had Derek been about to tell me?

He nudged my leg with his knee, then tapped a finger on the corner of his picture. In faint letters, he'd written:

Let's talk after class

I nodded, trying to remain calm, rational, sensible. I could do this. I could focus on my art project until he and I could talk.

Well, I *told* myself that . . . but as I waited, it felt like time was traveling backward. I swear, it was almost painful to glance up at the clock and see the stupid minute hand not moving at all.

Every couple of minutes I glanced at Derek out of the corner of my eyes, silently hoping to find him looking at me. But when it had actually happened one time, the impact had nearly smacked me with shock, since I wasn't expecting it. I'd jerked my gaze away from his piercing eyes, suddenly embarrassed.

Finally someone took pity on me and ended my misery by ringing the school bell. Trying not to appear too anxious and thus turn Derek off, I forced myself to calmly put my stuff away and gather my belongings. We headed out of class and down the hall, going slowly to allow traffic to pass around us.

I started to reach my hand over to grasp his, at the same moment he shifted his backpack on his shoulder. I jerked my hand back, cramming it in the pocket of my jeans so I wouldn't look stupid.

A hot burn swept over my cheeks. Was it just bad timing, or was he avoiding any purposeful contact with me now? Things couldn't have gotten bad that quickly after the spell had worn off, could they?

Once we were alone and everyone else had cleared out of the hall, I coughed lightly, hoping the sound would prod him to speak. It worked.

"So," he said, casting me a sideways glance, "we were talking about prom before we were cut off."

Oh God, I felt like I was going to hurl due to my bundled nerves. This was just crazy overwhelming. I forced myself to nod.

"Anyway," he continued, "is it okay if we go to dinner early and then over to my parents' house? My mom wants to see us together."

That was it? Whew—okay, he wasn't dumping me as his date. I forced myself to take several calming breaths before I answered. "Oh, absolutely. Sure, that's no problem. I'd love to see your mom again. I really like her. She's so sweet."

I was babbling, and badly, but I couldn't stop gushing. I wanted him to see how enthusiastic I still was.

"Great."

An odd thought took hold of me as we headed down the hallway. What would he do if I confessed about the spell Janet put on us? It was over now, so surely she couldn't have any problem with me discussing it.

If I told him, would Derek assure me of his love? Or would it turn him off that he'd been matchmade against his will?

Would he be mad at me for keeping it a secret for this long?

No, there wasn't any reason for him to be pissed. It's not like I'd cast the spell myself. Maybe I should unburden this load off my shoulders. Then, if I could assume his feelings were still the same, he'd realize that we were meant to be together and would assure me of as much.

I licked my lips, trying to figure out the right way to broach the subject. "Hey, Derek."

"What?" he asked me.

"Ummmmm," I said, then chickened out. We were so tentative right now that this might push us over the edge and break us up for good. And I just couldn't risk it. "Nothing. Never mind."

Derek sighed, frowning a little. I knew he could tell I was still keeping things inside, but he didn't say anything about it. He glanced at his watch. "I gotta go. I have to watch my brothers and sisters while Mom goes to her doctor's appointment this afternoon."

Disappointment gripped my gut. I shrugged nonchalantly, though, not wanting to show how I felt. Words babbled out of my mouth. "That's fine with me, since I have homework and stuff, anyway. You know, the House Nazi always has some new chore for me to do, like scrubbing stuff that no one wants to touch. Maybe you can call me later—if you get time, I mean. If you want."

He nodded.

Impulsively, I leaned forward onto my tiptoes and kissed him on the lips, relishing the sensation. "Maybe we can go out again soon. I'll give you a call later."

"Yeah, that should work." He smiled, said good-bye, then turned down the hallway, his steady gait moving him away from me.

I closed my eyes and pinched the bridge of my nose with my

thumb and forefinger, sighing heavily. As much as people liked to claim that girls were hard to read, I think I could prove that guys were even harder.

TGIF, and we were at Maya's house this time for our sleepover, since she wanted to stick close to her mom. I couldn't blame her—poor Mrs. Takahashi was like a zombie, wandering room to room with a dust rag and polishing furniture she'd already cleaned several times since I'd been there.

It was heartbreaking . . . and even more so because I understood her pain, her attempts to feel some sort of normalcy in her life even though everything was upside down.

No, Derek hadn't dumped me . . . yet. But with every day that passed, I could almost feel the ax coming down. Not that he was overtly doing anything cruel, but every gesture he made toward me felt like it had lessened in romantic intensity. Things were definitely different.

The best I could do was to try to act like nothing was wrong, to try to keep on moving forward and continue appearing confident and steady.

"I feel like seeing a movie night," Maya proclaimed, plopping her pajama-bottomed self down in front of the DVD shelf. "What should we watch? We can take it up to my room."

Andy, who'd just gotten back downstairs after changing into her nightclothes, shrugged. "Whatever you want. Just nothing with cars in it." She grimaced.

"Did you get a chance to call the dealership yesterday or today?" I asked her in a quiet voice. Not that I thought Mrs. Takahashi would call Andy's folks and rat her out, but one couldn't be too careful.

"I called them last night, but they told me I'd have to bring it in for them to examine." She rubbed the back of her neck, then pulled her hair into a loose ponytail, using the holder from around her wrist.

"Well, let's do that tomorrow," I suggested. I straightened the leg of my favorite pair of old flannel jammies that had gotten twisted somehow.

"Can't. Dad's gonna be home." Her voice took a shaky edge. "He's going to discover what happened, I just know it."

Poor Andy. We'd managed to sneak back into the garage and hold the bumper against the car with some bungee cables (which gave the illusion that the car was fine—a brilliant idea I'd had, thank you very much), but it was obviously only a temporary fix.

"How about you treat your parents to a special lunch—and while they're out, you can get the car fixed?" Maya suggested. "That way they can't refuse the invitation, especially if you've already made all the arrangements and reserved a table for them."

"That might work. This is getting *so* expensive, though." She dropped down beside Maya, releasing a big puff of air through her pinched lips.

"Hey, I like Maya's idea . . . what if you give them a Burger Butler gift card the next time you're at work? I'm sure they'd love that," I teased Andy.

She shot me a mock glare, wrinkling her face. "Oh yeah, that's a fabulous idea. We all know that's the gift that keeps on giving."

Maya and Andy picked a movie starring some new hottie actor, and we headed upstairs to watch it on Maya's big computer screen. The two of them squeezed in on her bed together, propping their backs up with pillows and draping a light blanket over their legs. I sat on the floor right in front of them, leaning back against the bed.

"Maybe this'll cheer me up," Andy said, rubbing her hands in anticipation. "The lead guy's supposed to be really good. And even better, he doesn't wear a shirt for, like, half the movie."

I groaned, giggling. "I should have known that's what appealed to you."

My stomach growled. Whoops. I never was one who could watch a movie without having something to chow on. Guess I had my body trained to expect food. I glanced over at the bowl of chocolate-covered pretzels beside me that was totally empty.

Maya faced me, eyes wide. "Holy crap, was that you?"

"Go get some food, girl," Andy said, one eyebrow raised. "You sound like you haven't eaten in a week."

"Hey, shut up, guys!" I shot back, crossing my arms like I was mad, for dramatic effect. "Just for that, I'm going to get ice cream and totally not share with either of you."

I headed downstairs toward the kitchen, where I grabbed a small pint of delicious rocky road ice cream and a spoon. I could almost taste the sweetness in my mouth and forced myself not to drool on the carton.

As I passed back through the first floor and toward the stairs, I noticed Mrs. Takahashi sitting on the couch, the dust rag draped across her sweatpants. Crap, she must have dug her sweats out of the back of her car before Maya could pitch them.

Following my impulse, I headed over to the sofa and sat beside her.

There was a sad silence between us for a long moment. Then she sniffled and said, "I'm okay, really. You can go upstairs with the girls, but thank you." She propped her small, sock-clad feet on the coffee table.

"I know I'm not a grown-up, but I know how it feels to be disappointed in love," I started, thinking about Derek. "And how you feel worried that your heart is completely out of your hands and in the grasp of someone who has the power to make you hurt."

She swallowed, nodding seriously in response. "Yeah, love isn't always what you think it's going to be."

That's one thing I really liked about Maya's mom—she didn't try to shoo me off or tell me to butt out of adult business, like some parents did. Yeah, I wasn't technically an adult yet, but I was close . . . and I'd seen and experienced more than my share of adult feelings.

I handed her the spoon and ice cream. "I think you need this even more than I do."

She took them, giving me a small smile of thanks. "Maybe we can share."

"Good idea." I ran back to grab a spoon from the kitchen, then sat beside her and propped my feet on the coffee table. We took turns eating delicious bites.

"Thank you for being such a good friend to Maya," Mrs. Takahashi said. "She's going to need you and Andy over the next few months—" She stopped, her voice sounding like her throat had closed up. After clearing her throat and sucking back a few sobs, she continued, "Because it's going to be a rough ride."

A rough ride. I'd heard someone say those words before. . . . Oh, wait. Maya had gotten her fortune told by Absinthia, a Goth girl at our school. She'd warned Maya that the next few months were going to be hard. "A rough ride," I think were her exact words.

She'd been spot-on in her tarot-card reading. Maybe I could scrounge up the courage and the cash to see if Absinthia would do a reading for me, too. She might have an interesting perspective about Derek that I hadn't considered . . . or at least give me a heads up on when the axe would fall.

I sighed, sinking further back into the couch and digging into another bite of ice cream. A couple of drops slid off my spoon and onto my pants. "Crap," I mumbled, wiping the mess off my leg. Great—that was totally going to stain. How very attractive.

Oh, well. What was the point of trying to look attractive,

anyway? It hadn't made Derek love me more. He hadn't responded at all to my makeover attempt. Maybe Mrs. Takahashi had the right idea, not caring about her looks and wearing whatever made her feel comfy.

I glanced over at her. Was this going to be me in twenty years—sitting on my couch, spilling food on my clothes and not caring? Or even sooner, should he and I break up?

The thought depressed me, and I blinked back tears. Maybe one can't change fate, regardless of what efforts are made. Mrs. Takahashi had worked her ass off trying to lure her husband back, to no avail.

"Felicity!" Andy yelled from upstairs. "Did you fall in a hole? You're missing all the shirtless scenes!"

"Go on back upstairs," Maya's mom said with a halfhearted smile, waving me away. "I'm fine, thanks. Just keep Maya happy tonight, okay?"

I hugged her quickly, then I went back to Maya's room, gently closing the door behind me.

"Sorry, guys," I said. "I got sidetracked talking to Maya's mom."

"How's she doing?" Maya asked, standing. "I should go down and check on her."

"It's okay," I said, tugging on her sleeve. "Your mom sent me up here and told me she's fine."

Which was a bald-faced lie. I knew she wasn't fine. Maya's mom knew it too. But for now, I'd respect her wish and help Maya have a good evening . . . even if I wasn't feeling too happy myself.

chapter seventeen

"Any calls for me?" I asked Mom when I got home on Saturday morning, bleary-eyed and half asleep on my feet. Maya, Andy, and I had sat up half the night yapping and watching movies, so I'd gotten almost no rest, a strategy I hadn't started regretting until I'd had to rouse my sorry self out of bed and head home this morning.

Boy, was I feeling it now. Blech.

Mom shook her head, moving toward the kitchen. "Nope. No calls."

I shrugged, trying to ignore the disappointed sting in my stomach, and followed her into the kitchen. "That's fine, thanks."

"Well, Derek knows you go to your sleepovers on Friday,"

Mom offered. She picked up the dish towel and slung it over her forearm. "I'm sure he'll call you today."

Was I that transparent? Or was she just that astute?

I blushed, suddenly embarrassed. "Things have just changed recently between us. You know how guys are, I'm sure."

She walked over to me, concern etched on her face. "You look tired," she said, sweeping the hair out of my eyes. "You should go back upstairs and get some more sleep. I'm sure that will help you feel better."

I nodded, glancing at my watch. Maybe she was right. Some rest would clear my mind and help me see things in a new light, and I could still get up in time to go with Andy to the car dealership this afternoon while her parents were at lunch.

"Okay." I gave Mom a quick hug and darted upstairs. Time to heed the siren call of my warm, awaiting bed.

As soon as my head hit the pillow, I conked out, not waking for two solid hours until my bedside phone rang.

"Hello?" I asked in a sleep-grogged voice, trying to clear the sleep from my eyes. Was it time for me to meet Andy already?

Though I squinted hard, I couldn't see the time on my alarm clock through my blurry eyes.

"Hey," Derek said, his low, familiar tone surprising me.

Instantly, I sat up in my bed, my pulse surging. "Oh, Derek. Hey!" I said, trying to sound perky and not like I was half-dead.

He cleared his throat. "I know this is last minute, but do you wanna grab a burger or something for lunch?"

Aw, crap! A golden opportunity, and I couldn't take it.

I slapped my forehead. "I would, if I hadn't already promised Andy I'd meet her. She . . . needs to get her car fixed," I said vaguely, figuring Andy wouldn't want me to embarrass her and tell the circumstances behind our visit. "Can we go out Sunday, though?"

"Sure, that'll work. Guess I'd better give you more notice," Derek replied, his voice light. "I had no idea you were so popular."

Me? Was he joking? Because we both knew that in our relationship, I was *so* not the popular one.

"*You're* friends with everyone in school, not me." I could feel the tension, the edge of jealousy, seeping into my voice, so I tried to relax. There was no way I wanted to get into another fight with him. "Though I bet the love spell I accidentally set on you probably had a small hand in it. Maybe some of the students are still madly in love with you."

He chuckled. "I sure hope not. I'm still trying to scrub the 'I heart Derek' graffiti off my mom's car."

There was a knock on my door.

"Felicity," my mom said, briefly poking her head in. "Andy's downstairs waiting for you."

"Okay, thanks," I answered Mom. "I gotta go," I told Derek, regret spilling into my voice. God, how badly I wanted to just run up and hug him tightly. I needed to feel his arms around me right now. But I couldn't tell him that without sounding desperate and clingy. Trying to keep my voice even, I continued, "I'll call you later, though, okay?"

I heard some mumbled talking in the background, which Derek responded to, his hand cupped over the phone. "Sure," he finally said to me. "Bye."

I placed the phone in the cradle and sat for a moment with my hand on the phone, mentally replaying the conversation. A sensation of paranoia swept over me. Derek wasn't usually one to ask me out on such short notice. And he'd seemed really distracted at the end of our conversation.

What did he want to talk to me about? He hadn't decided to end our relationship already, had he?

I toyed with the idea of not calling him back. Maybe if I stuck my head in the sand like a good little ostrich, all of this badness would go away.

Well, that's just dumb, I told myself, shaking my head in disgust. Better to man up—er, so to speak—and face this mess head-on. If Derek was going to break up with me, I was better off preparing myself for it instead of wishing it away.

Not that the idea didn't make me want to hurl all over the place.

Footsteps ran up my stairs and my door flew open, revealing Andy, who was twirling the key ring on her index finger.

"Hey, you ready to go? The bumper looks like it's going to fall off any minute," she said, then paused, tilting her head to the side. "What's with the weird look on your face? Are you sick?"

"No, I'm fine," I said brightly, pasting on a huge, fake smile. This wasn't the time to whine about my problems. Right now I needed to be a good friend to Andy and help her resolve the car issue.

At least that was something under our control.

"But is the owner of the car here?" Juan, the thin guy behind the counter, asked with one raised eyebrow, leaning forward to look over our shoulders.

Closing her eyes, Andy drew in a slow, deep breath. I could see a vein throbbing on the side of her forehead. Not that I could blame her. We'd been standing in line for twenty minutes to talk to the repairman at the dealership. And now that we'd finally gotten to the front of the line, he wouldn't listen to us at all.

"Look," Andy said through pinched lips. I could tell she was trying to keep her tone even so she wouldn't rip this guy a new butthole. Getting on his bad side wasn't going to help the problem. "I just told you, I'm helping out my parents by fixing the car for them. I have money, I promise, and will be more than happy to pay for the repairs in advance."

Juan shook his head. "Sorry, but we can't work with anyone but the owners of the vehicle. Since you're a minor, and not listed as an owner, there's nothing we can do to help you."

Andy turned and looked at me, frustration knitting her eyebrows together. I could practically see steam coming out of her ears.

"Give us just one second, please," I said to Juan, then pulled Andy to the side. "Okay, what now?"

Tears welled in her eyes, and she shrugged. "I'm screwed. No way will I be able to convince them to fix it. My dad will kill me when he finds out."

A lump clogged my throat. "I'm sorry. If you want, I'll come with you when you talk to him. Maybe he'll go easier on you if I'm there."

She sniffled.

I hugged her tightly, wishing I could take this bad situation away. She had to be dreading the inevitable.

I'd only seen her dad pissed off once before. When Andy and I were in fifth grade, we'd decided to play beauty shop and use his hair clippers to cut our Cabbage Patch Kids' hair. Yeah, not the brightest idea. He made us do chores around their house for two weeks to make up the cost of buying a new hair clipper.

Andy chuckled, as if knowing exactly what I was thinking. "I appreciate your offer," she said, mumbling into my shoulder, "but I think I'd better just face him on my own. He might not like me using you as a shield."

I nodded slowly. If only there were another way, but everything seemed to be conspiring against us.

We left the car repair shop in the Porsche and headed back to Andy's house, making sure to travel slowly and carefully. When we arrived, I gave her another huge hug, wished her good luck, and then headed back to my house.

Once there, I went up to my room and logged on to my computer to check e-mail. Nothing new but spam, of course. Then I loaded up my blog and created a new private entry.

I can't believe how chaotic everything is!

Poor Andy's going to be in deep, deep trouble when her dad finds out about his car. I hope he still lets her go to prom, because we've been planning this, like, forever. It doesn't seem fair to ground her from the only junior prom she'll ever get to go to, especially since she's willing to pay to fix the car.

And if she does get to go, I hope she doesn't get mad at Bobby because his brother is a terrible mechanic.

In just as horrible news, Maya's mom seems to have totally given up on true love. What a terrible place to be, to lose hope like that. She looked so bad when I saw her, so empty. Like a shell of who she used to be.

All I can do is hold on to my own inner strength . . . if there's even any left in me at this point.

I saved and closed the entry, then turned off my PC and worked on homework for a bit, staying near the phone to wait for

Andy's call. She was going to let me know what happened after all was said and done.

A full hour passed. I itched to call her, even picking up the phone twice and starting to dial her number, but it was probably a bad idea to interrupt whatever was going on.

Finally the phone rang. I jumped up and grabbed it.

"Hello?" I answered anxiously.

"Hey," Andy whispered into the mouthpiece, her voice thick and heavy like she'd been crying.

"Oh no," I breathed, heart thudding in my chest. "You sound awful. What happened? Are you okay?"

"Yeah, I'm fine. It was just very hard. I'm hiding in my bathroom right now, but I wanted to call you so you wouldn't worry. Dad was furious, but he appreciated my honesty with him. I'm grounded for three months, and I'm not allowed to drive." She paused. "Since I'm paying him back for the repair costs, he's going to let me go to prom."

"No way!" I squealed. "That's not too bad at all, Andy."

"No kidding. He's going to drop me off at prom and pick me back up at nine thirty. Which is superlame, but at least I get to go," she said. I heard some rustling. "Gotta go. We'll talk on Monday."

We hung up.

I pushed my homework to the foot of my bed and lay back, crossing my hands behind my head. Andy had faced the challenge head-on and had come out of it with some punishment, but not nearly as bad as we'd feared. For that, I was thrilled for her.

And so, so proud.

"So, I have something for you," I told Derek Sunday evening in my living room. He could only stop by for a few minutes since it was late, so I needed to get right to the point.

"Really?" Derek shifted on the couch, leaning back and giving me a curious look. His knees brushed against mine.

I swallowed, then dug into my pocket. I'd spent most of yesterday evening working on this project for Derek, inspired by Andy's gift to Bobby. But instead of just buying Derek something, I'd decided to make it.

Which, in retrospect, was not my best idea. It had taken me three attempts to get the necklace looking halfway decent. It still wasn't perfect, but if I'd kept going at it, it would never be done. And it was important to me to give it to him today.

I pressed the folded leather necklace into his hand. "Here. I made it. But if you don't like it, I won't be offended or anything, I promise." Geez, why was I so nervous? It wasn't nearly as impressive as his mosaic. It wasn't even in the same galaxy.

He stretched it out to its full length, and I saw all the lumpy flaws in it where my fingers weren't able to weave the leather tightly enough. I had to fight the urge to rip it back out of his fingertips. He'd probably think it was stupid or—

"I love it." He tied it around his neck, then leaned over and pressed a soft kiss against my lips. I saw him swallow. "No one's ever made me a gift before."

"It was no biggie, really." But his words made me feel better. Even if I wasn't as skilled at artistic endeavors as he was, at least he seemed truly appreciative. "I know it can't compare, but it's just a small thank-you for the mosaic you made of me." I paused, clearing my throat. "Um, speaking of, do you think it would be okay if I got to . . . have the portrait after the art show is over?"

"You want it?" he asked, his brows knitted. "Really?"

I blinked. "Are you on crack? It's amazing. I'd be honored."

He smiled softly, his finger brushing the leather of his necklace. "Then it's yours."

"Thank you." I knew I'd treasure the portrait he'd done of me always, regardless of what happened between us in the future. But at least right now, in this moment, we were sharing with each other and feeling happy.

And this was something I'd never forget.

Geez, was she *ever* going to get here?

On Wednesday night, I glanced at my watch for the thousandth time since I'd arrived at Pizza Hut, waiting for Rob's girlfriend, Annette, to show up. It didn't help that I was starving to death, too, and ready to order a massively large pizza. And the Coke I was chugging wasn't filling my stomach at all.

With all the drama going on in my life lately (hah, like *that* was anything new), I'd completely forgotten about doing the rest of my "interview" with Annette about being a female cop. Luckily, she'd asked me about it at Sunday dinner—and of course, since my whole family was there and staring expectantly at me, I couldn't back out of it.

So we'd agreed to meet, nosh on some pizza (my treat, since she was generously donating her time), and finish up our discussion.

However, it was now . . . seven fifteen, according to my watch. And she was supposed to have been here at seven.

I crossed my arms, sighing heavily.

Don't be so uptight, I ordered myself. After all, Annette was a cop. Maybe there was some kind of emergency that delayed her, like a bad accident on the highway. Those kinds of things should be her priority.

I suddenly felt bad about being so irritated. Not very grateful of me, especially since she didn't have to meet me at all.

Geez, what was happening to my attitude lately? Everything was sending me into extremes. This was getting out of control.

There was only one thing I could do.

I made a solemn, silent vow to myself, right there on the cracked red booth seat of Pizza Hut. I was going to show more tolerance, caring, and patience with the people around me. Time and time again, I'd seen how life's unexpected moments, no matter how big or small, could affect someone's life.

And it was my job as a decent human being to respond in the most understanding way I could.

Outside the window I saw a squad car pull into a nearby parking spot. Finally, Annette was here. And what fortuitous timing.

See? I felt a smile break out on my face. This new positive attitude was already bringing results.

Even though I knew it was a fake interview, I was looking forward to talking to her. This was a great opportunity for me to find out how her relationship with Rob was going, and from her point of view. I could easily tell how my brother had been affected, but I wanted to hear how happy she was too.

Annette, in the passenger's seat, talked animatedly to her partner, who was driving the car. Oh crap, the driver was Officer Banks, the guy who'd busted me outside the bar when I had spied on Rob.

I crossed my fingers and hoped he wasn't coming in, because I was soooo not wanting to deal with—

Right then Annette leaned over toward the officer and gave him a kiss on his mouth.

chapter eighteen

At first, a large part of my brain didn't seem to comprehend what was going on. It even tried to excuse the scene I'd just witnessed, but the other part of my brain knocked the excuse out like a prize fighter on steroids:

Delusional side of brain: Maybe Annette's just being friendly, and that's how she tells her partner good-bye. They could be good buddies.

Rational side of brain: Who tells a friend good-bye by sticking your tongue in their mouth? I've never told any of my friends good-bye like that, and for good reason . . . because that's called making out!

No, I knew exactly what had happened here. Annette had lost the flame she'd once carried for my brother. The cupid spell had apparently worn off. Which utterly sucked, because I knew beyond a shadow of a doubt that Rob was still madly in love with her.

In fact, I had talked to him not more than an hour ago to let him know my meeting with his girlfriend was still on, and he'd gushed about what a great time I was going to have with her. Poor Rob.

My stomach clenched in a tighter knot, and I fought another wave of sickness sweeping over me. I'd seen some crazy behavior from people I'd matchmade, but I'd never seen a person so brazenly make out with someone else on the day the spell had worn off. I doubted Annette had even had time to break up with Rob beforehand.

Annette finished licking the inside of Officer Banks's mouth and backed her way out of the car. She waggled her fingers good-bye to him, closing the door and strolling up the sidewalk. Toward me.

I couldn't do this. No way was I going to be able to get through dinner with her. My brain whirred, considering my options:

1. hide in the bathroom or under the table, where she can't see me

2. confront her about what I saw and risk her wrath

3. fake an illness and barf all over her

Well, it was too late for number one. The bathroom stood to the side of the front door, and she was coming inside now, walking toward me with her typical friendly smile. Her big, fat, lying smile.

"Felicity," Annette greeted me warmly. She slid into the booth across from me, and I heard her holster scrape against the back of the booth bench. "Sorry I'm late. Thanks for being so understanding, though."

Option two, or three? Two, or three?

I opened my mouth and let fly the first words that came out. "That's okay. Actually, I'm gonna have to bail. I feel like I'm going to be sick." With a dramatic groan, I clutched my stomach.

It was the truth. My stomach was churning like there was a tub of boiling butter inside it. Somehow, confronting Annette about what I'd seen seemed a lot less appealing when I was feeling icky. Plus, she had a gun on her. Not that I thought she'd shoot me or anything, but it was still intimidating.

She frowned, her back straightening. "Well, I'm sorry to hear that. Maybe we can finish your interview some other time."

Briefly, I wondered if she knew that *I* knew, or if she had grown suspicious. But given that she'd kissed Officer Banks so boldly, and right there in the parking lot, I highly doubted she cared about my opinion. She obviously didn't care what Rob thought, either, and he was supposedly her boyfriend.

I fought back the sneer that was trying to edge its way onto my face and rose from the booth, dropping a twenty-dollar bill on the table. "Here, please order yourself some dinner. After all, you did come all this way to talk to me." Then I turned and fled.

The whole ride home, I debated with myself about whether or not I should tell Rob about what I'd seen. Was it my place to tell him his girlfriend was playing kissy face with another officer? Part of me screamed that yes, if I were him, I'd want to know.

The other part reminded me of the cliché "don't shoot the messenger." There was a reason it was good to not butt into someone's love life in this way—because, inevitably, you ended up getting blamed yourself. And maybe this was something Rob needed to figure out for himself.

I pulled into the driveway, turned off the car, and trudged

through the front door. Mom and Dad were in the living room, watching TV.

"Hey," Dad said, glancing up with a smile.

I nodded in response. Wordlessly I handed Mom the car keys and made my way upstairs, draping across my bed with my head over the side, staring at the floor. A minute passed, and then there was a light knock on my door.

"Felicity, are you okay?" Mom asked through the thin plywood. "Can I come in and talk to you?"

"Sure," I mumbled, edging my body over on the mattress as she sat beside me.

"What's going on?"

"I have a bit of a conflict," I said, filled with a sudden urge to confide in someone. Mom often had good advice—when I asked for it, at least—and maybe she could help shed some light on what I should do. "I . . . saw something that's really going to hurt someone else. And I don't know if I should tell that person or not."

She sighed, rubbing my back. "That's a tough call. Sometimes people don't like it when you butt into their business. But there's something to be said for being honest. What do you think is the right thing to do?"

I leaned my face to the side, pressing my right cheek against my warmed bedspread. "I don't know. I guess I should tell."

We were silent for a moment.

Then she gently cleared her throat. "Sometimes, the right thing isn't always the easy thing."

Mom was right. I mean, look at Andy. It took massive courage to admit to her dad what had happened with his Porsche. And she knew for sure her confession was going to have a negative repercussion, but she still did it, anyway.

At least Rob would know I was telling him because I cared.

I sat up and hugged Mom. Yeah, she was a bit of a House Nazi, but she was still pretty darn smart. "Thanks. You're right."

She chuckled. "I have my moments."

"I should make a call," I said, picking up my phone. It was time to put on my big girl panties and deal.

"I'll leave you alone." She patted my back one last time and left the room.

Big girl panties or no, my hands were shaky as I dialed Rob's cell phone.

"Mom?" he said after picking the phone up.

"No, it's me, Felicity." I struggled to keep my voice calm and normal.

"Oh, hey. How did your meeting with Annette go?"

God, he sounded so full of hope and happiness, even just saying her name. And here I was, the brutal romance killer who was going to crush his heart by revealing the infidelities of his true love.

"I . . . left early," I said.

"Oh. How come? Don't you need to finish your interview?"

"Rob, I saw something I probably shouldn't have," I blurted out.

"Did you file a report?" he asked, instantly turning on his cop voice. "Was it some sort of crime?"

Only a crime against the heart. "No, it wasn't that kind of thing. It was . . . well . . ." Now that the moment was here, I wasn't sure how to say it.

I heard Rob's walkie-talkie go off, and a deep male voice spoke rapidly.

"Gotta go, Felicity. Police emergency. Can we talk later?"

"Sure," I whispered, closing my eyes.

Chicken! I could have told him by now if I hadn't stalled. Maybe there was time to say something, though, so he'd at least keep his eyes open.

"Rob," I continued, "just . . . be careful, okay? I'd hate to see you get hurt."

"Okayyy," he drawled. "Later."

Yes, later. I'd take some time to plan out my approach so I wouldn't be so tongue-tied the next time we talked. And there *would* be a next time.

Thursday, during lunch, I made up some lame excuse and sneaked away from Maya and Andy. There was no way in hell I wanted them to know I was going to consult Absinthia, resident super Goth, to get my fortune told. I remembered how much Andy had mocked Maya's reading. Even though I'd been skeptical myself, I couldn't deny Absinthia had been dead-on in her predictions.

I wound my way outside school and toward the steady streams of smoke pouring up from underneath the slats of the track field bleachers, her usual hangout.

"—you're crazy," one of the guys in her group was saying. He puffed on his cigarette, exhaling the smoke in an O shape from his mouth. "Hunter S. Thompson knew the effect he was having on his news reports, but he still chose to put himself right in the story."

"No kidding," Absinthia said, nodding in agreement. "He was a genius."

"Um, excuse me," I said, standing off to the edge behind them. "Can I talk to you, Absinthia?"

She turned to face me, pressing the stubby, ashy end of her cigarette on the ground. "So, you're back," she said, one eyebrow raised high. "What brings you out here? Does your friend need another reading?"

I cleared my throat. "Actually, *I'd* like one."

A dozen black-lined eyes fixed on me in disbelief. Obviously they'd remembered Andy's and my skepticism.

My cheeks flushed with embarrassment. Geez, I could see this was a dumb idea.

"But you're busy," I continued in a rapid speech, wishing I hadn't come out here in the first place. "See ya later."

"I'll do it," Absinthia said, standing.

Whew. I swallowed my relieved sigh, trying to keep cool.

"Let's go over to the other side of the bleachers. Do you have money?"

"Yup." I took the folded bill out of my pocket, handed it over, and followed her. We headed along the underside of the bleachers to where there was a flat concrete surface.

Absinthia sat down on it and crossed her legs, pulling the

cards, wrapped in velvety red fabric, out of her pants pocket. "Okay, I'm going to do a three-card reading of the major arcana. Have a seat." She pulled out the cards in question, shuffled them, then stretched out the red fabric and laid the stack of cards face-down on the cloth.

I did as she'd requested, my heart thudding painfully in anticipation as I watched her ring-covered fingers.

"Split the deck."

My hand shook as I reached over and divided the cards in two. She put them back together in reverse order, then fanned them out on the cloth. "Draw three cards. One will be your past, one your present, and one your future."

I studied the backs of the tarot cards, seeing if my intuition would tell me which ones I should choose. But nothing in me spoke up, so I simply picked three random ones and handed them to her.

Absinthia flipped the first one over in one deft turn. The Death card.

Crap. *Not* a good way to start this. My stomach lurched.

She smiled patiently, probably used to her clients freaking out whenever they got a horrible card. "Relax. This doesn't mean 'death,' per se."

Oh, that's right. I vaguely remembered her mentioning that when she did Maya's reading. I drew in a slow breath and forced myself to relax, shifting my legs. "So what does it mean, then?"

"You experienced an important change in your recent past, within the last few months. Something that upheaved your life drastically. It also caused unexpected pain as you felt the repercussions of that change."

She had to be talking about my cupid job, which for sure was a huge change . . . with its share of challenges. And pain. So many matches I'd made hadn't worked out. So many broken hearts.

I nodded. "Yeah, that makes sense."

"I sense you tried to force some actions in response to this big change, which didn't work." She raised that one eyebrow at me again, a small grin on her face. "Bit of a control freak, aren't you?"

Boy, two minutes into the reading and she already had me pegged.

"I guess so," I said noncommittally, not wanting to reveal all my weaknesses.

"Okay, this next card describes your present situation." She flipped over the next card. The Hanged Man.

Could the image staring up at me look any more miserable? Gee, this reading was making me feel *so* much better.

She clucked her tongue. "Things are a little . . . unbalanced for you right now, are they? Like the rug's been swept out from under you. I sense there's chaos in everything you touch . . . sometimes turning out for the good, but sometimes not."

"Very much so," I said, unable to prevent the emotional hitch in my voice. "But what can I do about it? How can I make things right? I've messed up a lot of stuff, and I don't know how to fix anything anymore."

Like how to make Maya's mom happy. Or how to make Derek love me without a spell influencing him. And the list went on and on.

She shook her head. "I think you're going about this the wrong way. Until you learn how to go with the flow, until you acknowledge and control your pride, nothing's going to get better for you."

Pride? Was it so wrong to have a sense of duty and satisfaction from making a good match or helping people? And wasn't that what Janet had hired me for?

"I don't see how I've done so badly here," I said stiffly. "I'm doing exactly what I'm supposed to."

"Hey, I'm just the messenger," she said with a casual shrug, raising her palms up toward me.

The messenger. She was right. How easy it was to get angry with the person just trying to help.

With a guilty twinge, I remembered how I'd hoped my brother would take the news of Annette when I finally got a chance to tell him. Not angry and resentful, like I was at the moment, but with an open heart and mind.

"Sorry," I whispered. "I'm a little sensitive about this topic."

"I can tell." She paused. "I sense there's someone else involved here, too . . . someone you're pushing too hard. You need to relax and trust in others. Let them handle things, too. For you, that may be the greatest sacrifice you can make. But once you do, you'll finally be righted on to your feet again."

Surely she was talking about Derek. Was she right—was I really forcing things with him? But if I didn't work hard, how was anything going to happen between us? After all, things slipped out of my hands and went down the crapper when I didn't fight to make the situation right. And even though he and I had some great, memorable moments together, they were becoming fewer and further between.

Eventually they'd just fade away altogether.

I was already seeing evidence of this happening. Derek didn't even try to find me in the mornings anymore. In fact, the only time I really saw him in school now was in art class. For the eight-billionth time, I rued the fact that I didn't even have a cell phone. We couldn't send texts to check in with each other, like most normal couples did.

I gave a begrudging shrug, not willing to believe what she was saying. "I guess."

"And now, your last card that shows the future." She flipped over The Sun. "This isn't a bad one at all."

I sighed in relief. It was about time. The whole reading so far hadn't been as gentle as I'd expected, or hoped. "So what does it mean?"

"The Sun means there's going to be a time of positive well-being in your future." She stopped and stared hard at me. "But those times will only come about so long as you are careful to adapt and remain flexible and not let your pride overrule you. Some pride is a good thing, but too much can make a person rigid and arrogant."

Okay, I was totally sensing a theme here, and I didn't like it. How many more times was she going to tell me what a bad person I was?

I stood. "Well, thank you very much for your time," I forced myself to say politely.

Absinthia wrapped up her cards and grabbed a pack of cigarettes out of her pocket, pulling out one and lighting it. Her face was neutral, but her eyes studied me with interest. "I don't normally tell clients this, but I can sense you're a very powerful person with the capacity to do great things. The cards you drew were strong, emotional ones."

I swallowed, staring at her silently.

She popped the cigarette in her mouth and drew in a big puff, then stood up and headed under the bleachers, turning to look at me. She gave me a small smile. "Once you learn balance and figure out how to get past this rough patch of your life, you'll be good to go."

Shame surged through me. She was obviously trying to leave me with a positive note, and I was being ungrateful. I didn't know what to make of her reading, but it didn't mean she was insincere in her efforts. Nor was she trying to force anything on me—she was simply reading what she'd seen in the cards.

"Thank you," I said humbly.

"Any time," she replied, then walked off to rejoin her group.

I made my way back into school, heading through the double doors right as the bell rang. Absinthia had said some stuff that stung, and other stuff that had to be flat-out wrong, but maybe within her message there was a grain of truth.

Now to figure it out.

chapter nineteen

Prom night had finally arrived, and I was a bundle of raw, excited nerves. I stood in front of my mirror and fiddled with my hair for the thousandth time. What would Derek think of my dress?

Of me?

I'd had so little time to talk to him over the past couple of days, and our only real correspondence was through e-mail, where he'd sent me a brief message about how swamped he was now that his mom was getting closer to giving birth. I wish he'd picked up the phone to call me instead, but I tried to push my insecurity aside and focus on here and now.

The only positive aspect about having so much time to myself this week was that I'd finished all but a small handful of my matches. Tonight would be the conclusion for our competition—though I had a strong gut feeling that Derek's lasting matches would greatly outnumber mine.

"Felicity, he's here," I heard my mom say from downstairs.

"I'm coming," I replied. With shaky hands, I smoothed my dress and headed downstairs to face my destiny.

Derek was standing in the living room, his face turned toward the staircase as I descended. His black tux fit him well, and the black vest hugged his torso nicely.

He smiled, bright teeth gleaming, and his eyes raked over me. My lips tingled under his appreciative gaze.

"You . . . look amazing." He handed me a plastic package. "Here."

I glanced down. There was a pure-white calla lily nestled with small sprigs of baby's breath and fresh greenery. I sucked in a deep breath, stunned at my corsage. Maybe he really did love me. "Holy crap, Derek. You did a nice job. This is beautiful." I didn't even know he was going to get me one.

"Glad you like it. I figured you were a 'simple flowers' kind of girl." He took it out of the package and stepped closer to me, his face mere inches from my mine. I closed my eyes and breathed in the light scent of his cologne.

Maybe things were going to be okay tonight, after all.

Concentrating on the task at hand, Derek pinned the flower to my dress. And he did it without even making me bleed. Was there anything he couldn't do?

"Okay, you two." My dad's voice interrupted the moment. "Face me so I can get some shots."

Derek's arm snaked around my back to rest on my hip. I leaned into his warm side. We fit perfectly together. Surely he was realizing it now, even without the benefit of Janet's cupid spell over us.

After about fifty billion more pictures, Mom and Dad finally let us go. Once outside, Derek opened the passenger door of his dark green Ford Focus.

Aw, crap. Something I hadn't banked on was how difficult it would be to get in and out of the car without flashing my goods. After all, this dress was a pretty close fit.

Derek solved the problem by holding out a hand, giving me the leverage to sort of slide my way in. I held on to his hand for a few extra seconds, just to make sure I was in the seat right. A girl couldn't be too careful, you know.

Once he'd popped into the driver's seat, he turned to me and smiled again, melting me into a pile of red-dressed goo.

We took off for the restaurant, making occasional small talk about unimportant stuff. I tried my best to sit as attractively as I could, praying he couldn't see my heart slamming in my chest.

A half hour later Derek pulled his car into a parking spot at P.F. Chang's China Bistro. Which just so happened to be one of my favorite places in the world. Their food was to die for, especially the lettuce wraps.

"Hope this is okay," Derek said. "I love eating here."

"Are you kidding?" I scoffed. "I'd eat here every day if I could afford it." Speaking of, I quickly peeked in my purse to make sure I had enough money. The restaurant had good food, but it was a little on the steep side.

We slipped into our seats. The waiter brought us water and took our orders.

"So, can you believe that about Alec?" I asked Derek a few minutes later, sipping from my glass. Alec was a freshman on my matchmaking list—I'd paired him a couple of weeks ago with Marie, the Hello Kitty girl. The two of them had kept a relatively low profile after being paired up.

Which was why we were all shocked when he'd tagged the side of the school with Marie's name and did a manga-style painting of her face with hearts around it. The principal had been furious, making Alec scrub the graffiti off and then suspending him for two weeks.

"I don't think anyone would have expected him to react so strongly to being matchmade. But Marie had helped him clean the bricks off, which was nice of her." He shook his head, smiling. "The things people do for love, right?"

So very true. I thought about the gorgeous art show portrait Derek had made of me while he was under the love spell. And the crappy leather necklace I'd made for him, now peeking through the collar of his tuxedo shirt. Or those stupid fake eyelashes I'd worn during my disastrous makeover phase.

Our food arrived, and I dug into my plate with gusto. Well, as much gusto as I could while wearing a form-fitting dress. I wondered if it would be tacky to ask Derek to store a doggy bag of the leftovers in the back of his car. Could they make it all evening in the car?

"You know, I'm glad we haven't done anything destructive while dating each other," I finally said, chuckling. "We don't need to get kicked out of school or anything."

Derek widened his eyes in mock nervousness and put his fork down. "Oh. So, you're not into that kind of thing." He paused dramatically. "As a completely unrelated side note, I think we should use the back entrance for prom."

I lifted an eyebrow. "Really? Is there another fun surprise waiting for me?"

He shrugged innocently. "Not anymore, I bet . . . the group of monkeys I trained to perform for you probably escaped the premises. Guess we should have eaten faster."

The rest of dinner went by all too quickly, with us trying to top each other about goofy public declarations of love we could make. When the bill came, Derek swiped it out of my hand. "I got it," he said.

"You don't have to. I have some money."

He laughed. "Mom would choke me if I let you pay. I'd never hear the end of it from her."

I laughed, too, but inside, I was wishing he'd offered to pay because of more romantic reasons. Maybe I was just making things worse with these heightened expectations. Things tended to go easier when I just let go, joked around, and didn't try to read into every word he said or action he did.

The bill settled, we left the restaurant and went to the prom hotel. When I saw the rows of limos pulling up to the front doors, my heart raced. How would things go tonight? Would Derek want to dance with me, or would he hang with his friends and ignore me?

Oh God, I'd be mortified if he ditched me like that. Even though things were going nicely now between us, I feared it could be a different story when his friends were around.

I quickly sent up a silent prayer—*Please, God, if you've ever, ever cared about me, don't let him dump me, tonight of all nights. He doesn't have to be head over heels in love, but don't let him hurt me.*

Derek escorted me to the door, his hand on the small of my back. I could feel his warm fingers through the thin fabric of my dress, and I wanted to turn around and lean against him. It took all the strength I had to keep calm and look normal. Not that I was totally normal in the first place or anything.

"Don't forget," he whispered in my ear, sending shivers across my skin. "Tonight's the night we see who won. Count up your matches, and I'll do the same with mine."

"Hey, man!" Toby, one of Derek's jock friends, said as we entered the front lobby, thumping him hard on the back.

Derek pulled away from me. "Hey," he replied to Toby, slugging him in the arm.

"We have a table in the back. Go sit with us. Catch ya in a bit." He headed off to the bathroom.

I hoped that meant I was invited to sit at the table, too. Otherwise, it was going to be a long night.

Derek and I wrangled our way through the crowd, trying not to trip in the darkened room. The disco light was in full swing, sending dots of white light scattering across the room. The DJ was playing some R & B song in the background, the singer's voice and a deep grooving bass pouring out of the speakers.

We found the table in question and sat in the last two available seats—the rest had jackets draped over the backs.

Derek helped me off with my wrap, then hung his jacket on the back of his seat. "Do you want something to drink?"

"Um, sure. Anything with caffeine is fine."

I sat at the empty table, drawing in deep, relaxing breaths. I couldn't believe how well the night was going so far. Maybe I could finally start to unwind and enjoy the evening.

"—and the cashmere sweater was on sale for dirt cheap," a voice said from behind me. But not just any voice.

I bit my lower lip and rolled my eyes, willing myself to relax. I could get through this. I'd known beforehand I was going to have to deal with her, so I might as well get it over with.

Mallory perched with two of her giggle-box friends in the seats across from me. Goody! "Oh, it's Felicity," she said, her eyes raking over my dress. She sneered slightly, wrinkling her nose. "What are you doing at our table?"

You'd think I'd chosen the seat just to torture her. "Derek's football buddies told us to sit here."

Her jaw tightened for a quick moment. Then she relaxed her face and glanced at her friends. They all rose out of their seats. "See ya," she said to me.

As they walked off, I saw their heads close together. One of the girls peeked back at me, shaking her head.

Great. I just loved being talked about by stupid, snotty girls. Then again, this was no different than any other day. Surprise, surprise—she was one of the unmatched people on my list who I couldn't seem to pair up with anyone.

"Here you go," Derek said at my side, coming out of nowhere. He placed a drink in front of me. "One heavily loaded caffeine drink, at your service."

I gave him a wan smile and took a small sip. "Thanks."

His forehead crunched up. "What's wrong?"

I stared into his eyes, debating whether or not to tell him what a total cow Mallory was. But bad-mouthing her wouldn't make me look any better. "Just waiting for Andy and Maya to arrive."

"I saw them and their dates at a table near the front," he offered.

"Derek!" his friend Toby hollered across the room, waving hard at him.

Derek turned to me. "Hey, let's go hang over there for a few minutes. Then we can go find your friends afterward."

I stood and swallowed, not wanting to go through the whole gig with his buddies yet again. I was still stinging from Mallory's rudeness. "I'll go find Andy and Maya. You can go talk to your buddies, okay?"

Giving him as genuine a smile as I could muster, I turned and left, weaving my way through small clusters of people milling around the room. The dance floor near the DJ was packed with happy couples grooving with each other on the floor, including Adele and Mike, who were getting separated every ten seconds by a teacher for "excessive closeness." As I counted my other matches, I noticed they were mostly couples made by Derek.

Of course they were.

Come on, this isn't the time to be down on yourself, I chided myself. It was prom, and I refused to be a crab ass. Besides, I'd already known going into this evening that I was going to lose the challenge.

I finally found Maya and Andy sitting close to their boyfriends at a table on the corner of the dance floor, smiling and laughing among themselves.

"Hey, guys," I said from behind them.

They both turned around, their eyes bugging out of their heads when they took in my dress.

"Oh my God! You look gorgeous!" Maya cried out, hugging me.

"How is Derek keeping his hands off you?" Andy said, giving me a hug too.

I swallowed, feeling tears of relief sting my eyes. I was so, so lucky to have such great friends. "When did you guys get here?"

"Just a little while ago," Andy said. She wound her arm through Bobby's. "Doesn't he look fantastic?"

Bobby's face turned beet red, and he gave an embarrassed grin, dropping his gaze to his lap.

I smiled, happy to see Andy wasn't holding the car fiasco

against Bobby. Really, it wasn't his fault. "I have to say, he rocks a tux better than you do," I teased Andy, since she has to wear a pseudo–tux at the Burger Butler.

"And Derek looks mighty fine in his, too," Maya said, one eyebrow raised. "How come you're not off swapping spit with him right now?"

My stomach clenched. "Oh, he's talking to his friends," I said casually, waving it off like I wasn't upset by it or anything. "I came over to chill with you guys."

"Need something to drink?" Scott asked Maya. His eyes twinkled in the disco light as he took in her dark plum A-line dress. Not that I could blame him for staring—Maya looked simply gorgeous.

Man, I wished Derek were there, gazing at me the way Scott was at Maya. It was my fault, though, since I'd told him to go.

Maya nodded at Scott with a smile, leaning over and kissing him on the cheek. "Thanks, I'll have a punch."

The R & B song ended, and an upbeat dance number started to play. I glanced around for Derek, hoping he'd remember it was my favorite dance song and come and drag me out onto the floor, especially since he'd put it on that mix playlist for the night of our outdoor picnic. But he was nowhere to be found.

Andy grabbed Maya's hand and tugged her out of her seat. "Okay, we have to dance to this," she proclaimed.

"Come on, Felicity, let's go!" Maya said.

My first impulse was to wave them away and wait for Derek . . . but dammit, this was my prom. I wanted to dance and have fun with my BFFs. I glanced around the ballroom one last time. Still no Derek. He was probably outside or something. Super.

"Okay, let's do this," I said, standing and smoothing my skirt.

We shook our booties for several minutes. My feet started to throb in my shoes, which were totally not made for dancing.

The set of fast songs ended, and a slow song came on. Out of nowhere, Scott and Bobby showed up to claim their dates, wrapping their arms tightly around Maya and Andy.

I stood on the edge of the floor for a minute, watching them and hoping Derek would show up, but my searching gaze couldn't find him at all. Maybe he'd forgotten he had even come to prom with me. Maybe he was talking to his friends about a way to break up with me. A lot could happen in the minutes since we'd gone our separate ways, right?

Maybe the last few molecules of cupid dust had finally evaporated from his system, and now I was history.

Seeing Andy and Maya cuddling with their boyfriends, their eyes glowing with love, was just too much to bear. A surge of tears flooded my eyes, and I left the dance floor and headed right to the bathroom, ducking into the closest stall and sitting on the toilet seat. I grabbed a wad of toilet paper and dabbed my eyes, then blew my nose.

Time to think clearly, rationally.

Honestly.

It seemed to me that right now I was at a crossroads in my life. Everything Absinthia had said was true, and I needed to admit it. I was a failure as a cupid, a failure as a girlfriend, and more important, a failure to myself—after all, the chaos around me had spiraled out of control because of my actions all along the way.

It was time to let go of all of this drama so I could finally move on past this stage in my life. And maybe the sacrifice I needed to start with was Derek. Should I be proactive and break up with him? Or wait for him to break up with me first? Until now, I'd been living in a limbo, waiting for the other shoe to drop. Waiting for him to finally proclaim he didn't want to be with me.

But Derek had proven time and again that he was a good guy and never wanted to hurt people. When I'd accidentally made the whole school fall in love with him, he was never mean to even the most obnoxious of his love-crazed suitors, despite the fact that he wasn't interested in dating them.

I shifted on the lid of the toilet seat. Maybe I'd simply become one of those suitors to him, all gaga and googly eyed whenever he came near. The thought broke my heart into a thousand pieces. But I guess the truth wasn't always easy to face.

I wanted him to love me so completely that he wouldn't let me out of his sight on a night like tonight. So deeply that he'd act like he had during the love spell and not slowly fade away from me as the days wore on and our relationship fizzled out.

Yes, I loved him. Yes, I wanted to be with him. But this wasn't the way I wanted our love to be—initially forced because of a spell Janet had put on us, with him stuck in a relationship because he was too kind to break up with me. And me too scared to ask him for more together time.

No, that wasn't going to cut the love mustard.

I wanted, and needed, more.

I tossed the wad of mascara-covered toilet paper into the tiny trash can attached to the wall. It was time to find Derek and face reality, once and for all.

My hand shook slightly as I pushed the stall door open and walked through. I left the bathroom, broken. Heart in throat, I scoured the ballroom in my search for Derek. I spotted him standing near the punch table with his jock friends and Mallory, whose date was nowhere to be found.

Courage, Felicity. I forced myself to walk over to Derek, who turned to me. His eyes were dark under the overhead light, unreadable. He certainly didn't look happy.

"We need to talk. Privately," I said, throwing a pointed glance toward his entourage. Of all the times in our relationship, now was when I had to put my foot down and insist they stay away.

He nodded. "Yeah, I think you're right."

We made our way through the hotel lobby and stood out front, where there was no foot traffic coming by. A light breeze blew, and I inadvertently shivered.

Derek took off his coat and wrapped it around my shoulders, the warmth from his body heat enveloping me instantly. It was a bittersweet gesture, given that we were about to break up, and I knew this moment would be trapped in my head and heart for a long time.

Crap. How was I supposed to start this? Stupid me, I hadn't thought about what I'd actually say.

"I think it's time for us to clear the air," Derek said slowly. He felt so distant to me, and I knew that with every second passing, he was slipping away from me even more.

I nodded slowly, ready to get the pain over with. "Yeah. Yeah, we do."

chapter twenty

"I just need to know . . . why have you been acting so weird around me?" Derek asked, his voice thick with emotion. "You're blowing hot and cold, and you've been so distant lately. Are you wanting to break up?"

"What?" I exclaimed in shock, heart slamming in my chest. Was he for real? That was not what I'd expected him to say. "Hey, *you're* the one acting all funky, not holding my hand or calling me or being as affectionate with me as you used to. And ditching me at prom to go talk to your friends," I pointed out.

Yeah, he'd only been gone a few minutes, but it still stung, and I wanted him to know that his friends had contributed to the wedge between us.

"I wasn't ditching you for them." He paused. "But I was gone for too long. You're right, and I'm sorry for that." Derek crossed his arms. "I think there's some massive confusion between us. What's going on here, Felicity?"

Drawing in a deep breath, I knew it was time to come clean. "I can tell you're not feeling as close to me anymore since the spell wore off."

Now it was his turn to be shocked. He reeled back, eyes wide. "What? You put a spell on us? Wait, wait—I didn't think that was possible."

"No, it's not," I said, shaking my head. Tears welled to my eyes again, and I blinked rapidly. "The day we . . . became boyfriend and girlfriend, Janet had put a cupid spell on us. Don't you see? That's the reason why you suddenly liked me. And that's why—" My voice broke. I stared at the ground, sucked in a breath, and forced myself to continue. "That's why when the spell wore off, you stopped feeling as strongly for me."

Derek said nothing for a long, painful moment. The only sound I heard was the whooshing of my heartbeat rushing in my ears.

Then he burst into laughter. "Really? You think Janet match-made us?"

"I don't see why that's funny," I said stiffly, my pride stung by his unexpected humor with the situation. "I'm sure she only meant it to be nice."

"No, no, no," he quickly said, then stepped toward me, pulling me close. He tugged my chin up, locking eyes with mine. "You don't understand. I've been crazy for you for a while . . . a lot longer than two weeks."

I swallowed, a small flutter of hope spreading from my stomach to my limbs. "Really? You have?"

"Absolutely. Janet didn't need to cast a spell to make me love you, Felicity. I loved you, anyway. In fact, I'd told her that right before we started dating." He leaned forward and pressed a soft, gentle kiss on my lips.

Oh my God, I think my heart just burst out of my chest with glee. "You have to know how I feel about you, Derek," I whispered when he lifted his head.

"I do." His eyes were warm, empathetic. "No wonder you've been acting so weird and distant. Carrying around that kind of perception about your relationship could drive a person crazy," he said slowly, shaking his head in wonder. "What caused you to think we were paired up?"

"Um, the day after we started dating and we went to her office,

I saw a planner with our names in it. There was a whole list of people, and I guess I assumed those were her matchmaking list." I laughed, feeling a weird mix of ecstatic relief and crazy giddiness, then pressed my cheek against his chest. "Oh my God, this whole situation has been a nightmare. I'm so, so glad that's out in the open now. And even gladder it isn't true."

It was actually embarrassing, thinking about my severe misperception. Derek had been steadfast and open and caring during our relationship, only I'd been too scared and crazy in love to see it at the time. How often had I come across to him as less than unwavering?

All this time I'd been working against my own happiness, keeping Derek at arm's length emotionally for fear of getting my own heart broken. And all this time I'd been hurting him in the process.

I bit my lower lip. Well, he was never going to have to doubt my true feelings again.

We held each other for another long moment, then linked fingers and headed back inside toward our table. I returned the coat he'd lent me, which he then hung over the back of his chair. The first few notes of a love song filled the air, and my heart seemed to bloom in my chest.

"Want to dance?" he asked me.

I nodded, and we made our way to the edge of the dance floor, where there was a smaller crowd, compared to the other side of the dance floor. Derek wrapped his arms tightly around me. I leaned in to him, closing my eyes and smiling blissfully to myself as we swayed in perfect rhythm.

What had started as a sketchy, nerve-wracking prom date had finally turned into the event I'd hoped for—dancing with Derek, the guy of my dreams.

"By the way, I think you won the bet," I admitted. "You have way more matches than I do. I'm prepared to fulfill my end of the bargain, so just pick where you want to eat."

"You don't have to do that," he said. "I'm not gonna hold you to it. But it's nice of you to offer."

"No, I insist." I paused dramatically. "I bet Andy would be happy to hook us up with a great table at The Burger Butler."

A loud laugh jarred me, and I peeked an eye over Derek's shoulder to see what was going on. It was Mallory's date, Doug, horsing around with some of his friends. Off in the distance I saw Mallory standing all alone with her back against the wall, looking forlorn.

Aw, man. As much as I didn't like her, I could totally feel her pain. No one wanted a date they felt was ignoring them. Maybe it was time for me to help Mallory out.

"Derek," I said, "can we go back to the table for just a second? I have a little . . . business to take care of."

He nodded knowingly and led me back to my chair, where I'd hidden my PDA in my purse under my seat. We sat down, and I fired up my good old LoveLine 3000, with Derek watching.

I sent a blank message to Mallory's and Doug's cell phones. "Now watch the magic happen," I said to Derek with a sly smile.

"You're a good person, Felicity." He draped an arm across the back of my chair and rubbed his hand on my shoulder.

"Not as good as I could be," I said, giving him a flirty smile as relished the sensation of his fingers on my bare skin. I turned off my LoveLine 3000 and tucked it back into my purse. "But I'll keep trying."

Mallory jumped a little and dug into her purse, pulling out her cell. She flipped it open and stared for a moment, then blinked rapidly and rubbed her chest.

Bingo.

A moment later Doug did the same. Their eyes met from across the room, and they headed right toward each other. Right in front of all the promgoers, Mallory mashed her mouth against his in a hot, furious kiss.

"Whoa," Derek said, blinking rapidly and jerking back in his chair.

I snorted. "No kidding. I guess she had some pent-up lovin' in her."

After a moment of make-out madness, Doug tore his mouth away and held up a finger for Mallory to wait where she was. Then he dashed madly onto the stage and whispered in the DJ's ear.

The DJ nodded, stopping the song that was playing and turning on the mic. "We have a special request," he said. "So everyone, make sure you have a partner and come out on the floor." Then, he handed the mic to Doug, who cleared his throat and stood ready, lipstick marks all over his mouth, as he stared intently at Mallory.

Derek and I exchanged glances, our eyebrows raised.

"What's this all about?" he asked me.

I shrugged my shoulders. "Hey, I just matched them. I can't control peoples' actions after that." A casual comment, but a lesson I'd learned the truth of all too well.

Derek tugged me out of my chair and led me to the floor again. "Let's get a closer view," he said, mischief dancing in his eyes. "I have a feeling we're about to see something really interesting."

The music started again, a fast groove that instantly got my attention. My jaw dropped. Oh my God, Doug was singing Beyoncé's song "Crazy in Love" to Mallory!

Mallory's friends ran in a giggle-rush toward her, clutching her hands as they all swooned en masse to his serenade.

"Got me lookin' so crazy right now," Doug warbled when he hit the chorus, swaying his upper body left, right, left, right.

His voice was amazingly bad, and we all stood riveted at the sight of his wide-open mouth and vibrating tonsils for a long moment. Even the adult chaperones and teachers were as shocked as we students were, staring at him as he gyrated on the stage.

Mallory, however, didn't care how bad he sounded. "Omigod!" she squealed loudly, clasping her hands to her bright-red cheeks. "That's, like, the most romantic thing ever!"

Derek tucked me against his side, shaking with laughter. I joined him, as did the other promgoers around me.

"It's so sweet!" one girl to the left of me exclaimed. She grabbed her date's hand. "We have to go dance!"

"His voice is horrible," Derek said, still chuckling.

"I know," I said, wiping tears from my eyes, "But what's scarier than his singing is that he actually knows the words to this song! There's no karaoke monitor up there for him to read from!"

He nodded, laughing hard. "This is true."

When the song ended, the entire room burst into thunderous

applause. Doug handed the mic back to the DJ, then jumped off the stage and plowed through the crowd toward Mallory, sweeping her off her feet and spinning her around the room. She squealed again, clinging tightly to his shoulders.

"Let's give one more round of applause to our serenader!" the DJ said, deftly turning on another slow song. "Stay on the floor and have another dance."

Someone bumped an arm into my back. "Sorry," I heard a familiar, throaty female voice say in a distracted manner.

I turned to see what was going on. It was Mrs. Kendel, leading Mr. Bakula, the guidance counselor I'd paired her up with, onto the dance floor. When the music started, she wrapped her thick arms around his skinny neck and tugged his face close to her massive bosom. Their bodies remained locked against each other as they rocked side to side.

With a knowing chuckle, I elbowed Derek in the side. "Check it out," I said, indicating my head toward them. "I finally found true love for Mrs. Kendel."

Derek smiled, then turned to me, his eyes deep, endless. He grabbed my waist and pulled me close. "You are the sweetest, most beautiful girl I've ever seen," he said, bending down to brush my lips with his. "How did I get so lucky?"

A hot flush swept over my cheeks. I kissed him back, then whispered, "I feel lucky, too."

"I'll never forget how beautiful you two looked in your dresses," Maya's mom said to me and Maya on Sunday afternoon. She'd offered to take us out to a late lunch at TGI Fridays as thanks for us helping with her makeover.

Well, Andy had been invited, too, but since she was grounded, she couldn't come. I'd told her I'd throw down some food on her behalf, to which she'd slugged me in the arm and called me a smart-ass (I guess boys aren't the only ones prone to violence). Sheesh, you just can't win with some people.

"Thanks, Mrs. Takahashi," I said, putting down my menu to check her out. Surprisingly enough, she was wearing one of the new outfits we'd picked out for her. "And thanks again for treating us to dinner. I . . . noticed you're not wearing sweatpants. Does that mean you've given them up?" I asked hopefully.

She laughed, rolling her eyes. "Well, I've decided to wear them only when I'm working out or cleaning around the house."

I nodded. "Fair enough. I'm glad to see you feeling better."

"Me too," Maya interjected. She smiled at her mom. "You look great."

"Thanks. I don't feel completely whole yet," Maya's mom said, "but I'm on my way. While you guys were at prom, I dug up some of my old high school pictures. I was so happy back then. I think it's time to start feeling happy again."

Maya reached across the table and squeezed her mom's hand. "I agree." She shot her mom a mock-serious look. "But I'll have you know there will be guidelines on what kinds of guys you can bring home to date, young lady."

Mrs. Takahashi shot Maya a skeptical look. "Yeah, it'll be a while before we have to worry about that."

The waitress arrived and took our orders. I got a sandwich and soup combo. Yum, I couldn't wait.

Maya's mom took a sip of water. "Your father and I won't be together anymore," she said to her daughter, tears welling up in her eyes, "but we're still going to do the best we can for you."

Maya slid out of her chair and hugged her mom. "I know. I never doubted it for a minute."

"Excuse me, guys," I said, moving out of the booth and into the bathroom. I wanted to give them a moment alone to talk.

And hopefully, start to heal.

chapter twenty-one

"Rob, I have something to tell you," I said, trying to ignore the vomity feeling in my stomach. I'd put this off for way too long. And he was due to come to Sunday dinner in about an hour. I definitely didn't want him bringing that skank Annette along, faking us all out with her niceness and then getting nasty with other guys behind Rob's back.

"Sure, what's up?"

I cradled the phone between my ear and shoulder, then drew in a deep, steadying breath. "When I'd told you before I saw something happen, I meant something about Annette." Oh God, please don't let him get pissed at me for being the messenger. "Um, when I was meeting her for dinner at Pizza Hut, I, um . . ." I floundered for a moment, then plunged straight ahead. "I saw her kissing Officer Banks."

There was a long, long moment of silence on the phone.

"Hello?" I asked tentatively.

Rob cleared his throat. "I'm here. Thanks for telling me."

"Do you . . . are you mad at me?"

"No," he said quickly. "I just need some time to think. Tell the folks I'm gonna pass on dinner. I'll talk to them later tonight."

My stomach sank, and tears sprang to my eyes. I sniffled. "Rob, I am so, so sorry. I was hoping Annette would be the one for you. I feel horrible." Yet another one of my brilliant matches, gone awry.

He sighed. "Don't be upset, Felicity. It's fine. I know it was hard for you to call me. I gotta go, okay?"

We hung up. I plopped backward across my bed and lay for a few minutes. Poor Rob. I wished I could fix this for him, but it was best if I let him handle his own love life from now on. Hopefully he'd open his eyes and heart to someone more worthy of his time and affection.

Monday evening, at my weekly work meeting, I handed the LoveLine 3000 back to Janet. "I think I'm ready to hang up my wings, so to speak."

She pursed her lips, disappointment clearly etched on her face at my news. "Really? Why?"

I leaned back in the chair across from her desk. "Wellllll, it's because I suck at it. Um, pardon my French. I don't think I'm a natural at the job, like you or Derek. But I do promise to stick to the terms of our contract and not tell anyone about being a cupid. Not that they'd understand it, anyway," I said in a droll voice.

Janet laughed, nodding her head knowingly. "Well, I'm sorry to see you go, but you're always welcome to come back in the future if you want. I thought you were a great cupid, for what it's worth."

"I appreciate that," I said, hoping my sincerity rang through my voice. Even if I knew I wasn't good at the job, it was nice to be treated so well by an employer. "I've really enjoyed working with you."

"Take care of yourself. I'll see you around, Felicity," she said, a mysterious smile on her face.

"Well, in that case, I'll be watching out for you first," I shot back with a wry grin.

"Felicity, can you run this iced tea to table four?" Miranda, the manager of The Burger Butler, handed me the chilled glass.

"Sure thing." As I squeezed past Andy in her butler uniform

behind the counter, I gave her a quick smile, then dashed to the table, my own butler jacket flapping.

Being a waitress who looked like a penguin wasn't the best job ever, but at least I wasn't holding the fate of people's love lives in my hand. Well, not unless I spilled boiling coffee in some guy's lap. Plus, I got to work with my best friend. And the tips weren't so bad, either.

Overall, not a horrible gig, if you didn't count the pervy old men who always sat at my tables.

When I finished handing off the iced tea, Andy tugged me by the arm and pulled me aside. "So, we're still on for studying tonight, right?"

"Absolutely," I said, nodding. "Maya's already promised to come over, and she's even bringing some food."

She sighed. "I wish Bobby could study with us, but with me still being grounded, I figured I wouldn't push my luck."

She and Bobby were going strong. I think it was the longest relationship I'd ever seen her in. Not the two people I would have paired up, but it worked for them. And you know what? Bobby was actually a decent guy, the more I was around him.

Plus, boy, did he care about her. At first I'd almost felt a little miffed that he got over his unrequited crush on me so easily, but since that was petty on my part, I tried to brush those feelings off. He was happy, she was happy, and that's what counted.

Besides, I was getting plenty of ego strokes these days, so who needed a crush to feel good about herself? Derek and I were doing great. Tonight was our six week anniversary of 'fessing up our feelings.

Yes, I was apparently *that* girl, the one who had anniversaries for every event in a relationship—first drink shared, first slow dance, first time swapping spit.

Lucky for me, Derek was a pretty patient guy and dug my quirks.

And also lucky for me, Mallory had totally backed off riding my ass all the time. On Monday after prom, she'd come up to me in the hallway in between classes and had apologized for being so snotty to me recently. She'd claimed it was extreme prom stress, which sounded totally stupid, but whatever. It was the closest I was going to get to a sincere emotion from her, so I'd take it.

Surprisingly enough, she and Doug were still dating, even though the spell had worn off. I guess love had softened her around the corners . . . a much-needed improvement, if you asked me.

"Felicity?" Miranda's soft voice jerked me out of my thoughts. "Wanna clear table nine now?"

"No problem." I grabbed the plastic container to dump the dirty plates into and glanced over at my supervisor.

She was pretty cute—slim body, cute blond hair pulled casually up, friendly smile. She looked to be in her early twenties.

And she was single, too. I'd overheard her talking to another server yesterday evening about it.

Unable to help myself, my mind started churning with the matchmaking possibilities. Even though I was out of "the business," as I'd come to think of it, I hated seeing nice people alone.

A few minutes later I heard the front door open, and my brother strolled in, his beat partner in tow. "Hey," he said to me, waving. "We came to make fun of you while we're on break. Any good doughnuts here?"

I laughed, happy to see Rob wasn't still upset about the Annette issue. He hadn't been around the house much since I'd talked to him about her cheating . . . and when he did stop by, he didn't bring a date or stay long. His only words to our folks on the subject were to let us know he and Annette had broken up.

Mom and Dad hadn't asked what had happened, sensing Rob didn't want to discuss it. Smart peeps, they were.

"You're a dork," I replied back to him, rolling my eyes.

Miranda walked over to Rob. I could see her look him up and down in a quick, sweeping motion. She offered him a small smile and waved her hand toward a booth. "Evening, officers. Would you like to have a seat here?"

My brother looked at her and paused for a moment, then grinned widely. "I certainly would."

Miranda walked away, stopping by me. "Is that your brother?" she whispered.

Well, well, well. Maybe Rob would turn out okay, after all. "Sure is. He's my very *single* brother."

She smiled. "I'll handle his table."

"No problem." I dumped the last glass in my container and walked away, chuckling to myself.

Relationships were a weird thing—some couples needed to be matched up to find each other, like Mallory and Doug, or even Derek and myself. Others, like Miranda and Rob, simply needed the right circumstances.

Love could conquer all, but thank God there were cupids to nudge it in the right direction sometimes.

Acknowledgments

This story wouldn't be out here if it weren't for my awesome agent, Caryn Wiseman. Thanks for continually supporting me, no matter what wacky ideas I throw your way. Also, a big fat thank-you to everyone at Simon Pulse for believing in this story—Anica, Guillian, the copyeditors, the cover artist, the marketing team, publicity, and the people who fetch coffee and doughnuts for the above-mentioned.

Family, friends, dogs, neighbors, coworkers, strangers on the street who listened to my inane mumbling—I also thank you from the bottom of my heart.

About the Author

Rhonda Stapleton started writing a few years ago to appease the voices in her head. She lives in northeast Ohio with her husband, two kids, and their lazy dog. Visit her website at rhondastapleton.com and follow her on Twitter at @rhondastapleton.

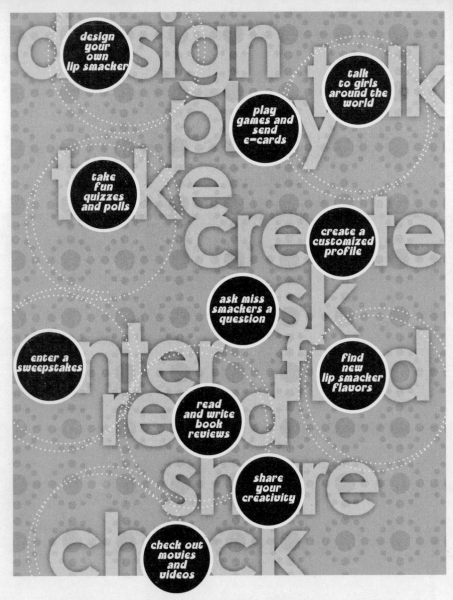

 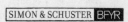

SimonTeen

Simon & Schuster's **Simon Teen**
e-newsletter delivers current updates on
the hottest titles, exciting sweepstakes, and
exclusive content from your favorite authors.

Visit **TEEN.SimonandSchuster.com** to
sign up, post your thoughts, and find out what
every avid reader is talking about!